Hertfordshire

D0540422

Mutual Friends

This book is gratefully dedicated
to the memory of
Dr Felix S. Besser and R. G. B. 'Bill' Milchem
who were both in their turn
Honorary Archivists to the Hospital for Sick Children

MUTUAL FRIENDS

Charles Dickens and Great Ormond Street Children's Hospital

Jules Kosky

Weidenfeld and Nicolson
London

Published in Great Britain in 1989
by George Weidenfeld & Nicolson Limited
91 Clapham High Street, London SW4 7TA

British Library Cataloguing in Publication Data
Kosky, Jules
Mutual friends: Charles Dickens
and Great Ormond Street Children's
Hospital.
1. London. Camden (London Borough).
Hospitals. Hospital for sick children
(London, England), history
I. Title
362.1′ 9892′ 000942142

ISBN 0–297–79673–9

Typeset in Sabon by BP Datagraphics Ltd

Printed and bound in Great Britain
by The Bath Press, Avon

Charles Dickens, the children's friend, first fairly set her on her legs and helped her to run alone, and in a few eloquent words which none who have heard can ever forget, like the good fairy in the tale, he gave her the gift that she should win love and favour everywhere; and so she grew and prospered.

DR CHARLES WEST
at a Great Ormond Street
Anniversary Dinner in 1867

CONTENTS

ILLUSTRATIONS

ACKNOWLEDGEMENTS

I am grateful to the Board of Governors of The Hospital for Sick Children for permission to quote from the Minutes and other archival records preserved in the Peter Pan Gallery, and to the Special Trustees of the Hospital for their support and the generous grant towards the cost of preparing the final typescript. I thank Mr Christopher Dickens for his permission to quote from Dickens's unpublished letters and others still in copyright. I wish to acknowledge quotations made from the following publications: the Oxford University Press for the Pilgrim Edition of *The Letters of Charles Dickens*, Norman and Jean Mackenzie's *Dickens, A Life*, H.House's *The Dickens World*, and *The Gladstone Diaries*, ed. H.C.G.Matthew; John Murray for Doris Langley Moore's *Ada, Countess of Lovelace*; Constable & Co. for Ethel Colburn Mayne's *Life and Letters of Lady Noel Byron*; Thomas Nelson and Sons for *The Letters & Diaries of John Henry Newman*, ed. C.D.Dessain; Victor Gollancz for Edgar Johnson's *Charles Dickens, His Tragedy and Triumph* and *Letters from Dickens to Angela Buirdett Coutts*; the Manchester University Press for *The Letters of Mrs. Gaskell*, ed. J.A.V.Chapple and A.Pollard. Dr David Parker, Curator of The Dickens House Museum, has been especially helpful, and I thank the staff of the Wellcome Library, the London Library, and Haringey Public Libraries for their assistance. Mr Peter D.Gratton, the Derbyshire County Librarian, and Miss Janet Halton, Librarian of Moravian House, were both generous in sharing their specialized knowledge. For advice and encouragement at the very beginning I must thank Professor Kathleen Tillotson and Mr David Dickens. Mr Ray Lunnon, Director of the Department of Medical Illustration at the Institute of Child Health, provided the photographs, and Mrs Roz Sullivan, also of the Institute, performed a minor miracle in reducing an untidy manuscript to neatness and respectability. Mrs Debbie Fisher and Mr and Mrs Harry Duggan patiently read through the book as it was written, thus providing a constant stimulus. Without Miss Eileen Power, and her help in the Peter Pan Gallery over the past year, the book would never have been finished.

—1—
THE CHILD FIRST AND ALWAYS

On 28 May 1883, a handsome woman in her forties, with beautiful auburn hair and a particularly sweet expression, visited The Hospital for Sick Children in Great Ormond Street. As she left, she signed the visitor's book in a firm plain hand, 'Kate Perugini'. She was Charles Dickens's youngest surviving daughter, his little Katey. Evidently she had not forgotten, thirteen years after his death, the Children's Hospital of which he had been such an enthusiastic supporter. As a child, she and her elder sister, Mamie, had been friends with Anny and Minny, the daughters of the other great Victorian novelist W.M.Thackeray. The girls were compatible in age, and the friendship was to become one of the closest and the longest-lasting of their lives. When Thackeray was away on a lecture tour of the United States in the winter of 1855–56, the Dickens and Thackeray girls all found themselves in Paris, where they went to and fro across the Champs Elysées to exchange confidences and chat over the latest news. This intimacy continued in London. This friendship between their daughters brought Dickens and Thackeray together, a relationship that survived the rift between the two novelists in 1858. It was Katey who finally managed to effect a reconciliation between the two men. And on that dreadful morning of Christmas Eve 1863, when Thackeray was discovered dead in his bed, it was Katey and her husband to whom Anny and Minny first turned. Katey was to be a great support to them over the next few days. Anne Thackeray, who was to write an account of The Hospital for Sick Children and of other children's hospitals that followed in its wake, became a novelist herself, and wrote some delightful and vivid recollections of their early years together, describing the incomparable joys of the Dickens children's parties.

Dickens and Thackeray had long been friends. No one who has read Jane Carlyle's account of the Christmas party organized by Dickens in 1843, 'the most remarkable party that I ever was at', and her description of the riotous behaviour of Dickens, Forster and Thackeray, could think otherwise. John Forster was Dickens's most intimate friend, his first and best biographer. He was, in a sense, almost his Boswell. When in 1857 the sudden death of their mutual friend, Douglas Jerrold, the dramatist and contributor to *Punch*, left his family in rather parlous financial straits, Dickens arranged for their benefit, among other things, a subscription performance of *The Frozen Deep*, and Thackeray gave a reading of his lecture 'Charity and Humour'. Fifteen years later, one of the Jerrold children, Blanche Jerrold, was to pay a most moving tribute to the great work Dickens had done on behalf of many charities and especially for The Hospital for Sick Children.

> But above and before all how he spoke for the sick poor children! The authorities in Great Ormond Street will tell anybody who may inquire, how his gallant and righteous spirit – how the warming light of his genius, plays about the cradles where the little ones lie! I can still catch the echoes of those tremulous tones in which he who created Tiny Tim, and melted the world's heart over the death of Little Dombey; pleaded for the sick and destitute children – conjuring the men at the table around him to think of the weeping mothers by the hospital cots: then of their own little ones at home; and then of the sick child fretting for lack of healing care and wholesome sustenance. Oratory was never sweeter nor more persuasive than this; and never fell from human lips pleading a holier cause. London does not include within its spacious bounds a more touching scene than that of The Hospital for Sick Children, nor a purer charity than that which covers helpless infancy.

Above and before all, indeed, were the needs, and the sorrow, and the laughter of children predominant with Charles Dickens. Great Ormond Street's later motto, 'The Child First and Always', would have received his wholehearted approval. It was a principle active in his labours both for charity and for the amelioration of social ills – here The Hospital for Sick Children may almost be said to stand as a memorial to his exertions – and in those creative works of genius whose pages preserve his memory throughout the world.

Much has been written on Dickens and his love of children. Numerous examples could be quoted from his works. It is more appropriate here to refer to Mamie's and Katey's descriptions of their father, and of how

> In all our childish ailments his visits were eagerly looked forward to, and our little hearts would beat a shade faster, and our aches and pains become

more bearable, when the sound of his quick footstep was heard, and the encouraging accents of his voice greeted the invalid.

And in Dickens's correspondence we find:

> Poor little Katey has been very ill. She is now recovering, thank Heaven, and goes out every night upon a Donkey. She would let nobody touch her, in the way of dressing her neck or giving her physic, when she was very ill; but her Papa. So I had a pretty tough time of it. But her sweet temper was wonderful to see.

This description of how patient Dickens was with his sick children can be confirmed by Anne Thackeray. She charmingly relates an anecdote showing another side of his appeal to children. In this Tennyson figures:

> I can remember vaguely, on one occasion, through a cloud of smoke, looking across a darkening room at the noble, great head of the Poet Laureate. He was sitting with my Father in the twilight after some family meal in the old house at Kensington; it was Tennyson himself who afterwards reminded me how upon this occasion, while my Father was speaking, my little sister looked up suddenly from the book over which she had been absorbed, saying in her sweet childish voice, 'Papa, why do you not write books like *Nicholas Nickleby*?'

Thackeray himself made gleeful use of this incident when, at New York in December 1852, he first gave that very lecture, 'Charity and Humour', which he was to repeat five years later in aid of the Jerrold family. In this he paid a memorable and generous tribute to Dickens and his love of children:

> As for the charities of Mr Dickens, multiplied kindnesses which he has conferred upon us all; upon our children; upon people educated and uneducated; upon the myriads here and at home who speak our common tongue; have not you, have not I, all of us reason to be thankful to this kind friend who ... made such multitude of children happy? ... Was there ever a better charity sermon preached in the world than Dickens's *Christmas Carol*? ... All children ought to love him. I know two that do, and read his books ten times for once that they peruse the dismal preachments of their father. I know one who, when she is happy reads *Nicholas Nickleby*; when she is unhappy, reads *Nicholas Nickleby*; when she is tired, reads *Nicholas Nickleby*; when she is in bed, reads *Nicholas Nickleby*; when she has nothing to do, reads *Nicholas Nickleby*; and when she has finished the book, reads *Nicholas Nickleby* over again. This candid young critic, at ten years of age, said, 'I like Mr Dickens's books much better than your books, Papa'; and frequently expressed her desire that the latter author should write a book like one of Mr Dickens's books.

> Who can? Every man must say his own thoughts in his own voice, in his own way; lucky is he who has such a charming gift of nature as this, which brings all the children in the world trooping to him, and being fond of him.

The novelist Hugh Walpole read *Nicholas Nickleby* in 1931. It particularly delighted him, and he decided part of its secret lay in the fact that 'Dickens never grew up. I believe the best authors never do.' This significant aspect of Dickens, which is important in explaining his interest in The Hospital for Sick Children, makes an interesting comparison with James Barrie, whose *Peter Pan*, the most generous gift the Hospital has ever received, became the archetype of all children who never grow up.

At the end of 1852 when Thackeray first gave his lecture, Dickens had already issued the tenth monthly part of *Bleak House*, in which Jo, the crossing-sweeper boy, gravely ill with an infectious fever, is discovered and carried to Bleak House. John Jarndyce then remarks, 'Is it not a horrible reflection . . . that if this wretched creature were a convicted prisoner, his hospital would be wide open to him and he would be as well taken care of as any sick boy in the kingdom.' Also in that December, Dr Charles West (who had fought, pleaded and planned for the idea of a children's hospital, the lack of which in the United Kingdom Dickens makes John Jarndyce rue) was gathering statistics and compiling the first annual medical report of his Hospital for Sick Children, which he had at last managed to open in Great Ormond Street the previous February.

To understand not only the intense sympathy which the idea of a children's hospital must have evoked in Charles Dickens, but also the great help Dickens gave to its promotion, Dr West's concise but significant report should be studied. 'At first, indeed, it seemed almost as if a Children's Hospital were not needed, for so few were the applicants that during the first month, only twenty-four were brought as Outpatients and only eight were received into the Hospital as Inpatients. The Hospital had its character to make among the poor.' It was Dickens, the loved and trusted champion of the needy and neglected child, who stood reference for its character, not only among the poor, but also among the highest in the land. Six weeks after Great Ormond Street first opened, Dickens published in *Household Words* an article, 'Drooping Buds', which not only forcibly argued the necessity of a Children's Hospital, but lovingly, touchingly and faithfully described the new institution in Great Ormond Street. This was the very first account printed of The Hospital for Sick Children. The effect of 'Drooping Buds' was immediately apparent. As Dr West continued in his report, 'Before long, greater numbers of children were brought ... and their mothers ... by degrees ... learned to place full confidence in its management, and to believe that those who asked for their suffering little ones were indeed to be trusted with so precious a deposit.'

A few weeks after 'Drooping Buds' was issued, Queen Victoria gave the Children's Hospital a generous donation and became its patron. Dickens had indeed made its character, both to the poor, despairing mother in the teeming slums of Clerkenwell, and to the royal mother, the Queen, in Buckingham Palace. It was Dickens's unique power of appealing directly and immediately across the whole spectrum of society that made him not only one of the greatest of all novelists, but one of the most powerful influences for social good in the nineteenth century. Dr West, always an admirer of Dickens and the man who described again and again how much Great Ormond Street owed to him, had quite likely read the December number of *Bleak House*, and perhaps had the episode of Jo in his mind when he wrote the next paragraph of his report:

> The Fever Wards of the Hospital have, as was expected, proved themselves, small though they be, one of its most important features. Twenty-five children have been received into them, of whom seventeen were suffering from scarlet fever or its immediate sequelae; and of the whole number only three died. Who shall say what would have been the mortality among these children, in the close apartments from which they came; or to what extent disease would otherwise have spread?

It is true that the fever from which Jo suffered, although not named by Dickens, was obviously smallpox, and therefore he would not have been admitted even to Great Ormond Street, but the threat of scarlet fever was a real and deadly peril both at that time and for many years afterwards. Six months before her marriage to Charles Dickens, Catherine Hogarth and her mother both contracted scarlet fever, and the worried Charles sent his brother Fred with blackcurrant jam, to relieve Catherine's throat, and chloride of lime. As Dickens quaintly wrote to her, the 'good it will do in purifying the atmosphere of your room, will more than counterbalance your dislike to its smell'. Fortunately, Catherine and Mrs Hogarth both recovered, but young children were more likely to succumb. Dickens and Catherine were greatly alarmed when their eldest boy caught scarlet fever at school in 1847, but the ten-year-old Charley came through the crisis. Mrs Gaskell, in her *Mary Barton*, published in 1848, gives a moving account, based on her own experiences, of John Barton's little son dying of the aftermath of scarlet fever, because he lacked good nursing and the proper diet which, *vide* Dr West, a hospital would have provided. In reality, the children of the rich were equally at risk: Mrs Gaskell again, in 1850, saw three little cousins, all siblings, die of the fever.

Children were in less danger from smallpox than from other infectious fevers, as West well knew from his matchless experience. Creighton, in *A History of Epidemics in England*, noted that after 1830 scarlet fever had become 'the leading cause of death among the infectious diseases of childhood' and that almost two-thirds of the deaths from it were among children under five years of age. Charles West could well congratulate himself that Great Ormond Street's low mortality rate was truly remarkable. Of the seventy-six boys and sixty-seven girls admitted as inpatients from February to December 1852, only nine boys and four girls died. These were really encouraging figures, especially when it is considered that fourteen of the children were under two years of age. This was contrary to the first tentative rules laid down for such admissions, and refutes claims by other children's hospitals, opened at later dates, to have been the first to admit infants of such a tender age. Dr West, in arguing the need for a children's hospital, had cited the appalling fact that of 50,000 persons dying annually in London, 21,000 were children under ten years of age. And in the sixth edition of his *Lectures on the Diseases of Infancy and Childhood*, published in 1874, West could still grimly remind his readers that 'so serious are their diseases, that one child in five dies within a year after birth, and one in three before the completion of the fifth year'. In the first year of its opening, The Hospital for Sick Children had allayed the fears of some of the more potent critics against the idea of a special hospital for children. At the Foundling Hospital, only 4400 of the first 15,000 children admitted lived to grow up. And these had been comparatively healthy waifs and abandoned babies. Such were the perils in those days of childish infections spreading unchecked by specialistic paediatric medicine and care.

The children whom Dr West and his colleagues had saved in that first year at Great Ormond Street were, of course, only a tiny drop in the ocean of need in London and throughout the kingdom. Even at the end of 1852, The Hospital for Sick Children had only increased its pitifully inadequate number of beds to thirty. West's original minimum requirements of a hospital with at least a hundred beds would take nearly a generation to achieve.

But the torch had been lit, and no one was more appreciative and more ready to carry it on than Charles Dickens, whose cry of 'Oh! Baby's dead' had begun the most moving passage of 'Drooping Buds'. It is beyond question that Great Ormond Street evoked the deepest response from Dickens, with its appeal to the most profound of his feelings and sympathies, the Children's Hospital was among the most favourite of his charities.

Dickens was the first great writer to give children a predominant place, and many of his memorable characters, from Oliver Twist onwards, are children. *Oliver Twist* itself was a massive force in arousing public awareness of the wrongs foisted upon deprived children, and gave impetus to a growing concern and encouragement for such reforms as those initiated by Lord Ashley.

In *Oliver Twist* a significant passage points to a theme which may be an explanation and an insight into the psychological roots of Dickens's sensitive response to the appeal of children. It is in Chapter 17, where Little Dick, who knows he is dying, begs to be remembered to Oliver:

> 'I should like,' said the child, 'to leave my dear love to poor Oliver Twist; and to let him know how often I have sat by myself and cried to think of his wandering about in the dark nights with nobody to help him. And I should like to tell him,' said the child, pressing his small hands together and speaking with great fervour, 'that I was glad to die when I was very young; for, perhaps, if I had lived to be a man and had grown old, my little sister, who is in Heaven, might forget me, or be unlike me; and it would be so much happier if we were both children there together.'

Apart from including a situation that Dickens was to use several times later, the child brother and sister, inseparable companions, and the sister dying young and waiting for her brother in heaven, as in *A Child's Dream of a Star* (or with the brother and sister roles reversed, as with Florence and Paul Dombey), this quotation shows the reluctance of the child to grow up, the thought that it would be better never to become an adult, and a looking backwards at the happy innocence of childhood. It was the time, in Dickens's case, before he was sent out to work at Warren's Blacking Warehouse – an episode which left so traumatic a mark on his memory that he spoke of it only to one person, his oldest friend, John Forster. And, perhaps, once to his wife. It was an episode he constantly recalled in his novels; and even after the most lengthy attempt at a catharsis, when he related the full story in *David Copperfield*, he is still haunted by it as late as *Edwin Drood*, when Neville Landless speaks of the childhood sorrows shared with his sister, Rosa: 'I have been stinted of education, liberty, money, dress, the very necessaries of life, the commonest pleasures of childhood, the commonest possessions of youth.'

This incident in Dickens's childhood has been commented upon at length by numerous scholars and biographers. What may also be of significance in explaining Dickens's sympathy with children is the half-hinted belief that it would be better never to have grown up – an attitude which, as previously noticed, is of peculiar interest to Great Ormond Street because of the debt the Hospital owes to *Peter Pan*. The words

Dickens gave to the dying Little Dick were written in 1837. The most recent biographer of James Barrie has written:

> If Margaret Ogilvy drew a measure of comfort from the notion that David [Barrie's older brother], in dying a boy, would remain a boy for ever, Barrie drew inspiration. It would be another thirty-three years before ... Peter Pan, but here was the germ, rooted in his mind and soul from the age of six.

Of course, such a feeling was not peculiar to Dickens and Barrie. One of the children who was often invited to the famous Dickens Christmas parties, the daughter of another celebrated Victorian, the artist William Frith, wrote in her old age: '"I wake in the night," said one of my nieces to me the other day, "and I cry to think I am growing old." Oh! foolish girl.' And a differing aspect of the same sentiment can be found in M. Ewin's *Savage Landor*:

> Landor could not foresee the tragic destiny of his passionate love for his children, though ... he was always aware, even in moments of most doting fondness, that he could not expect his unalloyed delight in his children to last beyond their childhood. Telling his sister Ellen ... how he wished never 'to be a day without any of them, while they are children', he added, as if with foreboding, 'they are different creatures when they grow up.'

Dickens not only lamented his own lost childhood, but there was something in him that sympathized with his old friend Landor. When his own children grew up, the crazy delirious days of love and play, of song, dance and kisses, faded, and father and child mostly grew apart. And as the magic of his own children one by one became lost to him, for whatever reason, and by whoever's fault, Dickens turned his love towards not only the dream children of his imagination, but also towards the real suffering children, towards the starving child and the fever-ridden consumptive infant, the frail, rickety children of the poor.

Yet Dickens, always so sympathetic and understanding in cases of real deprivation, always so punctilious in relieving distress, seemed sometimes in his more rhapsodical passages to use deliberately the image of a sick child as a kind of emotional organ stop, a *voix celeste*. Contemporary accounts of the sick children in Great Ormond Street can help us to understand something of the Victorian attitude towards illness and death. It is even possible that Little Nell and Paul Dombey were the fictitious catalysts that crystallized that attitude. Read again in that light, we may understand why these deathbed scenes were regarded as pinnacles of the writer's art by two such accomplished judges as Landor and Thackeray. *The Old Curiosity Shop* and *Dombey and Son* were both written before the founding of Great Ormond Street, the eventual opening of which owed not a little to the moral effect produced by these two books. To Charles Dickens, The Hospital for Sick Children would be an embodiment in the real world of some of his own imaginary children. And in its turn The Hospital for Sick Children is a valuable commentary upon Dickens. The children in its cots were a living justification of the validity of his creative powers, and even the few that, sadly, did not survive were with their little bodies a reminder that the grim poetry of death could move out from the pages of Mr Dickens's latest number. One of Great Ormond Street's most famous physicians of more modern times, Frederick J. Poynton, has said: 'Anyone who has ever seen the smile on the face of a dying child has had a glimpse of immortality.' Poynton, of all men, although devoted to children, could never be accused of meaningless sentimentality, and his words would not be out of place in a novel by Dickens. Hidden in the Hospital's reports and case notes are many stories that are truly Dickensian in tone. Some seem echoes from the novels already written; others foreshadow what was to come.

In *Nicholas Nickleby*, when Tim Linkinwater is describing the view of the court from his bedroom window, he tells Nicholas there is a double-wallflower in a cracked jug by the attic window of No. 6, where last spring there were hyacinths in an old blacking pot:

> 'They belong to a sickly bedridden humpbacked boy and seem to be the only pleasures, Mr Nickleby, of his sad existence. How many years is it ... since I first noticed him quite a little child, dragging himself about on a pair of tiny crutches? It is a sad thing to see a little deformed child sitting apart from other children, who are active and merry, watching the games he is denied the power to share in ... The flowers belong to this poor boy ... When it is fine weather, and he can crawl out of bed, he ... sits looking at them and arranging them all day ... He can't leave his bed now, so they have moved it close beside the window, and there he lies all day: now looking at the sky, and now at his flowers, which he still makes shift to trim and water with his own thin hands.'

Nearly thirty years after this was published, the Bishop of Lincoln described how his children had sent some snowdrops to Bishop Tozer's daughter, who was a nurse at Great Ormond Street:

> There was a little boy lying in one of the rooms of the hospital between life and death. He took no notice of anything. It seemed as if the vital power was slowly ebbing out. He lay patient, apparently insensible. This lady put some of the snowdrops in a glass, beside the bed. They caught the patient's eye, they roused him; a smile came upon his face. The medical man came his round soon afterwards and said, 'There is a great change here.' She pointed at the flowers and he saw at once what it was. That

> life was probably saved by those flowers which in the child's own house in London, he would never have seen.

The importance The Hospital for Sick Children had for Dickens was in its relationship and affinity to his subconscious stirrings and feelings about childhood, in its influence upon that self-exploration which, in an author, can alone bring about both the first faint, glimpsed outline of his theme and the later, fuller embodiment of his work. With Marcel Proust this was a deliberate and conscious process; but in Dickens, the product of many unconscious conflicts and contradictory philosophies. In his journalism and in his speeches, Dickens was always a stout partisan of worthy causes, and many were the charities he praised. Some schemes and philanthropic endeavours in which he became involved, either because of personal friendship with a forcible and active protagonist, or with patrons, as in the case of Angela Burdett Coutts, who possessed both the claims of friendship and of unlimited funds, made large and unconscionable demands upon his time. Angela Burdett Coutts, later Baroness Coutts, was a wealthy philanthropist. Dickens advised her and carried out many charitable and philanthropic schemes on her behalf. But, however much he agreed with these charitable aims, and no matter how tireless the energy and devotion he gave to them, it did not always mean that those charities which figure the largest in his public utterances, and in his correspondence, were those that were dearest to his heart. For any writer, the most important factor in his life must be his books. For a writer of genius, they become the overwhelming reason for his existence, and become in a sense almost sacrosanct. He may cheat, lie and live a life of deceit and selfishness; he may be a shameless sponger upon his friends or an unsavoury drunk, a violent or a fawning deceiver of women, a bad husband and a neglectful father, or a Pecksniffian hypocrite in his talk and correspondence. But his true work, his novels, his poems, or – in other arts – his music or painting, must all be stainless and without compromise, an expression of the truth as he sees it. It is not necessary, of course, to imply that Dickens indulged or did not indulge in some or any of these failings and vices. What is important is that we know that a Richard Wagner, a Dylan Thomas and a Verlaine did; but the operas of Wagner are nearly perfect masterpieces, and the poems of Dylan Thomas and Verlaine are mostly flawless gems. It is this contrast which allows us to believe that there must be profound significance and meaningful symbolism in something which Humphrey House points out in his study *The Dickens World*:

> A large proportion of the speeches . . . was delivered with the single object of raising funds for organized charities of one kind or another . . . His

letters to the press and other active work for Ragged Schools are well known. Yet in the novels and stories organized charity is almost universally condemned with effective acrimony; he rarely attempted to describe the working of an organized charity that he approved: the Children's Hospital in *Our Mutual Friend* is almost the only instance.

A few pages further on, House enlarges upon the theme:

> There is nowhere in the novels a charitable organization that deals in general almsgiving on the subscription and ticket method. The one set description of a good organized charity is of an institution doing work which could not be satisfactorily done by individual private benevolence. The children's Hospital described at the end of Chapter IX of *Our Mutual Friend* would have been unhesitatingly identified with the Great Ormond Street Hospital for which Dickens had made such an excellent speech at the Anniversary Dinner of 1858. The fiction, an attempt to recapture earlier brilliance, is not so good as the speech; yet it was a piece of plain propaganda for a specific object, and worth the deathbeds of Nell and Paul and Jo all put together.

What perhaps separated Dickens from all other contemporary novelists and writers is that he alone, as a child, had trembled on the verge of social destitution and utter loss. He alone had felt his very feet washed by that evil-smelling sea of poverty and helplessness which had overcome so many of his fellow creatures with homelessness and starvation, drowning them in its high tide, and only retreating to leave shapeless, huddled bundles of flotsam which were to be crammed hastily into the paupers' graves in the loathsome churchyards described in *Bleak House*. He had known this and not just through the medium of blue books or the exhortations of clergymen or other social workers. He was not merely a social reformer, clad in good serge and top-hatted, escorted by Sir Robert Peel's new police as he entered the maze of courts and slums on visits of compassion and enquiry. He had been a child, a child strangely innocent and inexperienced for his age, alone without real care or supervision, watching with awe and horror the life of the poor children who swarmed around Hungerford Stairs and elsewhere. A child left without hope or knowledge of what the future might hold. He was afraid and yet pitying, and always in later years burning with a secret anger.

As he had witnessed this world as a child and had been threatened with what seemed total loss as a child, so it was with the children of the poor that his deepest sympathies lay. And it was what he had seen of the truly poor and helpless that made Dickens impatient and intolerant of those, on the one hand, who had evaded their poverty by crime, and, on the other hand, of those who had been raised by circumstances or good fortune a little higher in the social scale but then behaved outrageously towards their less fortunate fellows. Dickens knew that the vast majority of the poor took upon themselves no evil course, and remained poor because of that, receiving from society only indifference and contempt. And for those who suffered the most through no fault of their own, the sick and crippled children of the poor, his sympathy and concern were overwhelming. It was not the fallen girls rescued by Burdett Coutts's Urania Cottage, nor the people of Bethnal Green rehoused in her Columbia Square, who were the first charge on his care. Not even the Ragged Schools of Saffron Hill, nor the victims of legal delay and circumlocution in Doctors' Commons and Chancery, really aroused his deepest emotions. The ill and fevered child from the foetid alleys of Drury Lane and Gray's Inn Lane, the child in a cot at Great Ormond Street, was to tug at his most secret heart-strings and invade the symbolic terrors of his deepest dreams. As Dickens wrote emotionally in his autobiographical fragment about his twelve-year-old self:

> No words can express the secret agony of my soul as I sank into this companionship; compared these everyday associates with those of my happier childhood; and felt my early hopes of growing up to be a learned and distinguished man crushed in my breast. The deep remembrance of the sense I had of being utterly neglected and hopeless; of the shame I felt in my position; of the misery it was to my young heart to believe that, day by day, what I had learned, and thought, and delighted in, and raised my fancy and my emulation up by, was passing away from me, never to be brought back any more; cannot be written. My whole nature was so penetrated with the grief and humiliation of such considerations, that even now, famous and caressed and happy, I often forget in my dreams that I have a dear wife and children; even that I am a man; and wander desolately back to that time of my life.

At the time when Dr Charles West became most active in his plans for a Children's Hospital, and during the period 1849–50 when its Provisional Committee first began to function, Dickens was preoccupied with the conception and the writing of *David Copperfield*. There is strong evidence that he was cognizant of and sympathetic to West's plans from the beginning, long before the Hospital actually opened. Many of Dickens's circle, including friends and relatives, were involved from the beginning. Norman and Jeanne Mackenzie, in a recent full-scale biography of Dickens, give an interesting interpretation of his mood and feelings at that time:

> Such a fantasy solution – the domestic paradise regained – was essentially utopian, and like all utopias it lay beyond the borders of magic. Dickens

provided such an artificial route to happiness in his novels because he knew no other. Caught emotionally at the threshold of adolescence, he kept transacting the unfinished business of his youth in his writings as if he might there discover some ending that had escaped him in ordinary life. The world he described was a child's world, bewildering, full of hidden terrors, inexplicable rejection, pathetic loyalties and lost loves, apparently senseless cruelty and unexpected benevolence. Seen through a child's eye, life is episodic, so full of rich detail, so brimming with energy and yet seemingly so purposeless. The problems of adult life cannot be properly stated let alone understood and solved by the cleverest child. And even the cleverest child cannot cope with them maturely, when his vision of the world is shaped by the perspective of childhood.

It is evident that the planning and the writing of *David Copperfield* were undertaken at a time when these memories and emotions were most strongly aroused. In May 1848, writing to Forster in a probable reference to his autobiographical notes, Dickens noted, 'I am more at rest for having opened all my heart and mind to you ... This day eleven years, poor Mary died.'

This returning obsession with the death of Mary Hogarth, his sister-in-law, who died in his arms in 1837, the shock of which Dickens lived over and over again in writing his child deathbed scenes, was to deepen, and his thoughts were forced towards episodes from his own childhood. By July, Dickens had realized that Fanny, his beloved elder sister, had only a few weeks to live. There is no doubt that Dickens's memories of playing with Fanny as a little child in the back garden of their childhood home at Southsea and elsewhere inspired the later *A Child's Dream of a Star*. 'His sister Fanny and himself ... used to wander at night about a churchyard near their house, looking up at the stars.' Dickens's letter to Forster of 5 July 1848 is a poignant record of his feelings:

> A change took place in poor Fanny about the middle of the day yesterday ... and, strange to say, she immediately became aware of her hopeless state; to which she resigned herself, after an hour's unrest and struggle, with extraordinary sweetness and constancy ... It was hard to die at such a time of life, but she had no alarm whatever in the prospect of the change; felt sure we should meet again in a better world ... Such an affecting exhibition of strength and tenderness, in all that early decay, is quite indescribable ... God knows how small the world looks to one who comes out of such a sick-room on a bright summer day. I don't know why I write this before going to bed. I only know that in the very pity and grief of my heart, I feel as if it were doing something.

Fanny's sickly and deformed little boy, for whom she and Dickens had been so concerned, did not long survive his mother, to his uncle's further and deep-felt grief. And during the last part of 1848 Dickens was musing more and more over the next book he was to write. How important *David Copperfield* became to him, a book which he claimed as his favourite child, and how great were the demands it made upon his secret self, can be seen in a letter written when he was within a few pages of completing the novel:

> Oh, my dear Forster, if I were to say half of what *Copperfield* makes me feel tonight, how strangely, even to you, I should be turned inside out! I seem to be sending some part of me into the Shadowy World.

The first number of *David Copperfield* was published in May 1849; the last number was to appear in November 1850. On 6 July 1849, Charles West, after vainly seeking support and encouragement in many quarters for the idea of a Hospital for Sick Children, wrote at last to Dr Henry Bence Jones, whose name had been suggested to him; and with the meeting of these two men, the establishment of a Children's Hospital began to pass from a dream into a possibility. And as West and Bence Jones gathered support and detailed help for the idea of an institution which was to be one of the greatest and most important steps forward in the history of paediatric medicine, so Charles Dickens continued to issue his masterpiece, which was to become the most personal of all his studies of childhood. To return again to Forster, who on this period and these matters is our important authority:

> The reader ... can judge for himself how far the childish experiences are likely to have given the turn to Dickens's genius; whether their bitterness had so burnt into his nature, as, in the hatred of oppression, the revolt against abuse of power, and the war with injustice under every form displayed in his earlier books, to have reproduced itself only; and to what extent mere compassion for his own childhood may account for the strange fascination always exerted over him by child-suffering and sorrow.

Among the earliest supporters of the idea of a Children's Hospital appear the names of Angela Burdett Coutts, Elizabeth Gaskell, Lady Noel Byron and her daughter Countess Lovelace, Dickens's own sister Mrs Austin, and Lady Kay-Shuttleworth. Among the men were the Earl of Shaftesbury, the Earl of Carlisle, and Henry Austin and Dr Thomas Southwood Smith. Dickens's own doctor and friend, Thomas Watson, was an early member of the Provisional Committee. Another medical friend, Dr Charles Locock, who had attended the birth of Dickens's seventh child, Sidney, in 1847, gave Charles West early support. There is some evidence that Dickens had been aware of Dr West's work at the Royal Universal Dispensary for Children in Lambeth from before 1847.

One thing Charles Dickens and Dr Charles West had in common was a love of fairy tales and a firm belief that they were good for children. In the little book *How to Nurse Sick Children* which Dr West published in 1854, there is a passage which I cannot forbear from quoting at length, because it not only illustrates this, but also demonstrates West's great affection for children, 'those little ones whom I so much love':

> If the child is older you may tell it stories to keep it quiet, and no one who really loves children will be at a loss in finding a story to tell. All children love to hear of what happened to grown people when they were young: – tell them of your own childhood – of what you saw and did when you were a little girl, of the village where you played, of where you went to school, of your church and your clergyman. Or tell the fairy tales that you heard, and your mother before you, and her mother before her in childhood – the tales of Goody Two Shoes, or Cinderella; Blue Beard, or Beauty and the Beast. I name them because I would not have you think that fairy tales are foolish to be told now that we have so many good and useful books for children ... God himself has formed this world full not only of useful things, but of things that are beautiful, and which, as far as we can tell, answer no other end than this, that they are lovely to gaze upon, or sweet to smell, and that they give pleasure to man. Your special business, however, when a child is ill, is to give it pleasure; such pleasure as it can then partake of; and in exact proportion as you can succeed in this, will you in very many instances promote the child's recovery. Trust me, too, for this; the innocent fairy tale which has beguiled your little patient of a weary hour will not leave you less able to tell, nor the child less ready to listen to, the story of Samuel or of Joseph ... Nor will it, I am sure, prevent the child from lifting his little hands with you when you repeat for him a prayer to his Saviour and ask Jesus, who so loved little children, to make him well again.

At the same time as Dr West was writing these words, or perhaps a little before, Dickens was writing his own defence of the fairy tale against George Cruikshank's attempts to turn everything into a temperance tract. In October 1853, Dickens published his paper, *Frauds upon Fairies*:

> We may assume that we are not singular in entertaining a very great tenderness for the fairy literature of our childhood. It would be hard to estimate the amount of gentleness and mercy that has made its way among us through these slight channels. Forbearance, courtesy, consideration for the poor and aged, kind treatment of animals, the love of nature, abhorrence of tyranny and brute force – many such good things have first been nourished in the child's heart by this powerful aid. It has greatly helped

> to keep us, in some sense ever young, by preserving through our worldly ways one slender track not overgrown with weeds, where we may walk with children, sharing their delights.

Later, in *Hard Times*, published the same year as Dr West's *How to Nurse Sick Children*, Dickens returned to the subject of the fairy tale and other stories of fancy, upholding them against the claims of merely utilitarian literature. It was not the first nor the last time that he and Charles West were to share the same attitude. The affinity between Great Ormond Street and some of the ideas held by Charles Dickens did not cease with his death. The Hospital for Sick Children has been responsible, directly and indirectly, for enabling more children to grow up without succumbing to the perilous diseases of childhood, than perhaps any other institution in the world. It may be considered as one of life's more pleasant little ironies, therefore, that it should have had as two of its chief benefactors, two authors who both, it could be said, had a Peter Pan complex. For J.M. Barrie, Peter Pan's creator, the wistful desire to remain a child was overt and confessed. In Dickens, it was a hidden conflict. If at the beginning the relationship between Dickens and The Hospital for Sick Children was a mixture of personal sympathy and what was almost mental symbiosis, it will be seen later, how at the climacteric period of Dickens's life, in 1858, his association and involvement with Great Ormond Street also reached a peak.

—2—

CHARLES DICKENS AND CHARLES WEST

The Hospital for Sick Children was the vision and the achievement of one man virtually alone, Dr Charles West. He dreamed of such a hospital when working among the poor in Lambeth and Southwark, but his dreams were shattered by the opposition of the local practitioners, who feared the loss of the pennies paid them by the mothers of the sick children – pennies gathered painfully and laboriously from long hours of charring or washing clothes, and pennies handed over to the local apothecary or surgeon with trembling hope for their threatened little ones, but not without a secret tear at the thought of the bread thus deprived them. West argued for a children's hospital against the reasoned objections of the leading physicians of the time, who pointed to the precedents and traditions of past generations. When, by his example and the respect gained from his growing reputation as a specialist in children's diseases West convinced his colleagues to support the creation of a hospital for children, the governing body of the Royal Infirmary for Children in Waterloo Road repeatedly turned down his proposals for converting the institution from a dispensary into a hospital. West finally achieved his dream only by constant pleading and canvassing in the consulting rooms of Marylebone and Mayfair. Many years later, when The Hospital for Sick Children was a much-respected and much loved institution, West wrote a new preface for the seventh edition of his *Lectures on the Diseases of Infancy and Childhood*. In this 1884 preface, West made a personal and rather sad statement, which revealed how much the hospital meant to him, and showed how much he personally meant to the hospital.

> The foundation of a hospital for sick children was the dream of my youth, and the occupation of thirty years of manhood ... and I trusted that when old age came I might be allowed to linger about the place to which my heart turns as a parent's towards his child. This happiness has been denied me to my life-long heartbreak; and it is now too late for me to hope for more than this – that when I have passed away those to whom my memory will still be dear may hear my name sometimes mentioned as the founder of the first children's hospital that ever existed in this country, and as having given the impulse to that movement which has led to the establishment of children's hospitals in almost every town in England and America, and has enriched the once scanty literature of the subject with contributions of surpassing value.

But as West was always ready to acknowledge, his dream would never have taken shape without the help of more influential men such as Dr Henry Bence Jones, the friend and first biographer of the eminent scientist, Michael Faraday, and later secretary to the Royal Institution founded in 1799. With this background together with his aristocratic family connections, Bence Jones was able to enlist the support of men of wealth and of social and intellectual renown. Indeed, the majority of the members of the first Provisional Committee, formed to propagate the idea of a children's hospital, were either friends of Bence Jones or friends of friends. But important and necessary as Dr Bence Jones's medical, scientific and social milieu was for getting the whole project started on a firm financial and practical basis, perhaps in the end the most decisive support, which made the hospital known to the public and enabled it to continue, was that given by Charles Dickens.

There is ample reason to believe that during his lifetime, and for a generation afterwards, the role that Dickens played in the fortunes of Great Ormond Street seemed in the eyes of the public almost a predominant one. A valuable and contemporary document in support of that view is an article printed in *The Family Herald* of 9 April 1859:

> The hospital has been in operation since 1852, but its objects and claims had been very little brought before the public, or rather ... lost sight of amidst the crowd of competing charities, till last year, when Mr Charles Dickens presided at the anniversary festival, and afterwards gave one of his 'readings' for the benefit of the institution. This helped to make it known to many who were not aware of its existence, although it possesses royal patronage, and includes the names of some noble, wealthy, and benevolent men in the list of its council and managers.

Half a century after the above extract was printed, the editor of a standard edition of Dickens's collected works could make the overwhelming claim that The Hospital for Sick Children was 'founded on a small scale over fifty years ago by Charles Dickens and a few others'. And in 1903, an authority such as F.G.Kitton could write in the catalogue of the newlyfounded Dickens Fellowship's Exhibition at the Memorial Hall, London, that the rare 1860 reprint of *A Curious Dance Round a Curious Tree* (a description of St Luke's Hospital for the Insane, City Road) was 'published in aid of the funds of the Children's Hospital, Great Ormond Street'. This was a most extraordinary error to come from such a source. It would seem that he assumed that any hospital with which Dickens was connected must *ipso facto* be Great Ormond Street. Statements such as these made at the beginning of this century, exaggerated though they may be, do illustrate a certain tradition of contemporary report and knowledge that Dickens moved in those circles which first supported the founding of a children's hospital, and that his sympathy and enthusiasm for such a cause dated back earlier and his active involvement in the institution was perhaps rather more than has hitherto been documented. For one thing, the slowly appearing volumes of the definitive and scholarly Pilgrim Edition of Dickens's letters make clear that the more that we know about Dickens, the more surely we realize how much we do not know, and that here are things we shall never know about him. Very few letters to Dickens have survived. There is some mention in the Hospital's archives of letters to him, the ashes of which must have been blown away among the Gad's Hill geraniums. What early letters written to him by Dr West and his colleagues may not have been recorded?

The Hospital itself was firmly convinced of Dickens's involvement. On 27 April 1908, *The Times* published a letter from Great Ormond Street announcing the proposed opening of the new outpatients department donated by William Waldorf Astor as a memorial to his youngest daughter, Gwendolyn Enid Astor, who had died of tuberculosis when only eight. This letter was signed by the Duke of Fife, the Hospital's president; Arthur Lucas, its chairman; John Murray, the vice-chairman, and J.W.F.Deacon, the treasurer. These four men, the senior governors of the Hospital, had been associated with it for many years, and had known personally some of the founder members. In this letter occurs a sentence which was indisputably the source for the claim made in the collected edition, mentioned above: 'The Hospital for Sick Children was founded on a small scale by that immortal friend of children Charles Dickens, Charles West, and a few others fifty-six years ago, and was the first hospital ever established in this country for children.'

It can confidently be assumed that early and late in its history, Charles West and Charles Dickens were both seen as having an important and special role in the development of The Hospital for Sick Children. But the stories of their lives and careers present a great contrast. Dickens, the world-famous writer, whose name and features were known to everyone, whose works were eagerly awaited and seized upon by avid readers: his lightest word and most trivial appearance were the subject of instant public interest and comment. West, a doctor respected by his colleagues, was obscure and unknown even in his chosen profession at an age when 'Boz' had long enjoyed glittering and international celebrity. His patients, young and old, admired him and adored him and never forgot him. But for over twenty years after he had resigned from Great Ormond Street, he lived in growing obscurity and sickness. He died almost forgotten by the world at large, although the obituaries in the medical journals paid unusual and handsome tribute to a man who had always been regarded as a difficult colleague.

Of course, one thing the two men had in common was a love of children. It was said of West that 'Children especially, with their wonderful faculty of recognizing those who love them, went to him at once.' And the most revered Matron of Great Ormond Street, Catherine J. Wood, wrote that 'There was no more touching sight than to see Dr West make his round; the little patients welcomed him as their friend, and the fractious or frightened child could not long resist the magic of his smile or the winning gentleness of his manner.' Another example of West's wonderful sympathy with children was that 'He would walk down a street behind a woman carrying a crying baby over her shoulder, and at almost the first glance the baby would stop crying and begin to laugh and hold out his little arms to go to him.'

But in addition to their mutual love for children, they both knew from their own experience of the wrongs suffered by children – they shared a concern for their helplessness and a deep awareness of the growing need for a change in those social structures which allowed the children of the poor to perish from want, bad conditions, neglect and preventable disease. They were both of the same generation, and had grown up in an age when the harsh conditions that existed in the new factories and mills and in the expanding cities were being realized and condemned by such men as Richard Oastler and, later, Lord Shaftesbury, who was to be connected with both West and Dickens in philanthropic work. It was in 1830 that Oastler was first made aware of 'the cruelties daily practised in our mills on little children'; he turned his attention from campaigning against slavery in the West Indies to starting a movement that first produced the twelve-hour bill and later fought for the ten-hour bill, both of which regulated the hours that children were expected to work in the mills. Dickens was then eighteen years old; West was fourteen. Both were at that time of youth and young manhood when it is full of noble enthusiasm. The growing social conscience of their age, which began to question the morality of allowing five-year-olds to work in the darkness of a mine as beasts of burden, or to labour for seventeen hours a day in the bedlam and dirt of a cotton mill, reinforced both of them in their already awakened awareness of the sufferings of the poor, particularly of children.

Charles West had finished his schooling at Totteridge and was about to be apprenticed to an apothecary at Amersham, where he had already been brought up in an atmosphere of Nonconformist philanthropy in the home of his father, a Baptist minister. He was now to come into close contact with the sick, the children of both the poor agricultural labourer and the comfortable farmer. This was the time when the high price of bread combined with low wages and unemployment, caused by the newly developed farm machinery, to produce extreme suffering in English villages, leading to riots, executions, and deportations, all of which did nothing to relieve the famished families or to improve their lot. Charles Dickens had already become personally acquainted with poor town children during his time at the blacking warehouse. But, strangely, he never seemed so aware of the starvation in the country which had caused so many to leave the fields and farms in the first place for the town slums and gaunt, dark mills, where they were surer of earning at least a pittance for bread, and where many were to find some improvement in their standards of living, at least in the good times. This was something of which his fellow novelist and friend Mrs Gaskell was well aware: Though she painted with bold strokes the grim mills of Manchester, she also, in *North and South*, referred to 'the difficulty of meeting with anyone in a manufacturing town who did not prefer the better wages and greater independence of working in a mill'. And in the same book she said of the lot of the agricultural labourer in the south that 'There is very hard bodily labour to be gone through, with very little food to give strength.'

When Charles West left school to become an apothecary's apprentice, Charles Dickens was already working as a reporter in Doctors' Commons, an experience which, together with his later spell as a parliamentary reporter, made him aware of the wrongs and deprivation caused not by poverty alone, but by the outdated and meaningless procedures and privileges of a law choked by its own ermine, and the comfortable complacency of uncaring, dull and selfish legislators. This was, of course, the time when the parliamentary struggle for the Reform Act was at its height. It was a recollection of those years that went into the creation of *Bleak House*, where in the first chapter Dickens's most despairing figure of helplessness appears, the unfortunate man who is apparently condemned to perpetual imprisonment because he cannot purge his contempt. He has been caught in a web of legalistic questions to which it is impossible that he could ever provide answers. The grim irony which records his brief appearance etches it indelibly upon the reader's memory, becoming the archetype of the law's delay and launching a theme which becomes a main stratum of the book. This first number of *Bleak House* appeared in March 1852, when The Hospital for Sick Children had been open only two weeks, and when Dickens and Henry Morley were probably contemplating 'Drooping Buds', published four weeks later in *Household Words*.

Dickens engaged in many schemes of philanthropy and reform, and gave his name and aid to many charities, with, as we have already seen, varying degrees of interest and sympathy. No cause was productive of more lasting good than the cause in which Charles Dickens and Charles West joined their respective talents. Urania Cottage at Shepherd's Bush, on which we know from epistolary evidence that Dickens spent an immense amount of time and labour, saved perhaps a few dozen girls and women from a life of prostitution or criminality. Of Great Ormond Street, a sober medical historian could write in the 1920s:

> Every year sees thousands of English tourists proceeding to Belgium to see the fields of Waterloo, but only very few realize how far more sacred are the few square acres in a quiet backwater of Holborn where this vast work was begun and achieved ... For of what campaign in our history could it be said that it had saved half the infant population of England? Yet such is the net result of the progress child welfare has made in a century – one child out of every two born in England today owes its life to the Great Ormond Street venture.

In West's and Dickens's day Great Ormond Street was indeed a quiet backwater. As Albert Smith wrote:

> Within the recollection of old inhabitants still extant we find that the ... neighbourhood between the Foundling Hospital and Red Lion Square ... and Gray's Inn Lane and Bloomsbury ... was once the patrician quarter of London. The houses even in their decay of quality have a respectable look ... All the furniture is rubbed up to the last degree of friction polish and the carpets are brushed cleanly threadbare. The window-curtains blanched in the sun of thirty or forty summers ... Even the ancient landladies have given the same conservative care to their flaxen fronts and remarkable caps. They are grave and dignified in their demeanour, for they believe Great Ormond Street still to be the focus of the West End.

In 'Drooping Buds' Dickens confirms this impression. 'Great Ormond Street belonged to our great-grandfathers ... It is cut off now from the life of the town – in London, but not of it ... Many stiff bows and formal introductions had those old walls seen, when Great Ormond Street was grand.' The final choice of Great Ormond Street as a site for the children's hospital was, however, not only influenced by its drowsy peacefulness, the large rooms from a more extravagant time, and the ample gardens still rustled by the breezes blowing down from the open fields and hills of Hampstead and Highgate. It was also near the meaner streets and alleys from which its little patients were to come. Some of the former pleasant retreats of Holborn were decaying fast. See how Dickens describes the square of Barnard's Inn: 'the dingiest collection of shabby buildings ever squeezed together ... the most dismal trees ... sparrows ... cats, and the most dismal houses ... in every stage of dilapidated blind and curtain, crippled flower-pot, cracked glass, dust and decay, and miserable makeshift'.

Holborn and its vicinity had long been notorious for harbouring some of the worst slums and rookeries in London. Charles West stressed that 'Sickness and suffering, poverty and disease, are commonplace enough, we meet them at every corner of the street ... We must remember that the first condition of the utility of a hospital for the poor is that it should be placed within their easy reach.' More than a century before this observation by West, Hogarth had drawn his *Gin Lane*. In the background is the characteristic spire of St George's, Bloomsbury, which had been recently erected because the respectable families of Holborn and Bloomsbury objected to having to pass through this infamous rookery on their way to worship at St Giles. The baby depicted by Hogarth as falling from its drunken mother's arms over the railing of the steps, and about to dash his head on the flagstones below, had no children's hospital to which he could be admitted. Even Dr Armstrong's Dispensary for the Infant Poor was not to open in nearby Red Lion Square until twenty-eight years later, in 1779. When Dickens could write of St Giles Rookery that still 'The filthy and miserable appearance of this part of London can hardly be imagined by those who have not visited it', no doubt other babies were still being overlaid or dropped by their stupefied mothers and nurses. But at least then, in 1836 when *Sketches by Boz* was published, Charles West was studying medicine in Paris and visiting L'Hôpital des Enfants Malades in the Rue de Sèvres, which had been converted from a foundling hospital into a true children's hospital in 1802.

It was this institution that no doubt first inspired him, and was certainly always an example to him, in his dream of a hospital for sick children in England. Although severely critical of some aspects of it, 'the extremely unfavourable hygienic conditions in which all children are placed', and even going so far as to refer to 'the wretched inmates of the Foundling and Children's Hospital at Paris', Charles West never forgot that it was the very first children's hospital of all, and despite its many faults, had contributed and was still contributing much towards that understanding of children's disease which only a hospital for sick children could provide.

West was still in Paris when *Oliver Twist* began to appear, and although neither he nor Charles Dickens realized it, Fagin and Oliver, picking their way through the mire of the Field Lane and Gray's Inn Lane slums, and Bill Sikes, lurching off to drink with fellow thieves at The Three Cripples in squalid and dirty Saffron Hill, were to become powerful factors in arousing public support for a children's hospital which was to serve the very courts and alleys in which their tale was set.

Holborn, together with Clerkenwell and St Giles, was important to Dickens, both in his life and as a setting for his characters. He lived there and wandered through the area as a child and a man. His numerous characters act out their comedies and their troubles in these streets. Mrs Gamp is made to live just round the corner from where the nurses of Great Ormond Street were to make her and Betsey Prig nightmares of the past. Gray's Inn, Lincoln's Inn and the other Inns of Court loom in the background of many of his works; sometimes, indeed, their cobble-stoned courts, crumbling arches and worn and dusty lawns become a predominant presence. The streets and buildings of Holborn are in his pages vested with as strong individualities as the humans he made pass among them. But one street, in reality, he was to help in giving the strongest identity of all, a street whose mere name would become throughout the world synonymous with help and care for those children he had described as wallowing half-naked in the kennels of the Seven Dials courts, where children and buildings were equally ill-proportioned and deformed.

Charles West had been spurred on in his endeavours to bring about a Great Ormond Street by his work among the sick children of the borough and elsewhere in London, and, above all, by his realization of the terrible ignorance that most doctors had about the nature and treatment of childhood diseases. Of all that has been written about the suffering and deprivation endured by the children of the poor in Victorian London, Dickens and certain others are usually quoted. But there is a little sketch written without melodrama or special pleading, which by its restraint gives a better and unforgettable picture of the lot of poor children. It dwells on no horrors and has no harrowing scenes. It was written by that other great novelist of the Victorian age, Thackeray, whose pages are not usually culled for such examples of sociological history. It is '*The Curate's Walk*', written for *Punch* in 1847. Dickens himself warmly admired it. It is based upon a pastoral visit made by Thackeray's friend, W.H.Brookfield, when curate of St Luke's, Soho. Three little girls, the eldest barely ten, the youngest five, look after themselves very neatly in their modest room while their mother is out charring. The eldest girl has taken charge of her two little sisters ever since their father, a journeyman binder, died four years ago.

> There was a big bed, which must have been the resting place of the whole of this little family ... And on the table there were two or three bits of dry bread, and a jug of water with which these three young people ... were about to take their meal called tea ... that little Betsey who looks so small is nearly ten years old ... and assumes command of the room during her parent's absence: has nursed her sisters from babyhood up to the present time ... and goes out occasionally and transacts the family purchases of bread, moist sugar, and mother's tea. They dine upon bread, tea and breakfast upon bread when they have it, or go to bed without a morsel. Their holiday is Sunday, which they spend at church and Sunday-school. The younger children scarcely ever go out, save on that day, but sit sometimes in the sun, which comes in pretty pleasantly; sometimes blue in the cold, for they very seldom see a fire except to heat irons by, when mother has a job of linen to get up.

The whole description of these three tiny girls 'content with small pittances, practising a hundred virtues of thrift and order', is handled with great tenderness and even whimsicality. Thackeray wrote nothing so touching as this picture of a 'little cockboat manned by babies venturing over the great stormy ocean' of life. These three small sisters were an example of the more fortunate and deserving poor, children who had almost nothing, although 'thrifty, kindly, simple and loving'. But the frail cockleshell of their starving existence could be upset by the slightest setback. Illness would bring utter disaster. It was such children to whom West was to offer help and hope.

It is difficult for us to understand how terrible it was to be a sick child in the first half of the nineteenth century, and to be a sick poor child was far, far worse. We shudder to think of the horrors of surgery before the days of anaesthetics and antisepsis, but forget that it was sometimes necessary to use the knife on children. John Flint South, surgeon to St Thomas's Hospital from 1841 to 1863 and president of the Royal College of Surgeons, describes his experience when he had left school and first began to study at St Thomas's in 1813:

> Soon after October I began to attend the operations in the hospital theatre; this was for sometime a very hard trial for me. I was always very anxious to see all I could, and soon got over the blood-shedding which necessarily ensued; and so long as the patient did not make much noise I got on very well but if the cries were great, and *specially if they came from a child*, I was quickly upset, had to leave the theatre, and not infrequently fainted.

It was not only the apprentice to surgery who was distressed by the thought of operating on children. The young South also attended the theatre at Guy's, where one of the greatest surgeons of the day, Sir Ashley Cooper, operated.

> For operating with alacrity, and well at the same time, I have not known his equal . . . With all his boldness in acting out his maxim that a surgeon should have an 'an eagle's eye, a lady's hand, and a lion's heart', I cannot doubt that Cooper did think of the suffering of patients on whom he operated; his kind and encouraging and patient manner with them was very striking, and not exceeded by any operator I have ever seen; and I cannot pass by one striking example of this which was told me by an old Quaker friend, from whose grandchild a naevus was to be removed. I do not know whether it was a lovely child or not, but when brought into the room it smiled very sweetly upon him, and Cooper burst into tears.

South had from his boyhood been well aware of the problems and shortcomings in treating the illnesses of childhood. His father had attempted some solution, a generation before Dr West had commenced working among the poor children of the same neighbourhood. The picture South draws in the opening paragraph of his *Memorials*, besides being a fascinating description of one part of a druggist's business, also helps in understanding some of the problems that West was to face, and is an indication that the poor worker, the small tradesman and others had an instinctive distrust – a distrust spread, perhaps by the rumour of experience – of the local doctors when their children were ill.

> I was the son of a druggist in the Borough, who lived forty years in the same house, in which he had made an excellent business, chiefly through the successful treatment of infantile disorders with very simple remedies; for, although he had not even attended a lecture of any kind, yet, seeing an immense number of sick children, and being a very intelligent and observant man, he had really attained very extensive empirical knowledge, which he used with much ability and judgement. The result of this was that his shop was filled from nine till twelve by people of all classes, with their sick children, waiting till they could be furnished with – now a two-penny powder of compound senna, and generally a grain of calomel to clean the alimentary canal; now an eightpenny ounce-and-half mixture of chalk with dillwater; and sometimes a little syrup of poppies, or a cough mixture of the same price, containing a little ipecacuanha wine and syrup of red poppies. The success of this simple treatment was very great, and brought him great celebrity; and he was often urged to become an apothecary and make outdoor visits, but he had too much good sense to be so persuaded, and continued his home practice throughout life.

How ignorant the medical profession must have been of childish complaints, if even these simple remedies were not prescribed by them; if they had been, South's father could hardly have earned such a local reputation. When, not so long afterwards Dr West joined the staff of the Royal Universal Infirmary for Children, the same local practitioners showed, in his opinion, the same lack of knowledge. West had in his boyhood apprenticeship with Mr Gray at Amersham learned two things: how to compound medicines, and Shakespeare, and he had often made up the same cough mixtures and medicines as used by South's father. The ignorance prevalent among practitioners as to the nature of their prescriptions was something Charles West always stressed, even in his later years. These remedies were for the simpler diseases of childhood. How much more serious were the consequences of the ignorance many doctors had of more complicated and perilous children's diseases?

In this Charles Dickens agreed with West. Apart from the passage in 'Drooping Buds' in which he describes doctors as being able to do little more than feel a sick child's pulse and 'shake their heads with vain regret over the little corpse, around which women weep so bitterly' (a passage directly influenced by West himself), there is the biting description of the doctor who is called to the inn when Little Nell faints. By prescribing no treatment except what he conjectures the landlady has already applied, an 'injunction, slowly and portentously delivered', the doctor leaves everybody dazzled and 'in admiration of that wisdom which tallied so closely with their own . . . a very shrewd doctor indeed'.

Charles West wrote, in the first announcement of an 'Appeal on Behalf of a Hospital for Sick Children', 'the diseases of children, owing to the limited opportunities of observing them, are but little studied and ill understood – an evil not confined in its effects to the poorer classes, for whose benefit such an institution may seem more especially needed, but extending to all ranks of society.'

This statement was soon to receive dramatic confirmation in the sad case of the little daughter of one of the most eminent of all Victorian statesmen. This child's sufferings in a household which had every comfort and assistance that rank, privilege and wealth could provide, emphasizes by contrast the greater distress of the seriously ill children of the poor. A few weeks before his first appeal for a children's hospital was advertised in *The Times*, Charles West had received a letter of support dated 23 January 1850 from Dr Charles Locock, one of the most eminent physicians of the day. Locock was first physician accoucheur to Queen Victoria, and had attended at the birth of all her children. As has been noted, Dickens had called in Locock when his wife Catherine suffered complications at the birth of her seventh child in 1847. In his letter to West, Locock agreed that a children's hospital would go far to improve the profession's knowledge of children's diseases. When this letter was written, William Ewart Gladstone's four-year-old daughter Jenny had already shown signs of developing her fatal illness, becoming passive and dormant, holding tightly to her mother, and suffering spasms and convulsions. Gladstone had described her two years previously as 'quick, thoughtful, very affectionate'. By March Gladstone was writing in his diary that Jenny 'is a wreck – we are thankful to be going near the best advice'.

But the best advice even for Gladstone was not to prove very helpful. Jenny was suffering from meningitis, but the doctors seemed to think it was some internal stomach trouble. On Good Friday the Gladstones became greatly alarmed at their daughter's condition, but were told it was 'apparently some unconquerable obstruction in the bowels'. Jenny became worse and then seemed to improve, but by Easter Monday, Jenny was again undergoing the fearful agony of convulsions. Gladstone wrote, 'Jenny had much pain. Last night we sent to Locock about 4.00 a.m. who when he came cheered us. In the morning thank God she was better.'

But Locock, who had written to West of the need to improve the knowledge of children's diseases, seemed also at first to misread the obvious symptoms. The next day, Tuesday, 2 April, Gladstone's diary entry reads:

> It was a day of much anxiety and pain. Last night the brain was in a fearful state of irritation and dear little Jenny spent it tossing, moaning and screaming, chiefly in Catherine's arms, the rest in mine ... Locock in the morning still held it most probable that the stomach was the cause. But at night he declared the head symptoms unequivocal. The moaning was much less but the head moved very constantly from side to side. The pulse was low, which he much disliked. The eyes very heavy. He says it is tubercular inflammation of the membranes of the brain, a most insidious form of disease.

At last Dr Locock had arrived at the correct diagnosis, but he was helpless, lacking all effective treatment apparently for anything more serious than blisters: a sudorific known as Dover's powder, of which opium and sulphate of potash were the constituents, and half a grain of calomel! Jenny's agony went on through the week, although there was some abatement, leading both Locock and her parents to false hopes. When on the Saturday night her racking convulsions started again, Gladstone went to Locock, 'who did not seem to regard them as of vital consequence'. No wonder Jenny's mother Catherine, worn out with watching, unable to help her little daughter's torment, was, as Gladstone reported, 'more cut up and tired tonight than I have yet seen her'. On Monday, Locock's last visit left Gladstone with no hope. 'Catherine and I with Mrs Baker sat in the room of death and watched the beloved child in her death battle, powerless to aid her.' Jenny's end was no peaceful exit like Little Nell's or Paul Dombey's. The excruciating convulsions increased, until 'there were scarcely any spaces of repose between the tearings and tossings of the conflict ... So many, many gasps, each of which it seemed must be the last; to see her in such an agony of battle, and to be by her side, and to be powerless to give her visible aid; to feel as we moistened her lips that it was a mockery ... this sight was sad and terrible to flesh and blood.'

Jenny's death at 2.00 a.m. on the morning of 9 April came as a blessed release to her parents. Her last conscious words were 'I want Mummy,' and Catherine, who had not broken down through all those nights, woke Gladstone a few hours later with her terrible weeping. Gladstone himself became half-mad with grief, and his family feared for his emotional balance.

Jenny's end, which neither her famous father nor her renowned physician could do anything to prevent or alleviate, emphasizes and underlines the real needs and motives that drove Charles West onwards to his mission to create a children's hospital in London. Even Charles Dickens, lacking those medical experiences and sights which confronted West every day, could not always appreciate the urgency and passion by which West was possessed, although Dickens could be equally possessed by his own need to write. In the pursuit of knowledge, in increasing his understanding of children's disease, West was indefatigable. At the last he could claim that his experience was based on the observations of 2250 cases and 650 post-mortem examinations. Similar and sympathetic as the two men were to each other, alike as they both were in espousing the cause of the distressed child, the fundamental difference between their two natures can be found in the astonishing contrast of their activities on the occasion of two of the most celebrated public spectacles in the first quarter of Queen Victoria's reign.

At the time of her coronation, on 28 June 1838, Charles Dickens was at the peak of the first full flush of his fame. *Oliver Twist* was approaching its final denouement, as the instalment containing chapters 33 and 34 appeared that June. *Nicholas Nickleby* had begun to appear in March, and the number just issued had described the first scenes at Dotheboys Hall, with its immortal portrayal of Squeers and his obnoxious family. In the November of the previous year, to celebrate the completion of the serialization of *Pickwick*, Dickens had given a dinner with Harrison Ainsworth, Samuel Lover, Serjeant Talfourd, Daniel Maclise, William Macready and John Forster among the guests. Two days after the dinner, in accordance with his growing prosperity, he opened an account at Coutts' Bank, in the first entry of which he is described as Charles Dickens, the author of *Pickwick Papers*, living at 48 Doughty Street. His circle of friends was enlarging to include other men of note and repute. Lady Holland and Lady Blessington, in advance of the more rigid and perhaps more respectable society hostesses, had been quick to assure themselves that the new young literary lion was presentable, and could conduct himself at a dinner party without embarrassment. A few days before the Coronation, Dickens, in company with Darwin, George Grote, Lord Lyttelton and others, had been elected to the Athenaeum, under the club's rule of selecting 'individuals known for their scientific or literary attainments'. 'Boz' had definitely arrived.

On the day of the Coronation itself, Dickens and some of his friends had come up to town from the house at Twickenham, which he had been renting for the summer, and in a third-floor front room, engaged for the day from a Mr Hawkins, had watched in comfort the royal procession pass beneath, sustaining themselves meanwhile with the contents of an ample picnic basket. The young Charles Dickens was not one to stint the supplies of cold viands and wine. On such an occasion, no doubt, ample bottles of champagne were a first requisite, and an indication of the success of their celebrations may be found in the letter that Dickens had to write to Mr Hawkins next day, politely requesting him to forward the hamper, which in the excitement of their festivities had been left behind. Probably Dickens's anxious haste to secure the basket may indicate that it and its cheerful contents had been supplied by Fortnum and Mason or one of the other fashionable caterers of the day.

In contrast to the glittering prospects and fame of the twenty-six-year-old Dickens, the twenty-two-year-old Charles West was unknown, except to a few professional friends, with no real future before him. The winter which had seen 'Boz' lauded with praise at the *Pickwick* dinner had also seen Charles West return to England after obtaining his doctorate in Berlin. His first venture at a settled medical career had not been successful: the buying of a partnership in a city practice which soon proved unprofitable. Not having many private patients to occupy him, West attached himself to the medical ward at St Bartholomew's Hospital, under Dr Latham, and his account of the typhus epidemic in the winter of 1837–38 attracted some attention when it was published in one of the professional journals. But the failure of his first attempt at general practice had still left him with ample time on his hands. His great interest in children's diseases made him offer his services, probably on an irregular, unofficial basis, to the Royal Infirmary for Children on Waterloo Road. As he said unequivocably in the first paragraph of his manuscript, 'Statement of Facts with Reference to my share in the founding of the Children's Hospital', probably written in the late 1880s: 'In

May 1838 my connection with the Children's Infirmary in the Waterloo Road began.' Here he saw, first in the dispensary and later in their appalling dwellings, the poor children of the surrounding slums. Nearby was the Marshalsea Prison, where Dickens's father had been imprisoned for debt. It was a district which had left indelible impressions on the boy Dickens, and which he was to make an integral part of *Little Dorrit*.

So it came about that on the day the young Queen was riding to Westminster to be crowned head of an Empire far greater than any the ancient or medieval world had ever known, and the young Charles Dickens was toasting her in champagne to wash down the cold chicken and game pies, the young Charles West, losing no opportunity of advancing his knowledge in his chosen field, was grimly performing a post-mortem *at the home* of a dead child somewhere in the slums of the Borough.

Perhaps it was a case of 'tubercular meningitis' such as that of seven-year-old Eliza Trewell from the same district, whose post-mortem West was to describe two and a half years later, recording her as 'the child of drunken parents living in the most squalid poverty' who had seemed in 'good health with the exception of an attack of pain in the head, fits and coma two years ago', and who, in January 1841, had been taken again, fatally, with another pain in the head. Poor little Eliza had none of the comforts and loving care that little Jenny Gladstone, whose symptoms Eliza had foreshadowed, was to have nine years later, but the result was the same for the poor child as for the rich child.

The post-mortem which West performed in a foul, unkempt room on Queen Victoria's Coronation Day was among the first of '180 post-mortem examination which I had observed at the dwellings of the poor in the district where I laboured'. Many more were to follow. By such relentless pursuit of paediatric medical knowledge, in conditions and circumstances which the modern reader can scarcely conceive, did Charles West advance towards his dream of a children's hospital for his poor young patients from the noisome and fever-ridden courts and alleys.

But in contrasting the widely differing activities of Charles West and Charles Dickens on that day of national rejoicing in June 1838, it should not be forgotten that the festive Dickens had also been brooding on the suffering and the waste, the inevitable concomitants of death in the young. Indelibly engraved on his memory, the wound still fresh without a cicatrice, was the completely unexpected and sudden death of his adored seventeen-year-old sister-in-law, Mary Hogarth, barely a year before. Separate though their careers had been, the thoughts, feelings and social consciences of the two men were never far apart even in the most contrasting circumstances. So it is not without significance that the June numbers of *Nicholas Nickleby* and *Oliver Twist* both show a concern with young death and the terror of its near approach.

Smike asks Nicholas Nickleby if he remembers the boy that died at Dotheboys Hall, and continues:

> 'I was with him at night, and when it was all silent he cried no more for friends he wished to come and sit with him, but began to see faces round his bed that came from home; he said they smiled and talked to him and died at last lifting his head to kiss them ... What faces will smile on me when I die! ... Who will talk to me in those long nights? They cannot come from home; they would frighten me if they did, for I don't know what it is and shouldn't know them. Pain and fear, pain and fear for me, alive or dead. No hope, no hope.'

Oliver Twist experiences, when Rose Maylie is taken suddenly and dangerously ill, emotions that exactly mirror Dickens's own emotion on that night when Mary Hogarth was dying.

> And what had been the fervency of all the prayers he had ever uttered, compared with those he poured forth, now, in the agony and passion of his supplication for the life and health of the gentle creature, who was tottering on the deep grave's verge!
>
> Oh! the suspense, the fearful, acute suspense, of standing idly by, while the life of one we dearly love is trembling in the balance! Oh! the racking thoughts that crowd upon the mind, and make the heart beat violently and the breath come thick ... the desperate anxiety *to be doing something* to relieve the pain, or lessen the danger, which we have no power to alleviate; the sinking of soul and spirit, which the sad remembrance of own helplessness produces; what tortures can equal these; what reflections or endeavours can, in the full tide and fever of the time, allay them? ...
>
> 'It is hard,' said the good doctor, turning away as he spoke; 'so young; so much beloved; but there is very little hope.'

The novelist Dickens, however, could do for Rose Maylie, what the man Dickens had been helpless to do for his sister-in-law. Rose Maylie is saved. Dickens muses in the last instalment of *Oliver Twist* the following April:

> I would show Rose Maylie in all the bloom and grace of early womanhood, shedding on her secluded path in life, such soft and gentle light, as fell on all who trod it with her, and shone into their hearts ... I would watch her in all her goodness and charity abroad ... I would summon before me, once again, those joyous little faces that clustered round her knee and listen to their merry prattle; I would recall the tones of that clear laugh, and conjure up the sympathizing tears that glistened in the soft

> blue eye. These, and a thousand looks and smiles, and turns of thought and speech – I would fain recall them every one.

Well could Dickens, probably very near in time to when the above was issued, in a letter to William Bradbury condoling him on the death of his child, mention Mary Hogarth and how he pictured her 'with every well-remembered grace and beauty heightened by the light of Heaven'. It is not often in a great writer that we have such an open and ardent wish-fulfilment in his prose; it is indeed, as Dr Slater remarks, the poet's 'golden world', of the old poets let it be remembered and even of the old philosophers; it was not until the time of *Dombey and Son* that Dickens realized that it was not enough to change the sorrows of the world by drawing a picture of an idealized world in which good triumphed and the wicked repented, even if it was only a reformed Scrooge sending a cab trotting off to Bob Cratchit in Camden Town with a prize turkey. And yet the sheer genius of the early Dickens, the power of presentation of social wrongs and injustice mingled with the eccentricities and laughter of comedy, the vividness of characterization in personages both good and bad, were in the end to produce a more lasting effect than those works 'in which a pervasive uneasiness about contemporary society takes the place of an intermittent concern with specific social wrongs,' as Professor Tillotson writes. Dickens himself realized this and his more active participation in actual movements of social reform were attempts to hasten reforms which even the unique power of his writings seemed unable to achieve immediately. It is a tribute to his good sense and innate inward gifts that Dickens never descended, as he might easily have done, into a mere writer of didactic and proselytizing novels. Dr Charles West looked upon the post-mortem knife as a valuable accessory to his true work of healing and succouring sick children. Did Charles Dickens sometimes regard philanthropic work as an accessory measure in advancing and inspiring his true task in life, the conception and creation of immortal tales?

Charles West's widow, whose letters to her stepson George A. Herbert West are an authority for West's practice of post-mortems, describes her husband as hating shows, and also mentioned that on the day of Wellington's funeral, that other great early Victorian public event, West had told her that he was again performing a post-mortem at the slum home of a dead child, whose mother, together with some neighbours, insisted on staying in the room to make sure her little daughter would not be needlessly cut up and mutilated. Bizarre and horrific as this seems today, it does show motherly love and concern.

By the date of Wellington's funeral, 18 November 1852, The Hospital for Sick Children had already been in existence for nine months. West's standing in the medical profession was totally different from the obscurity he had known in 1838. But it is evident that he was still ardently gathering knowledge in the same difficult way, even though the institution of which he had long dreamed was already a healthy infant, which would grow up to do all that West had envisioned and more. The Committee of Management had met on the eve of this solemn public spectacle, and the chairman, the Reverend Sir Henry Dukinfield, 'reported his attendance and inspection of the Hospital; expressing his unqualified approbation of the state and condition in which he found every part of the Institution'. The Committee then authorized the Matron 'to procure a Chest of Drawers and a Wash Stand for the Nurses' sleeping room' and 'directed that the weekly remuneration of the Errand Lad had been increased from six to eight shillings'. This last detail brings to mind the boy Dickens's remuneration at Warren's Blacking House.

But what was Dickens doing on that sunny but chilly day when the great eighteen-ton catafalque rumbled painfully and slowly along to St Paul's? He had refused a place in the cathedral to witness the ceremony, having already arranged to call back his eldest son from Eton to watch with him, from the windows of the *Household Words'* office, the long funeral cortège as it passed along the Strand to pause at Temple Bar. Perhaps he knew of West's activity on that day – they were now both together concerned with Great Ormond Street. And we may note that in this November number of *Bleak House* Dickens again took an opportunity to describe the deprived areas of Holborn and Clerkenwell to which The Hospital for Sick Children was becoming a beacon of hope, when he makes the former tinker Phil say, 'I took the business. Such as it was. It wasn't much of a beat – round Saffron Hill, Hatton Garden, Clerkenwell, Smiffield and these – poor neighbourhood, where they use up the kettles till they're past mending.'

The relative position Charles West and Charles Dickens occupied in the public eye was perhaps as disparate as ever. In some ways it was analogous to that which prevails today. The life of Charles Dickens has been written, rewritten and retold, discussed, analysed, and rehabilitated in countless volumes, only part of which would form a large library in themselves. The life of Charles West has never been told, apart from a brief paper or two in the medical journals. To the world at large, his name is as obscure as the hospital which he created is famous. Perhaps it may not be amiss to rectify a little of that ignorance and neglect.

—3—

CHARLES WEST AND CHARLES DICKENS

Charles West was born in London on 8 August 1816. In that year, John Bunnell Davies started the Universal Dispensary for Children at St Andrew's Hill, Doctor's Commons, which later moved to Waterloo Bridge Road in 1824, becoming the Royal Universal Infirmary for Children. This institution was to play a large part in the life of the newly born second son of thirty-eight-year-old Ebenezer West, a small businessman who was also a Baptist lay preacher. In that year, 1816, the four-year-old Charles Dickens and his family were still living in London at Norfolk Street, Fitzroy Square; the next year was to see the move to Chatham.

The little Charles West had, very briefly, a younger brother who only lived for six weeks. Perhaps Charles was too young to remember him, though Ebenezer and Jane must have grieved over their third child, so quickly snatched away from them, and with their deep and sincere religious convictions kept his memory alive to their two surviving sons. But Jane West surely forgot some of her sorrow when she gave birth to a daughter, who was named after her. Charles almost certainly doted upon his little sister, and appointed himself her playmate and careful guardian. In Chatham, the young Charles Dickens and his sister Fanny, the older by two years, were inseparable companions, sharing their joys, discoveries, sorrows, and schooling together. It is a fanciful thought that among the sturdy schoolboys playing happily in the field at Chatham, whom the rather sickly young Dickens used to watch wistfully and with admiration, was the little boy William Jenner, who later with Charles West was to be one of the first two physicians at Great Ormond Street.

In 1821 Ebenezer West received a call to become Baptist minister at Chenies in Buckinghamshire. It was an idyllic place, and for the five-year-old Charles a wonderful contrast with the streets of London which were all that he had known. The Baptist Chapel at Chenies, 'a good brick edifice', had been built in 1779. The village itself was described at length by the historian J.A.Froude, a friend of Bence Jones. Froude's account of Chenies was written over half a century after the Wests first came there, but it had not changed much, if at all:

> The village stands on a chalk hill rising from the little river Ches, four miles from Rickmansworth, on the road to Amersham. The estate belongs to the Duke of Bedford and is pervaded by serene good manners, as if it was always Sunday. No vulgar noises disturb the general quiet ... the oldest inhabitant can never have heard an oath spoken aloud or seen a drunken man. Dirt and poverty are equally unknown. The houses, large and small, are solid and substantial, built of red brick with high chimneys and pointed gables, and well-trimmed gardens before the doors.

Perhaps Ebenezer West, in answering a religious call, also had the more worldly thought that the new home would be beneficial to the children: seven-year-old Ebenezer, five-year-old Charles and baby Jane. But the fresh country air and peace of Chenies did not help little Jane, who died when she was four. Whether victim to a sudden childish infection or a sickly child we do not know. The loss of his baby sister certainly affected Charles West, who 'had at an early age determined to be a medical man'. Was it her early death, and the baby brother who had lived but a month and a half, that gave rise to this decision? Did his memories of them and of this mother's grief drive him on so hard for sick children and for the creation of a children's hospital? It is not too fanciful to look upon little Jane West as having been, in a way, responsible for Great Ormond Street. Childhood impressions, the intense but fleeting sorrows of our early years, can return and mean more to the grown man in retrospect when he is despondent or contemplating a great decision. As Charles Dickens wrote from Gad's Hill near the time when his domestic unhappiness was first confessed: 'I feel much as I used to do when I was a small child a few miles off, and somebody (who, I wonder, and which way did *She* go when she died) hummed the evening hymn to me, and I cried on the pillow.'

When the West family moved to Chenies, Charles was at that age when the attention of a small boy is first aroused to the meaning and consequence of the world around him, when he could say, with Pip in *Great Expectations*, 'it was the time of my first, most vivid and broad impression of things.' The beauty and the historical traditions of Chenies, the country pastimes and sports, it would be thought, were things which became important to the young Charles West, and remained in his memory in the same way as Chatham was important to the young Charles

Dickens. 'Here the most durable of his early impressions were received, and the associations that were around him when he died, were those which at the outset of his life had affected him most strongly,' Forster remarks of Dickens and his boyhood days at Chatham.

But Charles West had no biographer to remark upon his boyhood, and we can but surmise on the thoughts and activities that occupied him in those early years. The young Charles West would have wandered over the countryside in his free hours. With his brother and other boys, and without perhaps the water bailiff's permission, he fished the little river Ches, of which Froude fondly remarked, 'No river in England holds finer trout nor trout more willing to be caught.'

We know that in one sense his years at Chenies were not without result. The Duke of Bedford's name is to be found in the subscription list of the first Annual Report of The Hospital for Sick Children, and the successive Bedfords became regular and generous contributors to the funds of the Hospital. Nor are the names of other members of the Russell family lacking from the list, including Lady Mary Russell of The Grange, Chalfont St Peter, but a few miles away. All this must be an acknowledgement and an awareness of Charles West's links with Chenies, the Russells' former ancestral home, and the church where they all at the last were carried back to rest.

To supplement his small income, Ebenezer West started a school at Chenies, at which his sons were first taught. This became so successful that he later moved it to larger premises at Amersham, where eventually Charles's elder brother, Ebenezer, assisted his father in running the school. It is coincidental that Charles Dickens's first real schooling at Chatham, after attending a most ineffectual Dame's school, was also imparted by a Baptist minister, William Giles, of whom he retained favourable memories. But while Charles West was still in his first few years of schooling, Charles Dickens's education was in abeyance with the decline of his family's fortune and their departure from Chatham. In February, 1824, the twelve-year-old Dickens found himself labelling the pots in Warren's Blacking House. A few days later, his father was arrested for debt, and confined in the Marshalsea Prison. The boy Dickens was left almost alone in the daily round, struggling to make his scanty shillings keep pace with his needs and his childish inconsequence.

Charles West was never to experience personally the distress and problems of the young Charles Dickens. Around 1826, the ten-year-old Charles West was sent to Mr Wood's School at Totteridge. Charles West was to receive schooling far superior to that given to Dickens, but he could still possibly be challenged, when some of the more important medical appointments were under consideration, on the grounds of not being a product of the English public schools and universities. Dr William

Baly, his senior by two years, who had a somewhat similar career as a medical student, was actually opposed on the grounds of his educational background when seeking the lectureship on Forensic Medicine at St Bartholomew's Hospital. Dr Baly, perhaps not so abrasive towards his colleagues as his friend West, and, it may be, of a more diplomatic nature, not only obtained the lectureship, but went on to a highly successful career, becoming physician to Queen Victoria, a career which was cut tragically short by his death in a railway accident in 1861. Dr Baly, besides being an example used to illustrate certain aspects of West's medical training and to explain perhaps some of the difficulties the young Dr West seemed to have at first in obtaining a suitable position, deserves mention also because he was elected as one of the first members of the medical Committee at Great Ormond Street shortly before the Hospital opened in February 1852.

In 1831, at the age of fifteen, Charles West was apprenticed to Mr Gray, apothecary and general practitioner in Amersham, of whom passing mention has been made in the previous chapter. Mr Gray had been apothecary to St George's Hospital, London, and his experience gave West that thorough training in compounding medicines which was to prove invaluable when he came to prescribe for children. West was always grateful towards Gray, not only for this, but because he had first introduced him to Shakespeare. This was a dominant influence in the formation of that clarity, sweetness and eloquence of expression which were not only a feature of West's lectures and textbooks, but can be found also in his clinical observations and case notes.

Meanwhile, Charles Dickens was polishing his lines and improving his style in a series of letters and poems addressed to Maria Beadnell, with whom he was obsessively and hopelessly in love. Her father was the manager of a leading city clearing bank, Smith Payne and Smith of Lombard Street, and had no intention of ever allowing his daughter to marry a young man with no expectations and no career except the precarious one of reporting parliamentary debates for the daily press. But Maria was quite content to let Dickens dance attendance on her, and sigh in company with other young men in her band of admirers. For two or three years Dickens endured the pangs and frustrations of a young love never accepted, but never seemingly quite rejected. That it was his first and perhaps greatest love was evidently to be of great significance in his work and life.

Dickens never forgot his Maria, and when, over twenty years later, the famous author received a latter from his old love, he was as excited as he had been all those years ago. But, alas, the shock of seeing how his beloved and beautiful Maria Beadnell had changed into the corpulent and silly Maria Winter, rather over-fond of a little tipple, was traumatic for him. It was already the middle of what critics have come to regard as the 'dark period' of Dickens's works, which had started with the brooding intensity of *Bleak House* and had continued with the gloom of Coketown in *Hard Times*. Did Maria's reappearance remind the increasingly despondent and inwardly retrospective Dickens of how, despite his triumphs and success, the promises and dreams of youth had not really been fulfilled? Everything that he had loved and had seemed so beautiful in youth had been snatched from him, like Mary Hogarth, or had changed so much with the passing of the years. How even his own wife Catherine had altered! Was Maria Winter responsible for an upsurge of Dickens's always strong subconscious frustration at having to grow old, for the sudden impatience with those adult responsibilities which he had allowed to fall so heavily upon him? Did this secret nostalgic longing for an idealized childhood home clash with the overt memory of the miseries of a seemingly abandoned child? Was the whole Pandora's box of Dickens's contradictory desires and aspirations, his conflicting character and conduct, his alternations between euphoria and despair, all that complexity of personality in which lay the secret of his work and genius, flung open by Maria's return? It is significant that Forster tells us that it was while working on *Little Dorrit* that Dickens first began to feel and mention deep dissatisfaction with his then present mode of life. Two months after Mrs Maria Winter had dined with Mr and Mrs Charles Dickens, the first pages of *Little Dorrit* were being written!

We do not know of Charles West's young loves. The one great romance of his life of which we know happened, like Dickens with Ellen Ternan after he had long been married, was a father, and successful in his career. But these considerations did not prevent writer or doctor separating from the wife each had long cherished, from the mother of their grown-up children (although in Dickens's case his youngest child was only six). All this, however, was still far in the future.

Although hardly anything is recorded about Charles West's apprenticeship, some idea of his duties and activities and a detailed picture of medical practice in a market town at that time can be found in the reminiscences of Sir James Paget, one of the most famous Victorian surgeons. Paget, who was a fellow student and a life-long friend of West, had been apprenticed, one year before him, to a Mr Charles Costerton, a practitioner at Great Yarmouth.

Paget's 'deed of Apprenticeship to learn the art and mystery of a Surgeon and apothecary' cost a premium of 100 guineas. The usual term required by the Society of Apothecaries was five years. Paget says the time was too long, and certainly West only stayed about two years in his apprenticeship. It may be noted that West's apprenticeship and his later studies at St Bartholomew's, Bonn, Paris and Berlin all appear to have been somewhat shorter than the average. Whether this denotes a greater ability on the part of West, or a greater impatience, it is hard to say.

The two men who met at St Bartholomew's Hospital as students had much in common, and remained firm and life-long friends. When they were both old, Paget records having spent Christmas 1881 at Nice with Charles West and a few friends, when they cut an enormous Christmas cake and 'had a very pleasant time and some good music'. The Christmas cake, with its sugar-lace and fine colours, its dolphins and doves, standing two feet high, reminds us of the Twelfth Night cake sent by Miss Burdett Coutts for her godson, Charley Dickens, and which became the sensation of Genoa in 1845. Enjoying some 'good music' certainly casts a fresh light on Charles West! Much later, in 1896, the eighty-year-old West published a little volume on *The Profession of Medicine*, in which he praises the enduring charms of music: 'I should wish every student of medicine to cultivate music, were it only for the solace in worry, the refreshment in fatigue, which, as life goes on, it will be found to afford.' And West looks back wistfully over sixty-five years to his apprentice days at Amersham and remembers, 'In spite of its disadvantages, there were many compensating benefits which attended the old apprentice systems.' After he again enlarges on his favourite theme that then 'a young man did really acquire a knowledge of practical pharmacy, which is impossible in any hospital, infirmary, or dispensary, where all medicines are, of necessity, made up in large quantities, and according to special formulae', he goes on to an important aspect of a doctor's training that is often forgotten.

> Another advantage of the apprenticeship was that the pupil spent some time in a sort of medical atmosphere, in which he not only had the opportunity of becoming acquainted with minor surgery, but also with the manners, habits, and peculiarities of sick persons, mostly, indeed, among the poor; but still, between rich and poor, the difference in these respects, when illness comes, is not very considerable. The study of mankind is second only in importance, to the practitioner, to the study of his profession; for he must remember that he has to do not only with the disease, but with the sick person, his wants, his wishes, his fancies, and his fads; and this knowledge used to come to the apprentice almost imperceptibly, just as the infant gains his knowledge of the world around.
>
> But, for good or ill, that time, and those customs, have passed away, never to return.

With this last sigh, the old doctor bade farewell to the golden days at Amersham, but this valediction confirms what has already been glanced at, that it was in his apprentice days that Charles West first really came into direct contact with the sufferings of the poor. It was for the needy countryfolk he first drew upon his store of sympathy and humanity, which he was to bestow so largely upon the London children. Well could he write in the same slim volume, 'I have had more experience than most of the ways of the London poor.' Well could he implore the young physician to treat the poor outpatients at the hospital with courtesy and consideration, especially the girls and the women, and, with emphasis, even the sick prostitutes. 'Treat every woman – young or old, saint or sinner – as you would wish your own sister treated, if poverty and sickness befell her, and she were compelled to take refuge in a hospital. He who learns this lesson when a student, will need no change in his manners when he enters the bedchamber of a duchess.' The only sister Charles West ever knew was baby Jane, whom he lost when she was four, but he still remembered her all those years later.

In 1833, Charles West entered St Bartholomew's Hospital as a medical student. He had served only two years as an apprentice. James Paget, although two years older and serving a longer term, was not to enter St Bartholomew's until the following year. In some ways it seems strange that West should have chosen St Bartholomew's, where the main emphasis in teaching was surgical. There were three kinds of student: physicians in actual practice who accompanied the hospital physician into the wards and attended autopsies; graduates of Oxford and Cambridge who were proceeding to medical degrees, for, as Paget remarks, there was the feeling that none but Cambridge and Oxford men were deemed fit to be physicians to St Bartholomew's Hospital; and the most numerous group, apprentices or pupils of the surgeons, and apprentices from country practices who had come to study surgery. In 1820 there had been only three pupils of the physicians, and these three had all been medical graduates. Even in 1835 Paget remarked that there was very little clinical teaching of medicine except by Dr Latham. It was probably this Dr Peter Mere Latham who had attracted Charles West to St Bartholomew's. When West published his *Lectures on the Diseases of Women* in 1856, he dedicated it to Latham, 'Who first showed me how to study, and how to practise medicine; who has so often guided me by his advice; still oftener by his example; and smoothed by his universal kindness the early difficulties of my career.' This dedication was a sincere tribute to a man who had been his teacher and a friend, and later was to be a strong and active supporter of the idea of a children's hospital.

Peter Mere Latham had been elected Physician to St Bartholomew's in 1824. He himself explained his theory of teaching:

I have been physician here seven years. Having no formal lectures to give,

> I have considered my business to be expressly in the wards of the hospital, and I have thought myself expressly placed there to be a *demonstrator* of medical fact ... I have looked upon myself as engaged to direct the student where to look for, and how to detect the object which he ought to know; and, the object being known, to point out the value of it in itself and in all its relations.

In his case notes, lectures and medical papers, Charles West was to apply these principles which Latham had taught him. Even Paget, who was a surgical student, preferred to work in his second year in the medical wards with Latham, and in the outpatients' room with George Burrows, who had a decade before been a clinical clerk to Latham. Burrows (later to be knighted), together with Latham, joined the provisional committee of The Hospital for Sick Children. In March 1850, the first printed appeal, addressed directly to the medical profession for their approval and help in establishing such an institution, bore both their signatures above those of Bence Jones and Charles West. The fifth signatory was Robert Ferguson, the friend of Sir Walter Scott and Lockhart, who was appointed physician accoucheur to Queen Victoria in 1840, in partnership with Sir Charles Locock. It can be seen how important were West's student days at St Bartholomew's both for his later career and for the creation of The Hospital for Sick Children.

Charles West was, like Paget, a hardworking and model student, and was not led astray by the diversions of the London scene. He won the prize for medicine in 1834; the following year, the prize in forensic medicine and the first prize in midwifery. Already he had determined his specialized path in medicine – the treatment of children was considered an adjunct to that of women, as may be witnessed in the tradition of certain hospitals being described as for women and children.

The lecturer on midwifery was, in West's time, a Dr Conquest, who, although a highly respected practitioner, was at a loss to manage a class containing some rather obstreperous students, who interrupted him and bullied him until he was persuaded to resign in favour of Charles Locock. But even the great Locock only lectured for a short time before giving up. This is a reminder that all medical students were not as model as West and Paget, who in 1835 seemed to have monopolized the prizes between them. After all, it was only to be a year or two later that Dickens introduced Bob Sawyer and Benjamin Allen into *The Pickwick Papers*.

> 'In other words they're Medical Students, I suppose?' said Mr Pickwick. Sam Weller nodded assent.
>
> 'I am glad of it,' said Mr Pickwick, casting his nightcap energetically on the counterpane, 'They are fine fellows; very fine fellows; with judge-

ments matured by observation and reflection; tastes refined by reading and study. I am glad of it.'

'They're a smokin' cigars by the kitchen fire,' said Sam.

'Ah!' observed Mr Pickwick, rubbing his hands, 'overflowing with kindly feelings and animal spirits. Just what I like to see.'

'And one on 'em,' said Sam, not noticing his master's interruption, 'one on 'em's got his legs on the table, and is a drinking brandy neat, vile the t'other one – him in the barnacles – has got a barrel o' oysters atween his knees, wich he's a openin' like steam, and as fast as he eats 'em, he takes a aim with the shells at young dropsy, who's a sittin' down fast asleep, in the chimbley corner.'

'Eccentricities of genius, Sam,' said Mr Pickwick. 'You may retire.'

Dr Conquest, in having higher expectations of his students' behaviour than was justified, shared some of Mr Pickwick's illusions. Of course, Bob Sawyer and Benjamin Allen are not unlike medical students even of more modern times in some of their characteristics: their carelessness of attire, their ostentatious liking for strong drink and tobacco, their troubles with landladies, and their healthy appetites. They deliberately shock lay listeners with casual references to dissections and post-mortems, as with the leg which is 'a very muscular one for a child's,' not minding 'a brain, but I couldn't stand a whole head'; and repeat tall stories of impossible operations at Guy's, and of weird casualties brought into St Bartholomew's, like the boy who swallowed the large wooden beads and rattled so much 'when he walks about, that they're obliged to muffle him in a watchman's coat for fear he should wake the patients'. They belong to that great Gallery of comic characters, which Dickens created from his own acute observations, and owe much of their effect and humour to the fact that they can be related to the reader's own experiences.

Some of the conditions and teaching at St Bartholomew's at this time were not encouraging to students, unless they were strongly self-motivated. This is apparent in some of Paget's comments. And in the *Lancet* of 1837 there is confirmation. A generation before, James Flint South had experienced the overcrowding, jostling and total lack of consideration and courtesy which made conditions in the operating theatre appalling. It would appear that there was very little change in West's day. The *Lancet* mentioned that a year before, Mr Earle, one of the surgeons at St Bartholomew's, had promised that some rails should be erected for the purpose of keeping the area of the theatre clear during operations. However, as a letter from a student complained, these rails were still lacking, and on the Saturday last no less than thirty-four people had crowded into close proximity about the operating table. 'How deeply annoyed were the suffering patient and the students who endeavoured to look on from above may be easily judged . . . To seek redress from the surgeons for this grievance is useless.'

The *Lancet*, at this time, may be a prejudiced witness, and Paget particularly praised Earle. West was never to have a high opinion of some of the St Bartholomew's surgeons. In the same 1837 article, the *Lancet* claimed that another promise of Mr Earle's to the students had not been implemented for the past year: the promise that no post-mortem examination of interest should take place without prior notice being given to surgical pupils. In this respect Paget does remember adverse conditions for the students.

> The dead-house (it was never called by any better name) was a miserable kind of shed, stone-floored, damp, and dirty, where all stood round a table on which the examinations were made. And these were usually made in the roughest and least instructive way; and, unless one of the physicians was present, nothing was carefully looked at, nothing was taught. Pathology, in any fair sense of the word, was hardly considered.

It would give a false picture of Charles West's time as a student at St Bartholomew's to end on this rather dismal note. Paget says, 'My first year had passed happily and very prosperously, and I had made many friendships.' The same was true for West. Nor must the Abernethian Society meetings be forgotten, of which he and his friends all retained fond memories of the papers they had read and the discussions that had ensued, both as students and in the early years of their professional careers.

The year which saw Charles West enrol as a medical student at St Bartholomew's also saw the beginning of Charles Dickens's true career. In December 1833, his first published story, '*A Dinner at Poplar Walk*' (later entitled '*Mr Minns and his Cousin*') was printed in the *Monthly Magazine*. During the next year Dickens became parliamentary reporter for the *Morning Chronicle*, travelling during the recess to cover elections and political meetings as far afield as Edinburgh. The name 'Boz' appeared on sketches published in these and other periodicals. Dickens's father was again arrested for debt, but this time his increasingly successful son was able to rescue him, and felt prosperous enough to take chambers at Furnival's Inn, High Holborn, a short walk from Field Lane, Smithfield and St Bartholomew's Hospital. West's time as a student there was coming to an end when Dickens became engaged to Catherine Hogarth in April 1835.

In *Little Dorrit*, when John Baptist Cavalletto is run over by the Mail, near St Paul's, he is taken 'to the neighbouring hospital of Saint Bartholomew, where the disabled man was soon laid on a table in a cool, methodical way, and carefully examined by a surgeon', who makes his diagnosis 'with the thoughtful pleasure of an artist contemplating the work upon his easel'. And soon 'everything possible to be done had been skilfully and promptly done'. Dickens was as ready to recognize the good done at St Bartholomew's, as he had been to poke fun at it, in the person of the great Slasher in *The Pickwick Papers*.

Charles West's most grateful memories of his time as a medical student at St Bartholomew's may be found in the pages of an address which he delivered there on the opening of the medical session in 1850. Speaking directly to the students about to embark upon their long years of study, he said:

> If rightly used then what may not this hospital be to you? – a school, not of medicine only, but of the virtues; a place where you serve an apprenticeship that shall fit you for a life of more than the art of healing – in the heavenly arts of patience, and self-denial, and humility and love!

This highly moral view of the doctor's profession was in accordance with Charles West's philosophy of medical ethics. While it owed much to the example of men such as Latham, whom he had first encountered during the student years at St Bartholomew's, it most probably found more exact formulation and expression when West went to the University of Bonn.

As his father was a Baptist minister, Charles West was in 1835 precluded from going on to Oxford. Instead, West followed the recent example of his friend William Baly, who had gone on to study at Paris and Heidelberg and was to graduate at Berlin in 1836. This decision may have been determined earlier. Baly and West were regarded by their fellow students at St Bartholomew's as having an excellent knowledge of German, and both were to attract notice at the beginnings of their careers with translations from the famous Johannes Müller, Professor of Anatomy and Physiology at Berlin University. It is evident that the young Baly and the young West had thoroughly prepared themselves for the next stage in their studies.

Charles West's decision to go to Bonn in the summer of 1835 was influenced by the reputation of its obstetrics department and the facilities provided there. The university had a clinic or lying-in hospital for pauper patients, where on average at least two deliveries occurred each week. The medical students were obliged to attend to all the poor mothers who gave birth in Bonn, whether in the university clinic or around the town, which at that time had less than 15,000 inhabitants. The two most advanced students – and Charles West would certainly have been considered in that category – were also allowed to attend the local lunatic asylum at Sieburg, across the Rhine, during the vacations, and study there under the regular medical attendant. In all, the faculty of medicine had six professional chairs, to which ten professors were appointed.

It was at Bonn that Charles West first appreciated the greater scenic splendours of Europe, and he was in later life to take many walking tours in France, Germany and Switzerland. The best view of Bonn and its university across the broad Rhine, and of the beauties of the surrounding countryside, was that obtained from the craggy summit of the highest of the Seven Mountains above Koenigswinter. This spot was a favourite excursion of Prince Albert, already considered a possible consort for the future Queen of England, when, a year after Charles West had left, he became a student at Bonn University on 3 May 1837. A house belonging to Dr Bischof, one of the medical professors, was selected for Prince Albert and his brother. Bischof and West were on friendly terms and exchanged correspondence in later years, so Charles certainly knew the small neat house, with young trees before the windows, and a courtyard railed off from one side of the open ground near the cathedral. The Duke of Connaught once spoke of his father's deep interest in Great Ormond Street and of how as a child he was always taught to do little things for the hospital. Was Prince Albert's personal concern influenced by the knowledge that he and Charles West had been fellow students and almost contemporaries at the University of Bonn? At Bonn, Prince Albert would have surely heard from Dr Bischof, if from no one else, about the recent student from that country whose new queen was soon to be his wife. One reason why Bonn was chosen for Prince Albert was its reputation for the superior moral conduct of its students. This may also have influenced Charles West at a time when most Englishmen thought of German students, especially at Heidelberg, where his friend William Baly had elected to study, as being perpetually enveloped in a thick fog of tobacco smoke, quaffing immense quantities of beer, and fighting insane duels.

West remained at Bonn for a year, and gained the university prize for a Latin essay, 'The Female Pelvis and its Influence on Parturition'. But this academic distinction may not have been the greatest benefit West was to derive from Bonn. German literary and philosophic prestige, founded on the great names of Goethe, Kant and Hegel, was then at its height. A few years later, Charles Dickens, writing to a German literary scholar, Dr Keunzel, would enthuse:

> ... next to the favour and good opinion of my own countrymen, I value, above all price, the esteem of the German people. I honor and admire them past all expression. I know them to be, in their great mental endowments and cultivation, the chosen people of the Earth; and I was never

more proud or more happy than when I first began to know that my writings found favour in their eyes.

At Easter 1836, Immanuel Hermann Fichte was appointed Professor of Philosophy at Bonn. Immanuel Hermann was the only son of Johann Gottlieb Fichte, the famous philosopher and follower of Kant. The faculty of philosophy held a pre-eminent position at Bonn, and its influence was felt by all the students. Immanuel Hermann Fichte had written a life of his father, and was always ready to introduce students to his works. Charles West would have been sympathetic to Johann Gottlieb Fichte's statements of some of the fundamental problems of philosophy expressed in his *Science of Knowledge*, where science is described as having the twofold meaning of knowledge as a mental act and knowledge as a body of truth. One of his own pupils, who attended West's lectures at Middlesex Hospital, was to describe him as, 'This most honourable, high-principled accomplished physician', and remember that 'A more zealous instructor never was. His aid, night or day, was ever available for the student. He was still, to himself, essentially, a student, I think, all his professional life.'

Even if, though it is unlikely, West did not first become acquainted with Fichte's *On the Nature of the Scholar*, at Bonn, an English translation was published in 1848. *The English and Foreign Medical and Surgical Review*, to which West had become a regular contributor, reviewed it as part of an article on medical ethics, and this West certainly read. In this article there is a paragraph which would be a description of West's own personal ethos, and is also a statement of which Dickens would have heartily approved:

> The relief of the sick poor is a duty which has ever been diligently performed by the conscientious practitioner . . . Kindness, tenderness, and gentleness should, however, ever accompany the administration of public relief. Once the priest of the parish was the special guardian of the poor . . . Now it is the union surgeon or dispensary physician who is brought exclusively into this intimate relationship, and it is he who has to fight the battle of poverty against the proud man's contumely and the greedy man's avarice.

The example of his father's calling, the recollections of his childhood and schooldays, the contact with suffering he had known as a country apothecary's apprentice and as a student in London at St Bartholomew's, all had combined to make West sensitive to those higher moral purposes and meanings applicable to his chosen profession, which were being enunciated in the philosophy lectures at Bonn during the last few months of his stay. The next stage of his studentship was to determine irrevocably his selected path in medicine, which was to prove such a blessing and an example to the sick children, not only of his own land but throughout the world.

When Charles West arrived in Paris in September 1836, the French capital stood first in reputation among the Continental schools of medicine. Much of this was due to the reputation of men such as François Magendie. His pupil Claude Bernard and a provincial science-master named Louis Pasteur were to continue this reputation. It was Balzac's Paris, where crumbling houses, twisting streets, quiet courtyards with old trees and weed-filled alleys formed a background to the hurrying, crowded traffic of the main thoroughfares. A generation was to pass before the Second Empire cut through its tangled heart with the broad avenues and boulevards we know today.

There was quite a large English colony in Paris at that time. W.M.Thackeray had married Isabella Shawe at the British Embassy on 20 August 1836, and was living in Paris throughout West's stay. But Charles had little time for the social round which occupied his fellow-countrymen. To get the fullest benefit from the demonstrations at the principal hospitals, such as L'Hôtel-Dieu, or the lectures at the Collége de France, demanded long hours and early ones.

The medical lectures were overcrowded, and it was essential to arrive well beforehand to obtain a position in which it was possible both to hear and see. 'In the same way there are about two hundred students going round every morning with each of the best physicians at the hospitals. So that you are tolerably lucky if you get in a third row round the bed of a patient; the light by which you see a patient being moreover only that of a candle because it is so early in the morning.' James Paget, whose brother George had written this description two winters before, himself spent some time in Paris, at the same time as West, and was critical of many things, especially of the French medical student: 'I assure you the medical students here are the most ruffianly, ill-looking set of fellows I ever saw.' Paget had thought some of the English students bad enough! He also noted shortcomings in the French methods of studying in surgical practice and hospital practice, but admitted they were far superior in the science of medicine, concluding, 'On the other hand, the advantages they offer to anyone who wishes to study any one class of medicine are immense.'

There was one class of medicine which greatly interested Charles West, and for which the Paris of his student days gave unique opportunities – the study of children's diseases. In the Rue de Sèvres stood a group of old buildings, not particularly distinguished in appearance, but which were made more attractive by having large gardens and squares between some of the houses. Here, on sunny days, groups of children were seen, many of them lame or crippled, and all of them having the pallor of long and painful sickness. This was L'Hôpital des Enfants Malades, the very first true children's hospital, as distinct from a foundling institution or a dispensary. It had, indeed, originally been a foundling hospital itself. In 1751, a priest of St Sulpice started a school for young girls on the site of an old nunnery built in 1735 by Maria Leszcynska. The school was called La Maison de l'Enfant Jesus. During the Revolution it was converted into an asylum for female orphans, but in 1802, the year of the short-lived Peace of Amiens and when Napoleon was appointed First Consul for life, the Conseil des Hôpitaux, under the decree of the 18 Floreal, converted it into a hospital for children. In England that same year some awakenings of social conscience over the deprivation of children were seen with the passing of the Health and Morals of Apprentices Act, a first attempt to relieve the bad conditions in which pauper apprentices often existed. The winter of 1836–37 which first saw, in all probability, Charles West walk through the gates of 149 Rue de Sèvres – the first unconscious steps towards the creation of Great Ormond Street – also saw Charles Dickens begin his great crusade against children's wrongs with *Oliver Twist*, and a bitter depiction of the wrongs the pauper child still suffered in workhouse and apprenticeship.

L'Hôpital des Enfants Malades was a large establishment, with well over five hundred beds. Patients between the ages of two and fifteen years were admitted. So good was the reputation of the care and attention they received, both from the medical staff and the sisters of the religious order of St Thomas-de-Villeneuve, under whose care the children were nursed, that parents eagerly sought admission into the hospital when their children were ill. The wards were always overcrowded. Most of the wards were large and, by the standards of the day, well ventilated, but there were two or three which were damp and unhealthy. These wards and the overcrowding in the others, as Charles West was to comment later, often led to unhygienic conditions and a high mortality rate – one in every six of the children died. It was claimed that the children came from the poorest classes, were enfeebled already by hardships, and were often admitted in a hopeless or dying condition, suffering from consumption, pneumonia and the fatal tubercular meningitis, so prevalent in the Paris of that time. Great Ormond Street was later to demonstrate by example that even such disadvantages could be overcome successfully. But, as West realized, although many patients in L'Hôpital des Enfants Malades succumbed, far more children were saved who would have perished miserably had they been left to the inadequacies of their homes, or had lain isolated in the adult wards of L'Hôtel-Dieu, receiving scanty nursing and attention.

Something of this unsuitability of adult hospitals for children is conveyed in 'The Hospital Patient', a sketch published by 'Boz' in August 1836, when West was on his way to Paris from Bonn. Dickens describes how the dim light

> in the spacious room increased rather than diminished the ghastly appearance of the hapless creatures in the beds, which were ranged in two long rows on either side. In one bed lay a child enveloped in bandages, with its body half-consumed by fire; in another, a female, rendered half-hideous by some dreadful accident, was wildly beating her clenched fists on the coverlet in pain; on a third, there lay stretched a young girl, apparently in the heavy stupor often the immediate precursor of death: her face was stained with blood, and her breasts and arms were bound up in folds of linen. Two or three of the beds were empty, and their recent occupants were sitting besides them, but with faces worn, and eyes so bright and glassy, that it was fearful to meet their gaze. On every face was stamped the expression of anguish and suffering.

Dickens's ward could have been at the Middlesex Hospital or even at St Bartholomew's. Charles West would have been quick to contrast these with the wards at L'Hôpital des Enfants Malades, where, as visitors to the Rue de Sèvres often remarked, the devotion of the nursing sisters kept the tiny patients happy and quiet and rarely complaining. Visitors to Great Ormond Street were later to describe the same atmosphere there.

The impression L'Hôpital des Enfants Malades produced upon Charles West was profound. Many remarks in his later lectures and many passages in his writings lead to only one probable conclusion: that the physicians there could have had no more attentive student during their morning visits than this young Englishman. In the first months of 1837, the names of Guerseant, Baudelocque, Jaclelot, Bouneau, and Guérin (who that very year first established the early symptoms of rickets as general soreness, slight fever and profuse sweating) may not have all been familiar to Charles West, but within a decade his name was to join theirs whenever the study of children's diseases was reviewed.

Paget gives us a personal glimpse of Charles West in Paris. Towards the end of March 1837, Paget, West and some other English students spent three days walking in the Forest of Fontainebleau. Their French guide was appalled at the distances they covered and became utterly exhausted, declaring he would never again go walking with *les Anglais*. Paget's letter to his fiancée notes that on their return to Paris one of his friends left for Germany. This was Charles West, who in April arrived in Berlin, to follow the example of his friend William Baly, who had taken his doctorate there the previous year.

The University of Berlin was largely the creation of Wilhelm von Humboldt, the statesman and friend of Goethe and Schiller. In 1810 he had established it in the magnificent palace of Prince Henry of Prussia which faced the Opera House. The reputation of the University of Berlin had been greatly enhanced by the appointment, in 1833, of Johannes Peter Müller as Professor of Anatomy and Physiology. Müller introduced a new era of biological research in Germany, and pioneered the use of experimental research in medicine. Hermann von Helmholtz, the physicist famous for his work on optics and thermodynamics, who was one of Müller's most brilliant pupils, described him as a 'man of the first rank'. As Charles West would probably have agreed, Helmholtz held that knowing Müller as a student and a friend had 'definitely altered his intellectual standards'. Müller's previous researches into embryology had made him the most celebrated member of the Faculty of Medicine at Bonn, where he had studied and taken his doctorate in 1822. He had answered the first prize question which the faculty had posed: Does the foetus breathe in the mother's womb? Müller, in a series of experiments, demonstrated that bright red blood flows to the foetus through the umbilical vein, and that dark red blood flows back to the placenta through the umbilical artery. Further investigations on the evolution and development of the kidneys and their ducts and of the sexual organs had resulted in the early 1830's in the discovery that the embryonic duct, now known as 'Müller's duct', forms the Fallopian tubes, uterus and vagina; only rudimentary vestiges of it are found in the male. The tradition of Müller's work at Bonn, so important to his own chosen speciality, may have been another factor in Charles West's decision to spend a year there. At Berlin one of Müller's pupils, Theodor Schwann, showed in 1839 that the ovum was a cell, thus laying the foundations of the cell-growth theory. Another pupil, Rudolf Virchow, was to isolate the disease of leukaemia in 1845.

After six months at the University of Berlin, Charles West was awarded his doctorate for an illustrated dissertation on the female pelvis. The ceremony greatly impressed him. Nearly sixty years later he was to publish, in his last book, the oath taken by all doctors of medicine on their graduation at the University of Berlin. It evidently had a special significance for him.

West returned to England in the autumn of 1837, after over two years abroad. It is coincidental that in late August and September of that year Müller spent some time in England. During West's stay in Berlin, Müller had begun to work on another problem concerning pathological anatomy. As early as 1828 he had formulated the 'important law bearing his name, that the tissue of which a tumour is composed has its type in the tissues of the animal body, either in the adult or in the embryonic condition'. He now concluded that the traditional description of the various forms of tumours would lead to no further advance, and that chemical analysis and microscopic examination were the only means to be used if a method of distinguishing between benign and malignant growths was to be found. In 1838 Müller published the first and only part of *Über den feineren Bau und die Formen der Krankhaften Geschwülste*. It was this work that fostered the use of the microscope in the study of pathology formations and 'Müller thus founded pathological history as an independent field and provided physicians with diagnostic procedures that are now used in daily clinical work.' In 1840 Charles West published the first English translation, *On the Nature and Structural Characteristics of Cancer and of those Morbid Growths which may be confounded with it*, which evoked favourable comment. West's friend, William Baly, published the English translation of Müller's *Hanbuch der Physiologie*. This great work which Müller had planned in Bonn and completed at Berlin 'became a milestone in the history of European medicine'.

It was their translations from Müller which first really made West's and Baly's reputations, early in their careers, with their medical colleagues. The influence Müller had exerted upon the two English students from St Bartholomew's, who had both come to take their doctorate at his University of Berlin, was decisive. After his translation of Müller, West was considered as somewhat of an authority on cancer, especially in its feminine forms.

The two years West had spent at Bonn, Paris, and Berlin played a large part in the formation of certain aspects of his character, outlook and scientific approach. Like Dickens, West had grown up not in the rigid, prudish atmosphere of that Victorian age in England with which they were both to become associated, but in the freer moral manners of William IV's reign. The outlook of a Wellington, a Melbourne and a Palmerston on sexual mores, religious observances and, sadly enough, on social questions reflected that of an earlier generation, and really had little in common with the changes associated with the young Queen they supposedly influenced. Melbourne looked at *Oliver Twist* in compliance with the Queen's wish, but told her severely, 'It's all among Workhouses, and Coffin Makers and Pickpockets. I don't like that low debasing style!' Melbourne was unable, however, to turn Queen Victoria away from her continuing enthusiasm for Dickens's works.

West, although brought up in the rigid moral standards of a dissenting minister, and in his own light a very religious man, would have had little patience with charitable movements that made religious salvation a prime necessity for tiny children, white-faced, twisted and exhausted from their endless labours in the mills of Lancashire and Yorkshire, or starving and rotten with infection in the London Ragged Schools. West must have read with hearty approval Elizabeth Barrett's moving poem. *The Cry of the Children*

> Now tell the poor young children, O my brothers
> To look up to Him and pray;
> So the blessed One who blesseth all the others,
> Will bless them another day.
> They answer, 'Who is God that He should hear us
> While the rushing of iron wheels is stirred?
> When we sob aloud, the human creatures near us
> Pass by, hearing not, or answer not a word.
> And *we* hear not (for the wheels in their sounding)
> Strangers speaking at the door;
> Is it likely God, with angels singing round Him,
> Hears our weeping any more?

Or, if he had been privy to the letter, West could not have agreed more with Charles Dickens, when he wrote to Angela Burdett Coutts on the futility of insisting on religious catechism in the Ragged Schools, a letter which is best summed up in the account he gave to Forster:

> I sent Miss Coutts a sledge-hammer account of the Ragged Schools; and as I saw her name for two hundred pounds in the clergy subscription list, took pains to show her that religious mysteries and difficult creeds wouldn't do for such pupils. I told her, too, that it was of immense importance that they should be washed.

Elizabeth Barrett's poem was published in *Blackwood's Magazine*, August 1843; Dickens's letter on the Field Lane Ragged School was written only a month later. Charles West had, however, already been working for some years among the very children whom Dickens had described. Since 1841 he had been physician accoucheur to the Finsbury Dispensary, covering a district which, in his own words, 'included Golden Lane, and its purlieus, Saffron Hill and Field Lane'. This is the first time that their paths definitely crossed. West would have known of Dickens's visit to Saffron Hill, which was widely discussed in the neighbourhood. Did the famous novelist know of the young doctor who, week by week, had been giving to the children and their mothers care and attention far beyond the norm of a dispensary physician? Dickens had a shrewd habit of finding out those people who were doing the most practical good in any district or cause in which he was interested.

In that same year, 1843, West had published in the medical journals an 'Account of Some of the More Important Diseases of Childhood', and another paper, 'A Clinical and Pathological Report on the

Pneumonia of Children as it Prevails among the Poor in London', both based upon the child patients he had seen at his two dispensaries in Finsbury and Waterloo Road. These papers first established his reputation as a leading authority on children's diseases.

When the new young doctor, Charles West, had returned to England in the autumn of 1837, it was to a country with a new young queen, whose reign was to include the whole of his professional career. His years abroad had firmed his character and his outlook. He felt himself a part of the great advances in science and medicine which were being made. He had been made more aware and understanding of the frailties of men and women, and of the fear and incomprehension they had of their own bodies and of the organic mysteries of health and disease. Perhaps he was not always to be sympathetic to some of the attitudes and views of what was to be Victorian England. Charles West was certainly European in his outlook. He had mastered six languages. Bonn had imparted to him high ideals of scholastic standards and medical ethics, and had shown him the natural beauties of river, forest and mountain. Paris had given to him not only the dream of a children's hospital, but her tolerance, spirit and artistry. West, like Dickens, was always to have a special place for Paris and France in his affections. Berlin, in the person of Johannes Müller, had given him the most important gift of all – the presence and inspiration of a great scientist and medical researcher. Charles West had brought back from Europe far, far more than the average English student conventionally found there. It was perhaps inevitable that he had also brought back with him hopes and aspirations beyond the norm.

If his high ideals and expectations were not to be fully realized, if his estimation of his own worth and merits was not to be given that status which he thought his entitlement, if he sometimes viewed with a sense of personal injustice the more successful careers both of his contemporaries and of younger men, and if his insistence upon impeccable standards of medical conduct and care made him impatient with future colleagues and governing bodies of hospitals, the final consequence was to be of greater benefit and of greater credit. All the frustrations and disappointments endured by this complex but kindly man, who possessed at once the great contradictions of character and the great simplicity of soul which are often a concomitant of genius, as they were in Charles Dickens, made him in the end turn with deeper devotion and energy towards the main objects of his concern – the sick child, the neglected child, the despised and suffering child. In this mood, Charles West measured every philosophy, every faith and almost every scientific and medical advance against the preservation of the well-being, happiness and innocence of his little patients. Let us listen to his Lumleian

Lecture, which he gave, let it be remembered, in the very year when Darwin published his *Descent of Man*.

> I have lived among children, I have loved them as we all learn to love the objects by which we are daily surrounded. I have seen their suffering and sorrow, and no explanation but one could ever in any degree solve the problem which it suggests. I have found it in the belief that He whom an old book speaks of as the Holy child Jesus allows the young children 'whom in Palestine he had blessed once and for ever, to pass through this, only that they might meet the sooner'. The mystery of the suffering, indeed, is still in large measure incomprehensible, but an end is seen to it all; not the extinction of the weak for the sake of the strong, themselves to yield to the stronger; the race being all, the individual nothing, but the perfection of each individual of the race; – a perfection to be attained not here but higher.
>
> The last words of the gospel of the dreary creed to which I have referred, written by one whose intellectual gifts go far, whose moral excellencies go further still to disprove his own theories, and before whom, in both respects I bow in earnest admiration, are 'Man still bears in his bodily frame the indelible stamp of his lowly origin.' So be it, but we find it also written, 'The Lord God breathed into his nostrils the breath of life, and man became a living soul.'
>
> The humility of our origin we allow, the exceeding bitterness of tortured humanity we above all other men have to listen to, but to our joy we know the prayer, and we believe it has been answered.

Today, we may look upon Great Ormond Street and the contributions made to medical knowledge as another possible answer. West shared with Pasteur a simple but sincere religious belief. West's religion was not exclusive, at least for his child patients. He 'believed that every child ... Jew, Mahommedan, Pagan, or Christian, Catholic or Protestant, on leaving his world, goes straight to join their company who always behold the face of "our Father who is in Heaven"'.

— 4 —

TOWARDS A CHILDREN'S HOSPITAL

Catherine J. Wood, the most respected and the most influential of all the Lady Superintendents at Great Ormond Street, had known the hospital since she was a girl, living at her father's house in nearby Doughty Street where, earlier, Dickens had lived. She had been first a visitor to the hospital, and then a Lady Reader to the children in the wards, helping to divert a fretful child's attention away from its weary aches and pains, or keeping it still and quiet by telling it stories or explaining the pictures in a new book it could not read. Once, a little boy undergoing some painful treatment promised he would not cry if the Lady Reader sang to him, and the pact was observed all day long. Sometimes a letter was written from the dictation of childish phrases lisped a few words at a time between struggles for breath. Very young or very weak children could be amused by a toy monkey or soldier marched up and down the bed. And a little girl named Ada, her eyes temporarily bandaged, was once observed feeling carefully over a new doll, while her Lady Reader described all its glories of hair and dress, which the young owner was longing to see for herself.

Catherine Wood determined to devote her life to the care of such children, and in 1863, when she was twenty-two, she joined the hospital as a superintendent to one of the wards. After five years she became interested in a particular class of affliction, and with Miss Spencer Percival founded the Hospital for Hip-Joint Disease in Queen Square, only a few steps away from Great Ormond Street. But in 1870, at Charles West's suggestion, she agreed to become Lady Superintendent of The Hospital for Sick Children convalescent home, recently opened at Cromwell House, Highgate. She was appointed Lady Superintendent of Great Ormond Street in 1878, where she remained for ten years, laying the foundations of modern paediatric nursing and training. She and Charles West had great respect for each other. They had in common certain definite views as to the aims and organization of the Hospital and its nursing staff. Like West, Catherine Wood received no direct remuneration for all the long years of care and service so wholeheartedly given to the Hospital. There were few people more qualified by knowledge and experience to judge what Great Ormond Street had achieved, and what it meant to the poor sick children under her care. And no better description of the plight of such children before the advent of Great Ormond Street can be found than in the *Handbook of Nursing* she published in 1878. It went through many editions. I quote from the eleventh!

> About forty years ago, little children were hardly thought of as needing special nursing or treatment; they were either forgotten or passed over in the mass of patients that crowded into the general hospitals. They died as little infants in thousands, trampled down under feet in the race for life, or they grew up stunted and deformed, dragging on a weary, sickly existence, uncheered by the laughter or gaiety of childhood, unsolaced by the tender love of mother. If they claimed their right to the great medical charities of our city, their wee forms, strangely out of place in the large beds in the large wards, could hardly enforce attention; the child laughter or the child cry jarred on the older patients: and the little sufferer learned to bear its pain in silence, and was content to utter its plaint unheard. The doctors hardly knew how to handle these tiny frames. It was something like ausculating a turkey or percussing a goose; and their unspoken language of disease was hard to interpret. The quick, active life, difficult to treat at all, required patience, and patience is time-taking, and time is scarce in the hurry of a large hospital. The nurses resented the advent of these intruders, for they made large demands on their time, and larger still on their patience; and so they entered not at all or with difficulty, and still these poor little lives pined away, forgotten and neglected.

She then pays tribute to Charles West, which perhaps from anyone else would seem fulsome and sentimental: but she had worked with him for many years, and had known the benefits of his guidance and training. She best knew, in the wards of Great Ormond Street, his character and his wisdom, his kindness and concern, and she knew how much he had given to the institution which he founded.

> But some large hearts in that great city were thinking of the little children, and some ears were beginning to listen to their plaintive cry; some willing feet were already treading the alleys of that mighty place; some skilled hands were finding out the suffering babes, and with gentle coaxing touch were winning them back to life and love. And kind thoughts were busy

> for them, and great deeds were planned for them, until at last the little children had a hospital all to themselves. All honour to him who did it. The little children are weaving a crown for him; and each little soul that wings its flight from those walls carries a leaf with it to place there, or each little pair of feet that patter out of its doors to tread again the road of life, walk in his strength who has pleaded and won its cause. That man has built his own monument in his lifetime, and to him is given to see thousands pressing on and following in his footsteps even while he yet lives.

The opposition to children's hospitals had a long and almost respectable tradition. Dr George Armstrong opened what was the first children's clinic in Europe, the Dispensary for the Infant Poor, in 1769. The London Bill of Christenings and Burials had, a year before, recorded 16,042 baptisms and 8229 deaths of infants under two years of age. And this was a year without an epidemic of any kind. Red Lion Square, where Armstrong opened his dispensary, was in the combined parishes of St Andrew's-above-Bars and St George the Martyr (the very parish which had within its boundaries Great Ormond Street). In 1763, the poor-law governors of the parish had received into their care fifty-nine infants. By the end of 1765, only two of these helpless children had survived. It was the knowledge of such things that had determined Dr Armstrong to start his dispensary. But he was not in favour of special children's hospitals or even of admitting children as inpatients in general hospitals. In his *A General Account of the Dispensary for the Infant Poor*, 1772, he wrote:

> Several Friends of the Charity have thought it necessary to have a House fitted up for the Reception of such Infants as are very ill where they might be accommodated in the same Manner as Adults can in other Hospitals. But a very little Reflection will clearly convince any thinking person that such a scheme can never be executed. If you take away a Sick Child from its Parent or Nurse you will break its Heart immediately: and if there must be a Nurse to each Child what kind of Hospital must there be to contain any number of them? Besides, in this case the Wards must be crowded with grown Persons as well as children; must not the Air of the Hospital be thereby much contaminated?

Long after Dr Armstrong, and after Great Ormond Street and other children's hospitals had been opened in England, that great figure in nursing history, Florence Nightingale, was to repeat some of Armstrong's arguments. She dismissed children's wards in hospitals as making a demand for an excessive number of nurses, but 'where adults are mixed with them, the woman in the next bed, if the patients are judiciously distributed, often becomes the child's best protector and nurse'. And with that curious distortion of logic and attribution of false motivation which was so often a fatal flaw in that strong-minded woman, she casts scorn upon deducing the need for a children's hospital from an excessive child mortality rate, in words which would be taken as a direct criticism of Great Ormond Street's appeals.

> Upon this fact the most wonderful deductions have been strung. For a long time an announcement something like the following has been going the round of the papers – 'More than 25,000 children die every year in London under ten years of age; therefore we want a children's hospital' ... The causes of the enormous child mortality are perfectly well known ... in one word, defective *household* hygiene. The remedies are just as well known; and among them is certainly not the establishment of a child's hospital.

But in the same year as Florence Nightingale published her *Notes on Nursing*, where the above appeared, Dickens's *All The Year Round* for 19 November 1859, could observe:

> ... the want of such an institution in London, before the foundation of The Hospital for Sick Children in Great Ormond Street, was a large hole in our manners as a nation. We are not so civilized as we suppose ourselves to be if, instead of understanding that we ought to maintain in London five such hospitals, we should allow even this one to languish half-supported.

Charles West had to struggle arduously and long for his children's hospital, even after it was opened! And that the opposition could quote such authoritative and caring voices as Dr Armstrong from the past, or Florence Nightingale in the present, did not make it any easier. And always there loomed the fear of infections such as had swept through The Foundling Hospital.

Dr Armstrong's dispensary, which moved to Soho Square in October 1772, did not survive the personal misfortunes and ill-health of its founder, and closed in 1781. A more enduring monument to George Armstrong's pioneering work on the diseases of children was his 'Essay on the Diseases most Fatal to Infants', published in 1767. In the history of paediatric medicine, it was the appearance of Nils von Rosenstein's treatise at Stockholm in 1764 that is generally considered as a beginning; but it was not translated into English, under the title of *The Diseases of Children and their Remedies*, until 1776. George Armstrong will always hold his place in the history of children's diseases, especially in England.

After Armstrong, the first children's dispensary in Europe was founded by Dr Mastalier at Vienna in 1787. And as we have seen, Paris opened the first children's hospital in 1802. Over thirty years later, owing to the influence of Dr Friedeberg, Europe's second children's hospital was opened at St Petersburg in 1834, with sixty beds, which was increased the next year to one hundred. And in 1842, a similar establishment was opened at Moscow under the superintendence of Dr Kronenberg.

Meanwhile, a small hospital of only twelve beds had been started at Vienna, in 1837, by Dr Mauthner, at his own cost and risk; by 1840, the Empress Maria Anna was giving some financial support. Two years later she persuaded the state to take it under permanent protection and contribute some of the funds. In 1842 a second children's hospital, St Joseph, was also founded at Vienna, in the Wieden district.

It may be illuminating to list briefly the other children's hospitals which were opened in Europe during the 1840s. First in 1840, at Hamburg; in 1842, at Frankfurt, Prague and Stuttgart; in 1843, the Elizabeth Hospital at Berlin was followed there the next year by the tiny Louisa Hospital; Graz also opened a children's hospital in 1844; in 1845, no less than four children's hospitals were started – at Pest, Lemberg, Copenhagen and Turin, although this last was restricted to girls; in 1846, Brunn and Munich both opened small hospitals; and in 1847, the Sultan 'ordered the erection of a building on a convenient and healthy spot in Constantinople, which should serve for the reception, irrespective as to faith, of foundlings, and orphans, and for the care and restoration to health of sick children, as also for a vaccination institution'.

Only in England, the richest and most powerful country in Europe, did both government and private charity ignore the sick children of the poor. Furthermore, children were admitted only in tiny numbers to general hospitals in England. In 1843, a little over two dozen children under ten were counted among all the 2363 patients in the London hospitals. For a few years Guy's Hospital indeed had a children's ward, housed in a wooden building over the old stables. Meanwhile, in Europe, Stockholm's hospital department for sick children at the Almanna Barnuset attracted special notice in a survey of children's hospitals written in 1848.

As yet the few determined voices in favour of reform and a children's hospital did not always attract majority support. When Charles West was about to make his first strong efforts to found a children's hospital himself, a medical review in 1849 was still finding it necessary to put in a special plea against the opponents of such an institution.

> We believe ... so far as the *general body* of practitioners of all grades is concerned, there exists not a class of disease, relative to whose pathology

and treatment less exact information is possessed by it, than that which includes those more particularly affecting infants and children.

And the same article makes an attack on the easy solution to the problem of treating children's diseases, exemplified by South's father long before, and which was apparently still being advocated.

> We constantly have patients brought to us, who, we are informed, were at first taken to a particular counter prescriber, because he is said to be 'so famous for children' . . . Can . . . pneumonia or pericarditis be diagnosed by simply looking at a child in its bed or cradle, or can such diseases be treated by an aperient powder or syrup of quills?

But these arguments did not prevail in the most authoritative places. A year or so after these words were printed, the only children's ward in London, at Guy's Hospital, was closed when the outbuildings which housed it were demolished to make way for the new Hunt's House, which was opened in 1852. The historian of Guy's, Dr H.C.Cameron (who himself had in 1911 become Assistant Physician in charge of Children's Diseases) records:

> The cots were then distributed to the various women's wards, and the reason given at the time was that the children's ward required so many nurses that it was better to place them where the services of women patients could be utilized in their nursing and care.

That this attitude towards the care of children in general hospitals persisted long after Florence Nightingale had advocated such a solution (a solution which only perpetuated an unsatisfactory arrangement), and long after Great Ormond Street had shown it to be a fallacy, is also demonstrated by what happened at Guy's Hospital. Shortly after the completion of the new Evelina Hospital for Children nearby, Guy's Medical Council recommended in April 1870 'that the children's beds at Guy's be grouped together with a view of the more efficient study and teaching of Children's Diseases'. But nearly forty years later, in 1908, when the Committee on Specialism reported, it had to add a note, as Dr Cameron wryly remarks, 'This recommendation of the Medical Council has not been acted upon.'

In Britain, before Charles West and Great Ormond Street, the diseases of children were little understood and studied less. What has to be stressed, because it has not always been appreciated, is that the old attitudes and opposition lingered on. Great Ormond Street, although the mother of children's hospitals here, and in America and the

Commonwealth, was not a fairy godmother, who changed, at one wave of her magic wand, the grim and desperate surroundings of all her sick Cinderellas everywhere. The struggle was long and arduous, and in many deprived and famine-stricken countries today, the lessons that Charles West and Great Ormond Street first taught are still being fought for.

It was Dr John Bunnell Davis, who, with his Universal Dispensary for Children, revived the idea of a separate and special dispensary for children's diseases, twenty-five years after Dr Armstrong's Dispensary had closed. Like Charles West after him, he was influenced by what he had seen in France. Dr Loudon, in a paper on Davis, claimed that it was his institution which 'established the principle of charitable care for the sick children of the poor. Thereby it played a major part in the foundation of children's hospitals in England.' But Davis is not generally considered to have been in favour of children as inpatients. What his later attitude would have been, if he had not died early in his forty-seventh year, just before his enlarged dispensary was opened in 1824 as the Royal Universal Infirmary for Children, Waterloo Road, it is impossible to say. Lacking Davis's influence and example, the newly built infirmary continued without real vision, in a day-to-day fashion. Burdened with debts, grossly overcrowded by increasing demand, its staff and committee lacked the will and the foresight, or the energy, to pursue further development. It was the coming of Charles West and the work he did there that gives the Waterloo Road Children's Infirmary its important role in the establishment of children's hospitals in the United Kingdom. Had but John Bunnell Davis lived his allotted biblical span, perhaps he would have handed on the torch personally to Charles West, and Waterloo Road would have been, as Dr Loudon surmises, the synonym for a children's hospital instead of Great Ormond Street. As a letter from Charles West's widow, written in 1910, recalls:

> Dr West moved Heaven and Earth to get the authorities of Waterloo Road to make the place a hospital for children *only*, and I have always heard him say, 'it was an ideal site', as it was in the very centre of the poorest population and a thousand times more convenient for the Mothers to bring their children.

It should be remembered that it was West's second wife who was writing, and it is therefore evidence that, in his old age, West still retained affectionate memories of his time at Waterloo Road. It is sad to think of the ill Charles West in his final years seated perhaps on the Promenade des Anglais, Nice, where he passed so many of his last winters, looking across at the Mediterranean, and sighing as he thought of all the children in the slums of Lambeth and Holborn for whom he could no longer work. He was separated from them not only by illness, but also, as he would hold with strong self-justification, by the obstinacy or pusillanimity of the managing committees of the two institutions which he had served so well.

How West's connection with the Royal Universal Dispensary began is not known. Later, in 1870, replying to a royal toast on behalf of the medical staff at Great Ormond Street, he was to claim that it was mere chance; but the interest must have already been aroused, even if an accident gave him the opportunity. Almost immediately upon his return to England from his continental studies, West had attached himself to Waterloo Road in an unofficial capacity. He had purchased, as we have seen, a share in a London practice within the City. Charles West's father had evidently prospered with his school, or had prudently reserved some capital from his former business interest, to pay for his son's education. It has been estimated that at this time the cost of apprenticeship premium, hospital training, examination fees and other professional charges, plus living expenses, would total about £1000. And not every student, on qualifying, could afford to buy a partnership for £500 or more. It is not surprising that Charles West's partnership grew slack for lack of patients. Perhaps it was a case of a young doctor being led to purchase a share in a business that was almost nonexistent. There were quite a few examples of unscrupulous doctors repeatedly selling shares in a practice with little or no prospects of financial return. There were always eager young men with new qualifications who did not seek proper advice or guarantees. Henry Morley, who wrote so many of the medical articles for Dickens's *Household Words*, had encountered something similar. West should have had enough experienced medical friends to give him sound warning, however. He was only twenty-two, somewhat young to attract the confidence of private patients, especially as a physician accoucheur. In his early days there were too many medical practitioners in competition, and few could flourish or even gain an equitable share of the paying patients. These difficult times for young doctors and surgeons were to last for some decades. Dickens makes Mrs Badger in *Bleak House* utter some shrewdly perceptive observations on prospects in the medical profession: 'Young men, like Mr Allan Woodcourt, who take it from a strong interest in all that it can do, will find some reward in it through a great deal of work for a very little money, and through years of considerable endurance and disappointment.' But Allan Woodcourt himself, through lack of means, had to become a ship's surgeon, as Esther relates:

> He was not rich. All his widowed mother could spare had been spent

> in qualifying him for his profession. It was not lucrative to a young practitioner, with very little influence in London; and although he was, night and day, at the service of numbers of poor people, and did wonders of gentleness and skill for them, he gained very little by it in money ... he had been in practice three or four years, and that if he could have hoped to contend through three or four more, he would not have made the voyage on which he was bound. But he had no fortune or private means, and so he was going away ... We thought it a pity ... Because he was distinguished in his art among those who knew it best, and some of the greatest men belonging to it had a high opinion of him.

West's observation, under Dr Peter Latham, of the typhus epidemic in the wards of St Bartholomew's during the winter of 1837–38, already shows his awareness and concern with some of the social and nursing problems which were to occupy him later. He notes William Salter, a gardener from the country, twenty years old, who, out of work, had come to London in the first week of February 1838, and 'had since then endured great hardships, not having slept in a bed since he came to London, nor had for the last week other food than bread and water. On the 8th of February he caught cold from sleeping out of doors,' in the bitterest winter weather. William Salter died of typhus on 27 February, three days after he was admitted to hospital. How many others died shelterless, friendless and starving in the cold? Jane Ritchie, aged thirty-two, 'a maker of velvet, of temperate habits', recovered and was discharged after a month in St Bartholomew's. But Thomas Holten, fifty-two, 'a carpenter of intemperate habits formerly, when he was better off in the world, but of late has been destitute of many of the necessities in life', died after nine days.

West had no need to point the individual and social moral. He did comment, however, on the sad case of Elizabeth Gee, approaching her fiftieth year, a nurse in the hospital who had caught the infection a few days after Christmas 1837, but who did not, in the end, receive the attention she had given to others. 'The nurse, whose duty it was to attend upon her at night, appears to have neglected her, and in the morning she was evidently dying.'

Of the sixty cases of typhus fever West attended fourteen died, which, as he states, 'is a fearfully great mortality ... I do not know what to attribute the greater mortality among the women, unless it be the circumstance, that while the sister in the male ward was active and assiduous in seeing that the nurses did their duty in waiting upon the sick, she who had care of the female ward was indolent and inattentive.' Thus early in his professional career West demonstrated how much depended upon the nursing in the wards and their proper supervision.

After Queen Victoria's coronation in the summer of 1838, West travelled to Dublin, where he spent the autumn studying at the Rotunda Lying-In Hospital and at the Meath Hospital.

The Rotunda Lying-In Hospital was among the first of its kind, having been originally started by Dr Bartholomew Mosse in 1745. He was another example of a doctor, who moved by the sufferings of the poor, took what practical steps he could to offer relief. Dr Mosse, in his general practice, had seen how in the Irish capital the 'poor generally lodged in cold garrets open to every wind, or in damp cellars subject to floods from excessive rain, destitute of attendance, medicine, and often, proper food, by which hundreds perished with their little infants.'

The Rotunda was another element in the gradually developing concern over the fate of children. Captain Coram had opened his London Foundling Hospital at temporary premises at Hatton Garden in 1741. When the Rotunda's enlarged building was opened in 1757, it was in the presence of the then Lord Lieutenant of Ireland, the Duke of Bedford, who was already President of the Foundling Hospital, and had been foremost in its support. His tomb was to be visited by the boy Charles West in Chenies Church, and his descendants were to be patrons of Great Ormond Street.

When the Rotunda itself was completed, concerts and other events were performed there, as in the Foundling Hospital. Many famous musicians and singers gave recitals. Dickens himself appeared there when he visited Ireland on his first reading tour of 1858. He described the extraordinary success of his last night at Dublin:

> You can hardly imagine it. All the way from the hotel to the Rotunda (a mile) I had to contend against the stream of people who were turned away. When I got there, they had broken the glass in the pay-boxes, and were offering £5 freely for a stall. Half of my platform had to be taken down, and people heaped in among the ruins ... Ladies stood all night with their chins against my platform. Other ladies sat all night upon my steps. We turned away people enough to make immense houses for a week.

The Rotunda Hospital, as Charles West wrote in the Medical Gazette of January 1839 on his return to London, 'affords opportunities for investigating the diseases both of women and children far surpassing those presented by any other in the kingdom'. And in giving lengthy case histories of dropsy and peritonitis in the foetus observed there, he added, 'through the kindness of Dr Evory Kennedy he had an opportunity of examining all the children that were stillborn, or which died in the hospital'.

No doubt the poor in Dublin and the rest of Ireland were almost as deprived as they had been in Dr Mosse's day. They were soon to experience even worse suffering in the Great Famine. Thackeray, in *The Irish Sketch Book*, written four years after West was there, noticed between Kingstown and Dublin 'more shabbiness than a Londoner will see in the course of his home peregrinations for a year', and refers to 'the pretty buildings and gardens of the Rotunda'. But Dickens, in his letter to the *Morning Chronicle* of 25 July 1842, which bitterly attacked Lord Londonderry for opposing the Mines and Collieries Bill regulating child and women's labour underground in the pits, paints a much grimmer picture of poverty and parturition in an obvious reference to Irish conditions.

> A roofless cabin, with potatoes thrice a week, buttermilk o'Sundays, a pig in the parlour, a fever in the dungheap, seven naked children on the damp earth-floor, and a wife newly delivered of an eighth, upon a door, brought from the nearest hut that boasts one – five miles off!

Back in London, and lodging at Tavistock Place, West again spent some time at St Bartholomew's Hospital, this time working under George Burrows, who was then Assistant Physician with special responsibility for the outpatients. West, like quite a few promising doctors afterwards, served as Burrows's clinical clerk, an instructive experience. Perhaps he heard Burrows relate, as he was apt to do in his last years when knighted and Physician Extraordinary to Queen Victoria, his memories of an old physician, the last of those who retained the ancient procedure of examining patients in the wards. Seated in an armchair at the head of a long table, and with the apothecary and the ward sister standing to his left and his right, the old doctor would examine all the patients who could sit up, as they moved in turn towards him along the benches placed around the table. The matron was in attendance with a towel, and after examining each patient and giving a prescription, of which the apothecary noted the particulars, the physician would solemnly rinse out his mouth with water into a bucket, placed in readiness, and wipe his hands on the towel. Then, presumably still flanked by his entourage, he slowly walked round the ward examining those patients still confined to bed.

When Dickens visited the new East London Children's Hospital in December 1868, 'trotting about among the beds, on familiar terms with all the patients, was a comical mongrel dog, called Poodles'. On a second visit to this hospital (which eventually became part of the Great Ormond Street Hospitals for Sick Children Group) he saw Poodles again, acting in a manner which may irreverently recall George Burrows and his old hospital physician.

> Poodles has a greater interest in the patients. I find him making the round of the beds, like a house-surgeon, attended by another dog – a friend – who appears to trot about with him in the character of his pupil dresser ... a pretty little girl looking wonderfully healthy ... had a leg taken off for cancer of the knee. A difficult operation, Poodles intimates, wagging his tail on the counterpane, but perfectly successful, as you see, dear Sir! ... another little girl opens her mouth to show a peculiar enlargement of the tongue. Poodles ... looks at the tongue (with his own sympathetically out) so very gravely and knowingly, that I feel inclined to put my hand in my waistcoat pocket, and give him a guinea, wrapped in paper.

Burrows himself was to become a legendary figure who was 'constant in work and in his upright way of life, discharging every duty with exactitude; a man who permitted neither unpunctuality nor frivolity.' He once told a clergyman at St Bartholomew's, 'Many a man has been put in a lunatic asylum for much less nonsense than you preached to us today.' It was said that he used the same tailor and the same hatter for sixty-five years.

When West published his translation of Müller's *On the Nature ... of Cancer*, he wrote in the introduction, 'I rejoice in having this opportunity of owning my obligations to Dr G.Burrows for that unvarying kindness which he has shown me for some years.'

It was in May 1839 that Charles West renewed his association with the Royal Universal Infirmary, an association which, while not attaining official recognition for some three years, was to remain unbroken over the next ten years. West's own private practice could not yet have been very extensive, although, no doubt, he was beginning to be recommended by more influential and fashionable physicians to some of their married women patients. Despite his interest in the children at Waterloo Road, and his need to concern himself with his own practice, such as it was, he still had time left to work on the translation, not only of Müller's book, but before that on a work by Naegele, which was published in 1839. That both these works attracted attention, and added to West's reputation, can be seen from a review of the Müller book, which concluded:

> With reference to the translation we are bound to say that Dr West has acquitted himself very creditably. He has rendered some of the harshest and most crabbed German we ever read into smooth and pure English; and the few notes that he has added are all judicious and useful. Dr West was equally successful in his translation of Naegele's excellent work on Obstetric Ausculation.

Charles Dickens was occupied with *Nicholas Nickleby*. His visit to

Manchester had made him more aware of social problems other than that of the scandal of the Yorkshire schools, which dominates the first part of the novel in the person of Squeers. In Manchester he met the Grant brothers, who were surely the model for the Cheeryble brothers. No one who has heard the Reverend R.R.Carmyllie speak upon their claim in the Grants' home church at Ramsbottom could fail to be convinced by both the eloquence of the speaker and the silent testimony of the place. And did not Dickens in his preface write:

> But those who take an interest in this tale will be glad to learn that the Brothers Cheeryble live; that their liberal charity, their singleness of heart, their noble nature, and their unbounded benevolence are no creations of the Author's brain; but are prompting every day (and oftenest by stealth) some munificent and generous deed in that town of which they are the pride and the honour.

It was to individuals in the mould of the brothers Grant that Great Ormond Street and Charles West looked in the early years. But as Dickens was to write in his 1848 preface, 'The Brothers are now dead,' and although in their life they gave generous support to hospitals in their own neighbourhood, the children's hospital came too late for their active participation. Their influence, both by direct example and as even more powerfully transmuted by Dickens, was to remain.

At the beginning of 1839, the January number of *Nicholas Nickleby* shows Dickens's growing concern with social problems. When Nicholas and Smike arrive in London, he takes an opportunity to point out the contrast.

> The rags of the squalid ballad-singer fluttered in the rich light that showed the goldsmith's treasures; pale and pinched-up faces hovered about the windows where there was tempting food; hungry eyes wandered over the profusion guarded by one thin sheet of brittle glass – an iron wall to them; half-naked and shivering figures stopped to gaze at Chinese shawls and golden stuffs of India. There was a christening party at the largest coffin-maker's, and a funeral hatchment had stopped some great improvements in the bravest mansion. Life and death went hand in hand; wealth and poverty stood side by side; repletion and starvation laid themselves down together.

When Nicholas first enters the Brothers Cheeryble's counting-house, he sees on the wall, between the shipping announcements, 'designs for almshouses, statements of charities, and plans for new hospitals'. And in the very last number Ned Cheeryble bustles about, getting an 'unfortunate man into the hospital and sending a nurse to his children'. Those to whom the story of Great Ormond Street is familiar well know that

George Orwell's infelicitous sneer at the Brothers Cheeryble as being 'two gruesome old Peter Pans' not only completely misses its mark, but becomes an unintended compliment!

In the July of 1839, Dickens spoke at the dinner given to Macready when he retired from the management of Covent Garden. The chairman was the Duke of Cambridge, who was to be greatly interested in the Royal Universal Infirmary for Children as its president. It is one of the times when the veil between Charles Dickens and Charles West trembled, and seemed almost about to tear. Dickens was to meet the Duke again, perhaps several times, at the home of Miss Burdett Coutts, with whom the Duke and Duchess were on cordial terms. In July 1840, a worried Dickens sent a note to Edward Marjoribanks requesting advice on the correct dress to be worn at Angela Burdett Coutts's dinner party, where the Duke and his wife were to appear. It was probably in 1839 that Marjoribanks had introduced Dickens to Miss Coutts. Marjoribanks and Burdett Coutts were to be early supporters of Great Ormond Street. And the Macready dinner was to be by no means the only meeting or function chaired by the Duke of Cambridge at which Dickens spoke. Did the creator of Oliver Twist, and the Duke of Cambridge ever discuss the Infirmary for Children?

In the episode of *Nicholas Nickleby* written very shortly after the Macready dinner, Dickens does seem to present the deprivations of childhood in a more positive but less melodramatic manner. Ned Cheeryble is remonstrating with Ralph Nickleby over the treatment of Smike.

> 'What if we tell you that a poor unfortunate boy, a child in everything but never having known one of those tender endearments, or one of those lightsome hours which make our childhood a time to be remembered like a happy dream through all our after life ... what if we tell you that sinking under your persecution, sir, and the misery and ill-usage of a life short in years but long in suffering, this poor creature has gone to tell his sad tale where, for your part in it, you must surely answer?'

And when at last Ralph Nickleby learns that Smike was his own child, and slinks from the house towards his home, he passes by a burial ground which is a forerunner of those described in *Bleak House*.

> A dismal place, raised a few feet above the level of the street, and parted from it by a lower parapet-wall and an iron railing; a rank, unwholesome, rotten spot, where the very grass and weeds seemed, in their frowsy growth, to tell that they had spring from paupers' bodies and struck their roots in the graves of men, sodden in steaming courts and drunken hungry dens. And here in truth they lay, parted from the living by a little earth and a board or two – lay thick and close – corrupting in body as they

> had in mind; a dense and squalid crowd. Here they lay cheek by jowl with life; no deeper down than the feet of the throng that passed there every day, and piled as high as their throats.

In the same volume of the *British and Foreign Medical Review* which reviewed Charles West's translation of Müller, there is an article on '*Gatherings from Grave-Yards*' by G.A. Walker, which had been published in 1839. Dr Walker lived in Drury Lane and was convinced that the local prevalence of typhus was caused by the proximity of private and public burial places. He attended a poor man at 33 Clement's Lane, who had the fever of which 'this locality has ... so many examples ... through the windows of the room ... I noticed a grave within a few feet of the house ... made for a man in the room above who died of typhoid fever'. Whether or not the passage in *Nicholas Nickleby* was based upon Dr Walker's reports, it is evidence of how close West's and Dickens' influences were.

In 1840, West sought an appointment as Physician to the Royal Universal Dispensary for Children, but found he was ineligible, not being a Licentiate of the College of Physicians. The College did not award diplomas to candidates under the age of twenty-six, and West was only twenty-four. In this year, probably to increase his income, he began to contribute articles to the *Penny Cyclopaedia* and elsewhere in the medical and lay press. He now had rooms at Craven Street, Charing Cross. Another doctor had his consulting room further down the street. As an address it was in the vicinity of Charing Cross Hospital, and not too far from Waterloo Bridge for his constant visits to the Children's Infirmary. Craven Street was a Dickensian neighbourhood, running parallel with the old Hungerford Stairs of Dickens's sensitive boyhood memories. Opposite was Coutts & Co.'s Bank, where Dickens had his account.

Although somewhat of a disappointing year for Charles West, 1840 saw the inception and the creation of that story and character which were to influence the public most strongly in evoking feelings sympathetic to the idea of a children's hospital. At the end of February, Dickens and Forster went to Bath on a visit to Walter Savage Landor, and it was at the celebration of Landor's birthday 'that the fancy which took the form of Little Nell in *The Old Curiosity Shop* first dawned upon the genius of its creator. No character in prose fiction was a greater favourite with Landor.' So wrote Forster, and it is hard to exaggerate the extraordinary effect the story of Little Nell had, both at home and in America. In Germany it was at once preferred to *Oliver Twist*.

Much has been written of the 'legend' of tears shed for the death of Little Nell. There are powerful arguments on both sides. But it should not be forgotten that the success and interest aroused was already intense long before the development of the story gave any indication that Little Nell might die. Indeed some readers were highly indignant and angry at Dickens for this twist to the tale. One excited Irish gentleman called the author a villain, a rascal, and a bloodthirsty scoundrel! Quilp and Dick Swiveller were other characters who occupied a large part of the tale and were also popular; but Dickens's readers would see them both mainly in their relations to Little Nell.

Perhaps it was because *The Old Curiosity Shop* contained, allied to new psychological insights such as the curious relationship between Quilp and his wife, a strong, endearing fairy-tale atmosphere that it had such a hold on its readers. Little Nell is a kind of lost, legendary princess who is early described in her bed among the strange and dusty contents of the old curiosity shop, almost as if she were imprisoned in some enchanter's magic castle. And something of the story of Rumpelstiltskin with its malignant dwarf is present, even apart from the unforgettable Quilp. When Little Nell and her grandfather and Trotters are at the country inn, a tale is told of professionally retired giants being forced to wait upon the active dwarfs, who stick pins into their legs.

Even if a legend did grow of how strong men wept when reading of Little Nell's death, it was a legend that became accepted, and greatly aided the cause of Great Ormond Street. *Oliver Twist*, *The Old Curiosity Shop* and *The Christmas Carol* became a triumvirate in the public's mind which demonstrated most effectively Dickens's love of children and his concern for them.

It should be remembered that *The Old Curiosity Shop* was first conceived as a 'little child-story' for *Master Humphrey's Clock*, whose protagonist, crippled from boyhood, shuns the light of day and at once pervades the first numbers, and then the novel of *The Old Curiosity Shop*, with encroaching shadows and nocturnal images. At the end of *The Old Curiosity Shop*, when Master Humphrey is reintroduced to take a farewell of the story as a link for the forthcoming *Barnaby Rudge*, he describes London in darkness from St Paul's.

> I was musing the other evening upon the characters ... with which I had so long been engaged, wondering how I could ever have looked forward with pleasure to the completion of my tale ...
>
> Calm and unmoved amidst the scenes that darkness favours, the great heart of London throbs in its Giant breast. Wealth and beggary, vice and virtue, guilt and innocence, repletion and the direst hunger, all treading on each other and crowding together ... In that close corner where the roofs shrink down and cower together as if to hide the secrets from the handsome street hard by, there are such dark crimes, such miseries and horror, as could hardly be told in whispers ...

> The day begins to break . . . Those who have spent the night on doorsteps and cold stones crawl off to beg; they who have slept in beds come forth to their occupation, too . . . The jails are full, too, to the throat, nor have the workhouses or hospitals much room to spare.

There can be little doubt that Dickens is speaking in person. The contrasting city scene he was to use several times, and the regretful farewell to *The Old Curiosity Shop* is but an echo of his letter to Forster of 17 January 1841:

> After you left last night I took my desk upstairs and writing until four o'clock this morning, finished the old story. It makes me very melancholy to think all these people are lost to me for ever, and I feel as if I never could become attached to any new set of characters.

Perhaps the secret of Dickens's success as a novelist is that he believed in the reality of the people he created, with a belief as intense as that of his readers, both of his own time and today.

It was in 1841 that Charles West became physician accoucheur to the Finsbury Dispensary. The next year he also became an official physician at the Royal Universal Infirmary for Children. Charles Dickens has described for us the miseries of Saffron Hill and the streets served by the Finsbury Dispensary. Waterloo Road, also so familiar to him, and in a district so associated with Dickensian characters, was at this time described as one of the worst of neighbourhoods. West himself was to recall, over fifty years later:

> When young, I was physician to two dispensaries; the district of one included Golden Lane, and its purlieus, Saffron Hill and Field Lane; that of the other extended from the Mint in the Borough to Lambeth Church.

The aims of the Finsbury Dispensary were described as 'administering Advice and Medicine to the Poor at the Dispensary, or at their own Habitations, gratis'. It was his experience at Finsbury that brought West to introduce domiciliary visits at Waterloo Road after he had achieved an official position. It is an example of how underprivileged children were as patients that before West none of the medical staff at Waterloo Road seemed to consider it necessary to attend the children in their homes, an exception to the practice of normal dispensaries. The London Medical Gazette for 1832, warning young aspirants to such dispensary posts, comments, 'If he is a dispensary physician or surgeon in London, he must sit for hours prescribing for the afflicted poor, and then go to visit others in the filthiest situations.'

Dickens's visit to the Field Lane Ragged School has already been touched upon. He described the visit in detail, writing to Angela Burdett Coutts on 16 September 1843:

> On Thursday night I went to the Ragged School and a dreadful sight it is. I blush to quote Oliver Twist for an authority, but it stands on that ground, and is precisely such a place ... I have very seldom seen, in all the strange and dreadful things I have seen in London and elsewhere, anything so shocking as this neglect of soul and body exhibited in the children ...
>
> My heart sicks within me when I go into these scenes that I almost lose hope of ever seeing them changed ... The moral courage of the teachers is beyond all praise ... Their office is worthy of the apostles.

If the teachers at Field Lane were worthy of apostolic rank, what praise or comparison should be given to men such as Charles West and James Paget (who also joined the Finsbury Dispensary as Surgeon in 1841) for their care and treatment of sick children and their parents day after day in such fearful and hopeless surroundings?

In 1870, the Prince of Wales, speaking at the Anniversary Festival for Great Ormond Street, described West's activities in this field, although he was obviously referring to Waterloo Road, where the slums were as bad, or worse, as those of Saffron Hill:

> Before the hospital existed, when he was physician to another, it was he who visited the homes of many of the sick children, and did his utmost to alleviate their sufferings, and to render them every comfort in his power: and I may say it was he with whom the idea first originated of building a hospital for the purpose of nursing these children, and of calling the attention of the public to the want which had so long existed.

And ten years after this royal tribute, Sir James Paget, speaking on a similar occasion, enlarged upon this with all the authority of one who had worked side by side with Charles West, in the same streets and slums.

> I remember ... when Dr West worked among the sick poor in their own houses, worked with a marvellous amount of energy, with an enthusiasm unmatched, moved as he was both by his love of knowledge and by his pity for the sick poor; and I remember how when he worked he saw that knowledge was very hard to attain, hindered as it was at every step, and how his pity could never be satisfied.

Charles West's own case notes and papers have, hidden within their clinical observations and medical memoranda, much to tell of the service he gave to those children Dickens described, and could serve as a valuable commentary to the novelist's works. But we must not forget that many of West's medical colleagues also gave unstinting aid to the poor, men such as Dickens described in the person of Allan Woodcourt moving through the pages of *Bleak House*. It was Charles West's dedication to the cause of children and his determination and energy in bringing about a hospital for them which made him unique. West's case notes of the early 1840s show the unstinting dedication to children of which Paget spoke.

Among the children whom Charles West saw at his dispensaries was George Cole of 43 Easton Street, Spa Fields, five years old, who suffered from endocarditis. He recovered. But Anne Leach, aged ten, who lived at 50 Turnmill Street, Clerkenwell, around the corner from Saffron Hill, had parents who belonged 'to that class of poor who seldom pay much attention to their children's ailments. When brought to me she was greatly emaciated.' She died six months after first coming under West's care. These were only two of the many thousands of children he saw at Waterloo Road and Finsbury. The realization of how much was needed, the impossibility of children such as Anne Leach being treated adequately in their homes, made Dr West press as early as 1843 the question of inpatients at Waterloo Road, and in 1845 make the first attempt to turn it into a hospital; but in his own words, 'The attempt failed owing to the jealousies of local medical men.' This was not to be the last nor the only attempt West made over the next few years. What he knew could be achieved was perhaps exemplified twenty-five years later by the Bishop of Lincoln describing a visit to Great Ormond Street:

> I saw in the hospital, lying in their neat and beautifully clean beds, those who otherwise would have had nothing but a straw mattress, or even straw itself, upon the damp stones of a cellar, or in some mouldering attic. I saw those who must have been otherwise left almost without a mother's care – for what care can a mother give who has to earn bread for her children – attended by nurses, themselves ladies, whose care supplied every want and presented every wish; and I saw them – instead of being almost neglected, having, perhaps, the rare visit of the parish doctor, giving all he can give, which is very little – receiving all the attention which the greatest wealth could purchase for its own children.

In 1844 Charles West accepted the post of Consulting Physician to what was to become the New Asylum for Infant Orphans at Stamford Hill. Why this orphanage was founded is a demonstration of the irony that waits upon too much success, a demonstration of how, when the social prestige of a charity becomes so great, the originator, whose dream and child it was, feels that some or much of its original purposes are lost, and is forced into opposition. Originally, the Infant Orphan Asylum for fatherless children at Dalston owed much to the influence and inspiration of one man, Andrew Reed, pastor of the New Road Congregational Chapel and later of the larger Wycliffe Chapel. He conceived plans for its enlargement and removal to Wanstead, which received enthusiastic support at a public meeting presided over by the Duke of Cambridge, whose interest in the Royal Infirmary for Children should not be forgotten. The foundation-stone at Wanstead was laid by Prince Albert, and, in his absence, the completed Infant Orphan Asylum was opened in 1843 by Leopold, King of the Belgians – who curiously enough was Patron of the Finsbury Dispensary. The orphanage at Wanstead attracted not only royal patronage, but also that of the Bishop of London and the Archbishop of Canterbury. The governing committee insisted, despite Reed's opposition, that the Church of England catechism should be made compulsory. To Reed, a Dissenter, it meant that the children of his own faith and the children of other Nonconformists were thus declared ineligible for admission. He resigned from the board, but, in a demonstration of true charity, still gave the institution his patronage, leaving it a special bequest in his will. In 1844 he gathered support for a new orphanage which was founded first at Richmond, then moved to Hackney, and ended up in an old mansion on Stamford Hill. Baron Lionel de Rothschild was to become its treasurer. While the aims of the New Asylum were the same as those of the Wanstead Infant Orphan Asylum, the new orphanage laid down that:

> it shall be a rule absolute, beyond the control of any future general meeting, or any act of incorporation, that while the education of the infant family shall be strictly religious and scriptural, no catechism whatever shall be introduced, and that no particular forms whatever shall be imposed on any child, contrary to the religious convictions of the surviving parent, or guardian of such a child.

The story of the New Asylum for Infant Orphans shows how the charities of the early Victorian age were often vexed by the question of religion and denomination. Dickens was later to feel considerable distress and annoyance when Miss Burdett Coutts, discovering that the under-matron of Urania Cottage was a Dissenter, dismissed her forthwith without informing him. Such matters were to be argued further, of course, in the case of an orphanage than in that of a children's hospital. Great Ormond Street was successful in attracting to its support many of the individuals who had been on opposing sides over the two orphanages.

Perhaps it was typical of Charles West that he accepted a post in the new orphanage, which had been set up in opposition to the support of the royal personages who were patrons of the other two institutions to which he was attached. Most likely this aspect did not occur to him. There are men whose careers, either by ill-luck or by deliberate choice, are marred by a certain wilful neglect of polite expediency. As the son of a Baptist minister, West had already experienced the disadvantages of not belonging to the established church. His sympathies at that time would certainly have been with Andrew Reed and the aims of his New Asylum.

Charles West's involvement with an orphanage was a natural consequence of his work with sick children. It was also something that would draw him even closer to the sympathies and aims of Charles Dickens. In 1844 Dickens himself had, by subscription, become a Life Governor of the Orphan Working School. Perhaps West finally received an indirect benefit from his work for such charities and dispensaries. Many of the Rothschild children were to be his patients. As the medical historian Dr Loudon points out, at that time:

> Appointments as medical officer to charities and clubs ... were often the determining factor ... on a place to settle in practice. All of them provided benefits for a young practitioner, either tangibly as income, or intangibly as prestige and introductions which would lead to private practice. The intangible benefits were sometimes exaggerated.

However that may be, there is no doubt that Charles West's material position improved sufficiently in the summer of 1844 for him to marry Mary Hester, the daughter of W.B. Cartwright of The Field, Stroud, Gloucestershire. Cartwright seems to have been a man of some substance, living south of the town in one of the older and more noteworthy houses. For about two years now West had been living at Charterhouse Square, in the neighbourhood of St Bartholomew's Hospital.

Charles Dickens had become more and more directly concerned with social problems and injustices. In December 1840, Dr Southwood Smith had sent him not only some papers on the Children's Employment Commission, but also his proposals for a Sanatorium for the Lodging, Nursing and Care of Sick Persons of the Middle Classes. This was eventually opened in 1842 at York Gate, Regent's Park, nearly opposite Dickens's house at 1 Devonshire Terrace. Southwood Smith's sanatorium was in some ways a forward-looking institution, anticipating many of the social functions and purposes of the modern hospital. At that time, and for many decades after, hospital were only for the poor. All other classes expected to be treated in their own homes. The wealthy, with their large houses and establishments, could easily cope. The smaller professional and businessmen, or shopkeepers, living in more confined homes with, usually, large families and the assistance of but one or two servants, found sickness a more worrying problem and a strain upon their resources, especially the isolation and nursing necessary for the protracted periods of those infectious fevers which were then so common. And the plight of professional gentlewomen, such as governesses, living in other people's homes was much worse, as Dickens pointed out in a speech made in support of Southwood Smith's sanatorium. The venture, however, was comparatively short-lived.

It was the Children's Employment Commission that stirred Dickens most emotionally, and was the beginning of his personal involvement with Southwood Smith, Lord Ashley, Chadwick, Lord Morpeth, his brother-in-law Henry Austin, and Miss Burdett Coutts in schemes of social betterment and public welfare, many of them having as a primary purpose the protection of children and the amelioration of their condition. All of these associates were to be in some way connected with the beginnings of The Hospital for Sick Children.

Shortly after returning in the summer of 1842 from his American journey, Dickens sent, as we have already seen, a powerful letter to the *Morning Chronicle* in defence of Lord Ashley's bill restricting the employment of women and children underground in the mines. His indignation was probably heightened by the intense joy Catherine and he had at the reunion with their children after six months' absence. Their eldest son, Charley, fell into convulsions due to his excessive delight at seeing his mother, and Dr Elliotson had to be called in the middle of the night. In reporting this to an American friend in a letter from Broadstairs, Dickens mentions that Charley is well again.

> I can see him now, from the window at which I am writing, digging up the sand on the shore with a very small spade, and compressing it into a perfectly impossible wheelbarrow. The cliffs being high and the sea pretty cold, he looks a mere dot in creation. It is extraordinary how many hopes and affections we may pile up on such a speck; small as it is.

At such a time, when his delight in his own children was at a peak, Dickens's universal sympathy for children enlarged. Something of his joy overflows into the character of Tom Pinch in the fifth chapter of *Martin Chuzzlewit*, written in the middle of January 1843, just after Charley's glorious sixth birthday. Dickens was becoming more and more aware that all children were entitled to that love, happiness and protection which he lavished upon his own. That so many children in his day were denied even the merest vestige of such comforts was, he realized to his growing personal distress and concern, as much his individual responsibility and everybody's concern, as the fault of an abstract society and economic theory. Dickens was rapidly reaching that dissatisfaction with the world which would later make him close the chapter containing Jo's deathbed scene in *Bleak House* with the lines, 'Dead, men and women, born with Heavenly compassion in your hearts. And dying thus around us every day.' But although a powerful statement of everyone's involvement in a wrong done to a child, even the great master-novelist understated his case. It was not really 'thus'. Jo died in clean, comfortable and warm surroundings, with friendly care and medical attention. Not in the horrible filth of some squalid corner of a Tom-all-Alone's, as thousands of children had died every year in London for generations past.

Tom Pinch goes into Salisbury to meet Pecksniff's new pupil, Martin Chuzzlewit. He whiles away the time by looking at the bookshops.

> There was another ... where children's books were sold ... Robinson Crusoe stood alone in his might ... and calling Mr Pinch to witness that he, of all the crowd, impressed one solitary foot-print on the shores of boyish memory, whereof the tread of generations should not stir the lightest grain of sand. And there too were the Persian tales with flying chests and students of enchanted books shut up for years in caverns ... and there the mighty talisman, the rare Arabian nights ... Which matchless wonders, coming fast on Mr Pinch's mind did so rub up and chafe that wonderful lamp within him, that when he turned his face towards the busy street a crowd of phantoms waited on his pleasure, and he lived again, with new delight, the happy days before the Pecksniff era.

And when Tom goes on to play the great cathedral organ, the dream still lingers.

> Great thoughts and hopes came crowding on his mind as the rich music rolled upon the air, and yet among them – something more grave and solemn in their purpose, but the same – were all the images of that day, down to its very lightest recollections of childhood.

Dr West would have been delighted to read these pages and find how they concurred with his own thinking. *Martin Chuzzlewit* was the beginning of Dickens's flowering into his mature period. It was also the novel in which two of his greatest comic creations came to life: Mr Pecksniff and Mrs Gamp. Sarah, of course, cannot be left out of any account of what Great Ormond Street achieved. She must be discussed at large in a later chapter. Very soon after writing the Tom Pinch episode, Dickens, distressed by the second report of the Children's Employment

Commission which Southwood Smith had sent him, wondered in his letter of reply what could really be done.

> Want is so general, distress is so great, and Poverty so rampant ... that I scarcely know how we can step between them and one weekly farthing. The necessity of a mighty change I clearly see; and yet I cannot reconcile myself to reduce the earnings of any family – their means of existence being now so very scanty and spare.

A month later he was promising Southwood Smith that instead of the immediate pamphlet promised on the question, he would deliver a 'sledge-hammer' blow at the end of the year. Although the introduction of the two emaciated and twisted child figures of Ignorance and Want in the *Christmas Carol* went some way to fulfil this pledge, it was only with the following year's Christmas book, *The Chimes*, that Dickens struck out fiercely in the cause of the hungry, cold, oppressed and exploited poor of that time, defending them mightily against selfish men and the hypocrisy of economic theories and social attitudes, which complacently looked upon their suffering as an inevitable law of nature and decried personal charity and personal effort. Some of this had also been the theme of *Martin Chuzzlewit*, and is of course a facet of Scrooge in *A Christmas Carol*. In the *Carol*, however, the most memorable character was that of crippled Tiny Tim, the Dickensian child that came most frequently to the minds and lips of visitors to the early Hospital for Sick Children.

But Tiny Tim is a reminder that in some ways it is strange that Dickens, of all people, should have waited until stirred into indignation by Southwood Smith's reports. The agitation against the exploitation of child labour had been going on for years. In describing Dickens's and West's youth, mention has been made of how in the early 1830s Richard Oastler had commenced his powerful campaign. As *The Times* was to declare in 1843:

> With him originated the factory question and those ameliorations which have taken place ... if Oastler with his trenchant blade had not hewn his way through the positive mountains of obstructions which were raised to it in the early stages of this brilliant advance of humanity and justice, Lord Ashley would never have had a standing place.

Oastler was also critical of the New Poor Law Bill. Like Ashley and Disraeli, he was a Tory. And Disraeli, in a speech of 1839, gave utterance to similar sentiments, claiming that now the unfortunate labourer was being told that he had no legal claim to relief. Since 1832, Disraeli insisted, a new class had been given political power, but a class which wanted power with none of the responsibilities or the personal financial contributions which the assumption of such power entailed. They, concluded Disraeli, in a sweeping condemnation which would include as many members of his own party as those on the opposing benches, had 'not been bound up with the great mass of the people by the exercise of social duties'.

Oastler had another powerful claim on Dickens's sympathy. He was deliberately sued by his employer for debt and confined to the Fleet Prison in 1841. His first cell was number 12, Coffee Gallery, behind the Warden's House. When Mr Pickwick first enters the Fleet Prison, he is led by the turnkey, Mr Roker:

> Through an iron gate which stood open, and up another short flight of steps, into a long narrow gallery, dirty and low, paved with stone, and very dimly lighted by a window at each remote end ... Mr Roker then proceeded to mount another staircase as dirty ...
>
> 'There,' said Mr Roker, pausing for breath when they reached another gallery of the same dimensions of the one below, 'this is the coffee-room flight ... and the room where you're a-going to sleep tonight is the warden's room.'

Lord Ashley visited Oastler in the Fleet and noted in his diary:

> No man has finer talents or a warmer heart; his feelings are too powerful for control, and he has often been outrageous because he knew that his principles were just. The factory children, and all the operatives owe him an immense debt of gratitude ... His employer, Mr Thornhill, has used him infamously.

During the years of his imprisonment for debt, Oastler published a journal, *The Fleet Papers*, from 1841–44. Oastler's biographer, Carl Driver, describes them:

> There is a strangely Dickensian flavour in these papers. They abound in a robust pathos entirely foreign to our own age ... Here from the prison cell comes the pleading of one who has looked into the eyes of suffering and cannot forget what he has seen.

The Times published many extracts from the *Fleet Papers* as they appeared. Dickens and West would have read at least some of them. One such extract, which pleads strongly for children crippled in the mills, was, however, published on 11 January 1842, a few days after Dickens and Catherine had sailed from Liverpool for Boston.

> The Factory System
>
> But there are still thousands of victims of the accursed factory system unmentioned ... thousands of neglected, abject, forlorn, degraded, crippled, useless pieces of human lumber which the factory system has thrown out of its jaws, because they could minister no longer to the profit of the Leaguers, having been, though juvenile, 'used up' in the creation of wealth for their oppressors. To see these living crawling things (poor creatures, my heart bleeds for them while I write) in dark damp cellars, crouching upon filthy straw, huddled up, as I have beheld them, like lumps of waste skin and crooked stunted bones, so wretched that they are ashamed to mix even among their own kindred – the very outcasts of the destitute (for they feel themselves degraded below the human family) – to think, Sir, of the bodily and the mental anguish of those children of woe, even if they were in plenty, but now hungered almost to perishing ... I speak of the thousands of poor factory cripples ... poor, abject, wretched children ...
>
> Think of the injured ones, and of their sorrow – their pains in all their joints, and, in very many cases, nought but damp straw to lean on, on the cold stone floor ... In them you witness the foundation of our millionaires ... How strange that these poor worn-out factory cripples ... who are certainly the most deserving objects of charity ... should never have been thought of by any of the Christian philanthropists of our age.

Oastler suggested that the founding of a 'Royal Asylum for the poor factory cripples' would be the best solution to all the plans then being discussed to honour the new infant Prince of Wales. The royal infant would grow up to plead on behalf of Great Ormond Street. In the history of children's welfare, and of the movement which led to the opening of a children's hospital and other institutions caring for the youngest and most helpless members of society, the names of Ashley, seventh Earl of Shaftesbury, and of Charles Dickens are most frequently quoted. Richard Oastler, the 'Tory Radical', should not be forgotten. Lord Ashley was generous in his praise. Charles Dickens seemed strangely silent. Strangely silent, because the cause for which Oastler pleaded was the cause for which Dickens had spoken, and was to speak, so eloquently and so effectively.

Andrew Reed, to whose new Asylum for Infant Orphans Charles West was consultant physician, not content with devoting so much of his powers to the cause of orphan children, in 1847 started an Asylum for Idiots at Park House, Highgate. In addition to the adult inmates, arrangements were made for infants and children because they were considered the patients who most favourably responded to treatment. Its physician was John Conolly, whose associations with Dickens are well know. Dickens was later to visit Park House and write an article on it for *Household Words*. And a few years afterwards, Reed proposed a Hospital for Incurables. This also attracted Dickens's support – he spoke twice for its benefit.

The champions of the neglected child in early Victorian England were making their voices heard with increasing vigour, and these champions were not entering the lists alone. They were each of them recognizing the emblems emblazoned on the shield of their fellow fighters and were beginning to stand shoulder to shoulder. The names of Ashley, Dickens, Blomfield, Burdett Coutts, Reed, Southwood Smith, Kay-Shuttleworth, Chadwick, Oastler, and West – however much at times they would disagree among themselves – were beginning to come together and be seen in concert for various causes. One such cause, a hospital for children, was about to be argued with increasing force and confidence by its principal protagonist, Dr Charles West.

—5—
In Mid-Channel

For Dickens the writing of *A Christmas Carol* (a book described by Thackeray as 'a national benefit, and for every man and woman who reads it a personal kindness'), had been both exciting and exhausting. Over it, in his own words, he

> wept, and laughed, and wept again, and excited himself in a most extraordinary manner ... he walked about the black streets of London, fifteen and twenty miles many a night ... To keep the Chuzzlewit going and do this little book, the Carol, in the odd times between two parts of it, was ... pretty tight work. But when it was done, I broke out like a Madman.

The party for Nina Macready's birthday on 21 December 1843, four days after *A Christmas Carol* was published, at which Dickens's high spirits and gaiety were extravagantly displayed, was described by Jane Welsh Carlyle in a letter to her sister. Her letter explains much of the fascination Dickens had over children, and how he understood their world as few other grown-ups could, because he always kept in his heart some of the wonder and uncomplicated joys of childhood. The *Carol* had affected even Thomas Carlyle. When a friend sent him a turkey and some game, 'the visions of *Scrooge* had so worked on Carlyle's nervous organization that he has been seized with a perfect *convulsion* of hospitality'. The Macready birthday party, according to Mrs Carlyle, 'was the *very* most agreeable party that I ever was at in London'. Dickens performed conjuring tricks for a whole hour, aided by Forster, until the perspiration poured down their faces and they were drunk with success. The grand finale was boiling the raw ingredients of a plum pudding in a top hat, which 'tumbled out reeking – all in one minute before the eyes of the astonished children and astonished grown people!'

But in the middle of this uproar, laughter and intoxication, this atmosphere of boisterous adult indulgence in childish enjoyments which Dickens so loved, there was one person who may have found it exhausting and overwhelming, and could not have been too pleased at Thackeray and Forster being taken back to Devonshire Terrace after midnight to continue the revels. Catherine Dickens was over eight months pregnant. It was to be her fifth labour and at least one miscarriage endured within the space of seven years and seven days. It would be no wonder if she was beginning to show signs of that weariness and lassitude of which Dickens was later to complain so bitterly.

Catherine gave birth to Francis on 15 January 1844, and five days after her confinement Dickens wrote to Lady Holland:

> Mrs Dickens begs me to say, that she is much gratified by your enquiries; and that she is as well as is possible to be. We had some apprehensions beforehand, as she was exceedingly depressed and frightened; but thank God that all passed off before the reality.

Although Catherine was to give birth to five other children, besides miscarriages, between 1844 and 1852, it could be that a lack of true sympathy and understanding in the days immediately after the famous birthday party for Nina Macready held the seeds of the final estrangement between her and Charles. Catherine may well have thought that it was time for him to grow up!

It was something more than disappointment with the financial rewards from *Martin Chuzzlewit* and *A Christmas Carol* that made Dickens plan, early in 1844, to live abroad, and to pause for two years from the writing of novels. Forster hints at that. 'His temperament of course coloured everything, cheerful and sad . . . it was the turning point of his career . . . Much of his present restlessness I was too ready myself to ascribe to that love of change.' The growing and greater discontent with the social injustices of his times, which was to trouble Dickens during these years, may have also made him dissatisfied with the type of novel he had been writing. *The Chimes,* that loud peal of social protest, was one of the two Christmas books produced before he started *Dombey and Son.* And *Dombey,* as has been repeatedly said, shows a new maturity and a wider understanding of the economic and political pressures of the day.

Italy and Switzerland were also to bring mesmerism and Madame Emile de la Rue upon the scene, and the overt knowledge we have of Catherine's uneasiness, if not jealousy and suspicion, over Charles's relations with another woman. But like Charles West, the more Charles Dickens found his life unsatisfactory and full of problems, the more he turned towards the innocence and charm of childhood. It should be noticed that after *The Pickwick Papers,* every novel that Dickens wrote before *The Tale of Two Cities* was concerned wholly or partly with children deprived either by social conditions or by family estrangement and shortcomings. That this period covers almost exactly the years when he and Catherine were together may not be entirely coincidental. Dickens was not the only great novelist who, having attained fame and influence, found his views and feelings beginning to harmonize less and less with the wife he had loved in the days of youth and obscurity. In Dickens there was, however, a growing impatience with some of the more inconvenient details of domesticity and an intolerance of the problems that Catherine faced as a woman, a wife and a mother.

It was because Charles West had a great understanding and sympathy with Victorian women in their troubles, in their illnesses and in their many pregnancies that he first achieved worldly notice. Apart from his growing reputation as a specialist in children's diseases, he was becoming known as an authority on midwifery, and it was probably in that field that West first began to profit in his private practice. Apart from his brilliance as a diagnostician, his sensitivity to the needs of children, his empathy with their distress and their wants, and his love, which they felt instinctively, were probably of more help in assisting their recovery than many of his medical procedures and doses, which of necessity appear quaint and old-fashioned today. As the *Lancet* was to sum up in its obituary after West died in 1898: 'His success was due to the marvellous sympathy with suffering and power of inspiring the feeling that his whole mind and affectionate interests were his patients' for the time being.'

In 1880 Tennyson published a poem, 'In the Children's Hospital', and West's old patients seized upon the picture of 'our kindly old doctor' and the lines:

> I am sure that some of our children would die
> But for the voice of Love, and the smile, and the comforting eye.

They unhesitatingly identified this with their own beloved family doctor, Charles West, even though Tennyson was later to deny any personal knowledge of the hospital and its staff.

This talent for understanding his child patients, which earned him their life-long devotion, was also at the service of their mothers, and would arouse equal gratitude. Long after he had left Great Ormond Street and after spending some time abroad at Nice for reasons of health, he returned to London and set up his practice anew, at the age of seventy, in Harley Street. His old patients came back to him faithfully, even if too few new ones consulted the elderly physician.

> That skilful sympathy which children felt without recognizing drew older patients, and especially women in sorrow or distress, back to him year after year, not only for medical advice, but for help and counsel in the trouble of their lives. One old lady, to whom he had been a great help in sorrow, the widow of a very well-known artist, used to come to him regularly, and putting his fee on the table say, 'I have nothing the matter with me, but I want a talk, but I am not going to have it for nothing. You always send me home better and happier.'

A year after the *British Medical Journal* printed that anecdote in its obituary of Charles West, Freud published *The Interpretation of Dreams.* Like many other experienced medical men, West already knew and instinctively applied the theories and methods of psychoanalysis. It was evident that many wives found understanding and help in his consulting rooms which their husbands sometimes could not provide, even when they were in other ways as sensitive, observant and gifted as Charles Dickens. But it must be remembered that many husbands did in fact pay tribute to this side of West, realizing how much he meant not only to their children but also to their wives. Sir John Duke Coleridge, then Solicitor General, at an anniversary dinner for Great Ormond Street in 1869, particularly referred to 'those who know Dr West, those who have had the blessing of ever being attended by Dr West'.

That in the 1840s Charles West's reputation as a consultant in the diseases of women and midwifery stood high is evident from the recollections of the Surgeon General, Sir Anthony Dickson Home, VC, who remembered, when studying at the Middlesex Hospital in 1845 and 1846, how Charles West 'became the physician and lecturer in that branch of medicine [midwifery] of which he quickly rose to uncontested eminence ... This most honourable, highly principled, accomplished physician retired from practice in the zenith of his fame.' While Dickens was writing *Martin Chuzzlewit* and *The Christmas Carol,* West had devoted special attention to midwifery. With characteristic energy and foresight, knowing that it was in this subject that he was more likely to attain an influential position in the medical world, and thus further his ambition of starting a children's hospital in England, he compiled and prepared a full course of lectures on midwifery, against the future possibility of having the opportunity to deliver them. And in 1845 the opportunity arose, when he was appointed Lecturer on Midwifery at Middlesex Hospital, succeeding Dr Ashburner the next year as physician accoucheur. This appointment at one of the leading metropolitan teaching hospitals was an important step in West's career.

Charles West was already well aware of the shocking infant mortality of that time. What also concerned him was the large number of mothers who died in childbirth or soon afterwards from debility and exhaustion, or from infection and fever, leaving sometimes a newborn infant, and often several young children, to grow up lacking maternal love and care. It was a theme that Charles Dickens was to touch on in his next two novels, *Dombey* and then *Copperfield*. This is another example of how often West and Dickens seemed to move forward in step, as if both had an especial and sensitive response to the questions of their day. What is shown, without dispute, is how Dickens the novelist, the writer seated at his desk, was more responsive and understanding towards these women in their pain and sorrow than Dickens the man, who in correspondence and reported conversation could appear rather uncaring. It may be a truism to point out that without the novelist the man would be of little importance, but it should not be forgotten.

Another famous writer, to whom Great Ormond Street also owes much, brooded over the same sad problem. James Barrie, in his *Little White Bird* – the book in which, significantly, Peter Pan first appeared – made what may be considered a typically whimsical observation; but it is one which, like many of Barrie's whimsies, had much true perception and shrewd thinking behind it. Barrie's comment is very short: 'The only ghosts, I believe, who creep into this world, are dead young mothers, returned to see how their children fare. There is no other inducement to bring the departed back.' In the same way, Dickens's deathbed scenes have closely observed realism and fierce social criticism behind their sentiment. Not only the children of today, but their mothers as well, owe an incalculable debt to Charles West and his contemporary medical pioneers for removing from them many of the perils of that symbolic 'dark and unknown sea' which engulfed first Paul Dombey's mother prematurely, and then, within a few short years, her little old-fashioned son.

For six years, from 1843 onwards, Charles West was to urge the Committee of the Royal Universal Infirmary for Children to open the wards there to inpatients. The Committee appeared to agree in theory, for after all it could be argued that this was John Bunnell Davis's intention when planning the move from Doctors' Commons to Waterloo Road. But nothing was done, apart from the creation of a Hospital Fund to be used at a more auspicious time, at some purposely vague and indeterminate date in the future. No doubt these years of struggle against the natural procrastinatory propensity of the Royal Infirmary's Committee of Management increased Charles West's own inclination, in later years, always to be suspicious of any attempt to defer a decision by the committee of any hospital with which he was associated. This would explain the impression he gave, at both St Bartholomew's and Great Ormond

Street, of not always being an easy colleague. Certainly West did not appreciate that the setting up of the Hospital Fund was in itself a tribute to his growing reputation and influence.

Like other charitable institutions, the Royal Infirmary for Children found fund-raising public dinners, or anniversary festivals, a powerful instrument for obtaining urgently needed donations or subscriptions. Although Dickens spoke often and effectively at such functions himself, he could not always hide the sense of contradiction he felt at the gap between the participants of the dinner and his own deep knowledge of the distress suffered by the beneficiaries of the charity it was seeking to fund.

Perhaps an extreme example of the disgust he sometimes felt with such functions can be found in his description of the Seventh Anniversary Dinner of the Charterhouse Square Infirmary, held on May Day 1843. Dickens had particular reason to be grateful towards Dr Frederick Salmon, whose infirmary it was. About eighteen months previously, Dr Salmon had successfully operated on Charles Dickens for fistula. But even this sense of debt, although no doubt it prevailed on Dickens to attend the dinner and contribute towards the infirmary, could not prevent him giving full rein to his feelings in a letter to Douglas Jerrold.

> Oh Heaven, if you could have been with me at a Hospital Dinner last Monday. There were men there – your city aristocracy – who made such speeches, and expressed such sentiments, as any moderately intelligent dustman would have blushed through his cindery bloom to have thought of. Sleek, slobbering, bow-paunched, overfed, apoplectic, snorting cattle . . . I never saw such an illustration of the Power of the Purse, or felt so degraded . . . The absurdity of the thing was too horrible to laugh at.

It was a function of which Charles West must have been well aware. He was living at Charterhouse Square at that time, next door to the infirmary. He and Dr Salmon certainly consulted each other and conferred together, the more especially since Dr Salmon had been for a number of years House Surgeon at St Bartholomew's. And despite the letter, Dickens supported and championed the infirmary, and was always grateful towards Dr Salmon. In 1846 he sent him specially bound and signed copies of his four last books, including *The Chimes*.

It was *The Chimes* which first gave Charles Dickens a hint of how he could raise money for charity other than by speaking at public dinners. On 3 December 1844, having returned to London from Italy for a short stay to deal with necessary business concerning his Christmas book, he read *The Chimes* at Forster's house, Lincoln's Inn Fields, to a group of friends including Carlyle. The emotional response and the sensation caused by this private reading spread all over London. *The Chimes* was an undeniable success and its 20,000 copies were soon sold out. Its social message was clear and unequivocable. *The Chimes* was one of those books which helped to set the mood for continuing reform.

An immediate effect of *The Chimes'* reading was to reawaken in Dickens a desire to act, and he was at once arranging with Forster 'that a private play should be got up by us on your return from Italy'. But also born in that reading was an idea which later first found half-serious expression after Dickens had read the second number of *Dombey and Son* to a group of friends in October 1846.

> I was thinking the other day that in these days of lecturing and readings, a great deal of money might possibly be made (if it were not infra dig) by one's having Readings of one's own books. It would be an *odd* thing. I think it would take immensely.

Here, expressed for the first time, was something which was not only to be important in the story of Great Ormond Street, but was to have great and lasting consequences for the whole course of Dickens's career and life. These stirrings in Dickens's mind of readings and play-actings were further signs of his restlessness, and a seeking for something that would help to reconcile his dissatisfactions and despondencies with his outbursts of vivid enjoyment and delight. It seemed no longer enough to concentrate all his energies in his pen, in the creation of those works which we now know to be the true treasures of his life. However, although the diversion of Dickens's energies away from his books is something that may be sighed over and regretted, perhaps each activity was inextricably interwoven with others.

At Rosemont, Lausanne, he was not only dreaming of acting or of public readings. His letters to Angela Burdett Coutts began to develop their scheme for a refuge for the unfortunate young girls forced into prostitution, the girls Miss Burdett Coutts had watched with pity and helplessness from her windows at the corner of Stratton Street and Piccadilly. And almost as soon as Dickens had moved into Rosemont with 'its beautiful grounds, on the hill above the lake, with the whole range of the Alps towering before it', he was writing to Lord Morpeth, seeking some public post.

> I wish to confide in you, a very earnest desire of mine ... I have an ambition for some public employment – some Commissionship, or Inspectorship or the like, connected with any of those subjects in which I take a deep interest, and in respect of which the Public are generally disposed to treat me with confidence and regard. On any questions connected with the Education of the People, the elevation of their character, the improvement of their dwellings, their greater protection against disease or vice

> – or with the treatment of Criminals, or the administration of Prison Discipline, which I have long observed closely – I think I could do great service, and I am sure I should enter with my whole heart.

Lord Morpeth, as Earl of Carlisle, was to play a large part in the history of Great Ormond Street. He was a principal speaker at the first public meeting held in March 1851, to promote the founding of a children's hospital. He chaired the 1859 anniversary dinner in aid of the Hospital, the year after Dickens had first set the example. That someone of such political and governmental importance, who worked with Dickens on many movements for improving public health, sanitation and housing, was so concerned with The Hospital for Sick Children enlarges on the importance Dickens had for Great Ormond Street, and Great Ormond Street for him. In the Hospital for Sick Children, Charles Dickens did indeed find some employment connected with a subject in which he took 'a deep interest, and in which the Public are generally disposed to treat me with confidence and regard'.

But within a few days of writing this letter to Lord Morpeth, Dickens wrote to Forster, 'BEGAN DOMBEY!' It was, as Edgar Johnson, Dickens's most important modern biographer, writes, 'a turning point both in Dickens's life and in his literary art'. There had been a gap of two years since he had finished his last novel, *Martin Chuzzlewit,* whose public reception had been disappointing. *Dombey and Son* was a triumph from the first, and in another two years Dickens was able to write 'Dombey and Son has been the greatest success I have ever achieved.' It was while *Dombey and Son* was achieving its peak of popularity that the Royal Infirmary for Children announced that its 30th Annual Festival would be held at the London Tavern, Bishopsgate, on 23 February 1847. Its annual report for 1846, which had recently been issued, claimed:

> During the past twelve months, 5585 children have been admitted as patients on the application of their parents or friends, *without any recommendatory letter.* Of these children 4912 have come under the care of the Physicians or Surgeons, and in addition to receiving advice and medicine at the Institution, all whose dwellings were not too distant, and the nature and severity of whose ailments appear to require it, have been visited at their homes.

These were the domiciliary visits which Dr West had brought about by his example. His resolve to open a Children's Hospital, in which alone, as he well knew, the conditions could be found to treat successfully the children living in such places as Dickens described in his novels, was never more keen.

In advertising its 30th Annual Festival in *The Times* at the beginning of February, the Royal Infirmary for Children stressed another aspect of its claim for public support:

> The Committee appeal with confidence to the humane portion of the public for co-operation in their endeavours to apply the resources of improved medical science to numerous cases of severe bodily affliction and deformity, in which without prompt and skilful attention, the children of those who are destitute of the means to pay for medical assistance are left to die, or to grow up deformed and debilitated objects of pity and aversion.

Aversion! In *Nicholas Nickleby* Dickens had already touched upon this problem, in that unforgettable sentence which describes Nicholas's first sight of the pupils at Dotheboys Hall.

> Pale and haggard faces, lank and bony figures, children with the countenances of old men, deformities with irons upon their limbs, boys of stunted growth, and others whose long meagre legs would hardly bear their stooping bodies, all crowded on the view together; there were the bleared eye, the hare-lip, the crooked foot, and every ugliness of distortion that told of unnatural aversion conceived by parents for their offspring, or of young lives which, from the first dawn of infancy, had been one horrible endurance of cruelty and neglect.

After such extracts from Dickens's pages, it may not be so surprising, but it is certainly both exciting and tantalizing, to find, among Charles West's papers preserved at The Hospital for Sick Children, a sealed ticket for this very dinner of the Royal Infirmary for Children's 30th Annual Festival. A ticket that shows the list of stewards and is made out to 'Charles Dickens, Esqr.'

It is a document of which possibly too much could be made. But its very survival has a significance of its own. The date and time of the dinner, Tuesday, 23 February 1847, 'at six precisely', can arouse much conjecture and frustration. What cannot be denied is that it is the earliest piece of actual documentary evidence possibly linking Charles West and Charles Dickens together, five years before Great Ormond Street opened.

The Dickens family had left England for Switzerland the previous summer, and had remained abroad ever since, moving to Paris in November. Charles was in London for a week in December, attending to the publication of a new cheap edition of his works, and to the dramatization of his current Christmas Book, *The Battle of Life,* which was published on 19 December. He returned to Paris on Christmas Eve and had no intention of returning to England until the end of March. His house in Devonshire Terrace had been let until the middle of summer.

His residence abroad was, of course, well known to everyone, even apart from his friends and business acquaintances. But on Wednesday, 17 February 1847, he wrote to Forster in haste announcing his immediate departure for London, because he was 'horrified to find' the first chapter in the forthcoming number of *Dombey* was at least two pages short: 'I decide – after the first burst of nervousness is gone – *to follow this letter by Diligence tomorrow morning.* The malle-poste is full for days and days. I shall hope to be with you some time on Friday.'

On the Saturday afternoon, 20 February, Dickens wrote to his wife from the Piazza Coffee House, Covent Garden. After describing his stormy crossing from Boulogne, and the luck he had in catching 'the express train at Folkestone which brought us up in two hours and twenty minutes' (journey time that is not much improved upon nearly a century and a half later!), and news of their eldest son, Charley, then at school in Hampstead, he tells Catherine of his return arrangements.

> I shall be obliged to leave Folkestone on *Tuesday* by 3. By consequence I have no help for it but to sleep that night at Boulogne. I have engaged with the people at the Inn there, to take me a place on Wednesday's Malle Poste, if it can be got. If not, in the Wednesday's Diligence (Caillard & Co.'s) that leaves Boulogne at 11 in the forenoon.

From these intended plans and reserved places it would appear very likely that Dickens was in mid-channel or about to disembark at Boulogne when the Royal Universal Infirmary's guests began to arrive at the London Tavern at half past five that Tuesday evening. But there is no absolute proof! The next definite evidence we have of Dickens's whereabouts is in the letter written to Georgina Hogarth, his sister-in-law. It was sent from London, postmarked 1 March 1847, and could have been written the previous day, but not necessarily.

Forster wrote of this time, 'He had hardly returned to Paris when his eldest son was attacked by scarlet fever ... he and his wife at once came over.' It is possible to argue from this that Dickens may have delayed his departure from London until Wednesday, 24 February, and arrived in Paris on Thursday or Friday at the latest. The earliest information relating to Charley's scarlet fever is found in a note from Maclise to Forster, dated Friday, 26 February: 'I am anxious to know how little Charlie is ... Have you written to D---?' Departure from London on the Wednesday could agree with Forster ('he had hardly returned to Paris'), with Maclise's note, and with Dickens's letter to Georgina. She had been left in Paris with the children, when Charles, Catherine and Roche (the Dickens's courier) had rushed back to London, where they arrived at the Victoria Hotel, Euston Square, perhaps on the Sunday, but more likely on the Monday. Indeed a Sunday arrival seems unlikely, because as Dickens wrote to Douglas Jerrold a fortnight before, 'Now you can't cross to Boulogne on a Sunday, unless in summer-time.' The speedy railway journey from Folkestone allowed travellers to arrive in London on the same day as they made the crossing. It would appear that the letter to Georgina was in fact written on the day it was postmarked: Catherine would immediately send her sister the news of their safe arrival. Charles's letter, which survives, was obviously enclosed with Catherine's note.

Further confirmation can be found in a later letter of Dickens's, written to Emile de la Rue on 24 March:

> On the day before I left, Charley [then at School at King's College] was with me. On the very day I went away, he was seized with Scarlet Fever. On the day after my arrival in Paris, I received the intelligence, and started off again for England with his mother.

Even if Dickens had not arrived back in Paris until the Friday, and received the news from Forster on the Saturday, this would still allow the possibility that they could have reached London on the Monday.

All these journeys took place at a time when the railway from Paris to Boulogne was just about to be opened. The Paris to Amiens section had already come into use, but the Amiens to Boulogne extension was not opened until 14 March. On 19 December 1846, Dickens had written to Catherine from London, 'The Journey here was very long and cold. 24 hours from Paris to Boulogne. Passage not very bad, and made in two hours.' But writing to Forster just after Christmas, he describes his journey back to Paris, 'The malle poste, however, now takes the trains at Amiens. It is delightful travelling for its speed, that malle poste, and really for its comfort too . . . For two passengers (and it never carries more) it is capital.' However, the *malle-poste,* with its red barouche and four horses, because of this limitation to two passengers needed to be booked well in advance. Dickens's letter to Douglas Jerrold informed him that a place should be taken 'at least a fortnight before'. Dickens's intended booking for Wednesday, 24 February, 'if it can be got', made at the most with only five days' notice, stood very little chance of success. On the 17th it was already full 'for days and days'. Dickens knew, as he had told Jerrold, that there were 'plenty of coaches' for a diligence from Boulogne. His keeping the Wednesday morning reservation from Boulogne was therefore not vital. His first rushed journey to London, and his hurried return there on receiving the news of Charley's illness, showed that it was always possible to make the journey within two days, even if not by the fastest and most comfortable route, despite the inconvenience of tides and of railways which may or may not have been available over certain stretches.

This close examination of Dickens's travels between Paris and London – which perhaps may remind some older readers of Freeman Wills Croft's leisurely-paced detective novels, with their ingenious alibis and solutions based on a minute knowledge of railway timetables and coastal tidal waters – reveals a possibility at least that Dickens could have been in London on Tuesday, 23 February, and thus allows the further surmise that he actually attended the Royal Universal Infirmary's dinner. It would not be perhaps the first hospital or charity dinner which Dickens attended without attracting the notice of the press. But the mere fact that such a ticket was made out in Charles Dickens's name does raise more cogent questions.

It was known that Dickens was in residence abroad with no intention of being in London on the date in question – Dickens himself did not know it until the day before he left Paris – so why was such a ticket written out? A sealed ticket – one bearing a wax impression of the institution's or its officer's seal – was the contemporary equivalent of a complimentary ticket. It could be argued that Dickens's name was one which would be routinely included on the complimentary list of such a charity, and that it was automatically made out, but not sent to him. This is a feasible argument, but in that case why did Charles West preserve it among his papers, almost as something to treasure? In 1842 and 1845, Dickens was away from England, in America and Italy respectively, at the time when the Royal Universal Infirmary would hold its Annual Festival, but West preserved nothing from those years. What was different in 1847?

A mere glance at the names printed on the ticket provides an answer, and also an argument against the fact of its having been merely an automatic complimentary invitation. Indeed, as is known from the Great Ormond Street records, Charles West was always active and dominant in the preparations for such anniversary festivals. He was senior physician at the infirmary and would never agree to the sending out of unsolicited invitations to men of renown, which would not be welcome to the recipient and, certainly in Dickens's case, were often a source of considerable annoyance and inconvenience.

The chairman of the dinner was Lord Ashley, later the 7th Earl of Shaftesbury and first president of The Hospital for Sick Children. No more important association could possibly exist than that between him, Charles Dickens, Charles West and Great Ormond Street. The name of Lord Ashley alone would give good reason for this 1847 Annual Appeal having had a special significance and attraction for Charles Dickens.

Two members of the nobility head the list of stewards: the Duke of Rutland and the Earl of Ellesmere. Lord Ellesmere was a supporter of Great Ormond Street from its beginnings. The Duke of Rutland's name is first found in Great Ormond Street's subscription list among those who responded to Charles Dickens's 1858 appeal for the hospital.

William Hawes, surgeon to the Royal Universal Infirmary for Children, was also a steward at this dinner. A manuscript statement by Charles West, written over a generation later, records that in 1848 West made what was probably his most determined attempt to convert the Royal Universal Infirmary 'into a hospital. Some new members joined the committee, of whom one of the most active was Mr W. Hawes, brother of the late Sir Benjamin Hawes. The attempt failed owing to the jealousies of local medical men.' The sad background to that last terse sentence has already been enlarged upon. What is important here is that Sir Benjamin Hawes was the local Member of Parliament for Lambeth, who had become Under-Secretary of State for the Colonies in July, 1846. He and Dickens were in communication on the questions of Ragged Schools, emigration and articles for the *Examiner*.

The most interesting name is that of Samuel Cartwright, Surgeon Dentist to the Royal Universal Infirmary, who is listed among the stewards. He was Dickens's own personal dentist and friend. Dickens often dined at the Cartwrights', where Samuel Cartwright Sr, also a celebrated dentist, was well known as a host of many gatherings of the famous in literature, science, medicine, politics and society. The younger Cartwright was later to be directly responsible for Dickens agreeing to speak for Great Ormond Street eleven years afterwards. A William Hawes married the sister of Samuel Cartwright, and Dr Charles West's wife was a close cousin of these Cartwrights.

It can readily be seen that any or most of the above would have known that Dickens was abroad, and that surely, even apart from Dr West's influence, precludes the sealed invitation to Charles Dickens being issued merely as one of a standard complimentary list. It is also revealing that so many names should be linked with Dickens, West and later with Great Ormond Street. There are other likely-looking names on the stewards' list. A James Hunt is recorded among Dickens's correspondence. Dr Willshire, fellow physician with Dr West at the Royal Universal Infirmary, may have been a relative of the Emily Willshire whom Dickens mentions later on that year as being an applicant for the post of assistant matron at the proposed Urania Cottage Home for Fallen Women.

But it may be objected that, no matter how closely associated all the above were with Charles Dickens, how could they have known he was most unexpectedly in London for a few days at that time, and thus possibly available to attend the dinner?

Again, as so often, Forster provides an answer. Dickens, in his letter to Catherine of 20 February, had told her, 'And he [Charley] dines with us (I found him already engaged there) at Gore House tomorrow.' Gore House was the residence of that famous hostess, the Countess of Blessington. Forster recalls, 'This was on Sunday, the 21st of February, when a party were assembled of whom I think the French Emperor, his cousin the Prince Napoleon, Doctor Quin, Dickens's eldest son, and myself, are now the only survivors.'

Dr Frederic Quin, who started the Homeopathic Hospital (which coincidentally now stands next to The Hospital for Sick Children in Great Ormond Street), a friend of Dickens and Thackeray, was a frequent guest at Gore House, and a well-known figure at social and literary dinners. He moved in the same circles as the Samuel Cartwrights. Since 1845 he had been medical attendant to the Duchess of Cambridge, and the Duke of Cambridge's interest in the Royal Universal Infirmary for Children has already been explained. He was moreover a close neighbour of William Hawes in Arlington Street. It will be seen that Dr Quin was on several accounts in a position to tell Dickens about the proposed dinner in aid of the Waterloo Road Children's Infirmary, or to inform the infirmary itself that Dickens was in London. Dr Quin may already have known on the Saturday that Dickens was expected the next day at Gore House. As Dickens's letter indicates, Charley and Forster were 'already engaged there'.

It is now evident that it was possible for Dr Charles West and his colleagues to have made out the invitation to Charles Dickens, and with his knowledge, at almost the last moment. Whether Dickens agreed to attend, or made a half-promise to attend, either through Dr Quin or the other possible contacts; whether Dickens confused the day or the time of his still being in London; whatever happened, what is important, and beyond dispute, is the evidence that this sealed ticket brings to light of the close and intermingled links that already existed between Charles Dickens's circle, Charles West's colleagues, and those who were to be among the first supporters of Great Ormond Street. Most probable as it is that Dickens was in mid-Channel when the dinner took place, nevertheless this invitation made out to 'Charles Dickens, Esqr.', in view of all that has been explained above, has a value and a meaning in the mere fact of its existence and survival.

—6—

INTO HARBOUR

Dickens wrote to Emile de la Rue on 24 March telling him of Charley's illness, and explaining that they had not yet seen Charley because Catherine was 'going to be confined very early in May'. He then adds a comment in his usual rather jocular vein when discussing such matters: 'I thought it was a false alarm when you asked me at Vevey, but it turned out to be the real original Fire Bell.' Dickens did not know how real and great an alarm the confinement was going to cause. Her anxiety over Charley may have affected Catherine, for when her seventh child, Sydney Smith, was born somewhat earlier than expected on 18 April, she had a very difficult and dangerous confinement, and Dickens was greatly shaken and moved by her ordeal, as he wrote the next day to Macready:

> You will have heard I dare say, my very dear Macready, of yesterday – and you will have imagined what our anxieties were. Dr Henry Davis, whom I fetched wildly – getting hold of Locock at the same time – told me he had seen but one such case in his experience; and of course my dear Kate suffered terribly. But thank God she is as well today as ever she has been at such a time: as well as anyone *can* be: and sends all sorts of loves to you.

Near the time that Locock – a friend of West and a guest at Dickens's dinners – was sought out by Charles Dickens, Charles West had embarked upon a venture that was to be an important landmark in his career, and of great consequence in the founding of Great Ormond Street.

This was a series of lectures on 'The Diseases of Infancy and Childhood', which West delivered at the Middlesex Hospital. Each lecture was printed in the *London Medical Gazette*, starting with the issue of 30 April. He began by telling the students that 'children would form at least a third of all young patients, and so serious are their diseases that one child in five dies within a year of birth, and one in three before the completion of the fifth year.' Disease in childhood, he pointed out, 'not merely disturbs the present but its influence reaches to the future'. He warned them that they would 'have to study a new semiology, to learn a new pathology, and new therapeutics'. This was why he was giving this series of lectures: because it was too important a subject to be merely 'examined at the end of a course of lectures on midwifery'.

West's colleague at the Royal Universal Infirmary for Children, Dr W.H. Willshire, who was Lecturer on Materia Medica at the Charing Cross Hospital, had already begun publishing a series of lectures, 'Clinical Observations of some of the more Important Diseases of Children', in the *Medical Times* at the beginning of the month. In these he most generously drew attention 'to the able papers which have now and then appeared from the pen of my colleague, Dr West'.

Charles West's lectures were to bring him fame, to be translated into several languages and to acquire an international reputation. Dr Willshire's lectures faded into obscurity, although like West's they filled an important gap in medical instruction at that time. Willshire was not such an accomplished lecturer as West: he was more pedestrian and not so eloquent. As he acknowledged, Charles West was perhaps his superior in knowledge and observation. Later at St Bartholomew's, West's lectures were to be 'remarkable, not only for the keen observation and sound practical sense which they displayed, but for the graceful style in which the teaching was conveyed'. But what West also showed was an innate love, knowledge and understanding of children.

The late Dr Felix S.Besser, the honorary archivist of The Hospital for Sick Children, was fond of quoting the comment that Dickens's children were the victims of either the Benthamite economic view that the young were merely units to be trained for a useful role in a financially motivated and organized society, or of the Calvinistic view that children were unregenerate small imps of Satan; both views denied 'the Dickensian world of love and imagination'. Such views also denied Charles West's world of children, where love and imagination were not alone integral qualities, but also the duty and self-sacrifice on the part of the physician.

To his contemporaries, Dickens seemed to be the delineator and champion of children, and this is illustrated by an incident in the following December, when he spoke on behalf of the Mechanics' Institution at Leeds. When he came on to the platform the whole audience rose to him with deafening applause, and even after several minutes, when the ovation was beginning to subside, a gentleman called for 'one more cheer for the author of Little Nell', and a tumultuous and fervent burst of applause rang out again. Dickens was much moved by this experience.

In an age when every parent seemed to suffer a similar loss and a similar grief, Dickens had become a spokesman for their sorrow, expressing it in a language and a symbolic emotionalism beyond their own powers. They took comfort not only from the catharsis of the famous death scenes, but also from the scores of children scattered throughout his pages, almost as liberally as the fairies born out of the thousand pieces of a baby's first laugh in *Peter Pan.* From Joe, the fat sleepy boy in *Pickwick*, to little Johnny Tetterby in *The Haunted Man*, he had created a new generation of children, who were to console the fathers and mothers for their own lost children, much as a new baby will comfort a bereaved mother – comfort her, but never let her forget the child she had once cherished. Only by remembering this can it be understood what Charles Dickens's support would mean to Great Ormond Street.

Despite West's claim that it was in 1848 that an attempt was made to convert the Royal Universal Infirmary into a children's hospital, the 1847 Festival had also endeavoured to raise funds for this purpose. This is hinted at in a letter to West from Ebenezer Smith, a general practitioner near Fenchurch Street and surgeon to the Royal Maternity Charity. The letter is dated 19 February 1847, a few days before the dinner. He thanked West for sending him a new report on midwifery: 'I wish I could afford to aid with a Donation the valuable object of an Infirmary for Children.' He then suggests 'names of persons who might effect this very important and needful object, so far as subscriptions are concerned'. Whether or not West was successful in obtaining support from these names for the Waterloo Road Children's Infirmary, it is evident that he kept the list carefully: three of them – two most probably the wives of those 'rich and liberal' gentlemen – appear among Great Ormond Street's most generous donors in the very first annual report. In 1847, West moved to Wimpole Street, a sign of his increasing and fashionable private practice. In June 1847 Charles Dickens and his family returned to Devonshire Terrace, little more than a five-minute walk from Dr West. It may be permissible here to indulge in the fancy that West could have been called in as consultant when the Dickens children fell victim to one of their childish ailments. That some of the doctors within Dickens's circle knew West as a relative, a colleague and a friend has already been shown. It is likely that the Dickenses should have sought the advice of a leading authority on children's diseases who was most conveniently practising in the neighbourhood. In 1848, West's *Lectures on the Diseases of Infancy and Childhood* were published, he was elected FRCP, and appointed to St Bartholomew's Hospital as Lecturer on Midwifery and the Diseases of Women and Children. It was at first a joint appointment with Dr Rigby, but Rigby resigned early the following year and West became, in his own words, 'Sole Teacher on that subject'. All this made him a respected figure in his profession, whom no colleague would hesitate to call in or seek advice from when difficult and dangerous problems arose within the field of his special interests. The possibility that West visited Devonshire Terrace in a professional capacity cannot be entirely dismissed. Dr Chillip in *David Copperfield*, a book begun in 1849, may surprisingly offer further evidence.

In Forster's copy of *David Copperfield*, among the marginalia he made is a note against Dr Chillip, 'actual person'. Charles Dickens Jr, 'Charley', stated that Dr Chillip 'was based upon the little doctor who was attending them at the time the novel was being written'. In his number plan, Dickens wrote 'Morgan the Dr.'. The editor of the Clarendon edition tentatively suggests that this may be the name of his original, perhaps a Charles Morgan of Bedford Place, Russell Square, because he was the nearest practitioner named Morgan in the current medical directory. At this time Dickens did know of a Dr Morgan, who was the medical adviser of Mrs Leech, wife of the famous illustrator, John Leech. Dickens wrote to Catherine from Norwich that he had dreamed of Morgan in the night, and in view of her imminent confinement hoped it was not an ominous sign. But Mrs Leech's Morgan, practised at Earl's Court and Belgrave Square, rather too distant for Devonshire Terrace. And how usual was it for Dickens, experimenting with names for his characters and jotting them down on a number plan, to write down the name of an actual person?

Chillip is introduced in the novel as the 'meekest of his sex, the mildest of little men', a description that would in some ways hardly fit his contemporaries' view of Charles West. Like other characters in *Copperfield*, Dr Chillip, while being based on a living model, was most likely an amalgamation of reality and of Dickens's creative imagination. Mr Micawber, for instance, is much more than a mere portrayal of some of the characteristic mannerisms of Dickens's own father.

Charles West was short of stature. Twistington Higgins, who wrote a history of Great Ormond Street for its centenary in 1952, had access during his long career at The Hospital for Sick Children to much oral tradition and information from men such as Sir Thomas Barlow, who had actually worked with West at Great Ormond Street. It is significant that Higgins, in writing of the poor mothers and children attending West's clinic at Waterloo Road, should have used the phrase, 'they had faith in the little Doctor', words which echo Charley's own memory of the original Dr Chillip. Although West was by no means meek with his colleagues or hospital boards of management, he valued 'the quiet manner and the gentle voice' when treating children and he was unfailingly sympathetic to his women patients. Perhaps in contrast to some of the more ebullient and impatient practitioners of the day, West, when with his little patients, would appear to be the meekest and mildest of men. When David is overcome with grief after his mother's funeral, 'Mr Chillip talks to me; and when we get home, puts some water to my lips; and when I ask his leave to go up to my room, dismisses me with the gentleness of a woman' – exactly the same kindness with which West would have behaved in a like situation. It can be claimed in several ways – in some characteristics, speciality, professional acquaintance, and convenience of location – that Charles West would agree more with Charley's Dr Chillip than the unknown qualities of a Dr Charles Morgan from Russell Square. But, to adapt the opening words of *David Copperfield,* whether West shall turn out to be the hero, or whether that station will be held by anybody else, the future pages of another historian must show.

A shadow had fallen across Dickens before commencing *Copperfield* which he could not so easily dismiss with a flourish of his pen. After the triumph of his amateur productions of *Every Man in His Humour* and *The Merry Wives of Windsor* at the Theatre Royal, Haymarket, which had been attended by Queen Victoria and the Prince Consort in May 1848, their even greater acclaim at Manchester and Liverpool and the furore at Birmingham in June, Dickens returned to London at the end of the month. There he wrote to Mark Lemon, and after dealing with minor details of the tour and the productions added the news, 'Sir James Clark tells me my sister cannot possibly live many weeks. I have seen him this morning.'

Sir James Clark was Physician-in-Ordinary to Queen Victoria, and although now mainly remembered for his ill-chosen advice over the unfortunate Lady Flora Hastings and her supposed pregnancy, was a figure of much renown and respect in the medical profession. He was to be, incidentally, one of the most influential supporters of West in the proposals for a children's hospital, joining the Provisional Committee, and speaking at the first public meeting in its aid. Refusing to abandon hope, Dickens wrote the next day to his sister Fanny Burnett at Hornsey, arranging for her to see Dr J.Hastings, also a specialist in pulmonary diseases, because 'he has done wonders where Clark really did nothing'. Hastings's verdict did not differ from Sir James Clark's. In two months Fanny had died, 'and not by slow degrees'.

Perhaps some of this personal sorrow heightened the intensity with which Dickens attacked the neglect and maltreatment of children both in his Christmas book for that year and in his *Examiner* articles at the beginning of the next year. His fiercest passions were certainly engaged in the scandal of Drouet's baby farm at Tooting. Here 1400 children, boarded out by the guardians of the poor for the Holborn Union and other workhouses, were kept in the vilest and most horrific of conditions, on an inadequate diet where even the scanty potatoes were blackened and diseased. Those that could, clambered furtively over railings to pick out the scraps from tubs of hogwash. Emaciated and covered with boils and sores, the children easily fell victims to an outbreak of cholera, but were left without medical care, four in a bed, in foul damp rooms. One hundred and eighty-nine of these pauper children died, and the parish churchyard was too small for the great heap of tiny coffins. The author of *Oliver Twist* again sprang to the defence of the helpless workhouse children. Drouet's establishment, he wrote, 'was brutally conducted, vilely kept, preposterously inspected, dishonestly defended, a disgrace to a Christian community, and a stain upon a civilized land'.

Dickens was not alone in voicing indignation. The *Lancet* published a vituperative editorial on the inquest at Tooting:

> It must inevitably ensue from this investigation, that poor law guardians will be forced by the dread of public condemnation into more careful measures for the protection of the infantile poor entrusted to their care . . .
>
> Is it not monstrous that we should maintain an immense armament on the coast of Africa, to the destruction of the lives of our sailors, and the impoverishment of the tax-paying classes at home, for the purpose of capturing crowded slave-ships, while our white slave-children at home, under our very eyes, are packed by the hundred in rooms unfitted for the healthy existence of ten!

This may be a hint that Dickens's satire on Borrioboola Gha and Mrs Jellyby in *Bleak House,* three years later, reflected a growing public opinion. But Drouet, on legal quibble, was to be acquitted of any guilt of manslaughter.

A metropolis that could tolerate, until exposed, such places for the helpless orphan children of the poor would not be expected to lend a kindly ear and support towards the establishment of a hospital for such children. It was against this indifference, against, at the best, ignorance of these enormities, that Charles West had to fight for Great Ormond Street.

Dickens had expressed himself, at this same period, on a similar theme, in a book that foreshadowed the gloom, the discontent with his present role, and the vast impatience at the cruelties and inadequacies of the human race. *The Haunted Man* seems to suggest that in order to learn the true meaning and secret of life, one had first to be prepared to discard all memory, all learning, and become as an innocent child. It was a contradiction to the Dickens who had so longed for the university, that old foundation of learning, of which, like Thomas Hardy's later Jude the Obscure, he had felt himself unjustly deprived by the economic and social forces of an uncaring world; a contradiction to the Dickens who had spoken so eloquently and forcibly on the advantages of books and education at institutes up and down the country, invoking the cheers and applause of thousands of workmen and mechanics. This secret longing to return to the innocence of childhood was, of course, a powerful force in those hidden and obscure springs which gave the true motive power to those books, which we now realize were not only an Aristotelian catharsis for their readers, but even more so for their creator. 'The achievement brought him a kind of peace for which he had long been struggling vainly ... He resolved, for the time at least, some of the conflicts that struggled within him,' wrote Johnson of Dickens's mood on finishing *Copperfield*. It is another curious aspect of the Peter Pan symbol which Barrie made an enduring part of Great Ormond Street's image.

It was for the Christmas of 1848 that Dickens produced his last Christmas book, *The Haunted Man*, an eponymous identification with himself which is not always realized. Much of what he wrote about Drouet's Tooting baby farm is already to be found there, albeit in a more dramatic fashion.

In *The Haunted Man*, Dickens pleads that the whole world is responsible for the destitute, the orphaned, the sick and the depraved; that no power, no wealth, no learning, no presumption, even of moral goodness, allows anyone to walk past on the other side. Henceforth, this became a strong element of his social message. It was also the moral basis of the plea for a hospital for the sick and sad children of the poor.

The previous December, in the closing days of 1847, Dickens and Catherine were in Edinburgh and Glasgow. Dickens spoke at the Glasgow Athenaeum, where he praised 'its influence' which he knew 'must be felt for good downwards in ... those social miseries that can be alleviated, and those wide open doors of vice and crime that can be shut and barred'. He mentioned 'the energy and courage with which those who earn their daily bread by the labour of their hands or heads, come night after night'.

On the train between Edinburgh and Glasgow, Catherine had a miscarriage. Although sufficiently recovered to return to Edinburgh on the 30th, she had a severe relapse there, and a 'famous doctor' was summoned. This doctor was probably James Simpson, who was Professor of Midwifery at Edinburgh University. Only that year he had first demonstrated the use of chloroform in an operation, and had recently used it successfully in cases of childbirth. There is no doubt that Dickens first heard about this use of chloroform from the great pioneer of anaesthetics himself. And the next year, soon after the publication of *The*

Haunted Man, a book which showed that Dickens had lost some of the optimism he had expressed at Glasgow, what he had heard in Edinburgh from Simpson was put to the test. At the birth of his son Henry Fielding on 15 January 1849, Dickens insisted on the use of chloroform. Catherine, it should be noted, had suffered the ordeal of a very difficult delivery, a nasty miscarriage, and now this birth, which was by no means normal, all within the span of twenty-one months!

Dickens's letter to Macready describing Henry Fielding's birth was written two and a half weeks afterwards:

> Kate is wonderfully well – eating mutton chops in the drawing room – and sends you her dear love. The boy is what the Persian Princes might have called a 'moon-faced' monster. He did not, however, come into the world as he ought to have done (I don't know in what we have offended Nature, but she seems to have taken something in us amiss) and we had to call in extra counsel and assistance. Foreseeing the possibility of such a repetition of last time, I had made myself thoroughly acquainted in Edinburgh with the facts of chloroform – in contradistinction to the talk about it – and had insisted on the attendance of a gentleman from Bartholomew's Hospital, who administers it in the operations there, and has given it four or five thousand times. I had also promised her that she should have it. The doctors were dead against it, but I stood my ground, and (thank God), triumphantly. It spared her all pain (she had no sensation, but of a great display of sky-rockets) and saved the child all mutilation. It enabled the doctors to do, as they afterwards very readily said, in ten minutes, what might otherwise have taken them an hour and a half; the shock to her nervous system was reduced to nothing; and she was, to all intents and purposes, *well*, next day. Administered by someone who has nothing else to do, who knows its symptoms thoroughly, who keeps his hand upon the pulse, and his eyes upon the face, and uses nothing but a handkerchief, and that lightly, I am convinced that it is as safe in its administration, as it is miraculous and merciful in its effects. This the Edinburgh Professor assured me and certainly our experience thoroughly confirms them.

It is a fascinating letter. A description of the early administration of chloroform in childbirth, and by the premier writer of the age. Had it been made public perhaps it would have had as great an influence in making the use of chloroform respectable as had Queen Victoria's decision, four years later, to use it at the birth of Prince Leopold. If the 'extra counsel and assistance' called in meant that Dr Charles Locock was again summoned (and the precedent of Sydney Smith's birth should add great weight to the conclusion that he was), the highly successful outcome of Catherine's confinement may have influenced Locock and Sir James Clark in advising or consenting to the Queen being administered chloroform in 1853.

The letter also shows that Charles Dickens was now aware of the dangers and ordeals of childbirth, demonstrating a concern for Catherine such as he had hardly expressed before. The night of Sydney's birth had indeed been a frightening experience, not easily forgotten.

But who was the 'gentleman from Bartholomew's Hospital' on whose attendance Dickens had insisted? The Pilgrim edition of his *Collected Letters* identifies this physician as Dr Protheroe Smith, describing him as Assistant Teacher of Midwifery at St Bartholomew's. In 1849, however, Protheroe Smith no longer held that post. Since 1848 Charles West had been Lecturer in Midwifery at St Bartholomew's; and from early in 1849, when the expected resignation of Dr Rigby took place, he was, to quote West's own words, again, 'Sole Teacher in that subject'. This is confirmed by the St Bartholomew's Hospital and Medical College Students' Handbooks for the Sessions 1848–49.

Dr Protheroe Smith had indeed administered anaesthetics during labour many times, and claimed to be the first person in England to have done so. A paper of his, describing the use of ether in such cases, appeared in the *Lancet* during 1847. In April of the same year he had written to James Simpson from his London address:

> Ether here is at a discount among obstetric practitioners generally. I have, however, tested it ... and am satisfied of the justice of your opinions. I have written a paper advocating its adoption ... I am desirous to ascertain the number of cases in which you have employed this agent, and the result both to mother and child.

Protheroe Smith and Dickens are perhaps rather too hasty in condemning the London doctors. Before Protheroe Smith's letter, Dr Locock had himself written to Simpson on 8 March, and his letter shows a most reasonable attitude:

> Many thanks for your pamphlet on the ether inhalation, with which I have been much interested. People here and in Paris are getting frightened about it, as the arterial blood becomes black under its influence, and a few deaths have occurred. In time it will get to its level, after going through the annual preliminaries of over-praise and under-praise, and after the ordinary mischief from the injudicious application of a valuable discovery.

Simpson himself, writing in 1879 about the first employment of anaesthetics in midwifery in Great Britain, remembered what his late friend, Sir John Forbes, had said on the subject. Forbes, like Locock, was also a friend of West and one of his strongest supporters among medical men for the idea of a children's hospital. According to Simpson, Forbes held:

> The application of anaesthetics to midwifery involved more difficult and delicate problems than its mere application to dentistry and surgery. New rules required to be elaborated for its use – the time during which it would be given ascertained, its effect upon the action of the uterus, upon the state of the child ... all required to be accurately stated ... Moral or religious questions were also involved.

These moral questions aroused much comment in medical circles. The *Lancet,* reviewing a pamphlet by the medical officer of Queen Charlotte's Lying-In Hospital, seemed to agree thoroughly with some of his, to modern readers, more bizarre comments:

> Mr Gream also enters very fully into the question respecting the production of sexual excitement during labour in which chloroform is produced [was poor Catherine's 'great display of sky-rockets' a Freudian symbolism, after all?] ... On the testimony of many most respectable witnesses, there can be no doubt, that in some cases of chloroformization and etherization, sexual feelings are excited even in chaste persons of either sex ... These facts must be met, not evaded, by the advocation of anaesthesia in natural labour.

The religious objections were based upon the verse in Genesis, 'In sorrow thou shalt bring forth children'. Protheroe Smith, although described as a 'man of marked religious views, of the Evangelical School', attempted to meet this objection by publishing a pamphlet showing how the use of anaesthetics in labour could be justified by scriptural example.

Dickens was always ready to espouse the unorthodox in medicine. The more cautious professional approach to what was, at that time, a new and untested treatment, seemed in his eyes bigoted opposition. The physicians and obstetricians of Charles West's circle – Locock, Forbes and the venerable Sir James Clark himself – were not ready to risk the patients without full knowledge of all possible after-effects or the safety of the various methods of administering chloroform. Forty years later, after an abnormally high number of deaths by heart failure under the anaesthetic, doctors again began to question certain methods of giving chloroform. When Clark and his contemporaries were convinced, they were wholeheartedly in favour. Sir James Clark wrote to Simpson on 19 April 1853:

> The chief object of my writing to you, which was to tell you that the Queen had chloroform exhibited to her during her last confinement ... It acted admirably. It was not at any time given so strongly as to render

> the Queen insensible, and an ounce of chloroform was scarcely consumed during the whole time. Her Majesty was greatly pleased with the effect, and she certainly never has had a better recovery ... I know this information will please you and I have little doubt it will lead to a more general use of chloroform in midwifery practice ... than has hitherto prevailed.

In their own respective ways, Dickens and Queen Victoria, ignorant of each other's attitude, had eased the ordeal of women in labour. As Clark well knew, the Queen's example would give chloroform the last seal of approval. West's own attitude seems to have been cautious. It is interesting that he moved among the men who were at the centre of the controversy. Even the circumstances of his appointment to St Bartholomew's were inextricably entangled with its leading figures.

Protheroe Smith wrote to Simpson about the forthcoming appointment on 9 March 1848:

> My Dear Doctor, I presume you are aware that Rigby has resigned the office of Lecturer in Midwifery. Thinking it not impossible you may entertain some idea of removing to London, I have determined to ascertain your wishes as to the acceptance of the Obstetric Chair, before I decided on becoming a candidate for the appointment.

This was followed a week later by a letter written on behalf of three of St Bartholomew's doctors (not the entire staff, as is sometimes claimed):

> A vacancy is about to take place in the Obstetrics department of our school at St Bartholomew's, and you will readily believe that my colleagues and myself, the medical officers and teachers of the Hospital, think it should be filled by one whose abilities and skill have gained for him the highest professional character. Messrs. S--, P-- and myself have had a strictly confidential conference on this subject.
>
> Wm. L--.

Simpson refused to leave Edinburgh, and West received the appointment. Protheroe Smith, after his failure to get Simpson down from Edinburgh, and after failing to secure the appointment himself, seems to have concentrated his energies on the Hospital for Women which he had been responsible for starting in Red Lion Square. Dr Rigby, his senior at Bartholomew's, joined him at Red Lion Square. There were certain definite connections between The Hospital for Women, West and Great Ormond Street: Robert Ferguson, consulting physician at Red Lion Square, and Edward Futvoye, its honorary secretary, were members of West's Provisional Committee in 1850, and Futvoye was for many years an active member of Great Ormond Street's Committee of Management. In a way Protheroe Smith formed another link between West and Dickens, but through the mothers rather than through the children. Did West know about Mrs Dickens's confinement? His teaching post and connections with doctors possibly present make it not so unlikely.

West's election to the Bartholomew's post, and the proof that it gave of the respect and confidence of his colleagues, meant more to him than the affection for a hospital usually aroused in an old student. West did have the distinction of winning the prize for medicine the very first time it was awarded at St Bartholomew's. As a lecturer he was highly popular. When given the honour of making the introductory lecture for the medical school at the beginning of the 1850 session, it was reported: 'The theatre was so crowded in all parts that many visitors were unable to gain admission, and in our seat in the gallery we were not altogether without an apprehension of sharing in such a catastrophe as happened at the late Eisteddfod.' West gave his heart to the Royal Universal Infirmary for Children, to St Bartholomew's Hospital, and then to Great Ormond Street. And each of them in turn was to break it! But that is another story.

Two weeks after the birth of Henry Fielding Dickens, Dickens's nephew Henry Augustus, Fanny Burnett's crippled boy, died in his ninth year, barely five months after his mother. Dickens wrote to the doubly bereaved father:

> A child so afflicted, even with the inestimable blessing of a mother's care to support him, must, if he lived, be inevitably doomed to a great mortal anguish, to a weary struggle with the difficulties of life, to many years of secret comparison in his own breast between himself and more healthy and fortunate children.

It was because of children so afflicted that Charles West was now beginning to be preoccupied with a scheme that filled his thoughts more and more. He was convinced that the only way to get a hospital for children opened in England was to start one himself. He has left on record, in more than one version, the circumstances that encouraged that conclusion. After describing the abortive attempt to turn the Royal Universal Infirmary into a hospital, West recalled:

> In 1847, I gave a course of lectures on Children's Diseases at the Middlesex Hospital, the publication of which in 1848, together with my transference as one of the Medical Staff to St Bartholomew's Hospital gave me a position which I had not had before. In 1849, with a view to the establishment of a Children's Hospital, I visited all the hospitals in London, to ascertain their number of beds and the accommodation afforded by them for

children: and wrote with the same object to all the Children's Hospitals on the continent.

West wrote the above a generation or so after 1849, and the sequence and the timing of events may not have been exactly as described. But the motivation and the course of action he took are essentially what happened.

A valuable confirmation of this is a long and detailed letter in German to Charles West from Vienna, signed by Dr Mauthner, and dated 20 August 1849. In 1837 Dr Mauthner had, at his own cost and risk, opened a small children's hospital in Vienna. No more sympathetic and understanding correspondent could have been found for West's plans. Dr Mauthner agrees with him on the need to establish a children's hospital in London with one hundred beds, if possible. The reality was rather to resemble Mauthner's own modest beginnings. Mauthner recalls that when he was in London in 1838, there was not even one children's hospital. He refers to the Royal Universal Infirmary for Children, which he apparently visited. Elaborate details are also given as to the number of beds and the cost of maintaining them at the Children's Hospital in Vienna for every year from 1842 to 1848.

Similar letters to West from his London colleagues survive, but they seem to be of a later date. Some of their comments can be usefully considered here, however. W.H.O.Sankey, medical director of the New Fever Hospital, where Dr Southwood Smith was a physician, wrote:

> I have long thought that there was a great need of a Hospital for Children in London. I wished to have had wards appropriated in our New Building for our share of children's diseases, but I was strenuously opposed by one of our medical staff and the matter dropped. When we remember . . . the sources of all manner of infection that are kept alive in our alleys and streets by children, it is surprising that such a Hospital as you propose has not long ago been established.
>
> But for a Children's Hospital to be of any use – it ought to be on a very large scale, to contain at least 500 children. My notion is that it should be a little out of Town. If counties can build their asylums for lunatics, they ought at least in the Metropolis to build one for children.

About the same time, in March 1850, West received a letter from Dr G.Gregor, Physician to the Smallpox and Vaccination Hospital, King's Cross.

> We have not yet moved from King's Cross to Highgate nor do I calculate that we shall move before Midsummer.
>
> In the New Hospital at Highgate arrangements are made to receive

> 100 patients, and a special range [?] of Wards have been prepared for infants and children, capable of holding (comfortably) 14 beds.

And from the Westminster Hospital one of the doctors, whose signature cannot be deciphered, wrote: 'I have read the remarkable address which you have been good enough to send me; and only hope that it may be supported as it ought to be.' As West had recalled: 'The information thus obtained I embodied in what was afterwards the first Printed Appeal, with which in manuscript I called at the end of 1849 on all the leading London Physicians.'

There is no doubt that Charles West's efforts to start a children's hospital in London were arousing interest, some sympathy and some opposition. The medical journals of the time began to make more references to the arguments for and against such a hospital. A Dr Hess of Finsbury published an article in the *Lancet* towards the end of March 1849, on 'The Necessity of Practical Instruction in the Treatment of Diseases of Children':

> Some score of years ago, the treatment of these diseases was almost entirely left to ignorance and superstition, though it may be, kind, religious and conscientious mothers and nurses; the medical practitioner being called in for assistance only when the evil had assumed a threatening character by, or in spite of, the administration of some nostrum or family medicine.

After being summoned, the physician often found himself awkwardly situated in cases of which he was totally ignorant. In England medical students were taught only by lectures how to treat children's diseases; the great want was practical instruction: 'In France, Sweden and even in Russia, a great deal has been done to this end, by the establishment of clinical hospitals, wards and lectures; and at German Universities something at least is done by the institution of policlinics.'

A footnote explaining the practice at German universities is a reminder of what Charles West may have found particularly interesting when studying at Bonn:

> The elder students attend the poor inhabitants of some districts, or of the whole town, at their residence, under the inspection of the clinical professor and his assistants. More than fifty per cent of these patients are children.

Dr Hess concluded: 'I must leave more able hands to come forward with practical propositions concerning this subject.' The next month, *The English and Foreign Medico-Chirurgical Review*, in reviewing West's *Lectures* and other publications relating to children's diseases, commented, 'The great capital of this empire stands, in comparison with the continent, nearly alone in this want of a hospital for sick children.'

West was active in arousing sympathy and support for a children's hospital rather earlier than the manuscript recollections quoted here would suggest. After writing that he called on leading London physicians at the *end* of 1849, he continued:

> When I called on Dr Bright, he said to me, 'Dr Bence Jones was saying to me something about a children's hospital, the sister of his wife, Lady Millicent Bence Jones, wishes for such employment; go and talk to him.' I saw Dr Bence Jones . . .

West's 'Letter to the Governors of The Hospital for Sick Children', printed in 1877, probably some years before his more detailed manuscript statement, had given almost exactly the same account:

> I strove in the year 1849 to enlist the approval of the leading medical men in London in the attempt to establish a Hospital for Sick Children. While thus employed, and having already received assurance of cordial co-operation from most of the heads of the profession, I was informed by Dr Bright that Dr Bence Jones had talked to him of a similar undertaking. I saw Dr Bence Jones, who told me that a lady, a relative of his, had suggested it to him.

But when West first approached Bence Jones, in a letter dated 6 July 1849, he made no mention of Dr Bright:

> In conversation yesterday with Dr Robert Lee, I mentioned to him a proposal which has long engaged my thoughts for endeavouring to establish a Hospital for Diseases of Children. He informed me that the idea was one which you had been anxious to carry out, and suggested that I call upon you and talk to you about it.
>
> Though I cannot but feel very desirous to be allowed to co-operate with you, for a purpose which I have much at heart, I am yet sensible that with my very slight acquaintance with you it may seem almost intrusive if I call upon you about the subject without knowing whether you have any plans formed which you would prefer to pursue alone.
>
> If however I do not hear to the contrary I will take the liberty of calling on you in a few days.

It would seem from this letter that Dr Robert Lee was the prime instigator in getting West to approach Bence Jones. But the confident and twice-repeated statement made much later by West that it was Dr Bright cannot be ignored. Dr Robert Lee was a colleague of Dr Henry Bence Jones at St George's Hospital. As Lecturer in Midwifery, Lee would have been on close professional terms with West, who had an analogous position at St Bartholomew's. But if Bright had also spoken to West, why did he not mention him in the letter? The prestige and influence of Bright's name would have surely been far greater than that of Robert Lee. There is something of a mystery here. An explanation can perhaps be found in a forgotten episode involving the Royal Society.

The friendship that already existed between Richard Bright and Robert Lee was certainly strengthened when Bright strongly championed Lee after the Royal Society had ignored his obvious claims, and had awarded the Royal Medal of its Physiology Committee to Thomas Beck for his work on the nerves of the uterus.

> Bright's indignant voice was added to those who pointed out that it was Robert Lee who had done the pioneering work. Having studied all Lee's published works and long been fascinated by his obstetrical observations ... Bright felt justified in interfering. So he formed a special committee of enquiry.

Bright and his special committee confronted the Council of the Royal Society on 11 February 1847. Lee's claim was justified, and Dr Roget was dismissed from his post as secretary. In fairness it should be said that some sections of the medical press at the time thought the whole affair was a storm in a teacup, but the body of informed medical opinion was on the side of Lee and Bright. Bence Jones was already a Fellow at the time and would have known of the whole affair, and as his main interest was in the chemistry of diseases and medicine, he worked in the same field as Bright. Dr Peter Mere Latham, Charles West's old teacher at St Bartholomew's, was a neighbour of Bence Jones, who claimed that Dr Latham had introduced him to his first patient and the first seven guineas he had ever earned. Dr Latham had met Dr Bright in 1813 and remained his closest friend. There were more than sufficient contacts and opportunities for Bright to have known that Bence Jones's sister-in-law was thinking about a children's hospital. Perhaps the simple explanation is that Bright told Lee about this, and Lee told West what he had heard from Bright. West certainly for some reason had Dr Bright firmly fixed in his memory over this episode, and it is a happy thought that the great doctor should have helped in this way to get The Hospital for Sick Children started!

Bence Jones confirms much of what West wrote. Within a day or two of West's letter the two doctors had met. Bence Jones's privately printed autobiography is very definite about this: 'On July 9th 1849, we settled the objects we wished to obtain, the mode of our proceedings, and by the end of the year our plans had taken definite shape.'

This marked the real beginning of The Hospital for Sick Children (although it was not to open in Great Ormond Street for another two years). The long years during which it was only a vision in the mind of Charles West, and the long years of influencing public opinion by the labours of the reformers and the pen of Charles Dickens, had at last on that July day in 1849 come to fruition.

It was the very month when Dickens was working on that number of *David Copperfield* in which Mr Micawber was first introduced, and which with its account of Murdstone and Grinby's warehouse must be among the most autobiographical of the novel. On the very day when Charles West was writing to Henry Bence Jones, Charles Dickens was writing to his brother-in-law, Henry Austin, offering support for Austin in the controversy with the chief surveyor to the Metropolitan Commission for Sewers. This was an argument that continued while a cholera epidemic was raging: an epidemic that was to kill over 6500, a number which, according to medical opinion, would have been halved by better sanitation.

But against the gloom of the time, and against the fictional resetting of his bad childhood days, Dickens had, with that artistic sense of balance and true feeling for form and symbolism which shows throughout *Copperfield* prefixed to those chapters written in July a peaceful return to the enchanted beach at Yarmouth. In this chapter David's childish but deep love for little Em'ly is mirrored against the mature, calm and happy marriage of Peggotty and Barkis. Both events are shadowed by the recent sadness of David's mother's death, but it is a chapter which once again emphasizes an idyllic view of eternal childhood:

> I lay down in the old little bed in the stern of the boat, and the wind came moaning on across the flat as it had done before. But I could not help fancying, now, that it moaned of those who were gone . . . I thought of the sea that had risen, since I last heard those sounds, and drowned my happy home. I recollect, as the wind and water began to sound fainter in my ears, putting a short clause into my prayers, petitioning that I might grow up to marry little Em'ly, and so dropping lovingly asleep . . .
>
> . . . little Em'ly and I made a cloak of an old wrapper, and sat under it for the rest of the journey. Ah, how I loved her! What happiness (I thought) if we were married, and were going away anywhere to live among the trees and in the fields, never growing older, never growing wiser, children ever, rambling hand in hand through sunshine and among flowery meadows, laying down our heads on moss at night, in a sweet sleep of purity and peace, and buried by the birds when we were dead! Some such picture, with no real world in it, bright with the light of our innocence, and vague as the stars afar off, was in my mind all the way. I am glad to think there were two such guileless hearts at Peggotty's marriage as

> little Em'ly's and mine. I am glad to think the Loves and Graces took such airy forms in its homely procession.

David Copperfield had been conceived and begun at a time when, as we have already seen, Dickens's thoughts turned towards his childhood memories – memories strengthened and saddened by contemporary events in his personal life and even by the way in which the world around him was shaping itself. But after this fourth monthly part had been issued, his continuing labours on the book brought about an entirely different mood. Forster describes the next two years 'during the progress of what is generally thought his greatest book' as being 'what I think were his happiest years'. And during almost exactly the same period, Forster's comment could be applied to Charles West. After the long frustration of having his great desire and plans for a children's hospital repeatedly rejected or ignored, and after much searching among his colleagues for practical and active assistance in forwarding this dream, as apart from mere professional sympathy and encouragement, he had found in Dr Henry Bence Jones someone who not only immediately and constructively agreed with him and at once worked out with him the first necessary steps, but was in a position to bring their plans into being. It cannot be denied that these next two years 'were his happiest years', the time that West was engaged in what was his greatest work, the creation of The Hospital for Sick Children. West never forgot that it was Bence Jones who had in effect made his dreams possible, as he recalled nearly thirty years later:

> Dr Jones had influential friends out of the profession, while I had none. The meetings of the Provisional Committee were held at his house; many persons, whom I had no means of approaching, were induced by him to join it; and but for his aid, the establishment of the Children's Hospital would have encountered far more difficulties than attended it; the attempt might even altogether have failed.

—7—

NINE GENTLEMEN AND SOME FAMOUS LADIES

Henry Bence Jones was born in 1813, the son of Lt Colonel William Jones, of the 5th Dragoon Guards, and of Mathilda, the daughter of the Rector of Beccles, Bence Sparrow (who by royal sign manual in May 1804 had taken the name and arms of Bence). Henry's mother had a first cousin, the gallant and handsome Brigadier General Robert Bernard Sparrow of Brompton Park, Huntingdon. He married Lady Olivia Acheson, the daughter of Viscount Gosford, first Earl of Gosford. General Sparrow died in 1805, the same year in which his sister Mary married his wife's brother Archibald, later the second Earl of Gosford. Mary's mother-in-law, the Countess of Gosford, was an old friend of Lady Milbanke, the mother of that Annabella Milbanke who was to marry Lord Byron.

It was from Mary's house that the nineteen-year-old Annabella was introduced into her first London season in the spring of 1811, which led to her ill-fated marriage to the famous poet at the end of 1814. Mary, Lady Gosford, became Lady Byron's closest friend, and her most intimate correspondent under the initials 'M.G.'. When Mary died in 1841, Lady Byron looked upon her four daughters as her own, as she had during Lady Gosford's lifetime.

The youngest, Annabella, was named after her. The eldest, Mary, had in 1835 married James Hewitt, later Viscount Lifford. Olivia became Lady Byron's special favourite. It was the other sister, Millicent, who married her cousin, Henry Bence Jones, making the rather complicated family relationships even more involved. There must have been a strong attachment between the two cousins, for difficulties were raised about the marriage, which were only overcome by the aid of Lady Byron, but finally Henry and Millicent were married at the end of May 1842.

After their mother's death in 1841, the three unmarried Acheson sisters came under the protective guardianship of their aunt, Lady Olivia Sparrow. To describe this as 'subject to the tyranny of their formidable aunt',* is perhaps rather unkind. She had an authoritative personality and dominated her brother, the 2nd Earl. She was well known for her strong Evangelical opinions, and was friendly with many leading Evangelical families. Sister-in-law to the famous Governor General of Bengal, Lord William Bentinck, she was greatly interested in the movement's missions in India. Both her English and Indian religious acquaintances were to appear as supporters of The Hospital for Sick Children. Gladstone, when staying at Brampton Park, gently teased her about the contrast between the austerity of her religious convictions and the richness of her surroundings. But she was in her way kind, sympathetic to distress, and hastened to relieve it. She was not backward or hesitant in coming to the aid of her friends and those under her care, and worried not at all that fashionable gossip was amused by her apparent high-handed interference. Even Queen Charlotte speculated on what part she had played in one of the most interesting marriages of her day.

As Kitty Pakenham's best friend, Lady Olivia Sparrow had not scrupled in 1801 to write to Arthur Wellesley on her behalf. She was, indeed, largely responsible for Kitty's marriage to the future Duke of Wellington, who later told Mrs Arbuthnot that Mrs Sparrow (as she was then) had 'sent for him' on his return to England in 1805. The Arbuthnot family were to be generous in donations for Great Ormond Street. The Duchess of Wellington died in 1831 at the height of the parliamentary crisis over the Reform Bill. The mob that smashed the windows of Apsley House, because they were not illuminated in celebration of King William's dissolution of Parliament, were perhaps not aware that Lady Olivia's 'darling Kitty' was lying dead within, among all her husband's rich and magnificent trophies, of which she was so proud. Even as she lay dying she told another old friend, the Irish novelist and writer of children's stories Maria Edgeworth (whose friends and family were also to be part of the story of Great Ormond Street), that they were 'All tributes to merit – there is the value, and pure! pure! – no corruption – ever *suspected* even. Even of the Duke of Marlborough that could not be said.'

The Duke, as to be expected, was bitter about the mob, who 'did not care one pin for the poor Duchess being dead in the house'. Kitty's youngest son, Lord Charles Wellesley, and his wife are conspicuous in the Great Ormond Street subscription lists, and the later Wellingtons and Wellesleys were to be firm supporters of the Hospital.

* Ethel Colburn Mayne, *Life and Letters of Lady Noel Byron,* 1929, p. 382.

An engraving of Charles Dickens by W. P. Frith, made in 1859, when Dickens was 47.

Dr Charles West, 1816–98. Founder of the Hospital for Sick Children, Great Ormond Street.

HOSPITAL FOR SICK CHILDREN

The nursing staff in 1856.

A photograph of the original house where the Hospital first opened in 1852, at what was then 49, Great Ormond Street.

The silver inkstand – presented to Dr Charles West by Lady Byron.

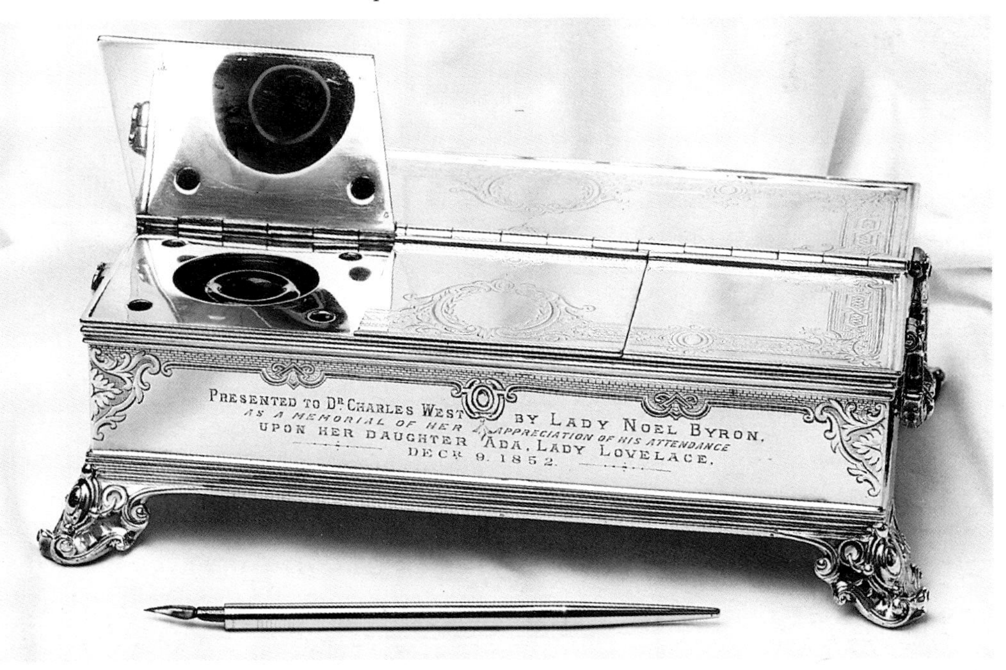

HOSPITAL FOR SICK CHILDREN.

PATRON—THE QUEEN.

Admit the Bearer ____________________

TO THE

FESTIVAL,

AT

THE FREEMASON'S TAVERN,

GREAT QUEEN STREET, LINCOLN'S INN FIELDS,

ON

TUESDAY, THE 9TH DAY OF FEBRUARY, 1858.

CHARLES DICKENS, Esq., in the Chair.

STEWARDS.

The Right Honourable the Earl of Shaftesbury.
The Right Honourable Lord Haddo, M.P.
The Right Honourable Lord John Manners, M.P.
The Right Honourable Lord Lilford.
The Right Honourable the Lord Chief Baron.
The Right Honourable Lawrence Sulivan.
The Honourable Mr. Justice Coleridge.
The Honourable Mr. Baron Watson.

The Honourable S. P. Vereker.
The Honourable Arthur Kinnaird, M.P.
Sir Stafford H. Northcote, Bart.
Col. Charles Kemeys Tynte, M.P.
W. Bovill, Esq., M.P., Q.C.
Robt. Hanbury, Jun., Esq., M.P.
A. J. Beresford Hope, Esq., M.P.
Arthur Mills, Esq., M.P.

Arbuthnot George, Esq.
Baillie, David, Esq.
Bathurst, Henry Allen, Esq.
Benham, James, Esq.
Bernays, Rev. Leopold J., M.A.
Bernays, Adolphus, Phil. D.
Bischoffsheim, H., Esq.
Bromehead, Crawford, Esq.
Coleridge, John Duke, Esq.
Corpe, George, Esq.
Cox, Leonard, Esq.
Currey, E. C., Esq.
Dickinson, F. H., Esq.
Eyre, G. Lewis Phipps, Esq.
Few, Charles, Esq.
Fox, Lieutenant-General.
Fox, William, Esq.
French, Colonel.
Frith, John Griffith, Esq.
Futvoye, Edward, Esq.
Gooden, J. Chisholme, Esq.
Göschen, Henry, Esq.
Gorton, Rev. R. G.
Groves, Major.
Harwood, H. Harwood, Esq.
Harness, Rev. William.
Hopkins, Thomas, Esq.
Kearns, William M., Esq.
Kelk, John, Esq.
Labouchere, John, Esq.
Loch, William Adam, Esq.

Lowe, Edwin, Esq.
Macready, W. C., Esq.
Maitland, J. Fuller, Esq.
Mansfield, George, Esq.
Marling, S. S., Esq.
Matheson, H. M., Esq.
Murray, John, Esq.
Nutt, D., Esq.
Owen, Rev. J. B.
Palmer, Roundell, Esq.
Parkin, G. Lewis, Esq.
Pashley, Robert, Esq., Q.C.
Pye, Kellow J., Esq.
Reid, Rawson, Esq.
Rimington, Alexander, Esq.
Robbins, George, Esq.
Rothery, Henry Cadogan, Esq.
Shadwell, Alfred, Esq.
Seymour, G. Edward, Esq.
Smith, Edmund James, Esq.
Sturgis, Russell, Esq.
Swinny, Rev. Hutchinson.
Teesdale, T. M., Esq.
Tennant, Rev. W.
Thomas, Rev. J.
Turner, John, Esq.
Uzielli, M., Esq.
Vincent, Rev. F.
Walker, Lieut-Col. Beauchamp.
Walker, James S., Esq.
Wallace, Lewis, Esq.
Westmacott, A. F., Esq.
Whitbread, Gordon, Esq.
Wilder, Edmond, Esq.
Wilde, Charles Norris, Esq.

The President of the Royal College of Physicians.
The President of the Royal College of Surgeons.
Ackland, H. W., M.D., F.R.S.
Arnott, J. Moncrieff, Esq., F.R.S.
Aldred, Henry Allen, M.D.
Alford, Stephen S., Esq.
Babington, Chas. Metcalfe, M.D.
Baly, William, M.D., F.R.S.
Brett, R., Esq.
Brodhurst, Bernard, Esq.
Browne, T., Esq.
Buchanan, George, M.D.
Burrows, George, M.D., F.R.S.
Burton, J. S., Esq.
Busk, George, Esq., F.R.S.
Carr, W., Esq.
Cartwright, Samuel, Jun., Esq.
Chenery, T., Esq.
Cholmeley, William, M.D.
Clark, Sir James, Bart., M.D., F.R.S.
Clayton, Oscar, Esq.
Collum, Robert, M.D.
Conolly, J., M.D., D.C.L.
De Mussy, A. Gueneau, M.D.
Dixon, James, Esq.
Dyer, H. S., M.D.
Evans, Thomas, M.D.
Evans, Herbert, Esq.
Falls, W. Stewart, Esq.
Ferguson, Robert M.D.
Forbes, Sir John, M.D., D.C.L., F.R.S.
Halley, Alexander, M.D.
Hawkins, Bissett, M.D., F.R.S.
Hawkins, Charles, Esq.

Henry, Mitchell, Esq.
Hetley, Frederick, Esq.
Hewlett, T., Esq.
Hillier, Thomas, M.D.
Hood, Peter, Esq.
Holmes, Timothy, K., Esq.
James, Thomas, Esq.
Jenner, William, M.D.
Johnson, Athol, Esq.
Jones, H. Bence, M.D., F.R.S.
Latham, Peter M., M.D.
Little, William J., M.D.
Lochée, Alfred, M.D.
Locock, Sir Charles, Bart., M.D.
Monro, H., M.D.
Newton, Edward, Esq.
Ormerod, Edward, M.D.
Paget, George, M.D.
Paget, James, Esq., F.R.S.
Partridge, Richard, Esq., F.R.S.
Pearse, Edmund, Esq.
Pope, J. H., Esq.
Quain, Richard, M.D.
Rigby, Edward, M.D.
Roberts, J. H., Esq.
Rolleston, George, M.D.
Shaw, Alexander, Esq.
Sharp, A. B., Esq.
Smith, Thomas, Esq.
Symonds, J. A., M.D., F.R.S.
Symonds, F., Esq.
Thompson, Seth, M.D.
Tuke, Harrington, M.D.
Watson, Thomas, M.D.
West, Charles, M.D.
Westall, Edward, Esq.
Williams, C. J. B., M.D., F.R.S.

No. ____________

Secretary.

Admission at Six o'Clock: the Chair to be taken at Half-past Six precisely.

The Hospital for Sick Children, April 1852 – the earliest known view of the wards – two months after the Hospital first opened. It closely compares with 'Drooping Buds'.

The girls' ward of the Hospital for Sick Children, April 1858. The two doctors on the left are William Jenner and Charles West, the latter is examining a little girl's leg.

Left: A list of Stewards and an admission ticket for the Dinner in aid of the Hospital, held on 9 February 1858.

Right: The girls' ward, summer 1858.

Bottom right: Her Royal Highness The Princess of Wales, as a 'Sister of Charity', visits the Hospital for Sick Children in October 1868.

Charles Dickens, reading at St Martin's Hall in 1858.

The leaflet announcing Dickens's reading of *A Christmas Carol* for the benefit of the Hospital for Sick Children in 1858.

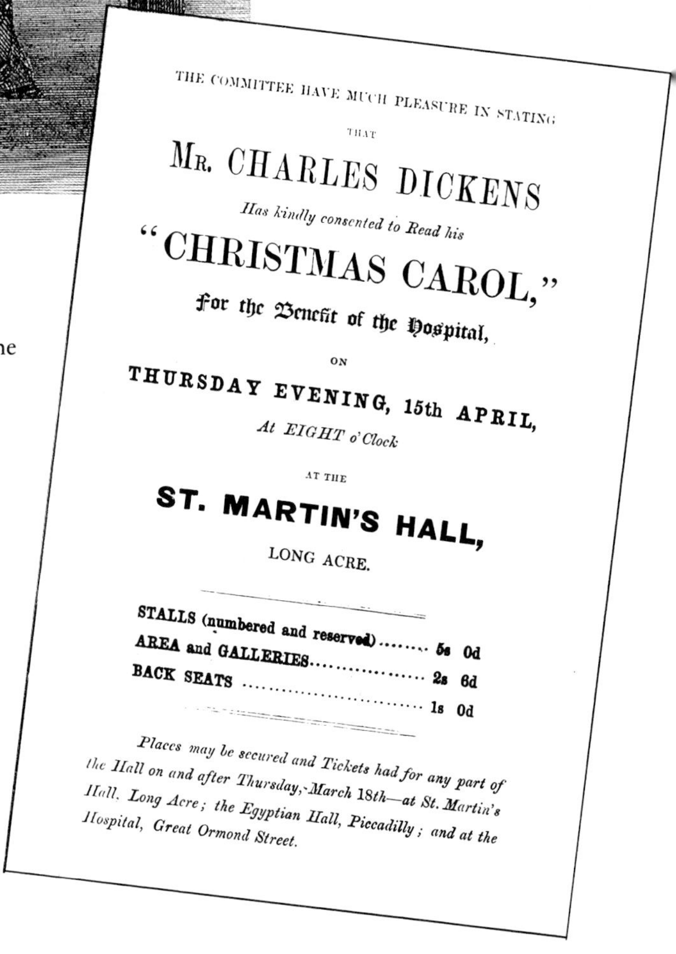

THE COMMITTEE HAVE MUCH PLEASURE IN STATING

THAT

MR. CHARLES DICKENS

Has kindly consented to Read his

"CHRISTMAS CAROL,"

For the Benefit of the Hospital,

ON

THURSDAY EVENING, 15th APRIL,

At EIGHT o'Clock

AT THE

ST. MARTIN'S HALL,

LONG ACRE.

STALLS (numbered and reserved)	**5s 0d**
AREA and GALLERIES	**2s 6d**
BACK SEATS	**1s 0d**

Places may be secured and Tickets had for any part of the Hall on and after Thursday, March 18th—at St. Martin's Hall, Long Acre; the Egyptian Hall, Piccadilly; and at the Hospital, Great Ormond Street.

SWAIN

The new hospital building was opened in 1875.

Had Lady Olivia Sparrow been so stern and formidable, would the newly married Millicent and Henry have stayed as they did for several months with her at Brampton Park? At the time of the marriage, Henry had been studying at St George's Hospital for some years. While at Brampton he went back to his old university, Cambridge, to take his MA. Lady Olivia Sparrow was very kind to Great Ormond Street; her donation of £50 was one of the very first contributions to its funds. And after Dickens's plea in 1858 she gave another twenty guineas. At present-day values these would represent a very handsome sum. Her personal example influenced many of her friends among the great in society and government to follow suit.

Apart from these family connections, Henry Bence Jones was able to call upon the support of many men of scientific and intellectual renown. When Charles West approached him, he was physician at St George's Hospital, and like West, had been a lecturer at the Middlesex Hospital, but on animal chemistry, not midwifery. Among his private patients were many famous names, including Sidney Herbert, whose fag he had been at Harrow. Sidney Herbert and Bence Jones were to be closely connected with Florence Nightingale and gave great support to her pioneering nursing work at Scutari in the Crimea. Thackeray and Charles Darwin consulted Bence Jones, and both left on record laments at their inability to follow the strict diet he set them. Lord Malmesbury was his patient. Disraeli used the remedies which Bence Jones had originally prescribed for Lady John Manners. Edward Fitzgerald, whose *Rubaiyat of Omar Khayyam* would have appealed greatly to Bence Jones, sought him out when ill, and recorded how Bence Jones remembered that Thackeray delighted a little too much in the company of the socially great. As secretary to the Royal Institution, Bence Jones himself corresponded with nearly all the famous names in science, literature, history, politics and society.

It was, as both Bence Jones and Charles West record, a sister of Lady Millicent Bence Jones who had expressed a desire to found some form of a hospital for children. The story behind this involved another prominent figure of the time, John Henry Newman. Lady Olivia Acheson, who was Lady Byron's favourite of the four younger Acheson sisters, had, despite her father's and her aunt's fervent Evangelicalism, or perhaps in reaction to it, become sympathetic towards Newman's religious views. Her youngest sister, Lady Annabella, was also influenced the same way, and both, despite what is sometimes said, were converted to the Roman Catholic Church in 1845, the very same year as Newman himself. It can be imagined that in the contemporary climate of opinion such a religious conversion caused great distress to their relatives and friends, especially Lady Byron and Lady Olivia Sparrow, who probably reacted rather fiercely. But again in the light of the founding of Great Ormond Street, it cannot be believed that relations between the sisters and their aunt and Lady Byron were as strained as most biographers assume.

When Archibald, 2nd Earl of Gosford, died on 27 March 1849, he left his unmarried daughters, Lady Olivia and Lady Annabella, £15,000 each, which they determined to devote to charitable purposes. Lady Annabella, however, died soon afterwards, on 26 July 1849, leaving her inheritance to her sister, Lady Olivia, to be used in promoting their joint philanthropic intentions.

It will be remembered that Charles West had first written to Bence Jones on 6 July, barely three weeks before Lady Annabella died. These dates are surely of great significance. What the sisters' charitable proposals were is hinted at in a letter written by Newman to Lady Olivia Acheson, on 5 February 1850. Lady Olivia was having moral doubts and scruples about her obligations over the inheritance from her sister, and had consulted Newman. He replied:

> It seems that your sister, when asked about any wishes she had about her property left all entirely in your hands – and whenever you spoke of the poor, did not indeed oppose such a direction of it (for your and her favourite project was a *hospital or refuge for destitute children in Ireland* [my italics], and Ireland, being so neglected was always your and her topic, more than the Irish in England) but only acquiesced on the condition that you should keep enough for yourself. Her fortune was not left by her express wish to the poor. She always seemed pained if you talked of alienating it from yourself.

Gosford Castle, the family seat, was in Armagh, Ireland. Newman went on to discuss the difference between offering all the property or only the income from it during her lifetime. When Dr Robert Whitty, the sisters' spiritual director, was at the Birmingham Oratory, Lady Olivia had talked about helping his charities and plans. Newman continued: 'Dr W. led us into the distinct idea that you were purporting to aid us in one of two or three purposes, not however disguising *that in the first instance you wished to found a hospital* [my italics].'

It would seem, no matter what Lady Olivia eventually decided and whatever was the fate of her and her sister's inheritance it would seem that the money was given to aid a Birmingham Oratory project, when Charles West first saw Henry Bence Jones, early in July 1849, the two sisters were intent on founding some sort of children's hospital, but whether in Ireland or London is not quite clear.

In connection with this question of a proposed children's hospital in Ireland, it is curious that in January 1848 a Belfast physician, Andrew Malcolm, wrote to West seeking information about hospitals for children. Had the two Acheson sisters, who knew even before their father died of their future inheritance, and had already decided on using it for charity, been making enquiries among the Belfast doctors when residing in Gosford Castle? It would seem that after their father's death, Olivia and Annabella for some reason had to leave Armagh and live in London. It is an intriguing thought that perhaps these changed circumstances made them consider starting a children's hospital in London. Throughout Great Ormond Street's history there always seems to be a fortunate congruence between need and event.

But the personal stories of Lady Olivia Acheson and Lady Annabella Acheson were sad ones. After her sister's death in July 1849 – her eldest married sister, Mary, also died in March of the following year – Olivia decided to become a postulant at Birmingham under Newman's direction.

Her family and friends were alarmed and greatly concerned that, with her consumptive tendencies, the stringencies of convent life would be harmful, if not fatal. Even apart from the divergent viewpoints on creed and Church, Lady Byron and the Acheson family held that on grounds of health alone Lady Olivia Acheson had taken a very foolish step. It is known that Henry Bence Jones himself together with Dr Thomas Watson (whose connection with Great Ormond Street and Charles Dickens should not be forgotten) examined Lady Olivia and were not at all satisfied with her condition, as a letter from Newman to Bence Jones reveals:

> I thank you for your kindness in telling me your and Dr Watson's judgement about Lady Olivia. It concerns me to find you still think seriously about her case ... I am obliged to speak as her spiritual adviser, just as you speak as her medical ... I have a deep conviction ... that, till she is here, she will not be happy; I do not believe that she will have a day of peace until she returns.

For Newman, with his vision so firmly fixed on the spirit and God, the weaknesses of the body were not important – illness and death were but vain things. His reading of Lady Olivia's character and attitude was not greatly mistaken. Lady Byron saw her favourite (who called her *Mütterchen*) for the last time in June 1851. She described this visit in a letter to a close friend, Caroline Bathurst, the daughter of Lady Caroline Bathurst. The Bathursts were already supporting Great Ormond Street. Henry Bathurst, indeed, was persuaded by Bence Jones (they were friends from Cambridge days) to be one of the first to join him and West in proposing a Children's Hospital. Bathurst became honorary secretary first to the Provisional Committee and then to The Hospital for Sick Children itself for ten years. He sat on the Committee of Management for many years afterwards and was one of its longest serving members. He was the last surviving trustee of Lady Byron's papers. Her letter to Caroline Bathurst revealed Lady Byron's true feelings towards Lady Olivia Acheson's religious conversion and Newman:

> Olivia said to me: 'I could not help thinking this morning how happy it would make me to see you a Catholic before I die!' You will conceive that this was to be met by sympathy, not opposition, and with tenderness and gratitude ... I was introduced to Newman. My mind was made up at once about his character. He is no Hypocrite – but a man in whom the elements are discordantly combined, and chiefly from great deficiencies ... I did not feel power in him – and he was evidently not at ease with me. Dialogue:
> N. You think Lady Olivia better, I hope.
> I. I do not – I suppose I must answer sincerely.
> N. But since – I assure you she is much better.
> I. Of that I can be no judge. I wish I could think her better.
> I was in my own mind displeased with him for having encouraged her to violate Dr [Bence] Jones's injunctions about going out, so we had a secret Antagonism, and he felt it.

When Olivia died at Birmingham on 28 March 1852, Great Ormond Street had only been opened a few weeks. Charles Dickens on that day had probably just finished correcting the final proofs of his article 'Drooping Buds' for *Household Words,* an article in which the British public were first told about the new children's hospital. It was the precursor to all those descriptions of Great Ormond Street which were to appear over the next few years, and which indeed have continued to appear during the last 137 years. The fact that it was Dickens who thus led the way surely has more than a mere symbolic significance. 'Drooping Buds' concluded:

> Is it too much to believe that the little beds in the great house will never be suffered to remain empty, while there are little shapes of pain and unrest to lie down in them; or that the wilderness in the garden will bloom with recovered infant health? Who that knows how part of home the children are – who that knows how ill our hearts can spare one child to Death, far less the dreadful and reproachful thought of one in three – can doubt the end of this so sorely needed enterprise! Its way to the general sympathy and aid, lies through one of the broadest doors into the human heart; and that heart is a great and tender one, and will receive it.

Lady Olivia Acheson's heart had been a great and tender one, and had she known that her and her sister's dream of a children's hospital had actually come into being, she would have rejoiced. Always at the back of her mind, despite Newman's counsel, was the thought that perhaps she had not been right to have taken a different path of charity. I believe that she did know: her sister, Lady Millicent, must surely have told her of what her husband and Charles West were doing. And, even more likely, Henry Bence Jones had told her himself. So perhaps her last days were illuminated not only by the spiritual consolations of her religion, but by the glowing thought of the poor sick children who were to receive such loving care at Great Ormond Street.

Dickens did not know of Lady Olivia Acheson, nor the part she played in making Great Ormond Street possible. Nor perhaps has the world known until now. If that heaven in which she firmly believed exists, and if she and her sister still have need of orisons for their souls, surely a goodly part of the prayers and grateful thanks, uttered or written so fervently by parents every day in the wards and chapel at Great Ormond Street, are the share of Lady Olivia and Lady Annabella. Without the two sisters' good and unselfish intentions, Charles West would have never been advised to approach Henry Bence Jones, and Bence Jones would not have listened to him.

Lady Byron was very bitter with Newman and the Catholic Church over Olivia's death. A few days after, she wrote angrily and fiercely to Lady Millicent Bence Jones (who had now lost all her sisters) in terms which may appal with their intolerance, but which in a way are very understandable, and may explain much of what has puzzled some biographers when her own daughter, Ada, died after long agony some eight months later. Lady Byron wrote of Olivia's death to Millicent:

> It has emancipated her from that tyrannical Church under which she suffered such thraldom ... They may say what they will of her happiness – we know better. I saw even as regarded myself that every affectionate feeling caused a painful conflict, and I thought it better not to awaken it latterly. Do not be shocked, if I rejoice that she is out of their power – that no Masses can any longer reach her – that she is *ours* more than before ...
>
> Mother never loved Daughter better than I did her ...
>
> There is one fact only on which you can dwell with unmixed gratification – your husband's generous devotedness – the more generous because, as I can testify, it was throughout unaccompanied by any illusion. He well knew she was absolutely in the hands of the Priests.

The bitterness in this letter did not last. The family and friends of Lady Byron had been and were to be involved with Charles West and Great Ormond Street, even apart from the story of Lady Olivia Acheson. In all the millions of words that have been written about Lady Byron and her marriage and the long years of her widowhood – for she was after all the poet's widow, short and bitter as their time together actually was before separating – the biographers have, on the whole, treated her harshly; in all those thousands of pages and years of research, her role in the founding of Great Ormond Street has never been revealed. The further development of this episode in Lady Byron's life may perhaps help us to re-evaluate her character. If she and Lady Olivia Sparrow were so religiously intolerant towards Lady Olivia Acheson and Lady Annabella's conversion to Catholicism, why were Lady Byron, Lady Sparrow, Lady Millicent and her husband so strongly supportive of the scheme to found a children's hospital? It was almost as if they wished the hospital to become a memorial to the two sisters. A bare three weeks after Charles West had first written to Henry Bence Jones, Annabella died. To judge from Newman's letter, it was Annabella who had seemed the most eager to start a hospital for children. It can safely be said that without Lady Byron's influence and strong support Henry Bence Jones would never have married Lady Millicent Acheson; and, in the words of Charles West, the attempt to establish a children's hospital 'might altogether have failed'.

The nine gentlemen who first formed a Provisional Committee for the establishment of a children's hospital, at Bence Jones's house in Grosvenor Street on 30 January 1850, were in the main friends of Bence Jones. That Edward Futvoye, a solicitor of 23 John Street, Bedford Row, was one of the earliest members is confirmed by a report in the *Surrey Advertiser* many years later, when a meeting was held in aid of the Hospital for Sick Children in the grounds of his Guildford home, Woodbridge House. Futvoye 'informed the gathering that while Dr Bence Jones and Dr West started the idea of the hospital, he was himself one of the first four who assisted at the founding of the institution'. Futvoye was speaking on the Thursday only two days after Charles Dickens had been buried in Westminster Abbey on 14 June 1870, and in paying tribute to Dickens's services to the Hospital described how he had stood beside the 'newly-opened grave . . . on Tuesday last'.

Thus we know that at least one of Great Ormond Street's original founders joined the ever-increasing stream of people who passed through the Abbey to mourn the great novelist and fill the open grave with flowers. And even after the grave was closed, as Dean Stanley wrote, 'There was a constant pressure on the spot, and many flowers were strewn upon it by unknown hands, many tears shed from unknown eyes.'

In 1850 and before, Futvoye was honorary secretary to the Hospital for Women, Red Lion Square, where Protheroe Smith and Edward Rigby from St Bartholomew's Hospital were physicians. If Futvoye had not known Dickens as a near neighbour from the Doughty Street days, the Hospital for Women was another likely means of introduction. The consulting physician was Robert Ferguson, from whom Bence Jones obtained a 'very influential' letter of support for the projected children's hospital, which was printed in the first prospectus. This may explain how Edward Futvoye became involved at a very early stage and remained an active and hardworking member of the Great Ormond Street Committee of Management until 1890.

It is not recorded who had the distinction of being the other member of 'the first four', but Bence Jones wrote, 'My old friend, Joseph Hoare, was the first treasurer, and another friend, Mr Henry Bathurst, became the Secretary.' It is a reasonable surmise that either or both joined the scheme as early as Futvoye. There is some evidence that Bathurst was the first. Joseph Hoare of Hampstead and Lombard Street was a member of the celebrated evangelical banking family. Barnetts, Hoare & Co. of 62 Lombard Street were originally with Herries, Farquhar & Co. of St James's Street, named as 'bankers of the charity'. Hoare, like Bathurst, had been a friend of Bence Jones since their Cambridge days. But his connection with the Provisional Committee was to be short-lived. When the very first public 'Appeal on Behalf of a Hospital for Sick Children' was printed in *The Times* of 16 February 1850, a little more than two weeks after the first meeting, it was read out a few days later by the secretary of The Royal Universal Infirmary for Children to his committee meeting at Waterloo Road. They were greatly alarmed and began a hospital appeal fund of their own, having ignored Charles West's pleas all these years. Bence Jones had his own recollections of what followed, and although he did not give the full story, he does explain why Joseph Hoare left:

> Arthur Barclay, who was treasurer of the Infirmary in Waterloo Road, objected to the new hospital, and as I had known him for years, Dr West and I had an interview with him at the Brewery. We were unable to persuade him to close his infirmary, and he was unable to make us give up our scheme. Joseph Hoare, who was his brother-in-law, was led to resign our treasureship, and Mr Labouchere accepted the office.

John Labouchere, well known as a philanthropist of the Evangelical school, was a partner in the banking house of Williams, Deacon & Co., of 20 Birchen Lane. One of the first invited to join the original nine members of the Provisional Committee, he accepted office as treasurer on 12 March 1850, and thus began a connection between Great Ormond Street and Williams, Deacon & Co. which remained unbroken through various mergers and changes of title until the present day. Before the advent of the National Health Service, a partner of the firm was always the honorary treasurer of the Hospital. With Labouchere as treasurer, Williams, Deacon & Co. took the place of Barnetts, Hoare & Co. as one of the two bankers of the charity. In less than a year however, a separate and senior branch of the Hoare family were to give Great Ormond Street their support, and Messrs Hoare of Fleet Street (the house said to be the model for Tellson's Bank by Temple Bar in *A Tale of Two Cities*) became the third bank to the Hospital.

Henry Bathurst's connection with Great Ormond Street was, in contrast to Joseph Hoare's, long and fruitful. Perhaps the most graphic illustration of this is to be found in the Hospital's annual report for 1884:

> The resignation of Mr H.A.Bathurst, owing to the increasing pressure of official business, has to their great regret deprived the Committee of another member who has been associated with the institution from its earliest years. Mr Bathurst was one of the original founders of the Hospital in 1850, and, for the first ten years, acted as Honorary Secretary, thus rendering special services in the original establishment and organization of the Charity.

The reference to increasing pressure of business is curious, as Bathurst was then in his sixty-fifth year. It is true that he became full registrar of the Admiralty Court when he was sixty, but it was a post he was to hold until 1890. A severe illness in the early part of 1883 made him retire from the board of The Hospital for Sick Children. Ralph Milbanke, Earl of Lovelace, wrote in his *Astarte:* 'Unfortunately the last of the trustees, Mr Henry Allen Bathurst, died a few years ago. His fidelity and affection for Lady Byron never waned, but difficulties stood in the way till the very last years of his life, when his health and energy were running out.' *Astarte,* the story of Byron and his half-sister Augusta, was first issued privately in 1905.

Henry Allen Bathurst was born in 1819, the fourth son of Lt General Sir James Bathurst, KCB. Henry was thus the grandson of Dr Bathurst, Bishop of Norwich, after whom he was named and whose favourite he was, and consequently a great-nephew of Lord Bathurst. His mother was Lady Caroline Stuart, daughter of Lord Castlestuart.

When Bishop Bathurst died in 1837, Lord Holland made the comment that he left very little in the way of fortune, a great reputation for benevolence and goodness, and three or four mad or eccentric sons. There was ample justification for Lord Holland's witticism.

Henry Allen's father, James Bathurst, was appointed assistant adjutant general to Wellington's Peninsular campaign. It is said that this was a return favour to the Richmonds, whose protégé James Bathurst was, for their services to Wellington's wife, Kitty. Lord Bathurst, the Secretary for War, had married the Duke of Richmond's sister. The links that held together the first supporters of Great Ormond Street were indeed forged in the early years of the century. James Bathurst had entered the army in 1794. He served under Sir Ralph Abercromby in his Egyptian campaign, was present at the sieges of Straslund and Copenhagen, and subsequently at the battles of Corunna, Talavera and Busaco. He served with the Russian army in 1807, the year of the battle of Friedland. But this fine record of military service has been forgotten – the solitary footnote in history by which he is remembered is the indisputable fact that in 1809 James Bathurst went mad, and had to be replaced by Ned Pakenham as military secretary.

Bishop Bathurst always insisted that this temporary mental breakdown was caused by worry over the uncertain fate of James's younger brother Benjamin. The good Bishop of Norwich certainly had very little joy in his sons. Benjamin Bathurst is the subject of one of the most famous unexplained disappearances in history. Travelling as envoy from the British government to Francis I, Emperor of Austria, he was about to enter his carriage outside the Swan Inn at Perleberg, a town between Berlin and Hamburg, when he vanished and was never seen or heard of again. One explanation is that he was murdered by Napoleon's agents for the sake of the confidential diplomatic papers he was thought to be carrying, but the exact circumstances of his disappearance do not allow such a solution. There was also an enigmatic report of Benjamin being seen on a boat crossing to Norway, but this came to nothing. Later, James Bathurst himself went to Perleberg, but failed to find any explanation. Several writers have offered various answers to the mystery, including a science-fiction story giving the inevitable extra-terrestrial explanation, but Benjamin Bathurst remains one of the most authenticated and puzzling cases of its kind in history.

Nor were his children spared what would seem to be the grim jest played by fate on the family. Benjamin's daughter Rosa, some years later, was riding with her uncle Lord Aylmer along the banks of the Tiber, when her horse apparently slipped into the river. She was drowned before the horrified eyes of her relative and friends, crying 'Uncle, save me!' Her body vanished. Not until six months later, when one of those friends, Charles Mills, had returned to Rome and was walking by the Tiber and thinking of her, did the river give up her body, almost in the same place, as he was passing. Rosa's brother was also killed in Rome, falling from his horse when taking part in a mad, reckless race. Charles Mills became a generous donor to Great Ormond Street. The story of Rosa Bathurst was often remembered. The great Victorian gossip, Augustus Hare, records in the sixth volume of his autobiography being told of her sad fate by Lady Sawle in 1888. Strangely enough, a little while before he had met Miss Laura Troubridge with an Adrian Hope whom she was soon to marry.

In 1888 Adrian Hope became secretary to The Hospital for Sick Children, thus continuing Henry Bathurst's work. Laura Troubridge was the granddaughter of David Gurney, Elizabeth Fry's brother. The Gurneys had been close friends of Bishop Bathurst, and the younger members early supporters of Great Ormond Street. Henry Bathurst lived long enough to see that Adrian and Laura Hope, their families and friends, gave their services and support to the Hospital in the same generous tradition he had begun all those years ago. And in view of Augustus Hare's reminiscences for 1888, it is a happy coincidence to find in the Hospital's subscription list for that year several collections entered under, 'Hare with a Few Friends'.

Henry Allen Bathurst, despite his influential friends and relatives, remains a rather shadowy and elusive figure. He was always very modest about the work he did for Great Ormond Street, but there is no doubt that much of the Hospital's success and its very survival was due to his unselfish and tireless activity. Alexander J.B. Beresford Hope, an early member of the Provisional Committee, who with his family was exceedingly generous in the Hospital's early and vital days, remarked in his speech at a Hospital dinner in February 1866: 'With regard to Mr Bathurst, we all know what he has done – that he has been the life and soul of the hospital from the first, and without him we know not what would become of it.'

Such a compliment from the eccentric Right Hon. A.J.B. Beresford Hope, MP who was at once one of Disraeli's oldest friends and a thorn in his side, is not lightly to be disregarded. Beresford Hope was very High Church in his views and thus a necessary leaven for the Evangelical opinions held by so many of Great Ormond Street's first patrons. He married Lady Mildred Cecil, the Marquess of Salisbury's eldest daughter, an important source of influence and patronage for the Hospital. Once when Lady Mildred fell into a deep fountain when showing a little boy how to fly a kite, her husband stared at her through his eye-glass, walked into the house, rang the bell for the footman and ordered him, 'Go and pick her ladyship out of the fountain!' Beresford Hope said of Dickens, 'With all his power of plausible writing he is a monstrous dangerous fellow'; and described Tennyson as 'A perpetual mystery and blister to the Vicar of Freshwater as he never goes to Church'.

Most of the references to Henry Allen Bathurst are found in connection with Lady Byron, whose name appears as one of the first donors to Great Ormond Street well before March 1850. Her daughter Ada appears in the first full subscription list of 1852, under the sad entry, 'The late Countess of Lovelace, £100'. It was a most generous and substantial donation, one of the highest. The story behind it is perhaps one of the most mournful if fascinating sequels to the Byron legend, in which his daughter's death seems almost as wasteful of genius and a unique talent, and certainly much more cruel, as Byron's at Missolonghi. It is part of the story of Charles West and Great Ormond Street, gathering Dickens within its orbit, and preserving to the present day a relic which is displayed upon the proudest of The Hospital for Sick Children's royal occasions.

Ada, Countess of Lovelace, died on 27 November 1852, after enduring months of agony from a form of cervical cancer. Doris Langley Moore, in her biography of Ada, gives a moving account of her last months; but she does not identify the Dr West who was called in by Dr Locock on 28 July, after Locock became alarmed over a hard swelling in the uterus. This was Charles West of Great Ormond Street, as we now know. After examining Ada, West, with Locock, told her husband, Lord Lovelace, that 'it must end fatally sooner or later'. Locock told Lady Byron that Ada might live for 'a couple of months'. West thought the symptoms had been present for possibly two years, and that Dr Lee had correctly diagnosed cancer over a year ago. Once again here is evidence of professional links between West, Locock and Lee. On 13 August, West reluctantly disclosed to Ada that 'there was no longer room for doubt as to the nature of her disease, nor grounds for expecting that indefinite prolongation of her life on which she seemed to have counted.' Three days later West described how she woke 'in a state of most maddenihg suffering; shrieked, talked deliriously, threw herself about, seemed almost out of her mind with it'. West was able to alleviate the pain temporarily with chloroform and opium. A few days after this, at Ada's most earnest wish, Charles Dickens came to see her. They had been friends for over nine years. He described this harrowing visit in a letter to Miss Burdett Coutts:

> I had a note from Lord Lovelace to tell me that Lady Lovelace was dying, and that the death of the child in Dombey had been so much in her thoughts and had soothed her so, that she wished to see me once more if I could be found. I went and sat with her alone for some time. It was very solemn and sad, but her fortitude was quite surprising; and her Conviction that all the agony she has suffered (which has been very great) had some design in the goodness of God, impressed me very much.

But the calmness and courage which impressed Dickens vanished the next night, when West recorded how she rolled in agony over the mattresses which covered the floor – she could not bear to lie in a normal bed. No wonder he wrote, 'The duty of the physician though necessary is a very grievous one; as the highest success he can hope to attain is to secure not recovery but euthanasia.'

The long ordeal was to last three months more. Doris Langley Moore condemns Lady Byron for attempting to discuss repentance and salvation with her daughter, writing, 'Of what use could it be to extract religious professions from a woman in so dreadful a plight?' But Ada had introduced such questions herself to Dickens.

> 'Do you ever pray?' Ada, Lady Lovelace asked him on her death-bed. 'Every morning and evening,' he answered.

Dickens's account of his sister Fanny's death-bed should not be forgotten. Dr West was the last person to praise mistaken attempts at dying repentance, but he had nothing but admiration for Lady Byron's words during Ada's last hours. And against the impression given that Lady Byron was too forward in reorganizing the Lovelace household, dismissing some of the servants and criticizing the nurses, is a little anecdote which Charles West related over forty years later, and which without doubt is a reference to Lady Byron and Countess Lovelace.

> I remember once assisting a peeress, whose daughter, of still higher rank than she was, was dangerously ill, to wash the medicine and wine glasses on the sickroom table, because the nurse considered it an office beneath her.

Certainly it would seem as if Lady Byron has been much maligned. Bence Jones, West and Bathurst are witnesses for her defence, and an independent voice can be added. When she died in 1860, the sculptor Thomas Woolner was asked to make a cast of her hands. He wrote to Tennyson's wife remarking that Lady Byron 'seems to have been almost adored by those about her'. Over twelve years before, Dickens had obtained Lady Byron's support for La Scuola Italiana, the school Mazzini had helped to establish at Clerkenwell for the children of poor Italian immigrants and which he had taken Dickens to see. But long before Dickens had involved himself in the Ragged Schools, Lady Byron was interested in the industrial and agricultural schools, opening one for the vagrant class at Ealing Grove in 1834. A history of the industrial school movement and of Emmanuel de Fellenberg's pioneering work in Switzerland was being written by Lady Byron when West and Bence Jones first met. The penultimate sentence read:

> The chief question that remained to be determined was how the leading classes of society, those who employ labour, could be trained to recognize the duty incumbent on them to educate the working classes and elevate

them morally in the same degree as they avail themselves of their labour to increase their own property.

Mrs Barwell, an old friend and the wife of the surgeon who had been in attendance with Dr West on Ada, wrote to Bence Jones the morning that Lady Byron died, to ensure he was among the first to be informed. Dr West never forgot Lady Byron or Ada. Among The Hospital for Sick Children's most treasured possessions is an elaborate Victorian silver inkstand, which the West family most generously presented a number of years ago. It is only taken out of the hospital safe when royalty or very distinguished visitors are expected. When the Queen or the Prince and Princess of Wales are signing the visitors' book they may notice the inscription:

Presented to Dr Charles West by Lady Noel Byron
As a memorial of her Appreciation
of his Attendance
Upon her Daughter, Ada, Lady Lovelace.
Decr. 9 1852

Only a few days before the date on that inscription, Ada had been placed, as she wished, in the Byron family vault, next to her father's coffin, the father who had left her and England when she was a helpless infant and never returned to wife, child or native land. So ended the tragic story of a poet's daughter. Ada is now remembered for her pioneer work with Charles Babbage on computers. The computer language ADA is named in her honour. That she and her mother belong to the story of Great Ormond Street is now acknowledged.

Lady Byron and Ada knew Florence Nightingale well. Florence counted Lady Byron among those who encouraged her work by previous example. When at Kaiserswerth, Florence Nightingale wrote home and named Lady Byron, Caroline Bathurst and Sydney Herbert among the people who would approve of what she was doing. Apparently Mrs Nightingale feared 'what people will say'. Mrs Nightingale, it must be remembered, when Florence wanted to take up a post as superintendent of nursing at King's College Hospital in 1854, suggested that if she wanted to do that kind of work, Great Ormond Street with its children would be much more suitable. Florence was not a great believer in children's hospitals, and in the immediate future the Crimea was to be her destiny. Dr Bence Jones had worked closely with Florence Nightingale at her Harley Street Institute for the Care of Sick Gentlewomen, and with Sydney Herbert, then Minister for War, gave her much advice and encouragement for her mission to Scutari. Sydney Herbert was a supporter of Great Ormond Street from the first. When the Nightingale

Fund was begun in acknowledgement of her services to the sick and wounded in the Crimea, Bence Jones was active in its promotion. He suggested that it should be used to set up training schools for nurses, employing special nursing tutors. Charles West, despite her criticism of children's hospitals, praised her. He had anticipated many of her views on nursing.

Mary Jane Kinnaird, whose husband, the Hon. Arthur Kinnaird, took a leading role in Great Ormond Street's management, had, with Lady Canning, sent nursing and other aid to the Crimea. There is no doubt that whatever views Florence Nightingale may have held about special children's hospitals and the excessive demands their tiny patients made upon nursing care, Great Ormond Street and the people who worked there, including such friends as Louisa Twinning, influenced her thinking. And in its turn Florence's own work was to have its effect on Great Ormond Street and its nurses, but that subject is important enough to be treated in a separate chapter. Lady Lovelace, who never lived to see Florence as 'The Lady with the Lamp', conceived an intense admiration for her. In 1851, she had written her a poem, 'A Portrait Taken from Life'.

I deem her fair – yes, very fair,
Yet some there are who pass her by,
Unmoved by all the graces there . . .

Her grave, but large and lucid eye,
Unites a boundless depth of feeling
With Truth's own bright transparency,
Her singleness of heart revealing.

A more complete and a more human picture of Florence Nightingale can be found in the letters of Mrs Gaskell, who was a close friend of the Nightingale family and often stayed at Lea Hurst. Mrs Gaskell was, of course, closely connected with Charles Dickens. On 31 January 1850, only one day after the Provisional Committee for a Hospital for Sick Children first met, Dickens wrote to Mrs Gaskell asking her to contribute to his projected new weekly journal, which became *Household Words*. Dickens averred, 'There is no living English writer whose aid I would desire to enlist, in preference to the authoress of Mary Barton.' Mrs Gaskell's contributions were to include a number of short stories, *Cranford* and *North and South*. The coincidence of the beginning of her association with *Household Words* with the start of what was to be Great Ormond Street is noted because in a letter from Mrs Gaskell later that year the two events are brought together, in what must be the first direct reference by a famous writer of that time to Charles West and his plans for a children's hospital.

The letter was to Lady Kay-Shuttleworth, dated 12 November 1850. Lady Kay-Shuttleworth and her husband Sir James were associated with Dickens in schemes for sanitary reform and universal education. It was at their house Briar Close, Windemere, that Mrs Gaskell had first met Charlotte Brontë the previous August, an event in itself of great literary significance. Lady Kay-Shuttleworth was to become a generous supporter of Great Ormond Street, and her son Dr Kay-Shuttleworth held a temporary appointment there. In the letter of November, after mentioning her story 'The Well of Pen-Morfa', which was to appear in the next number of *Household Words*, Mrs Gaskell continued:

> ... but one thing I must ask you, if you are at all interested about, or acquainted with the want of a children's hospital in London, and if you will sometime look over the accompanying papers; sent to me by Dr West.

What brought about Mrs Gaskell's knowledge and activity on behalf of Charles West's proposed Hospital for Sick Children? The names of half a dozen of her Holland relatives and of Dr Samuel Gaskell, her brother-in-law, appear in the early subscription lists. Dr Gaskell worked with Lord Shaftesbury on his Lunacy Commission. Mrs Gaskell persuaded him to help Florence Nightingale with her preparations for the Crimea. He was at first reluctant, but after meeting Florence became an enthusiastic supporter. Among the Holland contributions were a substantial one from Henry Holland, the royal physician, and an equally substantial one of thirty guineas from a Captain Holland RN, later described as of Ashbourne Hall, Derbyshire.

Captain Frederick Holland, Mrs Gaskell's cousin, was one of the nine gentlemen who were present at that first meeting for The Hospital for Sick Children in January 1850. His importance and influence as a founder member of Great Ormond Street lay not only in his relationship to Mrs Gaskell. A month after Mrs Gaskell's letter to Lady Kay-Shuttleworth, Dickens wrote to her about her new story for *Household Words*, which he had entitled 'The Heart of John Middleton'. The last sentence in this letter read: 'Mrs Dickens and her sister beg me to send their love. If Captain Holland should still be near you, pray remember us all to him very kindly.'

Dickens had evidently met Captain Frederick Holland, making yet another link between him and the beginnings of Great Ormond Street. But there is still another possible connection between Captain Holland and Charles Dickens. By one of those curious coincidences which, if not part of a general design, show a certain pattern of events occurring within a circumscribed period of time, the day before this letter to Mrs Gaskell of 17 December Dickens had written to Lord Denman, who had resigned as Lord Chief Justice ten months previously. Dickens wrote about the slave trade, mentioning papers received from Denman's son, Captain Joseph Denman. Captain Denman had played a prominent part in the naval blockade off the West African coast to prevent the shipping of slaves to the Cuban and Brazilian sugar plantations.

Captain Frederick Holland's second wife, whom he married in 1846, was Anne, the fifth daughter of Lord Denman. That Captain Holland formed a close professional relationship with his brother-in-law, Captain Denman, is confirmed in a letter from Mrs Gaskell to her daughter Marianne. Captain Denman became Commander of the Queen's royal yacht. Mrs Gaskell described a visit to Portsmouth and a tour of HMS *Victory.* She then 'Went to Royal Yacht and Lunched in the Ward Room with two or 3 officers – saw Cousin Fred's photograph'. This letter was probably written the year after Captain Holland's death, so that the display of his photograph in the royal yacht's ward room is of increased significance.

Lord Denman was an old and valued friend of Dickens. 'He is one of the noblest spirits in the world, and I have ever held him in great honour and regard,' wrote Dickens when Lord Denman had a final incapacitating stroke. Lord Denman had admired Dickens's work from the beginning, until he took exception to Mrs Jellyby and to the description of Chancery in *Bleak House.* Mary Russell Mitford wrote, 'Lord Denman studies *Pickwick* on the bench while the jury are deliberating.' She also describes his first cousin, Sir Benjamin Brodie, as reading *Pickwick* in his carriage between visits to patients, and that introduces another link between Lord Denman, Great Ormond Street, and possibly Charles Dickens, apart from Captain Holland.

Another of the 'nine gentlemen' was William Henry Baillie, whose mother, Lord Denman's sister, had married the great Dr Matthew Baillie, perhaps the finest physician of his age. Dr Matthew Baillie, with Hunter, was the founder of modern pathology. His *Morbid Anatomy* with its companion *Atlas,* published from 1793 onwards, formed the first comprehensive textbook on the subject. He was not without certain literary associations, some of them of a macabre kind. Baillie performed the post-mortem on Dr Samuel Johnson, who suffered from chronic emphysema, and it is said that the illustration in his *Atlas to the Morbid Anatomy* which shows the cut surface of a lung of such a case is probably that of the great lexicographer. Dr Baillie advised Lady Byron as to Byron's mental state. As the brother of Joanna Baillie, the poetess, he was known to both Lord and Lady Byron. Joanna Baillie and her sister Agnes are listed in a very early subscription list for Great Ormond Street, dated before 15 June 1850. They had lost no time in supporting the projected children's hospital in which their nephew was so interested.

Seven of the nine gentlemen have now been named. Before passing on to the remaining two, Captain Holland and his wife's first cousin W.H.Baillie deserve more detailed attention, not only in their own right as founder members of Great Ormond Street but because of their firm and definite place within the orbit of Dickens's circle at that time.

Captain Frederick Holland, son of Swinton Holland, was born in 1814. Edward Holland, MP, was his elder brother. Frederick obtained his first commission in the navy in August 1836, and joined the *Satellite* on its North American and West Indian stations. There, in 1839, he was given command of the schooner *Pickle*. He was advanced to the rank of commander in 1846, a few months after his marriage to Anne Denman. His health seems to have deteriorated while serving in the navy, and at the time of his association with Great Ormond Street he was on half-pay. At the beginning, Captain Holland was an active and useful member of the Provisional Committee, being on the first working subcommittee with Bence Jones, West, Hoare, Futvoye and Bathurst. But late in 1850 his name disappears. Whether it was because of ill-health or leaving London is not known. It is likely that both reasons played their part. Letters from Mrs Gaskell to her daughter Marianne in March 1851 mention in passing, 'Frederick and Annie Holland are gone to Rome, only to stay 2 months, however.' He therefore missed the first public meeting to promote a children's hospital which took place that same month, and in the printed report of the proceedings his name is omitted from the list of the Provisional Committee.

He was soon to settle in Derbyshire. Again a letter from Mrs Gaskell gives the news. Written probably in the April of 1852, a postscript adds, 'Captain Holland has bought Ashbourne Hall in Derbyshire, and is going to add to it considerably.'

> Ashbourne Hall, a square stuccoed erection, stands on a slope overlooking the little river Henmore. The mansion itself possesses few architectural excellences, but the gardens and pleasure grounds are laid out with considerable taste; and the river, as it winds ... through the park ... in a series of lakes and pools ... miniature waterfalls and cascades, adds to their sylvan beauty.

So a contemporary guidebook described Ashbourne Hall. From a very early period it was the seat of one of the oldest and famous Derbyshire families, the Cockaynes, whose last male representative, Sir Aston Cockayne, sold it to Sir William Boothby. Sir William offered its hospitality to the Young Pretender when he was on the march to Derby. Among the pictures which the Boothby family collected at Ashbourne Hall was that extraordinary painting by Fuseli, *The Nightmare*. Perhaps Fuseli, who also painted an allegory in memory of a young Boothby daughter, was sensitive to the atmosphere of the house. Some years later Meta Gaskell wrote that it was 'an old rambling house', haunted by one of the Madam Cockaynes 'who every night drives up the avenue in a coach and six – the spectral coachman and horses all headless'.

Captain Holland, although not in the best of health, played his part in the welfare of Ashbourne and its inhabitants. He soon became an assistant governor of the old Queen Elizabeth Grammar School, a magistrate and a churchwarden. He opened Ashbourne Hall's extensive grounds for the peace celebration at the end of the Crimean War, and in 1859, when the Volunteer Movement began, he formed the Ashbourne Company, the Dove Valley Corps.

But Captain Holland and Ashbourne Hall are now perhaps most noteworthy because of their associations with Mrs Gaskell. Only ten miles from Lea Hurst, the Nightingale home – Mr and Mrs Nightingale knew Captain and Anne Holland – Mrs Gaskell combined her visits there with a stay at Ashbourne Hall. Like Lea Hurst, she probably found the house with its pleasant gardens more conducive to literary work when her Manchester home, with her many family and social responsibilities, became rather irksome. Parts of *North and South* were written in these more congenial and peaceful surroundings. Ashbourne Hall was also near Stoney Middleton, the country home of Captain Holland's in-laws, the Denmans.

When, in October 1854, Florence Nightingale had left London for the Crimea, Mrs Gaskell wrote a letter from Lea Hurst to her friend Emily Shaen. It is an important document for the understanding of Florence Nightingale. It describes Florence as a little girl putting 'her 18 dolls all ill in rows in bed'. Florence's own words about the cholera epidemic when she was at the Middlesex Hospital are quoted: 'The prostitutes came in perpetually – poor creatures, staggering off their beat . . . One poor girl loathsomely filthy came in, and was dead in four hours. I held her in my arms . . .' Florence had formerly done much work among the villagers of Lea Hurst, 'who dote upon her. One poor woman lost a boy seven years ago of a white swelling in his knee and F.N. went twice a day to dress it.' But when the boy's mother later lost her husband, Florence only went to the funeral with great reluctance, urged there by her mother and sister. She refused to visit the poor widow again, despite her anxious pleas. Mrs Gaskell then describes Florence at work in Harley Street, where she did everything even to the rubbing of the ladies' cold feet at night in their beds. The greatness and contradictions of Florence Nightingale can be better understood after reading this letter, which concludes, 'I go to Captain Holland's Ashburne Hall, Derbyshire tomorrow and home on Tuesday week.'

Three days after this letter, Mrs Gaskell is writing to Florence's sister Parthenope from Ashbourne Hall itself, comforting her with the thought that for Florence 'all these steps in her life have been leading her on to this last great work'.

Perhaps Florence and the little village boy were in Mrs Gaskell's mind more than ten years later, when she was writing her last novel, *Wives and Daughters*. Mr Gibson, the doctor protagonist of the book, is thinking rather sadly of his second marriage and wondering if his daughter, Molly, is really happy with her stepmother and her stepsister.

> Five minutes afterwards he was too busy treating a case of white swelling in the knee of a little boy, and thinking how to relieve the poor mother, who went out charring all day, and had to listen to the moans of her child all night, to have any thought for his own cares, which, if they really existed were of so trifling a nature compared to the hard reality of this hopeless woe.

This quotation could also be applied to Dr Charles West, whose family were later to complain that he never gave much attention to their worries and needs. Saints, Florence Nightingales, and Dr Wests are sometimes rather awkward people to have in the family.

Mrs Gaskell's letters give evidence of Captain Holland's increasing ill-health. In December 1854, she wrote to his wife Anne, asking if Fred 'is sufficiently well for me to propose a visit from my husband to Ashbourne next week ... for he sadly wants a little rest and quiet, things impossible to be procured in our busy place'. When William Gaskell had returned, she wrote Anne Holland a thank-you letter in which from William's 'account of the improvement he saw in Fred's looks during his stay at Ashbourne, I cannot help hoping that he really has now met with the means of some permanent improvement; and that the new treatment will afford relief to this general health'. But in a letter of April 1859 she told Charles Bosanquet that long ago Captain Holland's knee-cap had slipped and become diseased having been badly replaced.

Finally, when Mrs Gaskell and her daughters were away in Germany, she received a letter from William Gaskell, dated 25 July 1860. 'You would perhaps hear at Kreuznach that Frederick ... died at the Victoria Hotel Euston Square on Saturday.' For Captain Holland's death at only forty-six years of age, the whole town of Ashbourne went into mourning, the shops closed, and all the blinds were drawn.

Ashbourne Hall became a hotel at the beginning of this century. Soon after the last war it was used for a block of flats, the grounds being much reduced and converted into a rather dull public park. Much of the house was destroyed or altered, but fittingly a branch of the county library was built on to its south front. A road had long been opened across the grounds, the traffic frightening away Madam Cockayne's spectral coach and horses. No doubt, Mrs Gaskell's accounts of Cranford and Milton are there issued to a new generation of appreciative readers. Yet Captain Holland's proudest claim to posterity must be as one of the founders of Great Ormond Street. In many ways he was an example of his time and class, one of those whose social conscience made them assume without question those duties and obligations which afforded some relief, even if not solving all their distress, to the poor. Throughout Great Ormond Street's history the support of the Royal Navy has always been prominent. Captain Holland was the first in a long tradition.

His wife's cousin and fellow-founder, William Hunter Baillie, had a much longer connection with Great Ormond Street; but then, in contrast to the ailing Captain Holland, Baillie, like his aunts, Joanna and Agnes Baillie, had the precious gift of longevity. When he died in 1894, an obituary in *The Times* described him as 'one of the few survivors of those born in the eighteenth century'.

He played a prominent part in the affairs of the Provisional Committee until January 1852, when its members 'having thus discharged the duties for which they were appointed, consigned the management of the Hospital to a Committee of Twelve Gentlemen'. Of the original nine gentlemen who had first met almost exactly two years ago, only Bence Jones, Futvoye and Baillie were named for the Committee of Management, with Bathurst as honorary secretary. West was modestly only on the Medical Committee. Not until 1855 was the Committee of Management enlarged to include those whose names were formerly to be found on the Medical Committee.

Baillie served on the Committee of Management for two years, until 1853. Yet his support for Great Ormond Street lasted until well past his ninetieth year, when his donation is recorded at a festival dinner chaired by the Bishop of Peterborough. His children made several collections, as did other members of his family. In addition to his famous father, W.H.Baillie came from a worthy medical background. His grandfather was Dr Thomas Denman; John Hunter and William Hunter (after whom he was named) were his great-uncles; and Sir Benjamin Brodie, president of the Royal College of Surgeons, was his first cousin once removed. He was intended for the law, following the example of his uncle, Lord Denman, but although called to the Bar, as the possessor of a comfortable income and property he never had the need or the urge to practise.

His interest in Great Ormond Street was but one example of his concern for the welfare of medicine. He was a member of the Middlesex Hospital committee and for a time its chairman. Both West and Bence Jones had lectured there. The Royal College of Surgeons and the Royal College of Physicians were beneficiaries of his interest. Although his work for the Middlesex and the two Colleges is recorded, his part in the history of Great Ormond Street, which could be held to be his most important contribution to the future good of medicine, appears to have been overlooked in the obituaries.

Before going on to consider the two remaining members of the 'nine gentlemen', it may be well to remember another famous lady who was most fittingly associated with The Hospital for Sick Children from its inception. She was described by Dickens as 'the noblest spirit we can ever know'. In what must surely be the earliest surviving list of donations and subscriptions, compiled up to 20 March 1850 – that is, only seven weeks after the nine gentlemen first met – is an entry showing that Miss Burdett Coutts donated £50. Later, through the century and beyond, a number of equivalent or larger sums are found ascribed merely to 'A Lady'. There can be no doubt that these refer to Angela Burdett Coutts, this being her favourite soubriquet when giving to charity. She had told Dickens some six years previously, 'What is the use of my means but to try and do some good with them?' It is not necessary to enlarge upon the charitable and philanthropic works she initiated, nor on Dickens's special involvement with many of these schemes. For a number of years, there was an intensive correspondence between them, an exchange of ideas and plans. Any participation by one in a charity was surely known to the other.

Of the years 1850 to 1852, when The Hospital for Sick Children was brought into being, the editors of the volume of the Pilgrim Edition of Dickens's letters covering this period, write: 'Many of the other interests Dickens pursued during these three years show his reforming zeal at its height, and most of them, as said, play an important part in *Bleak House*.' I have already drawn a parallel between that novel and Charles West's first annual medical report for Great Ormond Street. It should be noted that in these three years about 125 letters were written by Dickens to Miss Burdett Coutts.

It is probable that Miss Burdett Coutts made the very first gift of toys to the Hospital, a great distinction in the history of Great Ormond Street. Later, other gifts, including books and pictures, are recorded. During the Great Exhibition of 1851, hearing that Prince Albert thought that every child should have the opportunity of visiting it, Miss Burdett Coutts paid for all the boys and girls at her schools attached to St Stephen's, Westminster, to visit the glass palace in Hyde Park. There were nearly 450 children involved. Dickens, of all people, was ironic about the chaos such large numbers caused, describing a hundred infants crossing the crowded road at Kensington Gate towards the main entrance, dodging in and out of the clattering coaches and hurrying riders much to the horror and anguish of their monitors. 'They were clinging to horses, I am told, all over the Park.'

The Reverend William Tennant, the incumbent of St Stephen's, had been recommended to Miss Burdett Coutts by the Bishop of London. Tennant worked alongside Dickens on her charitable schemes, and was a hearty supporter of Great Ormond Street, preaching sermons and arranging collections on behalf of the new children's hospital. For these services he was made an honorary governor of the Hospital.

It was fitting that Miss Burdett Coutts also became a life governor of Great Ormond Street. Although Dickens had been so active in the home she had opened for rescuing prostitutes because 'the thought of such fallen women has troubled her in her bed' – a refuge which despite all Dickens's time and attention became somewhat diverted from its original purpose – he also spent much time and energy on other of her projects, which were to be of more relevance to the future patients of Great Ormond Street. Miss Burdett Coutts's sanitary and housing schemes at Bethnal Green and Westminster were to be of the utmost importance to the children of the poor. As Dickens wrote to her in 1854, explaining the article 'To Working Men' which had appeared in *Household Words*:

> Its meaning is that they will never save their children from the dreadful and unnatural mortality now prevalent among them (almost too murderous to be thought of) or save themselves from untimely sickness and death, until they have cheap pure water in unlimited quantity, wholesome air, constraint upon little landlords like our Westminster friend to keep their property decent. Under the heaviest penalties, efficient drainage, and such alterations in building acts as shall preserve open spaces in the closest regions, and make them where they are not now.

It could be argued that Charles West urged children's hospitals to reduce child mortality; Florence Nightingale improved housing conditions and hygiene. Dickens and Lord Shaftesbury, however, saw the importance of both and worked for the two causes; Angela Burdett Coutts gave them her support. Many of the arguments in favour of a children's hospital laid due emphasis on the horrid and dreadful conditions in which poor children lived.

The Hon. Joceline William Percy and the Rev. William Niven were the remaining two of the 'nine gentlemen'. That they are considered last and perhaps briefly as compared with the other founders, does not imply that they were of the least importance. Both Percy and Niven made important contributions to the inauguration and well-being of The Hospital for Sick Children.

The Hon. J.W.Percy was born in 1811, the second son of the 5th Duke of Northumberland, and thus brother of Algernon George, the 6th Duke. Another brother was Henry H.M.Percy, who was awarded one of the very first Victoria Crosses in the Crimea, and became an aide-de-camp to Queen Victoria. The Duchess of Northumberland had been Queen Victoria's first governess. Percy's family connections were obviously to be of great importance for the Hospital. His uncle, Rear Admiral William Henry Percy, was soon to join the Provisional Committee, eventually becoming one of the first members of the Committee of Management.

The Hon. J.W.Percy and the Reverend W.Niven were both lay members of the subcommittee which appointed Great Ormond Street's first medical officers, a responsibility that, looked at from the perspective of the Hospital's history, seems particularly awesome. That Percy and his uncle were conscientious in caring for Great Ormond Street and the welfare of its little patients may be demonstrated by the fact that their signatures appear on the opening page of the Hospital's earliest visitors' book.

Reverend Niven had been chaplain to St George's Hospital and was thus an old acquaintance of Bence Jones. He was perpetual curate of St Saviour's Church, Chelsea. Niven, like Percy, was active in the early but abortive approaches to the Royal Waterloo Dispensary. He was responsible, according to Bence Jones, for securing Lord Ashley for Great Ormond Street. Bence Jones wrote, 'Through my friend Mr Niven, Lord Ashley became Chairman.'

Lord Ashley, who became the 7th Earl of Shaftesbury in 1851, and Bence Jones 'were long on intimate terms', remembered Bence Jones's son. If Niven was responsible for Shaftesbury first becoming chairman of the Provisional Committee and then president of Great Ormond Street, by that act alone he had performed an incomparable service for the future Hospital for Sick Children. That such an influential reformer, much of whose concern was for the mitigation of childhood suffering and hardship, should become associated with the Hospital was to give its appeal almost irresistible authority. He and Dickens were the two most potent advocates of social reform in Victorian England, working for many causes together, as they were to do at Great Ormond Street. Shaftesbury had been one of the most generous and certainly the most important patron of the Ragged Schools movement, for which Dickens had done so much.

At the time when the Provisional Committee first met at Bence Jones's house, Dickens and Shaftesbury were preparing their speeches for the first public meeting of the Metropolitan Sanitary Association, chaired by Dr Blomfield, Bishop of London. The Bishop was later to plead passionately for Great Ormond Street. It may be instructive to quote from Dickens's speech at that meeting – he was seconding the resolution which deplored the number of deaths by preventable disease in London.

> They found infancy was made stunted, ugly and full of pain . . . Whoever breathed the same air as the inhabitants of that court, or street, or parish – so long as he lived on the same soil, was lighted by the same sun and moon, and fanned by the same winds, he should consider their health and sickness as most decidedly his business . . . No one who had any experience of the poor would fail to be deeply affected . . . by their sympathy with one another, and by the beautiful alacrity with which they helped each other in toil, in the day of suffering, and at the hour of death.

Dickens was to return to the theme of this last sentence in his 1858 dinner speech for the Hospital. It may be noted here that Lord Shaftesbury's connection with Great Ormond Street seems to have been totally ignored by his biographers. Exactly the same can be said of Lady Byron and Angela Burdett Coutts, but in their case it is more understandable. The history of Great Ormond Street has never been written in any detail, apart from Thomas Twistington Higgins's delightful little volume for its centenary in 1952. Therefore the names of the nine founders remain simply honoured names, except perhaps for West. If this chapter has given some substance to their hitherto rather shadowy figures, discovered some of the more famous women who helped or were associated with them, and pointed out the relationship so many of them had with Dickens, it is an overdue debt which The Hospital for Sick Children can now repay.

In Lord Shaftesbury's case, however, the neglect of his connection with the Hospital is rather puzzling. From 1850 until his death in 1885, Shaftesbury was associated with Great Ormond Street in all its most important changes, appeals and achievements, which were duly and amply noted in the press. While it is true that Shaftesbury gave his name and assistance to so many good causes that the mere listing of them is an onerous task, The Hospital for Sick Children is surely worthy of mention. It may not be amiss to record here the Hospital's own final tribute:

> The committee have to record, with the most unfeigned sorrow, the death of the late Earl of Shaftesbury, who had been the President of this Hospital since its commencement. Lord Shaftesbury took the deepest interest in the success of this charity, which he helped to found; and the Committee feel that the Hospital has lost one of its most valued supporters and warmest friends.

— 8 —
DROOPING BUDS

Dr West wrote to all the children's hospitals in Europe seeking information during the year 1849, after his first meeting with Dr Bence Jones in July. The letter from Dr Mauthner of Vienna has already been mentioned. Five days after that letter, on 25 August 1849, Dr Behrend wrote from Berlin to Charles West in German, apologizing for not replying in English. He recommended to West a book on children's hospitals in Europe by Dr Franz S. Hügel, published in Vienna the previous year.

Dr Hügel's book received a long and favourable notice in the *English and Foreign Medico-Chirurgical Review* for April 1850. Although West was a contributor to this journal, and a copy of the review can be found in West's own collection among the books he presented to Great Ormond Street, the more likely author was Dr Copland, who had taken West's place at Waterloo Road. And West is mentioned in this connection, Dr Hügel being 'indebted to a communication from the late Senior Physician to the Royal Infirmary for Children, Dr West'. The reviewer, in deploring the lack of a children's hospital in London, suggests:

> ... the persuasion of some patrician patrons so to 'assist' as the French say, at some fancy fair, or promenades in horticultural or botanic gardens, or *concert monstre*, or some such fanfaronade of fancy and fashion, that such an amount of means may be obtained, as shall enable the Royal Infirmary for Children to complete its original design of furnishing its now empty rooms, if it be only with a dozen beds. This surely is not asking too much to begin with.

It is chastening to read such an ironic comment, written nearly 140 years ago, upon the methods we have still had to employ to raise funds for Great Ormond Street's Wishing Well Appeal. Like Charles West, the anonymous reviewer could not forget the indisputable fact that right across Europe, from Paris to St Petersburg, children's hospitals had been opened and maintained at government expense. Dr Hügel's book included detailed instructions for organizing children's dispensaries and hospitals, and it is evident that many of West's plans and ideas for Great Ormond Street had their origin in its pages, as Hügel had no doubt made use of West's comments in writing it.

This review of Hügel's account of the European hospitals for children appeared at a time when Charles West and his colleagues had already launched their appeal for such a hospital in London, an event taken cognizance of by an evidently last-minute footnote added at the end of the review: 'Since the foregoing article has been in type, an urgent appeal in favour of the establishment of a Metropolitan Hospital for Children has appeared in the daily papers.'

One of the most interesting sections of Hügel's work, is the list of nine reasons he gives for the absolute necessity of hospitals for children as opposed to mere dispensaries. They are so pertinent and so close to what was being said by Dickens and other reformers all over England, and what would be said in the appeals for a Hospital for Sick Children, that they are worth reading in full. They also serve as a reminder of what West had observed in his student days at Berlin and Paris, that the plight of the poor child when sick was the same in all the cities of Europe where the pressure of growth and industrialization was relentless.

1. The localities frequented by the poor, close, confined, and damp, as they often are, as well as overcrowded, exert a prejudicial influence upon those residing in them even when in health; but in the case of the sick are the cause of great destruction.
2. The poverty of many families is so pressing, that many parents of sick children, to avoid starvation, are obliged to seek a livelihood by working from home; and thus, even with the best intentions, can bestow no care upon their offspring.
3. The domestic management of children is mostly performed by the mothers in the lowest classes with great awkwardness, carelessness, or want of affection; though sick children always require a certain amount both of discipline and forebearance.
4. The uncleanliness of the bed and body clothes, of the utensils for cooking and eating, or even their entire want.
5. The want of sufficient nourishment, etc., generally, or that of particular articles of diet for special diseased conditions.
6. The insufficient warmth of the dwellings, arising from the impossibility of procuring the necessary materials.

7. The entire desertion of so many children, who, left by chance, even when in health, upon the care of strangers, are considered as a burden; but when sick are regarded as a very great trouble, to be disposed of as quickly as possible.
8. The danger of infection in families, where several children are obliged to live in the same apartment, and that the only one.
9. The importance of possessing clinical institutions for the diseases of children, partly as being serviceable for the education of practitioners; and partly on account of the greater facility they afford of instituting anatomico-pathological investigations on the dead body, than is possible in private practice.

As Thomas Love Peacock said, 'There, sir, is political economy in a nutshell.' Apart from recommending Hügel's work, Dr Behrend of Berlin sent his London colleague a list of children's hospitals in the Germanic and Scandinavian countries with their current medical directors. He also gave detailed instructions for making contact with their fellows at St Petersburg and Moscow. And, if West wanted help with the foreign correspondence, Dr Behrend recommended a young friend, Martin Kalisch, a doctor of philosophy at Berlin University, who knew all the modern tongues, as well as Greek, Latin, Hebrew and Chaldean. He was living in London, and judging from the complicated address near the Monument, his lodgings may well have been the original of Mrs Todgers' Commercial Boarding-House, which Mr Pecksniff dived 'up the queerest courts, and down the strangest alleys and under the blindest archways' to find with difficulty. Charles West wrote to all the doctors named by Dr Behrend. Some of their replies, even from Russia, are still preserved in the Hospital archives. It would almost seem as if his Continental confrères were as eager as West for a children's hospital to be opened in London.

These letters from Europe are but part of the material relating to the founding of Great Ormond Street which has been preserved in the Peter Pan Gallery. One rather battered document, dating apparently from before 30 January 1850, gives the proposed composition of the Provisional Committee. In addition to five names of those who actually attended on 30 January, there are listed: Lord Ashley, chairman; Rear Admiral Sir Francis Beaufort; F.H.Dickinson; John Labouchere; the Marquess of Blandford; Lord Effingham; and Lord Gosford. Even more significant is the *omission* of the names of Charles West, Henry Bence Jones, Edward Futvoye and Henry Allen Bathurst! This would confirm Futvoye's claim twenty years later that he was one of the original four who first joined in the founding of the hospital, and suggests that Bathurst was one of the quartet.

A careful examination of the manuscript minutes of that first January meeting would suggest that this document was drawn up previously as an intended list of all who would be present in addition to West, Bence Jones, Futvoye and Bathurst, who most certainly compiled it between them. Higgins in his *Great Ormond Street* gives a fairly accurate transcription of the first three resolutions passed. The first, on the desirability of establishing in London a hospital for sick children, and the third, about Lord Ashley being chairman, Joseph Hoare treasurer, Bathurst honorary secretary and the two 'bankers of the charity', are exactly as Higgins transcribes.

The second in Higgins's transcription reads, 'That the following undermentioned gentlemen do constitute a Provisional Committee for the purpose of carrying out this project, namely, the establishment in London of a hospital for sick children'.

But the manuscript minutes of the second resolution actually read, 'That the following Noblemen and Gentlemen do constitute a Provisional Committee for the purpose of carrying out that object, viz. the establishment in London of a hospital for sick children.'

Noblemen and gentlemen! No nobleman was present. It would seem as if Lords Ashley, Gosford, Effingham and Blandford had already agreed to serve on the Provisional Committee and that it was the intention to write down immediately after the second resolution the names of everyone on the document plus, of course, Charles West and the other three. This is made more likely by an obvious blank space between the second and third resolutions, a gap which is otherwise without explanation. Should not all the names on that document, therefore, be regarded together with the nine gentlemen as the founders of Great Ormond Street? To West, Bence Jones, Futvoye, Bathurst, Hoare, Holland, Baillie, Percy and Niven, we must add Lord Ashley, the Marquess of Blandford, Lord Effingham, Lord Gosford, Sir Francis Beaufort, F.H.Dickinson and John Labouchere.

The most important step taken by the subcommittee, which met on 2 and 6 February 1850, was to agree on the printing of an 'Appeal to the Public', and on the form of the advertisement to be entered twice in *The Times*, the *Morning Post* and the *Standard*. Ten days later, on a Saturday, readers of *The Times* and the public at large were informed of the intention to open a children's hospital. Exactly two years were to pass before Great Ormond Street actually opened. At that time no one knew or guessed that Great Ormond Street was to become synonymous with a children's hospital all over the world – the exact site of the future institution was something that was to be argued over until time and chance gave the answer. The advertisement in *The Times* was headed 'Appeal on Behalf of a Hospital for Sick Children', was about 500 words long, and was preceded by a complete list of the Provisional

Committee. In addition to the sixteen names listed above, five new members appear. Three, Dr George Burrows, Dr Robert Ferguson and Dr Peter Latham, were friends of West and Bence Jones. Burrows and Latham knew West from his student days. All three, with West and Bence Jones, were to append their names to a separate appeal for support from the medical profession. The two other new members in *The Times*'s advertisement were the Reverend John Thomas, attached to Lambeth Palace as chaplain to the Archbishop of Canterbury; and Robert Williams, a prosperous business connection of Labouchere. The advertisement, which, like all the appeals and letters was largely written by Charles West, covers most of the reasons, statistics and arguments which were to be put forward over the next two years.

> In a metropolis pre-eminently distinguished by the munificence of its public charities ... it is not a little remarkable that hitherto no hospital should have been established for the reception of sick children. There exists in London only one dispensary for the ... diseases of children, whereas on the continent such dispensaries are found in large numbers even in the smaller towns.

The seventeen cities in Europe with hospitals for children are listed from Paris onwards, but not one 'exists throughout the British Empire'.

> ... of 5538 inmates of the London hospitals only 3½ per cent were children under 10 years of age, and at least one-half of these had been admitted on account of accidents ... not as the subjects of disease ... The diseases of children ... are but little studied and ill understood – an evil ... extending to all ranks of society. ... nearly 1000 deaths occur in the metropolis every week ... nearly half this number are children under 10 years of age ... the proportion of deaths in childhood is but little less than it was 50 years ago ... although vaccination was then unknown, and the ravages of smallpox were so fatal ... the mortality under 10 years of age is still as high as 442 in 1000 ... numbers of infants and children still fall victims to the ill-understood diseases peculiarly incidental to the early stages of life. ... It is intended to found in London a Hospital to contain 100 beds for children, between the ages of 2 and 12 years, and towards this object contributions are earnestly solicited.

It was signed H.A.Bathurst, Hon. Sec. We may wonder what the impact of this brief factual appeal was on the general public. The reiterated statistics of child mortality were perhaps familiar to a few readers as they had been quoted by other reformers, but their application to a plea for a hospital devoted entirely to children was novel.

The Times, during these years, bore many competing appeals and pleas for charity and relief, ranging from the optimistic and sometimes impudent personal seeker of alms to the great nationwide project of the 1851 Exhibition. Indeed, only four days after Bathurst's appeal had appeared, there was printed the huge second subscription list for that Exhibition, headed by Queen Victoria's contribution of £1000 and Prince Albert's of £500. And in the same issue of 20 February 1850 was an appeal for a monument to the late Lord Jeffrey, which lists among others Charles Dickens's personal contribution of five guineas, the same amount he gave, according to the advertisement, only two days before to the Metropolitan Sanitary Association. On this same Monday, a full page in *The Times* listed the many hundreds of signatories to a petition against Sunday labour at the Post Office! Many of the future supporters of The Hospital for Sick Children, and even some of those who had already pledged their support, had hastened to swell this monster petition, such as Lord Ashley. Their names can also be found appended to all the other appeals mentioned above as competing for interest against that for a children's hospital. But we know that the advertisement for a Hospital for Sick Children was noted by the secretary of the Waterloo Road Infirmary for Children, as we have seen the immediate reaction of its Committee and Bence Jones's account of a visit paid by him and Dr West to Arthur Barclay. The minutes of the Provisional Committee give a more rounded and intriguing sequel of events as far as relations with the Royal Universal Infirmary for Children were concerned.

On 12 March the Provisional Committee received a letter from Joseph Hoare offering his formal resignation as treasurer. John Labouchere then accepted the office, which is as Bence Jones remembers, but there were further references to Waterloo Road at that same meeting.

> A letter from HRH the Duke of Cambridge to Lord Ashley was read and also his Lordship's reply stating that no hostile feelings on the part of the Committee existed against the Infirmary for Children in Lambeth.
>
> Mr Niven was requested to draw up a letter to the Committee of the Infirmary for Children to be forwarded by Mr Labouchere.

That the old and ailing uncle of Queen Victoria – he died later that summer – was persuaded to write a letter of alarm to Lord Ashley is indicative of the panic aroused at Waterloo Road. Although perfectly aware of Charles West's impatience at their procrastination, the fact that he was actually able to bring a movement for a children's hospital into being seems to have surprised them. They did not appreciate his determination nor the influence he had acquired through his friends and standing in the medical profession. It was after all only three months since Charles West had resigned from his post at the Royal Universal Infirmary for Children.

There was, in fact, much coming and going between the Provisional Committee and Waterloo Road. When the Provisional Committee next met on 5 April, the minutes read:

> Mr Labouchere's letter to the Committe of the Infirmary for Children, and the acknowledgement thereof from Mr Barclay (not official and dated 30 March) were read.
>
> Mr Percy read a report of his visit to and inspection of the Infirmary for Children – Dr Bence Jones confirmed that report from his own inspection and informed the Committee that Mr Dickinson had also visited the Infirmary and had expressed an opinion of it in concurrence with theirs; after due consideration the Committee came to the unanimous opinion that the Infirmary for Children in the Waterloo Road is not adapted for and cannot be converted into such a Hospital for Sick Children as it is their object to establish.

There is no mention of Bence Jones and West calling on Arthur Barclay at the Brewery before Joseph Hoare resigned. When it is remembered that West, in his old age, regretted that the authorities at Waterloo Road would not turn it into a proper children's hospital, it is evident that he was not entirely convinced, as were his colleagues, that it could not be converted. Despite what has been written and said in the past, there was a strong and definite endeavour by the Provisional Committee to come to some *modus vivendi* with the Royal Universal Infirmary for Children. After all, for a committee who had no premises immediately in view, the thought of the empty rooms at Waterloo Road was tempting. Bence Jones's own account and what happened later makes it possible to infer that the Royal Universal Infirmary rather resented the newcomers. Waterloo Road did proceed with their own appeal and raised nearly £1200 in eight months, but again their committee delayed and it was not until 1856 that inpatients were officially admitted. Even then, under the terms of a bequest, women were treated as well as children.

The Provisional Committee had meanwhile extended the scope of its appeal by printing two leaflets. One was addressed to the medical profession; it was seven pages in length and was signed by Dr Latham, Dr Burrows, Dr Ferguson, Dr Bence Jones and Dr West. Much of this was devoted to countering arguments against children's hospitals based on the high mortality rate in the Paris institutions. The distinction between the Foundling Hospital and the Children's Hospital in that city was pointed out. Deficiencies, however, in the Paris Children's Hospital were admitted, but improvements based on the example of Vienna, St Petersburg and Moscow were stated to be possible. West's European experience was bearing fruit. The other, 'An Appeal to the Public on Behalf of a Hospital for Sick Children', had twenty pages in all, including a six-page 'Appendix of Letters from different members of the medical profession, expressive of the opinions On The Advantages and Probable Success of a Hospital for Sick Children'. These important letters of support were written by Dr Peter M.Latham, Dr Thomas Watson, Dr George Burrows, Dr Charles Locock, Dr Robert Ferguson and Dr John Forbes, and were dated between November 1849 and January 1850. The letters had been obtained between them by Bence Jones and West. Four of the doctors are described as physicians to the Queen; Watson was urgently consulted during Prince Albert's last illness. There are direct links between at least two of them and Charles Dickens, and all six were at the 1858 dinner, their names appearing on the printed list of stewards.

Both Appeals were printed and distributed in March. The 'Appeal to the Public' was reprinted some months later with a subscription list updated to 15 June. Donations by then had totalled over £1200, plus about 100 guineas pledged in annual subscriptions. West was getting far stronger financial support than were his late colleagues at Waterloo Road, something that was to rankle for some time, finding expression at the first public meeting for the new children's hospital the following March.

The 'Appeal to the Public', which earlier had been circulated by West in manuscript form, contained several arguments which were not included in the necessarily restricted scope of the first advertisement in *The Times*. It put forward the idea that the proposed hospital would also serve as a school for the training of nurses; argued that objectors to the separation of a child from its mother are 'those to whom the habitations of the poor are unknown'; and listed the conditions which were 'essential to the utility of a Children's Hospital':

> A situation sufficiently remote from the crowded parts of the Metropolis, to insure to the inmates of the building the advantages of pure air and good ventilation.
>
> A site sufficiently spacious to allow of the formation of a garden, or play-ground, for the exercise and amusement of those children who are convalescent.
>
> A building ... to provide for the complete separation from the rest of any children suffering from contagious fevers; and ... wards for convalescent children, in order that the quiet necessary for those who are seriously ill may be undisturbed.

West never forgot that amusement and play were essential for a normal child and that the sign of recovery in a sick child was this desire to play. The toys that were to be scattered so liberally throughout Great Ormond Street had a definite therapeutic purpose. West also urged (for it was he who really wrote the appeal) that apart from the physical benefit to the children from such a hospital, there was also moral improvement to be derived from it. He supports this belief with a charming anecdote, which Dickens was quick to seize upon two years later.

> ...nor can it be doubted by any when they read that the children who have been discharged cured from the Hospital at Frankfort hang about the gates to see those who tended them when sick, and beg as a special favour to be allowed to come into its garden again to play but that a Children's Hospital has been there, as it might be here, a means of moral as well as of physical good.

This 'Appeal to the Public' was soon noticed in the medical press, and the *Edinburgh Medical and Surgical Journal* printed a quite substantial article on it in its issue for 1 April. It pointed out something perhaps obvious but not dwelt upon in the 'Appeal', that of the high child mortality rate: 'by far the largest proportion falls upon the children of the poor', and even the child who survived would have been 'several times ill by one or more of the disorders liable to attack that early period of life'. And in further considering the most suitable site for a children's hospital, it debars one on the river or in closely populated parts of the city, plumping for 'the vicinity of Highgate or Hampstead, or in the line of that locality'. (For fifty years from 1869, Great Ormond Street had a branch at Cromwell House, Highgate Hill.) The review ends with a suggestion that looks forward to our contemporary approach to children in hospital, an approach that owes much to Charles West:

> ...it will be well to make provisions in many instances for the reception of mothers with their children. Though in many instances females in that rank of life understand little of the management of children, yet instances may occur in which infants and young children will be more easily managed with the aid of the mother than without. All this, however, will come in good time.

Over a century later, in 1959, the Platt Report urged the accommodation of mothers in children's hospitals, aware of the distress suffered by young children parted from their mothers. Certainly the early days of Great Ormond Street, when the influence of Charles West was preponderant, seem in many ways to have been more in line with modern views than those of the last quarter of the nineteenth century and the first half of this.

Meanwhile a site for The Hospital for Sick Children was proving very elusive. At the end of the year two premises, both near Baker Street and Regent's Park, were considered, as was the conversion of the disused

Chelsea Consumption Hospital, but all three sites were rejected. It was not until soon after the first public meeting, planned for March 1851, that a house was found. As long ago as May 1850, the holding of a public meeting had been postponed until the next year. A meeting of the subcommittee on 17 October 1850, with the original four friends – West, Bence Jones, Futvoye and Bathurst – plus Niven, considered the possible opening date of the new institution, and recommended that the Provisional Committee should open a temporary hospital before Lady's Day next. They were too optimistic by about a year.

The most difficult question that can be posed, relative to the theme of this book, is why Charles Dickens was not a speaker at that first public meeting in March 1851. When it is considered that the other speakers included Lord Ashley, the Earl of Carlisle, and Blomfield, Bishop of London, with whom he had been closely associated at various meetings in aid of reforms, especially that for the Metropolitan Sanitary Association, Charles Dickens would have seemed the most obvious and happy choice for a public meeting to launch a hospital for sick children. Although the Provisional Committee minutes record that at various times from the previous November through to February, Ashley, Blomfield and Carlisle were invited and their consent obtained, Dickens is not mentioned. 'A list of Noblemen and Gentlemen was drawn up who might be applied to speak at the meeting,' but the names are not recorded. Dickens may have been on this list, but it would seem that he would have had a specific and recorded invitation, had that been the case. Had he been interested in speaking – and he must have known through all these mutual friends of the intended meeting – this fact would have been prominently displayed and his name almost blazoned forth. In the absence of any record or paper it must be confessed that it seems that Dickens at that time was more concerned with other reforms. His preoccupation with amateur theatricals or his worry over Catherine at Malvern are not adequate explanations or excuses. In May 1851, barely a month after his little daughter Dora had died, Dickens was speaking with Ashley and Carlisle (Blomfield was unavoidably absent) at a second meeting for the Metropolitan Sanitary Association. His theme was again the inevitable spread of infection and pestilence, how the first reports of Chadwick and Southwood Smith over a decade previously had enlarged his realization of this, and how:

> If I be a miserable child born and nurtured in some wretched place and tempted ... to the Ragged School, what can the few hours' teaching I get there do for me, against the noxious, constant, ever-renewed lesson of my whole existence. But give ... light and air; give them water; help them to be clean; lighten the heavy atmosphere ... which makes them

> the callous things they are; take the body of the dead relative from the room where the living live with it,

then the children may listen to the lessons of morality and religion.

Had Dickens been present at the hospital meeting at the Hanover Square Rooms on 18 March he would have heard Lord Ashley – whom he would praise so lavishly in his May speech – utter the same sentiments.

> The mortality among children in the Metropolis was not to be traced only to the peculiarity of their diseases, but was also owing to the sanitary condition of the localities in which they lived – to bad water, imperfect ventilation, and all the noxious and pestiferous influences to which they were subject from their earliest years.

Although Dickens later would more than make up for not taking part in this meeting, it would seem that Lord Ashley had pre-empted any speech he would have made. Even the first resolution Ashley read out as chairman was couched in the same mood.

> That, as great and numerous evils are experienced by all classes of the community from the want of a hospital exclusively devoted to the reception and medical treatment of sick children, the formation of such an institution may be made, under the blessing of Almighty God, a means of relieving the sufferings of the poor, and of conferring important benefits upon society at large.

The Earl of Carlisle spoke of the worthiness and appeal to sympathy of a charity devoted to sick children, and paid tribute to Lord Ashley. 'In a soft and selfish age he has lived and laboured for the good of others, and especially of the weak and defenceless.' The Bishop of London pointed out that in the provision of hospitals 'we are still far behind most of the cities of the Continent.' He also stressed the misery 'presented when sickness first begins its ravages among the children of the poor ... in the cottage where lies, stretched upon the bed of sickness, the child of poor parents, who, bound down by penury, are mourning hopeless over ... their child'. He ended by expressing a hope which has been realized in every fund-raising event for Great Ormond Street, from the very beginning to the present Wishing Well Appeal, that not only a few large contributions were required but also a great number of small donations which would 'tend to excite throughout society at large a sympathy for our institution, and a desire to promote its welfare'.

Sir James Clark, the Queen's doctor, supported the resolution that a hospital for sick children should afford relief to the poor, promote the advancement of medical knowledge, and train efficient children's nurses. After Sir James had spoken, the meeting was diverted from its purpose by two unscheduled speakers who were not reported in the account of the meeting which the Provisional Committee published as a fund-raising pamphlet. The first was Dr Copland, who had taken over from Charles West at the Royal Universal Infirmary. He insisted that his institution was as well worth supporting as the new projected one. Let charity be shared, and the man who gave twenty guineas to the new hospital should give ten to the old one. This suggestion was greeted with both cheers and laughter. Dr Copland also urged the establishment of children's hospitals in Manchester, Birmingham and other manufacturing towns, where the increase of deaths among children was shocking. These cities, of course, were soon to follow Great Ormond Street's lead.

The other interruption was of a more eccentric nature. A Captain Acherley, described in the *Medical Times* as 'the genius of the lamp', insisted that the officers of the new institution should all be women.

> They alone were capable of attending to sick children; and he urgently called on the meeting not to allow any of the infamous medical men to be appointed to it, for they knew nothing of children's diseases, and killed more than half of those placed under their care. After many attempts to quiet the unhappy man the police were called in, and he was removed.

Captain Acherley, who perhaps anticipated some of Florence Nightingale's views as well as her honorific, deserves to be mentioned, not only for his entertainment value, but because he gave expression to some of the unease concerning the treatment of sick children at that time. Dickens would have surely made use of him as a model for a future character had he been there. And some of Great Ormond Street's present staff and governors may want to give a few hearty cheers to his memory on behalf of their fellow women.

Dr George Burrows enlarged upon the benefits to the medical profession such a hospital would confer, and emphasized the benefits obtained 'in training up women to be efficient children's nurses'. He proposed that a building fund should be raised for 'the erection of a suitable hospital . . . but that in the meantime a temporary hospital be opened for the reception of patients as soon as possible'. Great Ormond Street was decided upon within a month of Burrows's resolution.

Charles West drew upon the example of what had happened in Vienna and elsewhere in Europe as a good augury for the future of children's hospitals in England. He explained that the Royal Universal Infirmary for Children did not fulfil the conditions that were requisite for a hospital for sick children. Had it done so, 'we should have gladly gone there to work.' He confirmed what had been apparent from the first meetings of the Provisional Committee:

> Feeling this, we offer, as we already have done, most cordially and heartily to unite with the Committee of the other institution in founding a hospital in some proper situation, with all needful appliances, and with everything that can be required for the benefit of the sick poor. We will unite them in the good work, if they allow us; but if they decline, as hitherto they have done, to associated themselves with us, while in every good undertaking we wish them God-speed, we feel it to be our duty to persevere alone in carrying on our efforts in accordance with the principle that we have laid down.

It was reported that 'The meeting was but thinly attended, and chiefly by ladies.' At a collection, deliberately restricted to small sums, £12 17s 4d was raised. Lord Ashley and Lord Carlisle had to leave early for Westminster, and F.H.Dickinson took Lord Ashley's place as chairman.

The meeting of the Provisional Committee for 1 April 1851 was a landmark for The Hospital for Sick Children. The minutes record:

> Mr Pownall attended the Meeting and explained that in compliance with the request of the sub-committee appointed for finding suitable premises for a temporary Hospital he had looked over a house and premises in Great Ormond Street, Russell Square, at the corner of Powis Place, belonging to Mr Martelli and had put himself in communication with Mr Wyatt the agent of Mr Martelli, for the purpose of ascertaining on what terms they might be rented. Mr Pownall mentioned generally Mr Wyatt's views on the subject and as the Committee determined to inspect the premises more minutely in company with Mr Pownall (tomorrow Wednesday 2nd April) before making any offer to lease them.

After some offers and negotiation, the committee agreed at the end of the month to a rent of £200 per annum for a period of twenty-one years, terms that must have pleased Mr Martelli.

Many years later, at the Hospital's Anniversary Festival Dinner for 1874, West said:

> I remember some thirty years ago passing along Great Ormond Street, my head and heart full of the thoughts of little children and of little sick children, and I said to my companion with whom I was walking, as we passed No. 49, 'There, that is the future Children's Hospital.' Many a

> true word you know is spoken in jest and the young man's dream, thanks to your kindness, has come to be true.

This is a case where truth is more interesting than fancy. According to West, it must have been nearer 1844 when this walk happened, practically contemporaneous with his first attempts to persuade Waterloo Road to admit inpatients, not 1849, as Twistington Higgins (writing in 1952 for the Hospital's centenary) conjectured. The facts show that West did half-idly consider the possibility of No. 49 Great Ormond Street as a children's hospital at a much earlier date than Higgins realized. Whether this youthful idea of Charles West recurred to him before Mr Pownall told the committee that the house was available is something that cannot be known. Afterwards, of course, the coincidence must have amused him.

No. 49 Great Ormond Street had its niche in medical history long before it became The Hospital for Sick Children. It was the house of Dr Richard Mead, the famous physician to Queen Anne, whose library and museum, known to all the learned men of Europe, was housed in the spacious room which became the first Outpatients Department. Dr Johnson and other scholars of the day visited Great Ormond Street to consult some of the rare items Dr Mead had collected. In 1747 Mead had supported the practice of inoculation against smallpox, lending his considerable influence and authority to a movement that culminated in Edward Jenner and vaccination. A family tradition claims that at his death in 1754 Mead left a bequest intended to provide medical care for some of the poor children who lived in the mean streets of the neighbourhood!

In West's manuscript account of his share in the founding of Great Ormond Street, there is a passage which must be quoted here. It seems rather at variance with the sequence of events as described in the minutes of the Provisional Committee. This statement, written as it probably was about forty years after the acquisition of 49 Great Ormond Street, is perhaps not so reliable as the contemporary minutes; but the minutes, although invaluable, do not allow us to see behind the scenes, to the reasons underlying some decisions. Anything that Charles West says about the beginning of Great Ormond Street deserves respect, but it must be remembered that he had quarrelled bitterly with the Committee of Management in 1876 and this must be treated as an *ex parte* statement.

> In December 1850, a house (now pulled down) was found in Upper Gloucester St., Marylebone Road, which it was thought might be converted into a Hospital, and the plans were sent to me by Messrs Gregg & Pownall of the requisite alterations.

While this was under consideration I discovered the much more suitable house, 49 Gt. Ormond Street, on the site of which the present hospital stands.

The first paragraph cannot be quarrelled with; the second is open to question. It would indeed be most fitting were it Charles West himself who was responsible in the very first instance for finding Great Ormond Street. That he was the prime mover in most of the preparation necessary before 49 Great Ormond Street opened as The Hospital for Sick Children was always evident.

One of the most important appointments for the new hospital, and especially for a hospital for sick children, was that of matron. The post was advertised on 21 November 1851, offering a salary of £40 a year with board and lodging. Applicants had to be between thirty and forty-five years of age, 'single and without encumbrances' – a rather unfortunate if technically correct term for the first children's hospital to use! The other condition would have brought a wry smile to Charles West: 'She must be a Member of the Church of England.' Inured as he was to the disadvantages of Nonconformity in religion, he may have reflected that it was well that the same conditions did not apply to the physicians, otherwise he would have been ineligible. Mrs Willey was chosen as the first matron on 12 December.

Under the 1848 Nuisances Removal and Diseases Prevention Act, the General Board of Health's sanction and approval were required both for alterations to the premises and the opening of the hospital. On 1 July 1851, the minutes of the Provisional Committee record:

A letter from Mr Austin the Secretary to the Board of Health was read, notifying that Mr Grainger and Mr Austin had been appointed by the Board of Health to inspect and report upon the premises in Ormond Street and requesting plans of the proposed alterations.

Henry Bathurst and Charles West agreed to call on Mr Austin with the plans and discuss the alterations. Henry Austin, an architect, was Charles Dickens's brother-in-law, having married Dickens's younger sister Letitia. Dickens and Austin had known each other since 1833. Dickens had written to Lord Morpeth (the future Earl of Carlisle) supporting the appointment of Austin as secretary to the proposed Board of Health. On 8 July West told the Provisional Committee that together with Dr Baly (his old friend from St Bartholomew's Hospital who had become actively concerned with the new children's hospital) and Mr Perceval, he had met Austin and Grainger from the Board of Health at 49 Great Ormond Street and 'that the opinion of these gentlemen seems generally favourable'. They wanted, however, a statement of all the proposed changes and tracings of the plans, but promised to agree to some of the suggestions. West had convinced Austin that by slightly altering the proposed site of the mortuary it would be possible to preserve a magnificent old plane tree in the large garden. This plane tree was to become a treasured feature of the hospital, and many of the staff were photographed grouped under it, as were many of the children. In some of these photographs a handsome fountain can be seen, which was used by the children as a kind of wishing well into which they dropped their precious farthings and halfpennies, hoping they would soon get better and be able to run and play again. It was this that inspired the Wishing Well Appeal for the present rebuilding of the hospital. It is a pleasant fancy that if Dickens's brother-in-law had not agreed to West's suggestion about re-siting the 'dead house', there would have been no plane tree and perhaps no fountain and no Wishing Well Appeal!

On this same 8 July, Dickens was writing to the Earl of Carlisle to invite him down to Broadstairs for the weekend. On the 14th of the same month Dickens told Austin he was buying Tavistock House, and for the rest of the year numerous letters were sent to Austin concerning alterations and repairs to Tavistock House. Thus Henry Austin was responsible at the same time for overseeing both Great Ormond Street and Tavistock House, and it is evident that Dickens's new home gave Austin far greater trouble than did the new children's hospital. A Mrs Henry Austin was an early subscriber to Great Ormond Street's funds, but her identification as Dickens's sister cannot be verified. Henry wrote to Great Ormond Street that August announcing that, in confirmation with his report, the Board of Health had proposed to sanction the opening of the hospital, if, of course, the committee agreed to accept all their recommendations. Dr West, Dr Baly and Dr Fuller formed a subcommittee to supervise the alterations and 'see them done in the most economic manner'.

Henry Austin had supplied Dickens with most of the material for the articles on sanitation and public health which appeared in *Household Words*. Perhaps he gave Dickens the idea for an article on the new children's hospital, 'Drooping Buds', but that was not to appear until the following April.

It is an example of the closeness between Dickens and the events which led up to the opening of Great Ormond Street, that when on 21 January 1852 Henry Austin wrote to Henry Bathurst a letter enclosing the official sanction of the Board of Health for the opening of The Hospital for Sick Children – an official sanction signed by Edwin Chadwick and Dr Thomas Southwood Smith – on that very day Dickens wrote to Henry Austin mentioning both Chadwick and Southwood Smith. The letter was concerned with the Internment Bill and makes no reference of course to the hospital, but it is at least an interesting coincidence.

Now, alas, I must shatter the longest and most loved of The Hospital for Sick Children's proud traditions: that it opened on St Valentine's Day, 14 February 1852. This tradition was firmly fixed in its early years. In its twentieth annual report the committee emphatically stated it was 'opened for the reception of patients ... on February 14th, 1852 – a happy St Valentine's Day kept by the rich for the children of the poor'. But in fact the Committee of Management meeting on 12 February 1852 instructed the Secretary, Henry Bathurst, 'to inform the Medical Officers that the Hospital would open on the 16th inst.' – a date which was to be confirmed by Dr Charles West and his colleagues at the beginning of the report of the Medical Committee, which is printed in the very first annual report: 'We beg to lay before you the First Medical Report of the Hospital for Sick Children, from the date of its opening, on the 16th February, to the end of December, 1852.' The evidence from such primary and impeccable sources would seem incontrovertible! And it must be added that in 1852 St Valentine's Day fell on a Saturday, a day when no new hospital would open for the reception of patients.

How the error came about it is impossible to say, unless someone's hasty glance at the manuscript minutes misread the date, a very easy thing to do. Out of consideration for all the nursing staff at Great Ormond Street and others, who have always celebrated and particularly cherished St Valentine's Day, I offer a compromise which will perhaps satisfy both the demands of the historian and the understandable affection of Great Ormond Street for St Valentine's Day.

It was then the custom, prior to the formal opening of charities and such institutions as The Hospital for Sick Children, to throw open the premises to the public and invite inspection by its supporters and well-wishers. This practice was a useful source of fund-raising. What day would be more suitable for Great Ormond Street than Saturday, 14 February 1852? In this sense it may be true that The Hospital for Sick Children did open its doors to the public for the first time on St Valentine's Day!

About the time that Great Ormond Street opened, Dickens must have been checking the proofs of the first number of *Bleak House*. In the second chapter, in effective and artistic contrast to the London fog of the first, and yet a continuation of the mood set in that opening chapter, is a picture of Lincolnshire in flood under endless days of rain.

> The view from my Lady Dedlock's own windows is alternately a lead-coloured view, and a view in Indian ink. The vases on the stone terrace in the foreground catch the rain all day; and the heavy drops fall, drip,

> drip, drip, upon the broad flagged pavement, called, from old time, the Ghost's Walk, all night . . . My Lady Dedlock (who is childless), looking out in the early twilight from her boudoir at a keeper's lodge, and seeing the light of a fire upon the latticed panes, and smoke rising from the chimney, and a child, chased by a woman, running out into the rain to meet the shining figure of a wrapped-up man coming through the gate, has been put quite out of temper. My Lady Dedlock says she has been 'bored to death'.

This picture, the delight of a child's presence and the weariness of a life without children, was surely in Dickens's mind when shortly afterwards he was thinking of 'Drooping Buds' and its penultimate sentence, 'Who that knows how sweet a part of home the children are.' We have seen how numerous and how intimate were the links between Dickens and the people who helped to found Great Ormond Street, and how his work and message created the climate for it to open. Now in the pages of *Household Words* he was to bring to bear the whole weight of his influence and genius in the hospital's favour.

Much of 'Drooping Buds' was based on the various appeals and letters which the Provisional Committee had distributed nearly two years before, in some places using almost the same words – those words, facts and statistics which were compiled and written by Dr Charles West. But there cannot be a better example of the emotional appeal which a great and skilled writer like Dickens can impart to a familiar message, than the contrast between the printed hospital 'Appeal' and 'Drooping Buds'. Of even more moment was the circulation of *Household Words*, which enabled this plea for the new children's hospital to reach many who, before reading 'Drooping Buds', were not even aware that such an institution had been opened. Although never to achieve the vast circulation of *All the Year Round* – which, helped by such popular serials as Wilkie Collins's *The Woman in White*, more than trebled the highest *Household Words* printing of about 40,000 – 'Drooping Buds' drew the attention of that broad spectrum of interests and vast audience to which Dickens's works always appealed. It cannot be denied that after 'Drooping Buds' appeared, the knowledge and use of the hospital increased significantly, as I have pointed out in the first chapter. The Committee of Management were quick to realize this, and obtained permission to reprint it quickly, as 'From Dickens's Household Words'. It was always kept in circulation, reprinted as necessary. It is impossible to estimate what proportion of the support that Great Ormond Street received over the next few years was due to the influence of 'Drooping Buds', but it must have been responsible for many of the guineas, shillings and pennies sent to the secretary or the treasurer.

It must not be forgotten that 'Drooping Buds' was a collaboration with Henry Morley; but apart from passages like the apostrophic passage beginning, 'Oh! Baby's dead and will be never, never, never seen among us any more!', and the final peroration, which has already been quoted with regard to Lady Olivia Acheson's death, there are many passages which bear Dickens's personal stamp. 'Drooping Buds' cannot be neatly parcelled out between Dickens and Morley; it is evident that they discussed and revised it with more than usual care. What has not been appreciated is the accuracy of its description of Great Ormond Street and its little patients, an accuracy which can be shown by reference to contemporary records.

'Drooping Buds' begins starkly and abruptly by listing all the towns in Europe which have children's hospitals, from Paris to Constantinople: 'There was not one in all England until the other day.'

> No hospital for sick children! Does the public know what is implied in this? Those little graves two or three feet long, which are so plentiful in our churchyards and our cemeteries – to which, from home, in absence from the pleasure of society, the thoughts of many a young mother sadly wander.

The grim figures of child mortality in London, as given in the hospital's own appeal, lead to a passage which justifies the imagery of the title.

> Our children perish out of our homes: not because there is in them an inherent dangerous sickness (except in a few cases . . .), but because there is, in respect of their tender lives, a want of sanitary discipline and a want of medical knowledge. What should we say of a rose tree in which one bud out of every three dropped to the soil dead . . . ?
>
> Of all the coffins that are made in London, more than one in every three is made for a little child; a child that has not yet two figures to its age.

It is difficult for the doctor to treat children's diseases as compared with those of an adult:

> The infant can only wail; the child is silenced by disease; or, when it answers, wants experience, and answers incorrectly. Again, for life and death, all the changes in the sickness of a child are commonly very rapid: so rapid, that a child which suffers under an acute disease should be seen at least every five or six hours by its medical attendant.

The examples and facts are brought out much as Dr West had in his lectures and in his papers pleading for a children's hospital. Sometimes there is the new impact and force which only the practised writer can give.

> ... medical advisers, can in so many cases, do no more than sympathize with the distress of parents, look at a child's tongue, feel its pulse, send powders, and shake their heads with vain regret over the little corpse, around which women weep so bitterly.

The quiet backwater of the streets and houses of Great Ormond Street and its neighbourhood are a reminder of the old formalities, of the old minuets that once belonged to the fashionable families living there, especially at 49 Great Ormond Street.

> Many little faces, radiant in the wintry blaze, had looked up in the twilight, wondering at the great old Monument of a chimney-piece, and at the winking shadows peeping down from its recesses. Many, far too many, pretty house-fairies had vanished from before it, and left blank space on the hearth, to be filled up nevermore.
>
> Oh! Baby's dead, and will be never, never, never, seen among us any more! We fell into a waking dream, and the Spring air seemed to breathe the words. The young house-surgeon melted out of the quaint, quiet room; in his place, a group of little children gathered about a weeping lady; and the lamentation was familiar to the ancient echoes of the house. Then, there appeared to us a host of little figures, and cried, 'We are Baby. We were Baby here, each of us in its generation, and we were welcomed with joy and hope and thankfulness; but no love and no hope, though they were very strong, could keep us, and we went our early way!' – 'And we,' said another throng of shades, 'were that little child who lived to ... be the favourite ... of this great house ... until the infection ... from those poorer houses ... struck us one day while we were at play, and ... changed our prattle into moaning, and killed us in our promise!' – 'And I ... a sick child once, grew ... to be blessed with love, and then ... glided from the arms of my young husband ...' – 'And I,' said another shadow, 'am the lame mis-shapen boy who read so much by this fireside, and suffered so much pain so patiently ... I said to my fond father ... "O dear Papa ... it is better I should never be a man, for who could ... be so careful of me when you were gone!"' Then all the shadows said together: 'We belonged to this house, but others like us have belonged to every house, and many such will come here, now, to be relieved, and we will put it in the hearts of mothers and fathers to remember them. Come up, and see!'

When I said, in the first chapter, that Great Ormond Street invoked the most profound and the most personal of responses from Charles Dickens, the above passage, which most authorities hold to be Dickens's own, is an illustration of that claim. It is obviously based on the memories of his own private sorrows – the sudden death of Mary Hogarth, the slow dying of his sister Fanny, and the later loss of her crippled boy, Harry Burnett; and most recent of all, the unexpected death of his baby daughter Dora, not quite a year before. The memory of the night's vigil he had kept, with Mark Lemon, by the bedside of his dead baby, despite his protestation that he had resigned himself to the loss of 'our poor little pet', was overwhelming at times. Dickens could not easily find, as his readers did, an emotional compensation in his own characters. To obtain such a catharsis he had to endure the agonies and frustrations of creation, and all the bitter recollections conjured up by the mere stimulus of a writer's imagination.

Up the handsome staircase was the large and lofty old drawing room, now become a ward. It had an ornamented ceiling, and panels painted 'with rosy nymphs and children'. Light iron cribs with the half a dozen patients then in the Hospital were placed along the walls. Dolls occupied some of the vacant beds. 'A large gay ball was rolling on the floor, and toys abounded.' The neighbouring drawing room, also intended for a ward, was 'as yet unoccupied'.

> There were five girls and a boy. Five were in bed near the windows; two of these, whose beds were the most distant from each other, confined by painful maladies, were resting on their arms, and busily exporting and importing fun. A third shared the profits merrily, and occasionally speculated in a venture on its own account. The most delightful music in this world, the light laughter of children floated freely through the space. The hospital had begun with one child. What did *he* think about, or laugh about? Maybe those shadows who had their infant home in the great house, and had known in those same rooms the needs now sought to be supplied for him, told him stories in his sleep.

To the historian of Great Ormond Street, this passage is of absorbing interest, and not alone for the revelation that its unique atmosphere, its attitude towards the children and their swift response, was there in the beginning – the spirit of Charles West had immediately prevailed. One of the best-known Hospital traditions is that the first patient was a girl. As Higgins writes, 'On the 17th [of February] the first patient was admitted, Eliza Armstrong, a little girl of three and a half years suffering from "consumption".' Eliza was afflicted with 'phthisis', according to the surviving admissions register covering the period from 17 February 1852 to 8 August 1855, but she was not admitted until on or after 27 February. There are three other children listed in the admission register before Eliza Armstrong. The first, a tiny boy only two years old, George Parr, suffering from diarrhoea and catarrh, was the patient admitted on 17 February. Three days later an infant boy fourteen months old – thus early on the hospital rule admitting children only between two and twelve years of age was abandoned – named Charles Cooper, who had bronchitis and other pulmonary infections, became the second patient.

Charles West, speaking in 1868 on the hospital's beginnings, recalled, 'It is more than sixteen years since the first child admitted into it, for three days held solitary state there.' Dickens and Morley, writing within the first few weeks of its opening, knew that 'The hospital had begun with one child. What did *he* think about?' And knowing now of his being alone for three days adds a meaning to the imagined picture of the infant shadows telling him 'stories in his sleep'.

There can be no doubt that, on the evidence of the admissions register, confirmed by Charles West's recollections and Dickens's more contemporary description emphasizing the sex of the child, that to little George Parr belongs the distinction of being the first patient admitted into The Hospital for Sick Children.

Higgins, in repeating the Eliza Armstrong tradition, was following a long precedent that started only a few years after the hospital opened. One early example is Mrs Craik, who visited the hospital in December 1861, a few years after her *John Halifax, Gentleman* was published. The article she published describing her visit gave currency to this erroneous idea that the first patient was a girl.

It is possible to identify the six children described in 'Drooping Buds'. The child listed in the admissions register immediately before Eliza Armstrong – they probably came in on the same day – was a six-year-old Caroline Lambert. Her home was near the City Road, a locality familiar to Charles West from his Finsbury Dispensary days. Knowing the neighbourhood, where the closely packed streets and courts rarely allowed a direct ray of sunlight, and the scanty diet of the poor children living there, he would not have been surprised that Caroline had a bad case of rickets. Her entry is endorsed 'Recovered July 27', which makes it certain that Caroline Lambert was one of the five girls in 'Drooping Buds'.

The likely surmise is that Morley and Dickens (there is no actual documentary evidence that both went nor proof that they did not, but the accuracy and emotional content of the article is in favour of a joint visit) inspected the Hospital and wrote their account soon after 16 March. 'Drooping Buds' appeared in the *Household Words* number dated 3 April 1852, but the issue was actually available a few days before. There is some evidence that Dickens met Morley on 23 March, when they decided on the final shape and made any necessary alterations. The visit to Great Ormond Street could not have been made before 16 March, because only four girls had then been admitted. On the 16th two more girls came in, making a total of six girls since its opening; six boys had also been admitted, so five had come and gone by the time Dickens and Morley were there. There was a gap of ten days before the next child was admitted on the 26th, much too late to fit in with the writing, revision and printing of 'Drooping Buds'.

Martha Davy, who came in with a swollen axillary gland, was only thirteen months old, and nothing in 'Drooping Buds' allows us to think of one of the five girls as still a baby. It is highly probable therefore that the five girls were the Caroline Lambert and Eliza Armstrong already mentioned, plus Emily Harrington, a three-year-old from Marylebone Lane, another three-year-old, Mary Cassin from nearby Woburn Court, and Emily Compton, aged eight, from Upper Ashby Street, very near Goswell Road and the shades of Mr Pickwick and Mrs Bardell – again part of those Finsbury streets and alleys which West knew only too well.

The boy cannot be identified with such certainty – there seems to be no proper record of discharges extant. His description, however, gives a guide. He 'was not in bed and not at rest ... combining into patterns letters of the alphabet ... The solitary child was lonely ... its thoughts were at home ... it had not yet learnt to reconcile itself to temporary separation.' The last admitted boy was Thomas Hawkins, aged six, old enough even in those days of scanty or no education to have an interest in letters of the alphabet. Apart from being the only boy there, his loneliness was perhaps accentuated by the fact – of interest in itself – that his two younger brothers, William and James, had also been among the first patients in the hospital, and he was missing them. It is most likely that Thomas Hawkins was the sixth of the children described in 'Drooping Buds'.

'They had toys strewn upon their counterpane' – perhaps the very ones given by Miss Burdett Coutts. 'A sick child is a contradiction of ideas, like a cold summer. But to quench the summer in a child's heart is, thank God! not easy.' The wonderful courage and spirit of the desperately ill children in Great Ormond Street can be remarked upon today. 'Drooping Buds' shows once again its debt to Charles West's letters and appeals, by repeating the story of the Frankfurt children who beg to be allowed into their hospital's garden again, and using the same turns of expression.

The bathrooms are seen, including those upstairs which served the isolated rooms for fever cases, which have a modern system for ventilation, something in which Bence Jones was always interested. 'We came downstairs again, and passing through the surgery – upon whose jars and bottles our eyes saw many names of compounds, palatable to little mouths, we were shown through an excellent consulting-room, into a wide hall, with another of the massive chimney-pieces.' This was the room for outpatients, originally built for Dr Mead's famous library, and later used for balls and assemblies. The garden steps 'were short, suited to little feet'.

Ten years before, Chadwick in his great *Report* had stressed the children's need for gardens and parks, and the immense benefit to their health and well-being which would derive from the provision of more open spaces. And a year before Chadwick, Dickens in *Barnaby Rudge* had enlarged upon the delight and pleasure that country scenes gave the mentally retarded Barnaby: 'the bright red poppy, the gentle harebell, the cowslip and the rose'. So he was quick to seize upon the symbolism of the garden at Great Ormond Street.

> For means to plant the roses in the garden, and to plant the roses in the cheeks of many children besides those who come under their immediate care, the Hospital Committee has support to find. So large a piece of garden-ground waiting for flowers, only a quarter of a mile from Holborn, was a curious thing to contemplate. When we looked into the dead-house, built for the reception of those children whom skill and care shall fail to save, and heard of the alarm which its erection had excited in the breasts of some 'particular' old ladies in the neighbourhood, we felt inclined to preach some comfort to them. Be of good heart, particular old ladies! In every street, square, crescent, alley, lane, in this great city, you will find dead children too easily. They lie thick all round you. This little tenement will not hurt you; there will be the fewer dead-houses for it; and the place to which it is attached, may bring a saving health upon Queen Square, a blessing on Great Ormond Street.

How wide and great a blessing even the fertile imagination of Charles Dickens could scarcely conceive! 'Drooping Buds' concludes with that paragraph already quoted at length in the preceding chapter. In dwelling upon the debt Great Ormond Street owed to this article, the contribution Henry Morley made should not be forgotten. Morley is another example of the mingled threads which connect the founders of Great Ormond Street. He knew Mrs Gaskell, her Holland cousins and her brother-in-law Dr Samuel Gaskell. Trained for a medical career, Morley had suffered, like Charles West, by the purchase of a share in a doubtful medical practice. In financial difficulties, he wanted to start a school, and as he wrote in his memoirs, 'Friends were soon found, none more cordial and helpful than Mr and Mrs Gaskell. Mrs Gaskell had then just published *Mary Barton*.'

In the minutes of the Committee of Management of The Hospital for Sick Children for 8 April 1852 is recorded the very first acknowledgement of Dickens's services to the Hospital:

That the cordial thanks of this Committee be offered to Charles Dickens Esq. for the very able and interesting manner in which he has given so much additional publicity to this Institution and directed the Hon. Secretary to convey the thanks expressed in such resolution in a letter to Charles Dickens Esq.

—9—

INTO A GREAT COURSE

Sir James Clark, Dr Peter Mere Latham and Dr Thomas Watson, and three laymen, J.W.Percy, Arthur Kinnaird and W.Niven, together with John Labouchere the treasurer, joined in a subcommittee on 14 November 1851 to select and appoint the first medical staff for Great Ormond Street. On 15 December, Dr Latham wrote a letter to the Provisional Committee announcing the choice of Dr Charles West and Dr William Jenner as physicians, and Mr George David Pollock as surgeon.

The appointment of Charles West would seem inevitable and needs no comment. George David Pollock had been active on the Provisional Committee. His aunt, Lady Pollock, had an imposing house in Queen Square, a few yards from Great Ormond Street, and had in the early days been interested in the new children's hospital. The Lord Chief Baron and his son, Frederick Pollock, knew Dickens well, and he in consequence would have met their nephew and first cousin, George Pollock.

Pollock was interested in cleft-palate operations. There was probably very little opportunity for such surgery in the first days of The Hospital for Sick Children. When Pollock became assistant surgeon at St George's Hospital, he feared his increased duties would not allow him to continue at Great Ormond Street and he resigned, although of course his interest remained, and his advice and perhaps even assistance was always readily offered. By 1853 the surgeon to The Hospital for Sick Children was Athol Johnson, who held the post for nine years.

The first Resident or house surgeon was Mr Sydney Lynch. His services came without charge. As described in 'Drooping Buds', he was the 'young house-surgeon' whose name was 'a strange sound' in the ears of the newly engaged hall porter. As the chairman of the committee, Sir Henry Dukinfield, said in the testimonial he wrote on 22 July

1852 when Lynch's agreed term with 'great regret' came to an end:

> The admirable manner in which Mr Lynch has discharged his important duties has obtained for him the respect and kind feeling of all who have been connected with the establishment ... The high professional skill, and great tenderness with which he has uniformly treated his little patients ... will ensure to him a large share of success and reputation in any wider sphere.

Dickens and Morley would have agreed wholeheartedly.

The Hospital's first chairman, the Reverend Sir Henry Robert Dukinfield, had been vicar of St Martin's in the Fields, where he had been noted for his zeal and philanthropic spirit. It was he who was responsible for the bill which allowed public baths to be opened and maintained on the local rates – something of which Dickens would have known and strongly agreed with. A memoir by Lady Dukinfield tells how:

> At the instance of a friend he somewhat reluctantly joined the Committee of The Hospital for Sick Children, which was then in the course of formation. He soon began to take great interest in the institution, and at the urgent request of the same friend became Chairman of the Committee.

The friend is not named, but from other evidence it could be Henry Allen Bathurst or the Hon. J.W.Percy. Dukinfield's last sermon was preached in aid of Great Ormond Street.

Another member of that first committee who, despite some differences over Sunday observance and other Evangelical questions, worked with Dickens on many social reforms, was the Hon. Arthur Kinnaird. He was named after the Duke of Wellington, a family friend. Kinnaird became the 10th Lord Kinnaird and a vice-president of Great Ormond Street. He was publicly held to stand next to Lord Shaftesbury in his concern for social reforms. His wife, Mary Jane Kinnaird, was the daughter of the banker William Henry Hoare, and her activities in promoting many philanthropic schemes and missions led her daughter Emily to deny that her mother in any sense resembled Dickens's Mrs Jellyby. What is curious is that there were ties between the Kinnairds and the Clapham Sect, another Evangelical group, partly through John Labouchere, the Hospital's treasurer.

When Labouchere died, his partner in the bank of Williams, Deacon & Co., Henry Sykes Thornton, took over as Hospital treasurer in 1864. Sykes Thornton was the brother of Marianne Thornton, one of the most zealous members of the Clapham Evangelicals, and *she* was defended against a supposed resemblance to Dickens's Mrs Pardiggle. It is strange that both of Dickens's most effective satires against false charity and missionary work, in *Bleak House*, the very novel on which he was working during the first two years of the Hospital's existence, should thus have some connection with two of its most generous supporters. Nor does it end there. Mr Chadband, that savage portrait of religious hypocrisy, also from *Bleak House*, was held by some indignant Baptists to libel their famous preacher the Honourable and Reverend Baptist W. Noel, in whose Hornsey home his niece Mary Jane Kinnaird had elected to live when a young girl! Baptist Noel, like Dukinfield, preached on behalf of The Hospital for Sick Children. Such ramifications are, however, indeterminable.

William Jenner, with Charles West, did more for Great Ormond Street's sick children than any one else in its early years. He seems to have had no previous contact with the Provisional Committee. Like West he had been apprenticed as a boy to an apothecary, not in a country town but in St Marylebone, London. And there, after qualifying as a licentiate of the Society of Apothecaries in 1837, he started a general practice on his own account. This he relinquished when he graduated as a Doctor of Medicine from the University of London in 1844. In 1848 he became a Member of the Royal College of Physicians and was appointed professor of pathological anatomy at University College, and assistant physician to its hospital. Elected Fellow of the Royal College of Physicians in 1852, the next year he was made assistant physician at the London Fever Hospital, and thus held three active positions whose work all accorded well. It was said that his appointment to The Hospital for Sick Children gave him 'that intimate knowledge of the pathology and treatment of diphtheria for which his name will be famous, a subject in which his published works are still reckoned masterpieces of clinical research'. The lectures on rickets which Jenner delivered at Great Ormond Street contain 'observations concerning the habits of children [which] are veritable masterpieces of word painting'.

Dr William Baly, West's fellow-student at St Bartholomew's, who like him had first attracted professional attention with a translation from the works of the great Johannes Müller, and who was now a valued member of the St Bartholomew's staff, was a member of the Medical Committee at Great Ormond Street from the time the Hospital opened. In 1859 Baly was appointed physician to the Royal Family, as the elderly Sir William Clark had retired in 1860 at the age of seventy-three. But not long afterwards, Baly, considered by many to be the most promising doctor of his generation, was killed in a railway accident, with consequences that were to have a great effect on the relations between the Queen and her Ministers, and almost cause a constitutional crisis.

The Queen and Prince Albert were distressed at Baly's death. Albert wrote '*sehr traurig*' in his diary, not knowing how truly tragic the news was soon to be for him. Baly had inspired great trust in the Prince. Jenner was chosen a few weeks later by Sir James Clark as the replacement, but he lacked the confidence Prince Albert had put in Baly. At the end of the year when Albert fell a victim to typhoid, Jenner, acknowledged authority on the disease though he was, was unable to impose his comparatively recent medical authority on the Prince Consort. Influenced no doubt by Clark, Jenner seemed strangely reluctant actually to name the disease, and thus persuade Prince Albert to abandon his duties and keep to his bed, where perhaps even the inadequate nursing of valet, royal wife and daughter might have saved him. If Baly had been alive, the Prince Consort would have been under much firmer medical discipline and could not have refused. It is impossible to exaggerate the emotional shock the Queen suffered at Albert's death. If it is true that she took her four-year-old daughter Beatrice out of her cot, wrapped her in Albert's nightgown, and lay weeping with her until she fell asleep, it could be evidence of psychological disturbance. Jenner worried over her mental state, perhaps not without reason despite the reservations of some commentators. In the years that followed, when the Queen prolonged her absence from public life, causing great concern to her ministers and the country at large, Jenner was always ready to defend her. Gladstone in particular was publicly frustrated, and privately enraged, by the way in which the Queen shielded herself behind Jenner's medical advice. Gladstone's oft-quoted remark that if Jenner were his doctor, he would very quickly get rid of him, had its origin in this frustration; and Jenner, on his part, did not hesitate – as we know from Ponsonby, the Queen's secretary – to condemn Gladstone in a loud voice, or any others who sought to impose unwelcome duties on the Queen.

Jenner's royal duties had a consequence for Great Ormond Street. He resigned as physician there, but as the Hospital's eleventh annual report stated, 'He still remains a member of the Committee, and has withdrawn neither his good wishes nor his good offices.' One can but surmise what was owed to Jenner's influence in interesting royal patronage for the hospital, particularly that of the Prince and Princess of Wales. On Jenner's appointment, the Queen wrote to her eldest daughter that he was 'a great friend of our poor Dr Baly. He is extremely clever, and has a pleasing clever manner.' When Jenner died, many years later, the Court Circular described him as 'not only a most able physician but a true and devoted friend of Her Majesty's who deeply mourns his loss'.

How quickly Queen Victoria appreciated Jenner's loyalty and sympathetic nature can be seen from another letter to her eldest daughter, the German Crown Princess, written only three weeks after Albert's death. 'I send you a most beautiful little book by Tennyson which is a great comfort to me, which Dr Jenner spoke of to me – which is as if made for my misery.' The little book was, of course, *In Memoriam*.

A month after this, Jenner wrote to Charles West, in reply to an invitation to speak at the forthcoming Hospital anniversary dinner. It was dated from Osbourne, and written on Court mourning paper.

> My dear West,
> It would have afforded me the greatest possible pleasure to have returned thanks for the Medical Officers, but I am not I fear likely to be in London before the 1st of March. I feel I assure you the deepest interest in the Hospital. I believe it to be one of the best and most useful charities in London and I would now and always will do all in my power to promote its interests. As you think the appointment I hold would give weight to my expressions in its favour I am very sorry not to be able to say how high an estimate I attach to the value of the Hospital, the benefits it confers on the poor and its usefulness to Medical Science and so to everyone in the country. But my regret at not being able to stammer out something on these points is repressed by the consciousness that you will say all I would say and (from my lack of powers of speech) more than I shall be able to say and will say it so much better; but I should have been able to say something you cannot say, viz: how much the Hospital owes to you and to that I certainly should have liked to have borne public testimony.
> Yours very truly,
> Wm. Jenner.

As with West, the life of Jenner has never been written of, apart from a few scattered papers. The two doctors had certain things in common, besides their work for the children of Great Ormond Street. They were both strongly opposed to women entering the medical profession, and here Jenner certainly influenced Queen Victoria. In their younger days they had the same capacity for immersing themselves in their work, taking notice of neither public celebration nor national holiday. Jenner had an astounding capacity for work, and once exclaimed: 'Amusements! My amusement is pathological anatomy!' And in the same vein, 'The Derby! When I was a student I no more knew when it was Derby day than when it was Trinity Sunday!'

But their later careers could not have offered a stronger contrast. For the last twenty years of his life West lived in relative obscurity – although always honoured and respected by those who had been his contemporaries – wandering unhappy and ill between London, Nice and Paris. 'For the last few years of his life he suffered much from depression and from anxiety for the welfare of the Children's Hospital, a subject with which his mind was entirely occupied,' wrote his friend Dr R.L.Bowes at the end of an obituary. Jenner was made a baronet by the Queen in 1868, and as Sir William Jenner became the virtual dictator of his profession, president of the Royal College of Physicians from 1881 to 1887. He had great worldly success. When he died, like his friend Sir William Gull, with whom he had saved the Prince of Wales from his father's fate, he left what was almost an unparalleled fortune for a physician of over £300,000. West and Jenner both died in 1898. Whereas *The Times* devoted nearly two full columns to Jenner's obituary, some nine months previously it had given but two score lines to West.

Jenner's character is made elusive by the very glare of the luminaries with whom he shared the last thirty-five years of his life. Moving among royalty and in the shadow of Gladstone, Disraeli and others, perhaps it is in his connection with Great Ormond Street that we get a sight of the real Jenner. He was popular for his joviality and wit. Some of the anecdotes that Ponsonby, (Queen Victoria's secretary), perhaps a prejudiced witness, relates illustrate this. Children took to him, and many of the little patients glimpsed in this book, it must be remembered, received his care and concern. Charles West had a favourite story which from the circumstances of time, place and incident could only relate to Jenner, whose looks were not exactly prepossessing. One little boy, after being kindly and tenderly examined many times, took hold of Jenner's hand – 'little fingers,' as West said, 'not yet grown to the strength of after life put into our hands, and telling more than words could do' – fondly gazed into his face and exclaimed, 'You are so like my daddy!' Jenner was touched and flattered until he saw the boy's father who was 'most villainously ill-looking'. But he still, as West remembered, 'treasured up the thanks so given' and valued them as highly as any compliment received from the great ones of the world. And later, at Court, he would carefully check over the toys bought by the Queen and her family for Great Ormond Street every Christmas, to make sure that they would do no harm to the tiny patients.

Jenner received the spontaneous love and trust often given by children and animals. It was he who persuaded Queen Victoria to consent to the regulation and control of vivisection. There are two charming anecdotes of his love for animals. A colleague described how, when Jenner entered his London garden, the dusty town sparrows would flutter around him confidingly, knowing it was Jenner's great delight to feed them. He encouraged them by providing nesting places, nailing the boxes into place himself. And another colleague remembered how when several doctors held a number of consultations at the home of one of Jenner's old patients, a few minutes after the doctors had gathered for their conference the little collie of the house would trot into the room carrying a ball in her mouth, and Jenner always made time to play with her.

In some ways this resembles Dickens's delight and interest in Grip the raven and his successors, and in the many dogs that entered his life. After Great Ormond Street had opened, Dickens was mainly occupied with *Bleak House* until the summer of 1853, when it was completed at Boulogne. Wilkie Collins, who was to have a considerable influence on Dickens in their amateur theatricals, as a writer of tales, and as a new friend encouraging Dickens to a recovered sense of freedom, joined him at Boulogne. Like Dickens, Wilkie Collins understood children; some of the child characters in his novels are delightful little studies. At Boulogne that summer he and Dickens threw themselves wholeheartedly into preparations for a local children's fête. Wilkie described to his brother how for an entrance fee of about five pence an orchestra of forty players was provided, with thousands of lamps glittering in the dusk, various amusements such as sack races, greasy poles, donkey races, fireworks, balloons and a lottery. 'The children danced on the grass with the grown people sitting round them.' This was something they could enjoy nearer home if their 'stupid dignity' would allow it.

Wilkie Collins refers to Great Ormond Street in one of his later novels, *The Haunted Hotel*. Mrs Ferrari in London looks upon a £1000 banknote, sent her as compensation for the mysterious death of her courier husband in Venice, as stained with her husband's blood. It is finally given 'to the Children's Hospital' to add to the number of its beds. About the time this story was written Great Ormond Street had indeed been the recipient of several donations of £1000, sent anonymously, and probably by a rich eccentric recluse living near Rochester. A newspaper report on his death concluded, 'A thousand-pound note was found lying about the room as if it had been waste-paper.'

In 1854 *Fraser's Magazine* published an article, 'A visit to The Hospital for Sick Children'. It is possible that this was arranged by Athol Johnson, who had replaced George Pollock as surgeon there. It starts with the story of a case which was a strong justification for the Hospital's existence, throwing light on the conditions in which even the more industrious and fortunate of the poor lived.

> Not long since, a poor child, seven or eight years old, came under the writer's notice; she was thin and haggard, her eyes sunk, her face sallow, the glands of her throat enlarged, many of them forming open sores. She was under medical treatment, but still remained the same, or, if anything, got worse. At last we resolved to visit her at her own home. In a small back room, on the third floor, with a smokey chimney, and a suffocating atmosphere, we found the whole family. In one corner was the father at work, as a tailor, with two or three companions; in another was the mother, engaged at the wash-tub ... the remainder of the apartment was occupied by an old bed, in which lay, sprawling, four children,

including the little patient. This single room, miserably ventilated as it was, constituted the sole dwelling of the whole family.

The child was removed to the hospital [Great Ormond Street]; under the influence of fresh air, proper food, and the same medical treatment before adopted, she was well in three weeks.

Do not think this is an extreme case: it occurred in one of the best parts of London – in the parish of St George, Hanover Square.

The article is especially interesting for its description of some of the Great Ormond Street patients. Here is a picture of some of the convalescent children in the garden, which had evidently been tidied up since Dickens's visit two years before.

One merry young gentleman was trundling a hoop under difficulties – running after it with the assistance of a crutch: one of the little fellow's legs was, we learned, some inches shorter than the other, owing to severe disease of the hip.

Two or three laughing girls, hanging in a circle to a round-about, had just recovered from some serious affection of the chest ... A little boy, very pale, very delicate, and very sedate, seated on a bench ... told us that he had a bad knee – that he was better – that he did not know how long he had been ill, but he thought a very long time ... he had been in much danger of losing his leg, but happily it had been preserved to him.

A little further on, we came across a wee thing promenading in a dot-and-go-one fashion, with the aid of a nurse ... She was beginning to move again after an attack of paralysis.

An amputation case in the girls' ward follows, a child who would be Athol Johnson's patient and special care.

Not a single cry greeted our entrance. The kind looks of the nurses were responded to by a gentle and confiding air on the part of the patients ... In a corner bed, placed apart ... was a very pretty girl, pale, rather wan, but with a face having a sweet and interesting expression ... One of her legs had been amputated, a day or two previously, owing to incurable disease about the ankle. She was an orphan; and the timid, yet gentle manner in which she related her sufferings, and expressed her gratitude for all that had been done, was perfectly affecting.

And finally the boys' ward:

Still the same absence of peevishness and wailing; though, perhaps, a little more noisy merriment. Even a poor little fellow in a corner bed, with contracted limbs, who had recently undergone some operation ... was busily engaged ... with wooden bricks, to the wonder and amusement of a boy near him, who appeared to have only one eye ... Sculling himself along the floor, in a new-fashioned kind of go-cart, was another young gentleman ... to the intense delight of a small circle of patients, who were watching his progress, with as much interest as if they had heavy stakes depending on the result.

A few years later George August Sala, who worked with Dickens on *Household Words*, wrote a description of Great Ormond Street for another journal. In many ways the Hospital is best understood through the children themselves, in such fascinating and moving little scenes. The time of Sala's visit would have been very near that of Dickens's 1858 speech. Like most visitors, Sala found the girls' ward first.

Some wistful eyes followed us as a comely young nurse ... led me round the girls' ward; but in very many cases, alas! the little sufferers let us go by with listless mournful unnotice. One poor child, coiled up almost into a ball among the bed-clothes, could not bear the light ... and was always shrouding herself thus; another, covered with dreadful cutaneous sores, lay stark and rigid ... The nurse told me that this child was getting better wonderfully, and that hers was a very hopeful case indeed. The children were all in iron-work cribs ... with a sliding board on the top-rails, which ... formed an excellent play-table and platform for its toys. And its toys! ... The mantelpieces of the hospital – boys' ward and girls' ward – were covered; the cupboards were full, the tables and beds were sprinkled with toys. None of your penny monkeys that run up sticks ... but sound, honest toys ...

There was a case of typhoid fever, another of croup, a very sad one of rheumatism, but the most painful was a 'starvation' case. The child had been received a few days previously, in almost a dying state, from inanition and neglect, due ... more to the extreme and hideous poverty than to the cruelty of its parents. The face was like a diminutive death's head. The nurse drew up one sleeve of the child's bedgown, and showed me ... a bone just covered with integument. 'Lor', sir,' she said in answer to an expression of horror, 'it's getting quite plump to what it was a week ago.'

Sala draws a grimmer picture than most. The description of the boys' ward is very brief.

The boys were rather more lively ... two or three, who were convalescent, were clinging to the nurses' skirts. More were sitting up in bed, and one was playing in a most animated manner with a kitten. All who were able to do so, greeted us with a little airy wave of the hand that was full of genuine courtesy. Little children are little gentlemen.

... the nurses seemed full of gentleness and tenderness towards their infant charges, and there were not wanting some unmistakable indices on the part of the children themselves to show how lovingly grateful they were for the care and trouble bestowed upon them . . . Mrs Sairey Gamp and Mrs Betsy Prig . . . had no abiding place here.

In the October of 1854 a crisis came to a head at Great Ormond Street. In that month Dr Charles West sent a letter of resignation to the Committee of Management. It would seem that the dramatic increase in the number of outpatients had put an intolerable strain on the Hospital's small medical staff. In 1852 the total number of new outpatients was 1250; by 1853 it had reached 4251; and in 1854 it was to reach 6721. The number of actual appointments would, of course, have been considerably higher. As the Medical Committee had reported for 1853:

> In the autumnal months, when Diarrhoea was prevalent, and Cholera apprehended, as many as 146 new Out Patients have been admitted in a single week; and the attendances of old and new together have been nearly 710 [outpatients in the week] . . . total attendance, during four consecutive weeks of the autumn amounted to within a few of 2400.

With the number of beds still restricted to thirty, the inpatients had not increased so dramatically. Between 1852 and 1854 they had risen from 143 to 251. 'The full number of beds has been constantly occupied, and many parents have anxiously waited for vacant beds for their sick children.' Another passage in the second annual report illustrates the contrast the children found between the grimness and poverty of their homes and the comfort and relative plenty of The Hospital for Sick Children – 'The children themselves will even desire to remain, when they are sufficiently convalescent to return to their own homes.'

Charles West wanted the appointment of extra medical staff to help with a flood of outpatients that was overwhelming him and his colleagues. Henry Allen Bathurst, always ready to play the diplomat's role, wrote to West, pointing out that any disagreement between him and the lay members of the committee did not imply an aspersion as to his professional ability. It was reactions such as these on the part of West that probably gave rise to his reputation as a difficult colleague, oversensitive to criticism. But the impatience of medical men with the suggestions of administrators and directions from Whitehall is something we are too familiar with today, and not without reason. At the end of that October in 1854, Dr William Baly put forward a motion, 'That the Medical Committee recommend to the Managing Committee the appointment of Two Assistant Physicians to attend the Out Patients conjointly with the Physicians'. Dr Jenner had also supported a suggestion that the Medical Committee be merged with the Committee of Management because 'it is impossible for the Medical Committee always to embody in the compass of Resolution the various reasons on which their suggestions are based.' As both his apparent objectives had now been achieved, West withdrew his resignation.

What must be remembered is the background to these events of October 1854. The famous despatches from W.H.Russell, the war correspondent of *The Times*, had just exposed the shocking conditions in the Crimea. Florence Nightingale was gathering together her pioneer band of thirty-eight nurses, and left for Scutari that month. No doubt certain members of Great Ormond Street's Managing Committee felt that it behoved it to be cautious, as the war would bring hard times in its wake. They were not far wrong.

The two new assistant physicians were Dr C.Metcalfe Babington and Dr J.Russell Reynolds. Metcalfe Babington was to do much for Great Ormond Street. Many of his private patients, whom he saw at his consulting rooms in Hertford Street, Mayfair, were both rich and socially eminent. He became a full physician to the Hospital but was himself early stricken with a fatal disease.

One of Metcalfe Babington's last activities was arranging a benefit amateur theatrical performance at Campden House, Kensington in June 1860. At the same place five years before, Charles Dickens had produced Wilkie Collins's play *The Lighthouse* in aid of the Bournemouth Sanatorium for Consumptives. Babington's play was James Kenney's farce, *Fighting by Proxy*. It was announced as 'Under the immediate patronage of Her Majesty the Queen' and the list of lady patronesses included five duchesses, Countess Grey, Viscountess Palmerston, Baroness Mayer de Rothschild, and Lady de Rothschild, to name but a few. The performance raised £362.

Dr John Russell Reynolds was to have a longer and illustrious career, becoming president of the Royal College of Physicians, and created a baronet in 1895. The *Lancet*'s obituary for Jenner called particular attention to the fact that when at Great Ormond Street Jenner's junior colleague was Russell Reynolds. In a way Russell Reynolds was to be the very last link between Great Ormond Street and Charles Dickens: he was the London specialist who came down to Gad's Hill when Dickens had his fatal stroke.

In 1856, Samuel Cartwright Jr was appointed surgeon dentist to The Hospital for Sick Children. Dickens was his friend and patient. He and his father, also one of the most famous dentists of his generation, were largely responsible for the founding of the Royal Dental Hospital. The Cartwright dinners in Old Burlington Street were famous for the attendance of nearly all who were celebrated in science, art and literature. Dickens of course often went to them, but his friendship was really with the son, who was of his generation. George Eliot, in the second chapter of *Middlemarch*, makes Mr Brooke say, 'Sir Humphrey Davey: I dined with him years ago at Cartwright's, and Wordsworth was there too.' After the elder Cartwright had retired, Samuel Cartwright Jr was several times at Gad's Hill, and Dickens at Old Burlington Street. Quite a few of Dickens's letters to the younger Cartwright survive, of which only one or two have been partially published. They include some of Dickens's rueful comments on the difficulties he had with his dentures while on his American reading tour. There is no doubt that the friendship between them was closer than has been assumed. From Gad's Hill, Dickens writes, 'A line at any time to say you are coming will be sure to find a room ready for you, and me delighted to expect you. This county is really beautiful when the corn and hops are growing.'

Samuel Cartwright Jr was an old colleague of Charles West at the Royal Universal Infirmary for Children at Waterloo Road. They also had a close family relationship, as West's wife, Mary Hester Cartwright was his first cousin. At those celebrated dinners, at which Dickens was a guest, it would seem likely that old Samuel Cartwright would have invited on more than one occasion his niece and her husband, the doctor who was so interested in children, to meet the famous novelist, the supreme depictor of children and their great champion!

The difficulties the Hospital for Sick Children found in funding the institution, even on the very modest scale of the first few years, are seen in the comments made in its annual reports, the tone of which grew more urgent every year. The Crimean War had increased the cost of living, and this and other causes brought about a serious economic and banking crisis in 1857. Between 1853 and 1855 Great Ormond Street's expenditure rose: meat from £192 to £201; bread and flour, £65 to £88; cheese and butter, £43 to £57; milk, £46 to £49; grocery, £17 to £19; soap, candles, coals, wood and gas, £75 to £147. Medical supplies, i.e. the dispensary, drugs and surgical instruments, rose from £204 to £310. Some of these increases were due to the rising number of outpatients, and the annual reports over this period increased their pleas:

> The Hospital for Sick Children is no longer an experiment ... it has conferred incalculable blessings upon many thousands of sick and helpless Children; it has saved from a life of deformity many who were growing up under grievous bodily afflictions; it has preserved many lives; it has caused many a parent's heart to leap for joy ... May we not ask the especial sympathy of every parent, of every mother; may we not entreat those whose children, in a time of sickness, are treated with every comfort and alleviation which riches can procure, that they should cherish a compassionate regard for the children of their poorer brethren, who are sickening and dying around them?

A year after Dickens died, Charles West enlarged upon this plea when seeking to raise funds for the new hospital building which had been his constant dream and hope. His words show how close together were his and Dickens's thoughts on this question. Dickens, if he had still been alive, would have been proud to see West's words. It seems almost as if West said what he knew Dickens would have said, what he had often said, but words now emphasized by West's own unique knowledge, authority and experience.

> We cannot leave the children still in the crowded streets of London, in the ill-ventilated courts, in those places which members of our profession, like the members of the clerical profession, know too well, are but the hotbeds of disease whence it is propagated all through the neighbourhood, so that which arose at first in the neglect of the rich, comes at last to be their scourge. We cannot leave them there for this reason, that where illness does not end in death it ends in life-long sickness, and sickness amongst the poor is often worse than death.

—10—

THE DINNER AND THE SPEECH

When Dickens described in one of his 'Boz' London sketches the typical Victorian function, a public dinner, he little knew that in a very few years he himself would be the principal at many of these gatherings at which he had poked such gentle fun. The Cruikshank etching for the collected *Sketches by Boz* which illustrates 'Public Dinners' was strangely prophetic. It shows in jest the handsome young Dickens walking in procession with the stewards and surrounded by the children of the imaginary 'Indigent Orphans' Friends Benevolent Institution'. The Great Ormond Street dinner took place twenty-three years after the 'Boz' sketch first appeared, but the nature, function and arrangements of such dinners had changed little. Even the venue was still the same, the Freemasons' Hall in Great Queen Street. And, no doubt, on the evening of 9 February 1858, a crowd was still waiting outside the door, the crowd 'Boz' had described as waiting 'to witness the entrance of the indigent orphans' friends'. In 1858, however, Dickens would have been immediately recognized as taking the part of 'the noble Lord who is announced to fill the chair on the occasion'; there was little likelihood of his hearing 'it eventually decided that you are only a "wocalist"'.

'Boz' described the 'long tables for the less distinguished guests, with a cross table on a raised platform at the upper end for . . . the very particular friends of the indigent orphans'. This arrangement hardly changed, and many other things described by 'Boz' were almost the same at the Hospital dinner: the toastmaster, the vocalists, the ladies' gallery – 'the charity is always peculiarly favoured in this respect', the chairman's toast to the Queen and other 'loyal and patriotic toasts', and 'the most important toast of the evening – Prosperity to the Charity'. No doubt the menu itself was not much different. Henry Bathurst, whom we earlier surmised as recognizing a familiar scene and role in the description by 'Boz' of Doctors' Commons, perhaps remembered at the Hospital dinner that his present role as honorary secretary had also been described by the chairman when writing as 'Boz' all those years ago: 'After a short interval, occupied in singing and toasting, the secretary puts on his spectacles, and proceeds to read the report and list of subscriptions, the latter being listened to with great attention.'

Much nearer to the foundation of Great Ormond Street, Mark Lemon, like his old friend 'Boz', 'attempted to extract some amusement from a charity dinner'. Lemon's 'Recollections of a Charity Dinner, by a visitor to the Ladies' Gallery' also took place at the Freemasons' Hall or Tavern, as it was indiscriminately called. Its point of view, from the ladies' gallery, gave a new perspective of comedy and information, and being so much nearer the year of the Hospital dinner is of particular interest. The stewards still hold long wands to attend the chairman as he enters the hall, as depicted by Cruikshank and described by 'Boz'. The list of stewards at the Great Ormond Street function was so extensive that it seems most unlikely that they all solemnly marched in this fashion, escorting Dickens to the head table. Did a select band thus accompany him? The names of the stewards at the 1858 Great Ormond Street dinner are a roll-call of those who were active supporters of The Hospital for Sick Children and members of Charles Dickens's circle. It is by itself one of the most powerful documents illustrating Dickens's personal involvement with Great Ormond Street and his influence upon its progress.

Lemon's narrator, Laura Rubbleton, describes her dinner in a letter to her mother, and is bewildered by much of what happens. She is particularly baffled by the chairman and his speech. 'Lord Beeswing – a most liberal man they say, for he never misses a charity dinner if he can help it.' It is possible that Shaftesbury was the intended target here. Despite Lemon's more farcical view of a public dinner as compared with the gentle humour of the earlier 'Boz', there are many details which help us to picture the actual scene when Dickens spoke for Great Ormond Street.

There is, for instance, the grace, sung 'by a party of vocalists in the middle of the room', and other musical episodes. The book of words for the vocal music sung at Dickens's dinner still survives. A grace by W. Baley; the national anthem; glees by Hopkins, Novello, Bishop and from the German; songs and ballads by Hobbs, Cummings, Winn and Balfe (the perennial 'Come into the Garden, Maud') were all sung by a male quartet. Signor Errico Bianchi and his sister performed on the piano during the evening. The musicians' fees totalled twelve guineas.

Mark Lemon's Laura does not enjoy her evening: 'Never go to the Ladies' Gallery at a Public Dinner. It's so tantalizing to see all the men stuffing and drinking when you are feeling ready to famish with hunger or die with thirst.' Dr West and Great Ormond Street were a little more considerate of their lady patrons in the gallery, but the provision made was still very slight compared with the formal dinner for the gentlemen. After some bargaining over refreshments for the ladies, at a cost of six shillings a head – apparently the Ladies' Gallery at the Welsh Schools Festival had only cost three shillings a head – the caterers offered 'Tea and Coffee, Cakes, Ices, Oranges, Sandwiches, with Port and Sherry Negus' at the desired three shillings. The ladies were not expected to pay for these refreshments. The custom at these dinners was usually for the ladies to enter the gallery towards the end of the meal, but in time for the loyal toast and the speeches. The minute book of Great Ormond Street's Dinner Committee for 1858 provides what may be a rare insight into the preparations necessary for such an event, although it would seem that a modern committee arranging a hospital dinner today would be faced with much the same anxieties and decisions as Dr West and his colleagues.

The first meeting of the Dinner Committee was held at Charles West's house at 96 Wimpole Street. West was in the chair; Edward Futvoye, Dr Baly, Dr Jenner, Athol Johnson, Samuel Cartwright Jr, Dr Babington and Henry Bathurst were also present. Once again, at an important crisis in the history of Great Ormond Street, the names of those who had been active since its inception recur. Dr Bence Jones's name was lacking: he had rarely attended the Committee of Management during the past year. He was to be one of the stewards at the dinner, however. This meeting of 25 November 1857 came first to a resolution that was to be of the utmost importance not only in the history of The Hospital for Sick Children but for Dickens himself: 'It was Resolved, That Charles Dickens Esq. be requested to preside at the proposed Dinner: and also That S. Cartwright Esq. be deputed to convey the desire of the Committee.'

After fixing the stewards' liability at one guinea, and determining that February of the next year would be the most convenient time for the dinner, Dr West was asked to 'prepare a form of Letter to be sent very generally to members of the Medical Profession in Town; and to many in the Country'. He was also asked to draft a letter to the governors of Great Ormond Street, and to the public, and an advertisement. As he said many years later, West personally penned nearly all the appeals that went forth from The Hospital for Sick Children. How speedily West worked can be seen from a printed page proof of the letter to the medical profession, which was inserted in the minutes before the next meeting. The proof is dated December 1857, and signed by Bathurst. The day in February is left open, but that the dinner was to be held at the Freemasons' Tavern, and that Dickens had agreed to preside, was already settled.

The letter begins by referring to the appeal of nearly eight years before urging the establishment of a children's hospital, which was sent 'to nearly every Practitioner in the Kingdom'. Mention is made 'of the daughter institutions at Norwich, at Liverpool, and at Manchester' as evidence that the need for a children's hospital was a real one. The happy historical coincidence of Great Ormond Street being 'a house that, a century ago, had belonged to the great Physician, Dr Mead . . . seemed a good omen for the future'.

A Hospital for Sick Children 'with only 31 beds is quite unequal to supply the wants of the poor', but the original proposal of one with one hundred beds needed more abundant funds. In fact, 'the Hospital has been maintained to the present time only by a yearly diminution of the nearly exhausted Capital Stock of the charity.' Although not mentioned in this circular letter, Great Ormond Street's capital had been reduced to less than £1000. Room was also needed for a museum, and for 'a Library of Works on Diseases of Children, which has been presented to the Hospital, and waits only for suitable accommodation to be transferred thither'. This was West's own library, which was eventually given to Great Ormond Street in 1875 after the new building was first opened; it had been promised as early as 1857. Other arrangements for 'the advancement of medical knowledge, and thereby to the good of mankind', including 'the instruction of Nurses in the management of Sick Children', all needed and awaited 'ampler accommodation'. The letter concludes with a plea for help in these objectives and the formation of a Building and an Endowment Fund by becoming a Steward and attending the Dinner. 'But should distance or other causes prevent your compliance with their request, the Committee trust . . . you might confer the greatest benefit on the charity by explaining its objectives and advocating its claims among your patients.'

The Hospital for Sick Children was in real danger of closing because of inadequate financial support. The country's economic crisis of the past year had reduced the flow of donations and subscriptions. The feeble cry of the sick poor children of London was lost in the clamour of existing good causes. If the voice of Charles Dickens had not been raised again on its behalf, Great Ormond Street's doors, which had opened with such hope and vision a few years before, would have been shut against the mother hurrying from the neighbouring courts and alleys with a desperately ill child in her arms.

The fact that 'daughter institutions' had been opened at Norwich, Manchester and Liverpool was a shrewd argument in an appeal to medical men in town and in the country. As Lord Carlisle was to say in his 1859 speech for the Hospital, 'This institution shows that directly provision was afforded the highest medical knowledge and science was anxious to run in and fill the gap.' These other children's hospitals had indeed been founded directly because of Great Ormond Street's example. The great singer, Jenny Lind, had given a charity performance at Norwich, raising a considerable sum for the poor of that city. While the committee was considering how best to use these funds, their attention was drawn to the newly opened children's hospital. Great Ormond Street's second annual report, for 1853, remarked on this, and how 'Drooping Buds' had helped others beside themselves:

> It is with great satisfaction that your Committee have heard of another good result which has followed the establishment of your Hospital. In consequence of the appeal in Mr Dickens's 'Household Words', chiefly through the generous benevolence of one Lady, decided measures have been adopted for the establishment of a similar Hospital in the City of Norwich.

Dickens was a great admirer of Jenny Lind, whom he met socially on several occasions, and this must have given him particular satisfaction. Nor should it be forgotten that Otto and Madame Goldschmidt (Jenny Lind and her husband) shortly afterwards appeared in Great Ormond Street's subscription list as contributing the by no means negligible sum of thirty pounds.

Later Dr West was to claim, 'Our first born, if I may so say, was the hospital at Norwich; and, as you have heard, the gentle woman, the sweet singer, Jenny Lind, stood sponsor for it.'

Manchester's children's hospital also owed its establishment to the influence of Dr West's example, and perhaps to another famous lady greatly admired by Charles Dickens. Mrs Gaskell, when she sent in 1850 Dr West's papers to her friend Lady Kay-Shuttleworth, added: 'You will be glad to hear that before Christmas, a trial public nursery will be established in Manchester; the subject is taken up very warmly.' By none was it taken up more warmly than by Mrs Gaskell herself. It was from her urging and early knowledge of Charles West's proposed children's hospital that the movement which opened public nurseries in Manchester soon developed, fortified by Great Ormond Street's success, into the foundation of a children's hospital there.

It is illuminating and chastening to find that these newer children's hospitals were soon in a much stronger and sounder financial position than Great Ormond Street, which, as West said in 1872, was outstripped already 'by a daughter institution . . . they are building at Manchester a children's hospital on a large site'. He claimed the secret of this sudden rapid growth was the habit Manchester people had of filling up cheques for their hospital 'with three figures instead of two'. Dr West recommended this habit to the London gentlemen. 'Or, still better I think it would be if they would sign their names, and hand the blank cheques to the ladies to fill up.'

It was at the second meeting of the Dinner Committee, on 1 December 1857, that Samuel Cartwright announced that Dickens had 'kindly consented to take the Chair on the occasion of the Dinner'. Four days later the committee accepted a tender from the Freemasons' Hall for dinner, desert, Moselle, sherry, port, champagne and coffee at 20 shillings a head, on the understanding that waiters and ices were included in the charge. On 8 December (the committee was meeting very frequently) Cartwright was asked to 'wait on Charles Dickens, Esq., and invite his inspection of the Hospital prior to the Dinner, and to request the favour of a short letter from him, to be lithographed for issue'. Ten days later Cartwright, although absent, sent a note received from Dickens 'desiring to be excused writing any note for issue in lithographed form'.

By the end of the year Bathurst was able to announce that a 'Total of upwards of 2100 Letters, including 531 Reports have been sent out'. One result of this was that the names of 117 stewards could now be listed. In the end 153 names, many eminent, were to be printed.

There were sixteen noblemen, judges and Members of Parliament, including Lord Shaftesbury, Lord John Manners, the Lord Chief Baron Pollock and the Hon. Arthur Kinnaird, all associates of Dickens. Next are listed the sixty-six gentlemen who do not qualify for the first group. Of these the Reverend William Harness and the Reverend W. Tennant are particularly of Dickens's circle. Harness was one of the small group of intimates to whom Dickens read *The Chimes* at Forster's house. A steward who was an even greater friend of Dickens was W. C. Macready, the famous actor. We know he was not present, but he was to be a steward at more than one Great Ormond Street dinner in the future. And of course many of the faithful Great Ormond Street supporters from the committees and meetings were also listed. Lastly, seventy-one medical men are given their own section. Again, apart from old friends of the Hospital, there are names which have a special significance for Dickens, such as Dr H. Monro, Dr Richard Quain and Dr J. Connolly. John Connolly formed an important link between Charles Dickens and Charles West. His close connections and friendship with Dickens are well known. What is not remembered is that Charles West was greatly interested in the mental disorders of childhood and some of his conclusions and interpretations were in agreement with Connolly, whom he often consulted. This section of the stewards' list is of especial interest. As the Hospital's annual report for 1858 was to emphasize, 'thanks are due in an especial manner to the members of the Medical Profession . . . 71 of their number, among whom were the most distinguished Physicians and Surgeons in England, officiating as Stewards at the Festival.'

There were quite a few stewards as well as Macready who did not attend the dinner, as they lived too far away. It is frustrating not to know who actually came. According to the very first printing by the Hospital of the 'Speech of Charles Dickens, Esq.', about 150 sat down to dinner and 'Later in the evening all the seats in the gallery were filled with ladies interested in the success of the Hospital.' This is the same as the number of stewards, but not everyone at the dinner was a steward, although it is possible that the majority were. There are one or two fascinating questions about the unnamed guests. Complimentary, or sealed, tickets were issued, and the list is headed by 'The Friends of Charles Dickens, Esq.' and next by 'W.M.Thackeray Esq.', the prominence given to the two novelists being most interesting. There is nothing to show that Thackeray actually attended, but there is nothing we know that would have prevented him. It was well before his estrangement from Dickens. Mutual acquaintances such as Pollock and Russell Sturgis were there. Only a few weeks before, Thackeray and his daughters had spent Christmas at Russell Sturgis's grand country house. The tickets for the press arouse more positive speculation, as we find that one was sent to *The Examiner* for Forster. Of all Dickens's biographers, Forster gives most prominence to his Great Ormond Street speech and reading. His description of the effect produced by Dickens at the Hospital dinner, is surely written from personal experience.

> Dickens threw himself into the service heart and soul. There was a simple pathos in his address from the chair quite startling in its effect at such a meeting: and he probably never moved any audience so much as by the strong personal feeling with which he referred to the sacrifices made for the Hospital by the very poor themselves . . . The whole speech, indeed, is the best of the kind spoken by him.

And Dickens's words, spoken on that night, still have the power today, as the Wishing Well Appeal showed, to awaken a response for Great Ormond Street in every corner of the land and far overseas.

It was on 18 January 1858 that the Dinner Committee again asked Cartwright to fix a definite appointment for Dickens to visit the Hospital and to ascertain whether there were 'any friends of Mr C.Dickens' to whom he would 'desire Tickets to be sent'. It was in the following week, on 25 January, that sealed tickets were allocated, and although no date was recorded for Dickens's visit it could be that Cartwright had an answer to the query about tickets. It is curious that the actual date of Dickens's visit seems not to have been recorded anywhere by the Dinner Committee, nor in any of the other Hospital minutes. The customary time for the chairman at a charity dinner to visit the institution for which he would plead was the day before the event or on the morning of the dinner. And no doubt Dickens followed this customary procedure as he did on other occasions.

The committee on 25 January also settled the toasts to be given at the dinner. There was one novel loyal toast. After the Queen, the Prince Consort and the Royal Family, the minutes list 'The Prince and Princess Fredk. William of Prussia'. On that very morning, the Queen's eldest daughter, Princess Victoria, had married the Prussian prince who would become the ill-fated and short-reigning Emperor. The ceremony took place in the Chapel Royal, St James's, where, almost exactly eighteen years before, her mother had married Prince Albert. For the Queen, her first-born's wedding was an event that ranked with her own. The public enthusiasm could be seen in the cheering crowds before Buckingham Palace when the newly married pair appeared on the celebrated balcony. Some of the day's excitement seems to have transmitted itself to Bathurst, who, in writing the minutes, forgot and had to squeeze in the names 'Fredk. William'.

At the dinner itself, a fortnight later, Dickens was able to use the wedding in a neat compliment to the Queen, when proposing the loyal toast:

> It was a most happy coincidence that her patronage should be extended just as she was about to part with her eldest child; and it was most important the example of supporting such an institution should be set by a mother who was a Queen, and moreover a Queen whose example had always been for the advancement of charity, and exercised for the good of her people.

The newspaper report describes the reference to the newly married princess as being greeted with cheers. Dickens was not to know that the new Prussian princess was herself to become, and remain, a staunch patron of the Hospital. As Crown Princess of Prussia she visited Great Ormond Street with her sister-in-law the Princess of Wales. She never failed to think of the children's hospital whenever she revisited England; as late as 1898 the name of Victoria, Dowager Empress Frederick, is found in the visitors' book.

On the first day of February, the Dinner Committee received a letter from Messrs Reed, Robesan and Co. and agreed to 'their engagement at a Fee of Three Guineas, to furnish a verbatim Report of the speeches of the Chairman; with condensed notes of the other speeches at the

Dinner'. It was Thomas Allen Reed himself who actually took the shorthand report. With hindsight, the three-guinea fee was the best investment the Hospital ever made. When Charles West and his colleagues invited Dickens to be chairman, they expected to have a speech somewhat above the level normal on such occasions. What they heard, to their intense surprise and delight, was the greatest speech he ever made.

George Eliot, long before she became known as a novelist, saw Dickens acting as a chairman at a meeting in 1852 in support of the editor of the *Westminster Review*. Her account, which is unflattering and not well known, may present a more accurate picture than other more fulsome descriptions. 'Dickens in the chair – a position he fills remarkably well, preserving a courteous neutrality of eyebrow, and speaking with clearness and decision. His appearance is certainly disappointing ... not distinguished looking in any way – neither handsome nor ugly, neither fat nor thin, neither tall nor short.' But at the time of the Dickens dinner in February 1858, George Eliot had received his letter in praise of her *Scenes of Clerical Life*, and was saying, 'There can hardly be any climax of approbation for me after this.' After hearing his speech, The Hospital for Sick Children felt exactly the same.

> It is one of my rules in life not to believe a man who may happen to tell me that he feels no interest in children ... I know, as we all must, that any heart which could really toughen its affections and sympathies against those dear little people must be wanting in so many humanizing experiences of innocence and tenderness, as to be quite an unsafe monstrosity among men ...
>
> I suppose it may be taken for granted that we, who come together in the name of children, and for the sake of children, acknowledge that we have an interest in them; indeed, I have observed since we sat down here that we are quite in a childlike state altogether, representing an infant institution, and not even yet a grown-up company. A few years are necessary to the increase of our strength and the expansion of our figure; and then these tables, which now have a few tucks in them, will be let out, and then this hall, which now sits so easily upon us, will be too tight and small for us.

It was this allusion to the empty chairs left at the lower end of the room when the diners moved up to hear Dickens which aroused some comment on the sparse attendance. The Freemasons' Hall, although by no means overcrowded, was not really so empty for a hospital dinner. Many chairmen after Dickens would speak to smaller audiences. The real purpose of the dinner, raising funds and increasing public awareness of the Hospital, was only bettered in the matter of money by the Prince of Wales in 1870.

> Nevertheless, it is likely that even we are not without our experience now and then of spoilt children. I do not mean of our own spoilt children, because nobody's own children were ever spoilt, but I mean the disagreeable children of our particular friends. We know by experience what it is to have them down after dinner, and across the rich perspective of a miscellaneous dessert, to see, as in a black dose darkly, the family doctor looming in the distance. We know ... what it is to assist at those little maternal anecdotes and table entertainments ... We know what it is when those children won't go to bed ... when they become fractious, they say aloud ... our nose is too long ... We are perfectly acquainted with those kicking bundles which are carried off at last protesting. An eminent eye-witness told me that he was one of the company of learned pundits who assembled at the house of a very distinguished philosopher of the last generation, to hear him expound his stringent views concerning infant education and early mental development, and he told me that, while the philosopher did this in very beautiful and lucid language, the philosopher's little boy, for his part, edified the assembled sages by dabbling up to the elbows in an apple pie ... having previously anointed his head with syrup, combed it with his fork, and brushed it with his spoon.

Three years later Mr Pocket in *Great Expectations* is described as 'a most delightful lecturer on domestic economy and his treatises on the management of children and servants were considered the very best text-books on these themes'. Previously the egregiously inept management by Mrs Pocket of their four little girls, two boys and a baby, and of the cook and servants was related at length, introduced by their neighbour, Mrs Coiler, making 'admiring comments' on the children's 'eyes, noses, and legs'. Up to now, Dickens's speech had been frequently punctuated by laughter and cheers. From this point the mood is changed – the serious part of the evening is at hand and the picture is painted in darker colours, the emotional appeal rises to its height in images which hark back to the grimmer parts of *A Christmas Carol* or *The Chimes*.

> But, ladies and gentlemen, the spoilt children whom I have to present to you after this dinner of today are not of this class. I have glanced at these for the easier and lighter introduction of another, a very different, a far more numerous, and a far more serious class. The spoilt children whom I must show you are spoilt children of the poor in this great city – the children who are, every year, for ever and ever irrevocably spoilt out of this breathing life of ours by tens of thousands, but who may in vast numbers be preserved, if you, assisting and not contravening the ways of Providence, will help to save them. The two grim nurses, Poverty and Sickness, who bring these children before you, preside over their births, rock their wretched cradles, nail down their little coffins, pile up the earth

above their graves. Of the annual deaths in this great town, their unnatural deaths form more than one-third. I shall not ask you, according to the custom as to the other class – I shall not ask you on behalf of these children, to observe how good they are, how pretty they are, how clever they are, how promising they are, whose beauty they most resemble – I shall only ask you to observe how weak they are, and how like death they are! And I shall ask you, by the remembrance of everything that lies between your own infancy and that so miscalled second childhood when the child's graces are gone, and nothing but its helplessness remains – I shall ask you to turn your thoughts to these spoilt children in the sacred names of Pity and Compassion.

It is passages like these, spoken with the deepest of feeling, which emphasize (as I have already pointed out) that it was such children, and especially the sick child in its cot at Great Ormond Street, which awakened Dickens's most secret emotions. The next paragraph is perhaps the best-known of all the speech; the little Edinburgh boy in his 'wretched cradle' of an egg-box has been quoted many times. It is curious that four years before in *Hard Times*, Mr Bounderby in false boasts of his childhood miseries makes great play of his grandmother keeping him in an egg-box: 'That was the cot of *my* infancy; an old egg-box.' The reader is invited to smile at Bounderby's vainglorious hardships. Dickens's genius, like Charles Chaplin's, moved quickly from pathos to comedy and back, from laughter to tears in a moment. It is one explanation of their unique, universal appeal.

Some years ago, being in Scotland, I went with one of the most humane members of the humane medical profession, on a morning tour among some of the worst-lodged inhabitants of the old town of Edinburgh. In the closes and wynds of that picturesque place – I am sorry to remind you what fast friends picturesqueness and typhus often are – we saw more poverty and sickness in an hour than many people would believe in a life. Our way lay from one to another of the most wretched dwellings – reeking with horrible odours – shut off from the sky – shut out from the air – mere pits and dens. In a room in one of these places, where there was an empty porridge-pot on the cold hearth, with a ragged woman and some ragged children crouching on the bare ground near it – where, I remember as I speak, that very light, reflected from a high damp-stained and time-stained house wall, came trembling in, as if the fever which had shaken everything else there had shaken even it – there lay, in an old egg-box which the mother had begged from a shop, a little feeble, wasted, wan, sick child. With his little wasted face, and his little hot worn hands folded over his breast, and his little bright attentive eyes, I can see him now, as I have seen him for several years, looking steadily at us. There he lay in his little frail box, which was not at all a bad

> emblem of the little body from which he was slowly parting – there he lay, quite quiet, quite patient, saying never a word. He seldom cried, the mother said; he seldom complained; 'he lay there, seeming to wonder what it was a' aboot.' God knows I thought, as I stood looking at him, he had his reasons for wondering – reasons for wondering how it could possibly come to be that he lay there, left alone, feeble and full of pain, when he ought to have been as bright and as brisk as the birds that never got near him – reasons for wondering how he came to be left there, a little decrepit old man, pining to death, quite a thing of course, as if there were no crowds of healthy and happy children playing on the grass under the summer's sun within a stone's throw of him, as if there were no bright moving sea on the other side of the great hill overhanging the city; as if there were no great clouds rushing over it; as if there were no life, and movement, and vigour anywhere in the world – nothing but stoppage and decay. There he lay looking at us, saying in his silence, more pathetically than I have ever heard anything said by any orator in my life, 'Will you please tell us what this means, strange man? And if you can give me any good reason why I should be so soon, so far advanced on my way to Him who said that children were to come into His presence, and were not to be forbidden, but who scarcely meant, that they should come by this hard road by which I am travelling – pray give that reason to me, for I seek it very earnestly and wonder about it very much'; and to my mind he has been wondering about it ever since. Many a poor child, sick and neglected, I have seen since that time in this London; many a poor sick child have I seen most affectionately and kindly tended by poor people, in an unwholesome house and untoward circumstances, wherein its recovery was quite impossible; but at all such times I have seen my poor little drooping friend in his egg-box, and he had always addressed his dumb speech to me, and I have always found him wondering what it meant, and why, in the name of gracious God, such things should be!

Then, immediately after the slowly developed flowering of this pathetic and appealing picture, with practised and deliberate rhetorical effect Dickens moves to the main purpose of his appeal in a phrase which recalls the final sentence of 'Drooping Buds' about 'one of the broadest doors into the general heart; and that heart is a great and tender one':

> Now, ladies and gentlemen, such things need not be, and will not be, if this company, which is a drop of the life-blood of the great compassionate public heart, will only accept the means of rescue and prevention which is mine to offer. Within a quarter of a mile of this place where I speak, stands a courtly old house, where once, no doubt, blooming children were born, and grew up to be men and women, and married, and brought their own blooming children back to patter up the old oak staircase which stood but the other day, and to wonder at the old oak carvings on the chimney-pieces.

The old oak staircase had recently been altered as part of the enlargement of the facilities in the outpatients', where the numbers attending had increased almost eight-fold in the last five years.

> In the airy wards into which the old state drawing-rooms and family bedchambers of that house are converted are such little patients that the attendant nurses look like reclaimed giantesses, and the kind medical practitioner like an amiable Christian ogre. Grouped about the little low tables in the centre of the rooms are such tiny convalescents that they seem to be playing at having been ill. On the dolls' beds are such diminutive creatures, that each poor sufferer is supplied with its tray of toys; and, looking around, you may see how the tired, flushed cheek has toppled over half the brute creation on its way into the ark; or how one little dimpled arm has mowed down (as I saw myself) the whole tin soldiery of Europe. On the walls of these rooms are graceful, pleasant, bright, childish pictures. At the beds' heads, are pictures of the figure which is the universal embodiment of all mercy and compassion, the figure of Him who was once a child himself, and a poor one.
>
> Besides these little creatures on the beds, you may learn in that place that the number of small Out-patients brought to that house for relief is no fewer than ten thousand in the compass of a single year. In the room in which these are received, you may see against the wall a box, on which it is written, that it has been calculated that if every grateful mother who brings a child there will drop a penny into it, the Hospital funds may possibly be increased in a year by so large a sum as forty pounds. And you may read in the Hospital report, with a glow of pleasure, that these poor women are so respondent as to have made, even in a toiling year of difficulty and high prices, this estimated forty, fifty pounds.

This passage was especially remarked upon by Forster for the unprecedented emotional reaction it produced on Dickens's audience. And it was certainly greeted with cheers. Forster could not know of a most happy and charming incident connected with the Hospital collecting box, which if told by Dickens would have made the Freemasons' Hall resound and re-echo with approving thunder. An episode in the earlier *Dombey and Son* describes the day of little Paul Dombey's funeral. In the street outside the house, the funeral cortège attracts a crowd. A juggler who was going to perform delays out of respect, and waits with 'his trudging wife, one-sided with a heavy baby in her arms'. The funeral moves slowly down the street, and is scarcely out of sight when the juggler begins his act, taking advantage of the chance-gathered audience. 'But the juggler's wife is less alert than usual with the money box, for a child's burial has set her thinking that perhaps the baby underneath her shabby shawl may not grow up to be a man, and wear a sky-blue fillet round his head, and salmon-coloured worsted drawers, and tumble in the mud.' A year or two after the Hospital opened, 'A Man About Town' described in his regular column how late one night he was walking down Great Ormond Street behind a troupe of street acrobats arguing over their takings. As they passed the children's hospital, the youngest member of the troupe, a small boy, lingered behind, drew some coppers from his pocket, furtively counted them, ran over to the door of the Hospital, pushed the money through the slot of the collecting box, and then pattered after his still disputing and gesticulating elders on their way to mean lodgings off Gray's Inn Lane. It almost seems as if the baby boy of the juggler and his wife did grow up to wear motley and tumble in the mud like his father, and then stepped out of the pages of *Dombey and Son* to support the Hospital his creator loved. In any case, it is a touching example of how the poorest children came to realize what Great Ormond Street was doing for them and gave their own mite, perhaps in gratitude for a brother, a sister, or a friend Dr West and his colleagues had saved.

Dickens went on to explain more exactly what the Hospital was doing:

> In the printed papers of this same Hospital, you may read with what a generous earnestness the highest and wisest members of the medical profession testify to the great need of it; to the immense difficulty of treating children in the same hospitals with grown-up people, by reason of their different ailments and requirements; to the vast amount of pain that will be assuaged, and of the life that will be saved through this Hospital – not only among the poor, observe, but among the prosperous too, by reason of the increased knowledge of children's illnesses, which cannot fail to arise from a more systematic mode of studying them. Lastly, gentlemen, and I am sorry to say, worst of all – (for I must present no rose-coloured picture of this place to you – I must not deceive you); lastly – the visitor to this Children's Hospital, reckoning up the number of its beds, will find himself perforce obliged to stop at very little over thirty; and will learn, with sorrow and surprise, that even that small number, so forlornly, so miserably diminutive, compared with this vast London, cannot possibly be maintained unless the Hospital be better known; I limit myself to saying better known, because I will not believe that in a Christian community of fathers and mothers, and brothers and sisters, it can fail, being better known, to be well and richly endowed.
>
> Now, ladies and gentlemen, this without a word of adornment – which I resolved when I got up not to allow myself – this is the simple case. This is the pathetic case which I have to put to you; not only on behalf of the thousands of children who annually die in this great city, but also on behalf of the thousands of children who live half-developed, racked with preventable pain, shorn of their natural capacity for health and enjoyment. If these innocent creatures cannot move you for themselves, how can I possibly hope to move you in their name?

> The most delightful paper, the most charming essay, which the tender imagination of Charles Lamb conceived, represents him as sitting by his fireside on a winter night, telling stories to his own dear children, and delighting in their society, until he suddenly comes to his old solitary, bachelor self, and finds that they were but dream-children, who might have been, but never were. 'We are nothing,' they say to him; 'less than nothing, and dreams. We are only what might have been, and we must wait upon the tedious shore of Lethe, millions of ages, before we have existence and a name.' 'And immediately awakening,' he says, 'I found myself in my arm-chair.' The dream-children whom I should now raise if I could, before every one of you, according to your various circumstances, should be the dear child you love, the dearer child you have lost, the child you might have had, the child you certainly have been. Each of these dream-children would hold in its powerful hand one of the little children now lying in the Child's Hospital, or now shut out of it to perish. Each of these dream-children should say to you, 'O help this little suppliant in my name; O, help it for my sake!' Well! – And immediately awakening, you should find yourself in the Freemasons' Hall happily arrived at the end of a rather long speech, drinking 'Prosperity to the Hospital for Sick Children', and thoroughly resolved that it should flourish.

The speech was indeed a triumph. Reading it, we understand Anthony Trollope's encomium of Dickens as an orator. 'And he had another gift – had it so wonderfully, that it might be said that he has left no equal behind him. He spoke so well, that a public dinner became a blessing instead of a curse, if he was in the chair.' There is one important detail about the dinner which is only found in the Hospital's first printing of the speech, which must have been issued within a few weeks. John Duke Coleridge, who became an eminent lawyer and Lord Chief Justice, who was such a close friend of Forster that it was said a place was always laid for him at Forster's dinner-table, who was to play a large part in the affairs of Great Ormond Street and to be Dr Charles West's stoutest champion, had a special duty at this 1858 dinner.

> In the course of the evening Mr J.D.Coleridge proposed the health of the chairman, and paid an eloquent and graceful tribute to his high literary reputation, and to the purity as well as the power which characterize all his writings.
>
> In replying to this toast Mr Dickens most kindly offered to 'read' for the benefit of the Hospital, an offer which the committee have gratefully accepted.

A footnote announced that the reading would be at St Martin's Hall, on the evening of 15 April, and that the *Christmas Carol* would be read. Tickets were five shillings for the stalls and two shillings and sixpence for the area and gallery; back seats were one shilling.

It will be seen that Dickens volunteered to give that important reading, and almost immediately after making his main speech. He was not asked at a later date, as has always been inferred. The treasurer, John Labouchere, in replying to another toast, paid tribute to their late chairman of the committee, Sir Henry Dukinfield, who had died suddenly a few weeks before. It was Henry Allen Bathurst who announced the contributions, which came to nearly £3000. About £900 of this had been given by the ladies in the gallery, including a contribution of £500 from 'Mary Jane', the largest single donation the Hospital had every received. Dickens proposed the final toast to 'The Ladies'.

> In doing so, he said, he coupled it with a special compliment to 'Mary Jane', and an emphatic good-night to all. Without the ladies little good could be done in the world. He had once been reminded of all Robinson Crusoe had done in a state of single blessedness, but on careful investigation of the authorities he found that worthy had, in reality, had two wives.

'Mary Jane', as she was described in the newspaper report, has been identified with Mary Jane Kinnaird, the wife of the Hon. Arthur Kinnaird, an identification which has seemed perfectly feasible and sound. But following Dickens's example, a 'careful investigation of the authorities' has found that it was not Mary Jane Kinnaird, although on every ground of philanthropy and personal wealth she seemed the only possible candidate. But the name 'Mary Jane' was only a reporter's mistake or Bathurst's misreading from the list of contributions. In the Hospital's sixth annual report issued in 1858, the list of donations and subscriptions includes the contributions made or pledged at the dinner, and among them is '"Jane Mary", per E.C.Currey, Esq. £500 0 0.' 'Mary Jane' was in fact 'Jane Mary'. E.C.Currey, was a lawyer and, like Bathurst, was based at Doctors' Commons. He had been a supporter of the Hospital from the days of the Provisional Committee, and was one of the two auditors of the very first Statement of Income and Expenditure, a duty he was to perform again in later years including on the accounts printed in the report when 'Jane Mary' was first listed. This entry in the donation list was reprinted every year without alteration until the sixteenth annual report, printed early in 1868, which read, '"Jane Mary", the late £500 0 0.'

Mary Jane Kinnaird lived on until 1888. It is evident that Dickens's 'Mary Jane' must be sought elsewhere: some charitable and wealthy lady, named Jane Mary, who had died after the first quarter of 1867 and before March of 1868, whose lawyer was probably Edmund C. Currey, and who may have had a special reason in February 1858 for being aware of Great Ormond Street's urgent need. Five hundred pounds in 1858 was a very respectable sum. There was one lady, who evidently lived a very retired life, who sought neither notice or renown, who even hid her charity under a name whose inversion must have amused her when it deepened her anonymity, and who only attracted attention and passing mention after her death by the generosity of her charitable bequests.

Miss Jane Mary Tottingham of 130 Harley Street fits all the conditions. She died on 21 October 1867 at the age of eighty-three. She left nearly £100,000, over a quarter of which, besides the residue, she left to a number of charitable institutions. One of the executors was 'Edmund Charles Currey, Esq., of Doctors' Commons'. Thus three of the main conditions for identification are met. As for the fourth condition, the will itself was dated 5 February 1858, and as among the many asylums, hospitals and other charities named was Middlesex Hospital with a legacy of £500, it needs very little imagination to suppose that when drawing up the will, E.C. Currey pointed out that if The Hospital for Sick Children had to wait until her decease to benefit, there was a great possibility that it would close for lack of funds. So it would be likely that the £500 to Great Ormond Street was in anticipation and in lieu of a proposed bequest. And her neighbours on either side in Harley Street were Mrs Ricardo and Mrs Alexander, who themselves were benefactors of Great Ormond Street. Miss Jane Mary Tottingham, I would hold, can safely be remembered as Charles Dickens's true 'Mary Jane'.

She was the surviving daughter of a Colonel Tottingham who had died many years before, and was probably, like Thackeray's Colonel Newcombe, in the service of the East India Company, in which her mother and two sisters were listed as shareholders. This is reflected in her many bequests to foreign missions, the main beneficiary being the Moravian Mission London Association with £5000, with others having an Indian interest also remembered. It can intriguingly be said that the full list of bequests includes many charities in which Mary Jane Kinnaird was also interested, so it is likely that Mrs Kinnaird and Miss Tottingham were acquainted. In 1898, ten years after Lady Kinnaird (as she then was) died, a contribution of £1000 towards the purchase of the site of the Hospital of St John and St Elizabeth for Great Ormond Street was made by the 'Law Executors of the late Mrs Mary Jane'. This was forty years after Charles Dickens had concluded proceedings at the dinner with that tribute to 'Mary Jane'.

Three days after this tribute, the Hospital's Committee of Management met on 12 February, and paid their own tribute to Dickens.

> The Committee resolved that a Special Note of Thanks be presented to Charles Dickens Esq. for his eminent services to this Hospital in presiding at the Dinner at Freemasons' Hall; and the Honorary Secretary was requested to convey to Charles Dickens Esq. this resolution.
>
> It was resolved, being proposed by S. Arbuthnot Esq., and seconded by Dr West, that it be recommended to the Court of Governors this day, 'To elect Charles Dickens Esq. an Honorary Governor of this Hospital'.

The following Wednesday evening, Dickens sat down at his desk at Tavistock House and wrote a letter to Bathurst.

> I beg to acknowledge the receipt of your obliging letter, and to assure the Committee, through you, of the gratification I derive from this generous recognition of my most willingly rendered services. It will give me great pleasure to become one of the Honorary Governors of the Hospital.
>
> In the matter of my public reading for its benefit, I will personally consult the friend who was Honorary Secretary to the Jerrold Remembrance Fund (for which I read in London last year), and who has a better practical experience of the management of such things than perhaps any one in London. When I shall have taken counsel with him as to time, place, and prices, I will communicate with you again. You will of course understand in the meanwhile, that I only desire to redeem my pledge in the most advantageous and most profitable manner.

The friend was Arthur Smith, who became the very able manager of Dickens's public readings, arranging all the details of performances and tours. This letter is a reinforcement of Forster's claim that the Hospital reading influenced Dickens's decision to undertake a series of readings for his own profit. The fact that it was as early as February that Dickens approached Smith to consult him about arrangements for the Hospital, shows that his thoughts turned more firmly in that direction somewhat earlier than we are led to believe by Forster and others. We know that from the middle of March, the arguments for and against the commercial readings loom large in Dickens's correspondence. The enthusiastic reception at Edinburgh of his reading of *A Christmas Carol* on the 26th, in aid of the Philosophical Institute, had him writing to Forster, 'I had no opportunity of asking any one's advice in Edinburgh. The crowd was too enormous, and the excitement in it much too great. But my determination is all but taken.' The Queen, although nothing came to pass then or later, was also 'bent upon hearing the Carol read'. Arthur Smith, when asked for his opinion about reading for profit said, 'Of the immense return in money I have no doubt. Of the Dash into the new position, however, I am not so good a judge.' What finally, according to Forster, 'closed the attempt at further objections' was Dickens's letter to him of 9 April:

They have let five hundred stalls for the Hospital night; and as people come every day for more, and it is out of the question to make more they cannot be restrained at St Martin's Hall from taking down names for other readings.

But to return to Bathurst and the events of February. On the 19th of that month, he read out to the Committee Dickens's letter of Wednesday, the 17th. He also read a letter from Dr Henry Bence Jones 'intimating his inability from multiplied engagements to attend the duties of this Committee, and desiring to have his place filled up'.

Although this closed a most important page in Great Ormond Street's history, it does show that Bence Jones's active connection with the Children's Hospital he and West had founded lasted much longer than has hitherto been assumed. He had told West in 1849 that although he agreed to join him in his plans, it was his firm intention not to be involved in the active work of the institution once it was opened. He was much better than his word.

A transcription of the shorthand report of the speech was sent to Dickens for his approval. Dickens returned it to Bathurst on 21 February, with appreciative comments.

I send you the speech, with a few slight corrections. It is extremely well done, and with great fidelity. If you should have an opportunity of making my approval known to the gentleman who took it down, I would beg you to do so.

Tomorrow or next day, I do not doubt to be able to write to you in detail on the subject of the reading.

Dickens, as a former parliamentary reporter, would of course be appreciative of the work of Thomas Allen Reed, to whom Bathurst apparently sent the letter in accordance with Dickens's wishes. The letter from Dickens which he promised for the next day has not survived, but we know of its contents from the committee meeting of 26 February:

The Honorary Secretary read a Letter from Charles Dickens Esq. proposing to fulfil his kind promise to read for the benefit of this Hospital, on Thursday the 15th April, at St Martin's Hall, and recommending that the arrangements be superintended by Mr Alfred [sic] Smith, of Egyptian Hall – the committee requested the Honorary Secretary to see Mr Dickens and consent to any arrangement deemed necessary.

The Committee authorized the printing of Mr Dickens's Speech at Freemasons' Hall, from the Reporter's copy – proofs to be obtained as speedily as possible.

That no time was wasted over the proofs is evident in Dickens's letter to Macready of 15 March:

> I have safely received your cheque for three guineas this morning, and will hand it over forthwith to the honorary secretary of the hospital. I hope you have read the little speech in the hospital's publication of it. They had it taken by their own shorthand-writer, and it is done verbatim.
>
> You may be sure that it is a good and kind charity. It is amazing to me that it is not at this day ten times as large and rich as it is. But I hope and trust that I have happily been able to give it a good thrust onward into a great course.

At the end of the month in discussing with Forster possible arrangements for the contemplated course of readings, he said of the advertisements, 'they should always mention me as a third person – just as the Child's Hospital, for instance, in addressing the public, mentions me.' Ten days before the Hospital reading he sent Thomas Beard one of the four complimentary tickets sent on by Bathurst.

After all his doubts about the wisdom of the announced readings for profit, Dickens must have been particularly pleased by *The Times* of 16 April.

> Last night, at St Martin's Hall, he read his *Christmas Carol* in aid of The Hospital for Sick Children, and such was the assembled multitude that the sum produced must have been sufficient to physic all the sick children in the United Kingdom. But, notwithstanding the sympathy that every one will feel for the infantile invalids in whose cause Mr Dickens laboured so strenuously and so successfully last night, a more general gratification will be produced by the announcement that the benevolent 'reader' is at last about to employ his elocutionary talents for his own advantage.

And that same morning the Hospital Committee, 'being informed of the successful Meeting at St Martin's Hall last night', passed a resolution 'That the cordial Thanks of the Board be presented to Charles Dickens Esq. for his kindness in reading his "Christmas Carol" for the benefit of the Hospital'. In that year's annual report, written before the reading, the real value of Dickens's services to Great Ormond Street is emphasized, explaining what the dinner had really achieved.

> Gladly would they believe that that event did but inaugurate a new epoch in the history of the Hospital; for the liberal response of the guests to the Chairman's beautiful and touching appeal has enabled the Committee to advance a step towards placing the Institution on a permanent basis, by commencing two Funds, the one for its endowment, the other a Building

Fund to provide for its further increase. Still it is but one step, and that but a small one, which has yet been taken towards the accomplishment of this object.

Mr Dickens, to whom the Committee tender the expression of their most heartfelt gratitude, feels this; and in order further to help the Charity, has offered to give a 'Public Reading' for its benefit – an offer made so gracefully as doubly to enhance its value. Their friends will, doubtless, feel with him, that success cannot be won by any single effort, but must be the reward of long sustained and untiring exertion.

The dinner raised £2850; the reading, £165 8s 0d. There were two smaller sums worth noting: five guineas each from Charles Dickens and the proprietors of *Household Words*.

—11—

FROM MRS GAMP TO OUR JOHNNY

Early in 1861 Dickens had decided upon the title of the novel which was to follow *Great Expectations*. And he stood by this title, *Our Mutual Friend*, as Forster remarks, in the face of three years of unfavourable comment and alternative suggestions, until the serialization began in May 1864. Some of Dickens's easy facility and readiness in writing had gone from him: 'I am exceedingly anxious to begin my book . . . I want to prepare it for the spring . . . if I don't strike while the iron . . . is hot, I shall drift off again, and have to go through all this uneasiness once more.' So he wrote to Forster in the late summer of 1863. It was very different from those happy days in Doughty Street, when he could bring his current task into the drawing-room and steadily write on, amid the distractions of friends and family. The difficulties he found in starting his new book were not only due to the encroachments made upon his time and strength by the demands of public readings and *All The Year Round*, nor the consideration of a possible tour in Australia for which he was offered £10,000 and only refused after some hesitation, nor the inevitable decline in energy and animal spirits as he grew older. Writing a novel was something that could no longer be the spontaneous inspiration and improvisation it had been with *Pickwick, Oliver* or *Nickleby*.

Dickens had, since *Dombey*, a more serious attitude towards his profession and the purpose, scope and message of his novels. Whether his later works equal the earlier in the happy flow of story and character, or whether his later, more conscious style seemed rather obscure and turgid at times to his readers, almost like the London fog which opened *Bleak House* or the Thames at the beginning of *Our Mutual Friend*, is something that can be argued over by the critics. No doubt there were both gains and losses. It is, however, generally agreed that *Our*

Mutual Friend is the most carefully designed of his later works in the symbolism of its events, setting and characters. This makes the tribute paid to Great Ormond Street in its description of Our Johnny's admission and death – the very last of Dickens's such pathetic scenes – all the more important and sincere. Here his dream children and the little sufferers of reality merged together, as they always did when Dickens wrote or spoke of The Hospital for Sick Children. In *Our Mutual Friend* the creator of Mrs Gamp moved on to praise good nurses who devoted their lives to children.

This was not to escape notice at Great Ormond Street. The Hospital's report for 1865 put on record, 'The best thanks of the Committee are due to the Author of "Our Mutual Friend".' Fourteen years later, a Mr Herbert C. Saunders, speaking at the anniversary dinner, paid this tribute to Dickens's influence in improving the standard of nursing:

> I cannot help here alluding to the very vast difference that I have seen, even in my lifetime, in the character of nursing done by ladies, and I may also say by paid nurses. No doubt that is in part owing to the immortal Charles Dickens, for from the days when he stamped the name of 'Mrs Gamp' upon old-fashioned nurses there has no doubt been a rapid and continuous improvement in the character of nursing throughout the country. From the royal lady upon the throne ... down to the humblest person who had to nurse by a sick bed there has not been a person who has not endeavoured from that time to this to improve in every possible way the character of the nursing of the country.

In invoking the example of the Queen, it is apposite to remember that at the end of the year in which Dickens decided on the title of *Our Mutual Friend*, Prince Albert died of typhoid. It is held that a main reason why the Prince of Wales, exactly ten years after his father's death, successfully came through a severe attack of the same disease was that he had, as the Prince Consort did not, the attendance of professional nurses. In 1880, Dr W. H. Dickinson, who had taken West's place as senior physician to The Hospital for Sick Children, reminded his audience at the Hospital dinner that year, 'It is not by medical treatment that patients with typhoid fever are preserved – it is not by the doctor but by the nurse.' Forty-three years before, Charles West had made much the same observation at St Bartholomew's Hospital, in one of his very first published papers. And in his old age, in the very last book he wrote, *The Profession of Medicine* of 1896, he was able to comment upon the advances in nursing he had seen, in examples which are most apt to the present theme.

> The old nurse of the Sairey Gamp style is no longer to be found; ignorance,

> dishonesty, and intemperance are abolished, and the account of the class given by Dr Ferrier of Manchester, many years ago, in his paper on the *Treatment of the Dying* [1798], is so horrible as to seem almost incredible. The nurse of the present day is an educated woman, free from all the vices of her predecessors; deft in handling the sick, with considerable technical knowledge, and, sometimes, also with large experience. And from these good qualities there are no drawbacks in the case of trained hospital nurses, who are well disciplined ... I have heard that, on the Prince of Wales's recovery from the illness which kept all England watching for the news as if he were everyone's brother, Sir William Gull said to him, 'Your Royal Highness has been nursed as well as if you had been in a hospital.'

How slowly such nursing reforms were to evolve in reality may be seen in that, eighteen years after the creation of Mrs Gamp, no professional nurse was in attendance on Prince Albert, because neither wealth nor position could guarantee adequate nursing. Mrs Gamp herself was based on the nurse who attended the companion of Miss Burdett Coutts. If the wealthiest woman in England could not provide a decent nurse for her friend, nor the Queen for her husband, even after Florence Nightingale had set such a magnificent example in the Crimea, it was no wonder that wives, mothers, daughters and sisters were still needed in the sick-room.

Perhaps because Mrs Gamp was a comic figure as well as a horrific example, the lesson Dickens intended to be drawn from her took rather long to strike home. Sairey Gamp is one of the great characters of comedy rather than a moral warning – as so often happens in Dickens, where laughter overpowers his original didactic purpose. As George Meredith wrote at the beginning of his own masterpiece, *The Egoist*: 'The Comic Spirit conceives a definite situation for a number of characters, and rejects all accessories in the exclusive pursuit of them and their speech.'

It would be hard to find in English literature – apart from Mrs Malaprop, who is conceived on a much smaller scale – a character as dependent for comedy on the idiosyncrasies of her speech as Sairey Gamp, or as successful in the happy awryness of words and phrases, and the glorious muddle of her syntax. In apparent contradiction to what has just been argued, in the long view it is because Mrs Gamp is conceived in the spirit of laughter rather than of nightmare that she did in the end prevail as a type and a warning, becoming almost a part of folk-memory and tradition. As Forster says, 'That which endearingly stamped upon his page its most mirth-moving figure, had stamped out of English life for ever one of its disgraces.'

The realization that Sairey Gamp, as a great figure of fun, would arouse the reader's partiality at the expense of the warning she was intended to be, surely made Dickens give to old Martin Chuzzlewit a rather conventional denunciation of her.

> 'Mr Sweedlepipe, take as much care of your lady-lodger as you can, and give her a word or two of good advice now and then. Such,' said old Martin, looking gravely at the astonished Mrs Gamp, 'as hinting at the expediency of a little less liquor, and a little more humanity, and a little less regard for herself, and a little more regard for her patients, and perhaps a trifle of additional honesty. Or when Mrs Gamp gets into trouble, Mr Sweedlepipe, it had better not be at a time when I am near enough to the Old Bailey to volunteer myself as a witness to her character.'

Well might Mrs Gamp clasp her hands, turn up her eyes, and fall into a walking swoon while muttering, 'Less liquor! – Sairey Gamp – Bottle on the chimney-piece, and let me put my lips to it, when I am so dispoged!' Mrs Gamp, as always, was convinced that her conduct was beyond reproach and patients benefited from her attendance. The charge of excessive drinking would amaze her. She defends her preference for Brighton Old Tipper ale, 'it bein' considered wakeful by the doctors', and enjoins the chambermaid at The Bull in Holborn not to bring more than 'a shilling's worth of gin and water-warm when I rings the bell a second time'. She removes the pillow from her helpless patient – on Betsey Prig's advice be it remembered, 'The easy-chair an't soft enough. You'll want his piller' – and tells herself, 'Now he's comfortable as he can be.' Under the happy influence of the supper tray, with its pickled salmon, cucumber and vinegar, and her 'warm shilling's worth', she had already reflected, 'What a blessed thing it is to make sick people happy in their beds, and never mind one's self as long as one can do a service!' Mrs Harris was amazed the 'any woman could sick-nurse and monthly likeways, on the little you takes to drink.'

It should be understood that Mrs Gamp was not a professional hospital nurse, 'being, in the highest walk of art, a monthly nurse, or, as her sign-board boldly had it, "Midwife"'. She was careful enough of her interests in this field to mark in a 'small almanack' on her chimney-piece the dates at which her ladies were 'expected to fall due'. When in 1847 Dickens toyed with the idea of reviving Mrs Gamp in a 'Piljians Projiss' to raise further funds at the benefit performances of *Every Man in His Humour* at Manchester and Liverpool, it was this aspect of her profession he intended to emphasize.

> 'I am informed as there is Ladies in this party, and that half a dozen of 'em, if not more, is in various stages of an interesting state. Mrs Harris, you and me well knows what Ingeins often does . . . may I not combine my calling with change of air, and prove a service to my feller creeturs?'

Allied with this calling was a strong partiality for events at the other extreme of life's span, 'a performer of nameless offices about the persons of the dead ... she went to a lying-in or a laying-out with equal zest and relish.' Her role as a 'sick-nurse' was a means of earning extra money, 'half-a-crown a day' according to Betsey Prig's own fees. Laying-out was 'eighteen pence a day for working people, and three and six for gentlefolks – night watching ... being an extra charge,' as Mrs Gamp emphasizes. Betsey Prig, 'a day nurse as was recommended from Bartholomew's; and well I knows her', could be considered the expert. When the two friends quarrel, Betsey, apart from being upset at not being allowed to help herself freely to the spirits (kept in a teapot 'from motives of delicacy'), is hurt in her professional pride by the offer 'to take me under you' in attending to Mrs Gamp's patient, Chuffey.

No doubt Thackeray had Mrs Gamp's weakness in mind as well as his own experience when he describes Arthur Pendennis being nursed by the attendant laundress in his Temple Chambers:

> Pen's condition had so much alarmed her that she was obliged to have recourse to the stimulus of brandy to enable her to support the grief which his illness occasioned. As she hung about his bed and endeavoured to minister to him, her attentions became intolerable to the invalid, and he begged her peevishly not to come near him.

Certainly Dickens's other fellow novelist, Wilkie Collins, remembered 'She was a fat old woman, this Mrs Gamp,' when in *The Woman in White* he wonders 'whether hired nurses, proverbially as cruel a set of women as are to be found in all England, were not, for the most part, also as fat a set of women as are to be found in all England'.

Despite Mrs Gamp's endearing habits of clutching patients by the windpipe when pouring their draughts down their throats, holding down their arms by their sides in ghoulish anticipation – 'Ah! he'd make a lovely corpse!' – or carelessly dropping her snuff into their gruel or broth – 'It don't signify. It stimulates a patient' – or grumbling at delirious patients for waking her up when she is supposed to be acting as night nurse, she is convinced that she has carried out all her duties and followed the doctor's instructions. She is not in any way a pious hypocrite like Mr Pecksniff. Her ample figure heaves its way across the pages, through Kingsgate Street and High Holborn, relishing the thought of her tasty snacks and the spirituous comfort of her bottle.

Despite the high standard which West demanded of the staff at Great Ormond Street, some incidents were reminiscent of Mrs Gamp. One of the first Hospital porters was dismissed for bringing in beer for the nurses. More hilariously in Sairey's own style, when the housekeeper was discovered intoxicated and unfit for duty, Bathurst, according to the minutes for May 1859, was asked 'to see her and give her the opportunity of explaining her conduct to the Board, which she declined to do'. That was the last of the housekeeper! But comedy turned to tragedy ten years later when night nurse Roberts in the fever ward swallowed some belladonna liniment, mistaking it for brandy, and died. The inquest returned a verdict of accidental death. The day nurse was admonished by the Medical Committee for the delay in calling the house surgeon. The Committee of Management paid for Nurse Roberts's funeral 'on finding that the family of the nurse were poor'. It would appear that some nurses in the fever ward were more inclined to Mrs Gamp's failing than most. Very soon after Dickens had given his 1858 speech, a visiting governor reported, 'Everything satisfactory, except that the Matron reported to me that the nurse in the Fever Ward on her return to the Hospital on Sunday last was intoxicated.' But on the whole the true picture was that given by the Matron in her report of 28 October 1852. The future pattern of the Hospital was set in its very first year.

> ... the Nurses and Servants are fulfilling their respective duties properly, and the parents of the discharged patients have expressed their grateful thanks for the great care and attention shown to the Children during their sickness. And the Matron considered the affairs under her control are going on satisfactorily.

In 1867, for the Collected Charles Dickens Edition, Dickens wrote a preface to *Martin Chuzzlewit*, which concluded:

> Mrs Sarah Gamp was, four-and-twenty years ago, a fair representation of the hired attendant on the poor in sickness. The Hospitals of London were, in many respects, noble Institutions; in others, very defective. I think it not the least among the instances of their mismanagment, that Mrs Betsey Prig was a fair specimen of a Hospital Nurse; and that the Hospitals, with their means and friends, should have left it to private humanity and enterprise to enter on an attempt to improve that class of persons – since, greatly improved through the agency of good women.

The 'good women' not only included Florence Nightingale and her circle. The nurses at Great Ormond Street would also have been in his mind. Apart from 'Drooping Buds', there was the 1858 speech which described The Hospital for Sick Children, those things which were, Dickens specifically states, 'as I saw myself'. Much of that speech, as Forster points out, found its way into the ninth chapter of the second book of *Our Mutual Friend*. The new preface to *Martin Chuzzlewit* was written over two years after that ninth chapter was published. In 1862 Morley had written, with Dickens's most evident approval and agreement, 'Between the Cradle and the Grave' for *All the Year Round*, which revisited Great Ormond Street ten years after 'Drooping Buds'. In that article Morley mentioned 'an old nurse who has been in the hospital since it opened'. He was not the only visitor to pay particular attention to Nurse Mooney, as we shall see. Nurse Mooney and her fellow workers were obviously known to Dickens; he had them in view when writing the *Our Mutual Friend* passages, which are the most easily accessible to the casual reader of all Dickens's descriptions of Great Ormond Street. No excuse is necessary for quoting them here at some length.

Betty Higden's orphan grandchild Johnny is dangerously ill. Betty is reluctant to let him be taken from her cottage to what she thinks is a form of the workhouse infirmary which she has loathed and fled from all her life: 'I understand too well. I know too much about it, sir. I've run from it too many a year. No! Never for me, nor for the child, while there's water enough in England to cover us!'

Mrs Boffin, who has interested herself in Johnny, with a view to his possible adoption, calms Betty and reassures her.

> 'We want to move Johnny to a place where there are none but children; a place set up on purpose for sick children; where the good doctors and nurses pass their lives with children, talk to none but children, touch none but children, comfort and cure none but children.'
>
> 'Is there really such a place?' asked the old women, with a gaze of wonder.
>
> 'Yes, Betty, on my word, and you shall see it. If my home was a better place for the dear boy, I'd take him to it; but indeed it's not.'
>
> 'You shall take him,' returned Betty . . .
>
> At the Children's Hospital, the gallant steed, the Noah's ark, the yellow bird, and the officer in the Guards were made as welcome as their child-owner. But the doctor said aside to Rokesmith, 'This should have been days ago. Too late!'
>
> However, they were all carried up into a fresh airy room, and there Johnny came to himself, out of a sleep or a swoon or whatever it was, to find himself lying in a little quiet bed, with a little platform over his breast, on which were already arranged, to give him heart and urge him to cheer up, the Noah's ark, the noble steed, and the yellow bird, with the officer in the Guards doing duty over the whole, quite as much to the satisfaction of his country as if he had been upon Parade.

This paragraph and its continuation, as given below, enlarge in detail Dickens's description of the ward, its cots and little patients which he had given in his speech for the Hospital over six years before. What particularly impressed him, unusually for Dickens, seems to have been the bright religious pictures on the walls, pictures which were very probably given by Miss Burdett Coutts. These may have given the same impression of the Christ child which Dickens tried to convey to his own children in the story written for them in 1849, *The Life of Our Lord*, 'who was once a child Himself, and a poor one,' as he said in that speech in 1858.

> And at the bed's head was a coloured picture beautiful to see, representing as it were another Johnny seated on the knee of some Angel surely who loved little children. And marvellous fact to lie and stare at: Johnny had become one of a little family, all in little quiet beds (except two playing dominoes in little arm-chairs at a little table on the hearth): and on all the little beds were little platforms whereon were to be seen dolls' houses, woolly dogs with mechanical barks in them ... tin armies, Moorish tumblers, wooden tea-things, and the riches of the earth.
>
> As Johnny murmured something in his placid admiration, the ministering woman at his bed's head asked him what he said. It seemed that he wanted to know whether all these were brothers and sisters of his? So they told him yes ...
>
> ... he had to be washed and tended, and remedies were applied, and though these offices were far, far more skilfully and lightly done than ever anything had been done for him in his little life, so rough and short, they would have hurt and tired him but for an amazing circumstance which laid hold of his attention. This was no less than the appearance on his own little platform in pairs, of All Creation on its way into his own particular ark: the elephant leading, and the fly, with a diffident sense of his size, politely bringing up the rear. A very little brother lying in the next bed with a broken leg, was so enchanted by this spectacle that his delight exalted its enthralling interest; and so came rest and sleep ...
>
> From bed to bed a light womanly tread and a pleasant fresh face passed in the silence of the night. A little head would lift itself up into the softened light here and there, to be kissed as the face went by – for these little patients are very loving – and would then submit itself to be composed to rest again. The mite with the broken leg was restless, and moaned; but after a while he turned his face towards Johnny's bed, to fortify himself with a view of the ark, and fell asleep. Over most of the beds, the toys were yet grouped as the children had left them when they last laid themselves down, and, in their innocent grotesqueness and incongruity, they might have stood for the childrens' dreams.
>
> The doctor came in too, to see how it fared with Johnny. And he and Rokesmith stood together, looking down with compassion on him.
>
> 'What is it, Johnny?' Rokesmith was the questioner, and put an arm round the poor baby as he made a struggle.
>
> 'Him!' said the little fellow. 'Those!'
>
> The doctor was quick to understand children, and, taking the horse, the ark, the yellow bird, and the man in the Guards, from Johnny's bed,

> softly placed them on that of his next neighbour, the mite with the broken leg.
>
> With a weary and yet a pleased smile, and with an action as if he stretched his little figure out to rest, the child heaved his body on the sustaining arm, and seeking Rokesmith's face with his lips, said:
>
> 'A kiss for the boofer lady.'
>
> Having now bequeathed all he had to dispose of, and arranged his affairs in this world, Johnny, thus speaking, left it.

Whether the doctor who so speedily grasped Johnny's last wish was based on Charles West himself is something which cannot be determined, but which would be most fitting. In such understanding and concern West set the example which was emulated by all the younger physicians who served under him. In the same way, although it is not possible to identify the nurses – 'the ministering woman at his bed's head' and the 'light womanly tread and a pleasant fresh face' – we know they were all of the mould and standard set by Charles West. Indeed, the whole atmosphere of loving care and sympathy, which Dickens conveys so vividly, was in a way West's creation. His manuscript draft entitled 'Hints for Rules' embodies what were in essence the official regulations of The Hospital for Sick Children, especially the section headed 'Nurses':

> As the duty of attending on Sick Children calls not only for the ordinary amount of patience, gentleness and womanly kindness, necessary in the case of all sick persons; but also for a freedom from prejudice and a quickness of observation seldom found among the utterly uncultivated, no woman be admitted as a nurse who cannot both read readily and write legibly, and who cannot repeat the Lord's Prayer and Ten Commandments, and who is not acquainted with the principles of the Christian religion.
>
> It shall be the duty of every nurse not merely to watch the children with care, and to tend them with kindness, but by all means to keep them cheerful and contented; and while impatience, ill-temper, or anger towards the patients, will be followed by dismissal; also mere inability to make children happy will be regarded as of itself a sufficient cause for not retaining a Nurse in the service of the Hospital.

West's unending vigilance and personal responsibility in improving and upholding the pattern of perfection he set for the nurses at Great Ormond Street is confirmed by that impeccable authority on the subject, Catherine J. Wood. Her letter to the *British Medical Journal*, written in response to West's obituary notice – although it refers to a period somewhat later than Great Ormond Street's beginnings, but one especially relevant to the time of *Our Mutual Friend* – shows his attitudes to and care for the nurses. And we know that it was thus from the very start.

> He it was who, in 1862, introduced the trained and educated gentlewoman into the wards of the Children's Hospital, and from that year may be dated the immense advance that took place in the nursing of children's diseases. Dr West from the first superintended the new arrangements himself, and he gave the most unremitting attention to all the details of the nursing; nothing escaped his notice; he knew each nurse; and he constantly inquired as to their progress and aptitude for the work. A nurse was not only to be proficient in her work, but she was to succeed in making her patients happy and in winning their confidence, or she was not worthy to be on the staff. Having had the privilege of working with Dr West, and of being trained under his eye, I can speak from my own experience of the earnest devotion that he threw into the art of nursing, and the enthusiasm with which he inspired all engaged in the work.

In 1854 West published anonymously – it was later to appear under his own name – a small octavo volume of seventy-nine pages, *How to Nurse Sick Children*. It was, as the subtitle states, 'Intended Especially as Help to the Nurses at The Hospital for Sick Children', although he hoped it would prove of 'Service to All who have Charge of the Young'. As the late Dr Felix S. Besser pointed out, 'It is noteworthy that Dr Charles West anticipated Florence Nightingale's *Note on Nursing* by five years.' West at once confirmed Catherine Wood's memory of his regard and care for the nurses at Great Ormond Street by addressing them at the very beginning of his little book as 'My Dear Friends', which was somewhat different from the usual contemporary attitude of doctors towards the humble hospital nurse. He charmingly describes his own qualifications for writing the book, and then the qualities necessary in a children's nurse:

> It is written by a person who has seen a great deal of little children, especially of little sick children, who loves them very much, and believe that you would not have undertaken to nurse them, unless you loved them too.
>
> Indeed, if any of you have entered on your office without a feeling of very earnest love to little children – a feeling which makes you long to be with them, to take care of them, to help them – you have made a great mistake in undertaking such duties as you are now engaged in . . .
>
> There is a great difference, as you must by this time have found out, between a child when well, and the same child when sick. When well, it is all life, and merriment and fun . . . But if illness comes: first the child loses its merriment, though it still shows just every now and then

> a sad attempt at playfulness, and then, as its illness increases, it grows more fretful; so fretful that nothing can go right with it. It cries to be laid down in its bed, and then no sooner have you placed it there, than it cries to be taken up again; it is thirsty, and asks or at least makes signs for drink, but nothing that you offer pleases its taste, and it pushes away the cup, irritated all the more by what you have so kindly done to promote its comfort. For day and night this continues, but yet you bear it, losing your own sense of weariness in anxiety for the life of your little charge. At length amendment comes, but as the anxiety you had felt passes away, you are disappointed at finding that, instead of being more loving and more fond for all that you have done for it, the little one is more cross and fractious than ever, and it is only by degrees that its childish ways come back to it, and that you discover that the illness did not destroy, but only took away for a short time, the little loving heart . . .
>
> But besides this, the delight of seeing a sick child recover; of watching all its little baby ways come back one by one; of feeling that you have its confidence and love; – for in spite of all their cross and naughty tempers, little children's love is not hard to win, nor hard to keep; – this is a source of pure and daily returning happiness, such as no other occupation brings with it, such as ought, I think, to make for you, what a good man called 'music at midnight'. And though there are some exceptions to it, yet very generally the parent's gratitude is not wanting; and a mother's blessing whose heart you have made glad is a blessing indeed; one which money will not purchase, one of which poverty, and sickness, and death itself, will not rob you.

As Dr Besser said, 'Years have passed and the world and with it medicine have undergone many profound changes. Yet the message which this book transmits is as valid today as when it was written.' The great tradition of love and high ideals in the care and nursing of the sick child, that tradition of which Great Ormond Street is so proud, was formulated in these pages. As with the remarks on fairy tales quoted earlier from the little volume, many of these sentiments would find an echo in Charles Dickens.

One of the nurses to whom West addressed his book was Ann Mooney. She had been at the Hospital since its beginning, as Morley remarked. The Medical Committee on 17 March 1852 noted: 'The Matron having reported that Ann Mooney had served a month as a probation nurse, and the Medical Officers having expressed their satisfaction with her conduct, her permanent engagement was authorized.' Her salary was probably £12 per annum to begin with. Later it was raised to £20. This included, of course, board and lodging, but the nurses had to provide their own tea and sugar. Later one of the Lady Visitors was to remark that she thought the committee could afford to supply the nurses with these, the more especially as their 'wages are not, I think, sufficient to admit of a Nurse saving anything for her old age'. It was not the only time a similar sentiment was expressed. Louisa Twining, one of Florence Nightingale's circle, knew Ann Mooney well. Her autobiography, published in 1893, relates:

> In 1858 and 1859 I had a great desire to learn something of nursing in the Children's Hospital, in Great Ormond Street, of which I had seen the commencement under Dr West. Vast indeed are the changes which have taken place there, as elsewhere, in the years since then. The fine old houses, with their noble staircases, have both disappeared, and with them all the arrangements of those days when a kindly matron had for many years superintended a staff of, I believe, untrained nurses, or at least what we should consider such at the present day. For some time I went there every morning, and was chiefly under the instruction of a good, kind elderly Irish woman, who at least had learnt her art by experience, if not by scientific teaching . . . I found that nursing was a vocation I could not follow . . . and I was impressed then with a conviction that I have never lost – that it is far more sad and trying to witness disease and suffering amongst little children than in adults.

In 1860 when a scheme was started for the committee to receive monthly reports from the Lady Visitors on their tours of inspection, the first report was made by Dr West's wife, Mary. She found in the boys' ward, as in the girls' ward, a lack of bags for keeping each child's clothes separate, and suggested that some should be made. The closets she found very neat, but without enough room for the medicines. 'It seemed to me these should have a separate closet if possible.' Beds were in nicer order than in the girls' ward. The water closet, however, was wet on the floor. The boys' ward was Nurse Mooney's responsibility, and the next month Mrs Shadwell, the wife of one of the most active and influential members of the Committee of Management, wrote, 'In the boys' ward there were 2 very bad cases and I was quite delighted with the way in which Moonie [sic] was attending to one little boy.'

The next reports were written by Miss Bell and Miss Twining, who were both influenced by Florence Nightingale. They were written at great length and like the others full of suggestions which are now part of normal ward equipment and procedure. In contradiction to the earlier Lady Visitors, married women who had known and helped the hospital from its beginning, they found the boys' ward untidy and the beds not quite clean, and although recognizing that Mooney was overworked with patients needing careful nursing, both of them criticized her for keeping the boys' rather smelly old boots in the clothes cupboard. Louisa Twining, although admonishing her old mentor, 'would like to get some warm slippers' for the boys. Nurse Mooney was wise enough in the ways of the poor to realize how precious even an old broken pair of boots was to a child. She had seen too many bare-footed urchins in her time. When the floor was being scrubbed in the boys' ward – 'the work had been delayed on account of a sudden death in the night' – Louisa Twining was 'reminded of Miss Nightingale's remarks about old board floors, by the very unpleasant smell that proceeded from these; but this is I suppose unavoidable here'. This was indeed one of the drawbacks of the old houses. A few days later she records: 'I have always met with so much kind and friendly feeling from every person in this Hospital, and such readiness to listen to everything I said, that I feel a great unwillingness to say anything which may seem to be finding fault.'

These reports by the Lady Visitors are fascinating documents of the Hospital from 1860 to 1862. In that year, as Catherine Wood remembered, 'the trained and educated gentlewomen' came into the wards, and from that November the reports lost their unique and personal character, being written in the third person and signed by the chairman. Even from the glimpses given above it can be seen that Great Ormond Street, like every human institution, was not all sweetness and light, but subject to human frailty, as when it is reported that the Matron, Mrs Rice, never presided over morning prayers, as was her duty, because she never got up before ten o'clock. But then, like Nurse Mooney, Mrs Rice was getting old.

In February 1862, we are given another glimpse of Nurse Mooney in *All the Year Round*, when she is described in 'Between the Cradle and the Grave'.

> Not only here, but among the fifty sick children in the hospital, we heard not a cry or a murmur of fretfulness ... Love carries the key of such mysteries. Upon a bit of wall over a table in one of the sick wards, is a cluster of little cheap daguerreotypes of children. They belong to an old nurse who has been in the hospital since its opening. They are gifts from children or from mothers of children, whom she made happy on the sick-bed or the death-bed. She can tell you, with a love yet fresh, and never dying tenderness, the tale of each, is as proud of her decorations as if she were a general, and they were medals won upon the battle-field. As truly they are. In the war against all spirits of darkness that fight horribly against the flesh and soul of childhood, this good nurse has fought, and every decoration here speaks of a battle and a victory. This nurse herself is drawing near the day when she may also need the soothing help she has so freely given. When the good time shall be so nearly come, that all is done that ought to be done for the Children's Hospital, it will include among its means a superannuation fund for old and faithful nurses.

A similar sentiment and description, which names her, was published in *Sunday at Home*, a few years later:

> But one of the kind watchful nurses came. They seemed ever at hand to soothe or attend to the children's wants. And they all seemed so fond of the nurses, kissing and keeping hold of them with their hands. Nurse Mooney seemed like a dear kind granny among the children. Long and tenderly has she nursed the relays of sufferers, and many are the daguerreotypes of grateful little patients that form her picture gallery of love. Nurse is getting old. May she never want the care she has shown to others! How very nice it would be if there were some almshouses built for aged nurses.

There was an unexpected response to this. Major Vereker, speaking at the anniversary dinner for 1865, was able to claim:

> It was only recently that some articles that appeared in the 'Sunday at Home' were read ... in the presidency of Madras – and they led to so much sympathy with us that we were sent over little dolls in Hindoo costume worked by the Hindoo girls in that presidency, with a request that one nurse who had been named in the articles should receive a special mark of their regard.

But others had noticed that 'Nurse is getting old.' At the end of November 1866, the Medical Committee was asked by the Committee of Management to report upon Nurse Mooney's 'alleged incapacity for duty from increasing infirmity'. Charles West was in the chair, and present were Gee, Hillier, Buchanan, Dickinson and Thomas Smith, all names of fame and renown in the world of medicine. Their report was in its way a unique tribute to Ann Mooney.

> ... all the Physicians present coincided in the opinion that Nurse Mooney discharges her duties efficiently and kindly; and, though not equal to great fatigue of body, it was thought that with similar help to that recently afforded her by a junior assistant, she may yet continue to fulfil her duties to the satisfaction of the Medical Officers. The Committee considered it doubtful, whether, in a position so responsible, and for which it is difficult to secure proper oversight, if any other person were appointed, the duties would be so well discharged or the Patients so carefully attended to.

Nurse Mooney finally retired in May 1868. The previous month, at Dr West's suggestion, she was allowed a pension of £12 per year, and the expenses of her return home to Ireland were also paid. That members of the Committee also contributed in the end to her pension is indicated many years later in 1880 when a 'statement of the account of Nurse Mooney's pension fund' was submitted, and a letter from Dr West contributing £5 17s 0d to it was read. One committee member having 'discontinued his Contribution, Mr Craufurd kindly undertook to become a contributor to the fund'. West had left Great Ormond Street and was now living at Nice, but he had not forgotten his old hospital nurse.

In January 1886, the committee were informed of Nurse Mooney's death. She had been sixteen years in the service of the Hospital and had enjoyed her retirement for nearly eighteen years. She was a nurse who in West's words had indeed 'a feeling of very earnest love to little children' and exemplified in her own person the essential truth of Dickens's picture of Our Johnny's last hours.

> The greatest portrayer in modern times of human nature, and more especially of the peculiarities of children, a man whose name will go down to posterity, as his works have done, as a household word ... I mean Charles Dickens ... has told the history and pleaded the cause of this hospital in words of eloquence and of truth which have never been equalled, and can certainly never be surpassed; and when, in *Our Mutual Friend*, he told the eloquent story of poor Johnny's sufferings ... as ... in the last moments of his life he turned round to the doctor near him and made a sign, which only the doctor understood ... Dickens, in those few words, told a story unequalled in its simplicity.

This tribute to Dickens and *Our Mutual Friend* was loudly cheered at the Hospital's anniversary dinner in 1874. It was spoken by Baron Henry de Worms when proposing the 'Health of the Medical Officers' with which the name of Dr West was coupled, so it may have a hidden significance. In replying, West made his own reference to Dickens's work for Great Ormond Street: 'Charles Dickens stood godfather to it, and a true and a generous and kind-hearted sponsor was he to his child, so long as he lived.'

The annual report printed that year mentioned 'arrangements for the opening of an adjacent house' intended for the 'systematic training of young women' as children's nurses. It is from this time and from this house that the beginning of Great Ormond Street's School of Nursing (now named in honour of Charles West) is usually dated; but it was earlier, in 1858, that Dickens's speech and reading enabled the Hospital for Sick Children to begin such training. With the money that Dickens raised, the Hospital had sufficient funds to buy the neighbouring premises at 48 Great Ormond Street for £1600. Hitherto, its original intention of providing 'instruction for nurses ... was rendered almost impracticable by the inability to lodge Pupil Nurses in the house'. And this same 1858 report went on to say that with the acquisition of No 48 it was now 'in the power of the Committee to offer a home within the Hospital to young women desirous of instruction in the care and management of Sick Children'. Charles Dickens not only paid tribute to the nurses of Great Ormond Street in *Our Mutual Friend* – he had been directly responsible for making their original training possible, two years before the Nightingale School for Nurses was opened at St Thomas's Hospital in 1860.

Nevertheless, when, as Miss Wood described, West introduced his trained and educated ladies into the wards at Great Ormond Street in 1862, the influence of Florence Nightingale was apparent and readily acknowledged: 'We, in this hospital, have succeeded in obtaining assistance of the same sort as that which Florence Nightingale gave to the Military Hospital in the Crimea.' This was said at a Hospital dinner shortly after the new arrangements began. But the high ideals of nursing which Charles West brought to Great Ormond Street had an influence on Miss Nightingale, even if it was not openly acknowledged. It has been seen how some of her close circle were involved with the Hospital for Sick Children, even if later, like Miss Twining, they were to be at variance with her over certain aspects of nursing. Three of the seven named by Florence Nightingale herself in her 1856 letter to Sydney Herbert as executors with him of the Nightingale Fund had been more than usually involved in Great Ormond Street's beginnings – Lord Ellesmere, Sir James Clark and Dr Bence Jones. And in 1877 Florence Nightingale wrote to Charles West, lamenting 'that after 20 years we shall be put on our trial again as to the training of Nurses . . . I own to much apprehension as to their results; unless, as I trust, good men and true like yourself will try to guide them.'

—12—
CHANGES OF GLORIOUS LIGHT

For twelve years Dickens was to experience the delight and emotion of the enthusiastic response audiences here and in America gave to his readings. And everywhere the most popular reading was that which, despite being first read in aid of the Birmingham and Midland Institute at Christmas 1853, remains so associated with The Hospital for Sick Children. *A Christmas Carol* with Tiny Tim had, and continues to have, an irresistible appeal. Although there are many descriptions of the impression produced by Dickens on his audience, perhaps here it would be most fitting to record the memories of a child, a poet's daughter, Longfellow's twelve-year-old Allegra, and the intense delight with which she remembered Dickens reading on those magical nights at Boston in the winter and spring of 1867–68.

> Sam Weller and Mr Pickwick, Nicholas Nickleby and the old gentleman and the vegetable marrows over the garden wall. *How* he did make Aunt Betsy Trotwood snap out, 'Janet, donkeys' – and David Copperfield yearn over the handsome sleeping Steerforth. How the audience loved best of all the Christmas Carol and how they laughed as Dickens fairly smacked his lips as there came the 'smell like an eating house and a pastry cook's next door to each other, with a laundress's next door to that', as Mrs Cratchit bore in the Christmas pudding and how they nearly wept as Tiny Tim cried, 'God bless us every one!'

No wonder Dickens broke down and wept at his very last reading in London on 15 March 1870 – tears which so alarmed his little granddaughter Meketty, already upset by the strange voices and expressions of her familiar 'Wenerables'. He could barely control himself to say a few words: 'From these garish lights I vanish now forevermore, with a heartfelt, grateful, respectful, affectionate farewell.' These last readings had been permitted, only on the understanding that no long journeys were involved, by Sir Thomas Watson, who had been consulted the previous April when Dickens became seriously ill after collapsing when on tour. Twenty years before, Sir Thomas Watson had been one of the distinguished physicians who signed the first appeal on behalf of a Hospital for Sick Children, and had written a powerful letter in support. After examining Dickens that April in 1869, Watson told Dr Beard that the symptoms 'showed plainly that Charles Dickens had been on the brink of an attack of paralysis of his left side, and possibly of apoplexy. It was, no doubt, the result of extreme hurry, overwork, and excitement, incidental to his readings.' Although Dickens demurred somewhat at this strict warning and the doctors' injunctions, he quickly recognized the truth behind Watson's diagnosis, and wrote to him later, 'Your friendly aid will never be forgotten by me; and again I thank you for it with all my heart.'

Did Dickens remember in the emotion and stress of his last public reading that immediately after the triumph of that reading for Great Ormond Street, which as he knew had finally set him on that momentous course, he had written to his friend Yates complaining of how he was pestered by various charities, 'but never anything like what I suffer now'? The tone of that letter was at once comical and bitter. 'Benevolent men' hiding by his gate have 'their pot-bellied shadows projected on the gravel. Benevolent bullies drive up ... Benevolent area-sneaks get lost in the kitchen.' And with dialogue that only the creator of Sam Weller could have put down, he reports what his servant said at the local public house: 'When all the Christian virtues is always a-shoulderin' and a-helberin' on you in the 'all, a-tryin' to git past you and cut upstairs into Master's room, wy no wages as you couldn't name wouldn't make it up to you.'

It has been seen before how impatient Dickens could be with the importuning of various unwelcome charities. It was the consequence of his unique reputation. This makes the support he gave his chosen charities all the more important and significant. To the Christmas of 1858 belongs what would appear to be the only surviving letter from Dickens to Charles West. He is sorry that he cannot come as he is reading on Christmas Eve, but 'you may perhaps be free to come and see (and hear) me instead.' Had West invited Dickens to join in the Christmas festivities for the children at Great Ormond Street?

In future years, The Hospital for Sick Children twice asked Samuel Cartwright to approach Dickens to see if he would speak again at the anniversary dinner. His replies are not recorded. In 1863, Bathurst received two letters from Dickens relating to a request to use his influence in asking Bulwer Lytton to preside at the next year's anniversary dinner. An entry in the minutes gives an abstract of the second. 'Mr Dickens recommended a direct application to Sir Bulwer and authorizing the use of his name.' But Bulwer Lytton declined the invitation. The previous year Dickens had written 'withholding his concurrence in the proposed reading of the "Wreck of the Golden Mary" by A.F. Westmacott'. Westmacott, a member of the committee, was arranging his own reading in aid of Great Ormond Street. A few weeks later, Dickens wrote to Bathurst confirming that Henry Morley had indeed written 'Between the Cradle and the Grave' which had recently appeared in *All the Year Round*, agreeing that Morley should be made an honorary governor of the Hospital, and granting permission for the article to be printed for the benefit of the Hospital. There is evidence that other letters were exchanged between Dickens and the Hospital at various times.

'Between the Cradle and the Grave' deliberately made a contrast between the Great Ormond Street of 'Drooping Buds' and the Hospital ten years later. It began by stressing the high mortality that still existed among London children. Morley made the telling simile that in London enough young children die in a year 'to make an unbroken line of corpses ... along the kerb-stone on each side of the way, from Bow Church down to Bow Road, through ... the whole length of Holborn and Oxford Street, to beyond Kensington Gardens'. The next year, continuing the tradition started by Dickens of presiding at the anniversary dinner, the Earl of Shaftesbury returned to the subject. 'It is a monstrous thing to say that of half the children born in London, more than one half die under five years of age.' In the country and the more favourable colonies 'so far from half the children dying under ten years of age, you will find that nearly the whole number pass that age and rise into adolescent manhood.' Morley describes the day-nursery, where working mothers can leave their babies, their 'small parcels of humanity'. Here girls from Miss Twining's nearby domestic training school for workhouse girls were taught to mind a baby, of which they knew so little that, in a scene which could have come straight out of Dickens's pages, 'one was stopped in the act of hoisting a baby by its head'. Another reminder of Dickens comes from *Dombey and Son*, where Mr Toodles's children gather round him as he eats his evening meal, 'on the look-out for irregular morsels ... These he distributed now and then to the expectant circle, by holding out great wedges of bread and butter, to be bitten at by the family in lawful succession, and by serving out small doses of tea in like manner with a spoon.' Morley describes the little ones being fed in Great Ormond Street's day-nursery:

In the middle of the floor ... is the circle of tiny seats into which babies

> can be shut, built ... around a central stool. The feeding nurse sits in the middle of the nest with basin and spoon; fourteen of the fledglings can be settled around her; and she then proceeds to revolve on her stool, filling mouth after mouth – finding mouth one, as well as mouths two, three and four, empty and open by the time fourteen is filled.

Morley goes on to remark upon something which was confirmed by another writer who visited Great Ormond Street at almost the same time. 'Not only here, but among the fifty sick children in the hospital, we heard not a cry or a murmur of fretfulness.' Mrs Craik, the author of *John Halifax, Gentleman*, wrote an article, 'The History of a Hospital', which was published in *Macmillan's Magazine* in July 1862. She actually visited The Hospital for Sick Children on 19 December 1861. The nurse she describes could very well be Ann Mooney.

> 'How exceedingly good they all seem' was noticed – as, indeed, no one could help noticing, who was at all acquainted with the difficulty of managing such children ...
>
> 'It's curious, ma'am,' replied the nurse, 'but they almost always are good. The amount of pain some 'em will bear is quite wonderful. And they lie so patient like; we hardly ever have any crossness or whimpering. Maybe, it is partly because, considering the homes they come from, they find themselves so quiet and comfortable here. But, unless they're very bad, they scarcely ever cry. Poor little dears!'
>
> There were tears in the woman's own eyes – God bless her! She, like one or two more of the establishment, had been there from its commencement. She was evidently a great favourite, and a most important person. Her little patients, we heard, when discharged cured, continually come back to see 'Nurse' and the hospital; looking upon it as a pleasant, happy home, instead of a place to be shuddered at and avoided.

It is no wonder, with a spirit like this prevalent, that a decade later an American, R.H.McDonald from New York, who visited Great Ormond Street with his three sons, all 'attending school in Germany', could sign the visitors' book with the comment, 'This institution I believe is one of the most deserving I have seen in London or elsewhere.'

Morley's simile of the infants gathered like birds in a circle around the nurse feeding them with a spoon is also described in an article in *The Leisure Hour*. Although printed in August 1877, the anonymous author, Richard Rowe of *Episodes in an Obscure Life*, based part of it on earlier memories of Great Ormond Street, when he visited the Hospital with the late Dr Thomas Guthrie, the philanthropic Scottish divine. Dr Guthrie was a strong supporter of that other cause close to the heart of Charles Dickens, the Ragged Schools. When the Ragged School Union supporters set up the Reformatory and Refuge Union to modify the Reformatory Schools Bill, Dr Guthrie was on the committee. Among the first members and subscribers were Lord Shaftesbury, Arthur Kinnaird, R.C.L.Bevan, John Labouchere and Lady Olivia Sparrow, all prominent in the early history of The Hospital for Sick Children. This is how Richard Rowe described Dr Guthrie among the little patients.

> I well remember how the little ones, well enough to toddle about, instantly appropriated the grand old man, clustering about and clinging to his legs like iron filings to a magnet, whilst he fumbled in his packets for lozenges for them – how confidingly they looked up to his beaming face, which hung over them like the sunlit top of 'some tall cliff', and how the normal hiatus between his loosely-tied neckcloth and tumbled shirt widened when he flung one of the wee-est up high over even his silvery head. I can hear his chuckling 'heck!' of amused delight when he entered the creche, and saw the infants seated in a circle round the good-natured, laughing nurse, gaping like little birds as she fed them in turn with her well-filled spoon. I can see, too, the good old doctor's blank look of disappointment when, after searching all his pockets, he found that, so far as lozenges went, previous extravagance had left him hopelessly insolvent.

Rowe has also recorded for us some of the children at the time of the article:

> As strength comes back to them, they indulge in plenty of fun. They play at doctors, looking at one another's tongues, feeling one another's pulses, and poking pencils, to represent thermometers, under one another's arms, gravely pretending afterwards to read off the registered temperature; they cuddle and dress up their kittens like babies, and put their dolls' hair in curl-papers; they pipe away like little larks; they chirp like little sparrows; some, alas! – or ought I to use a more jubilant interjection? – of the little male redbreasts begin to peck at one another like little robins ...
>
> But in spite of the loving care ... and the flower-like way in which those who are getting over their sufferings open to the sunshine, sadness must be the dominant outcome of a walk through the wards ...
>
> The little shoulders are so very narrow to bear, or sink under such heavy loads. This mite of a girl has lost one leg, and is destined to lose the other. Her pride in the perambulator in which she takes her airings ... as her own private carriage, is the way in which the wind is tempered to the shorn lamb. Another is waiting for the surgeon to free her from a hideous tumour on the head; a third shrimp is crying, not so much on account of her own sufferings ... as because it is washing day at home, and she cannot be there to mind baby!

The Hospital's convalescent home, Cromwell House at Highgate, was visited and described by Rowe:

> When walking up Highgate Hill on a sunny Sunday morning, it is very pleasant to hear the little inmates' voices floating out through the open windows in psalm or hymn; very pleasant on weekdays to hear them ringing merrily in their playground; though if you hear them from the wards the pleasure is damped by the sight of the poor little chronic patients, some of them literally tied by the leg, with chain and weight for the straightening of a limb, like lamed captive little birds ... From the pleasant garden behind ... the eye can wander for miles over the champaign of grass and wood and water, unbroken save for a few sprinkled houses and Hornsey's ivied church-tower.

Highgate was where David Copperfield and his Aunty Betsey Trotwood lived when he came to London, and Hornsey Church where Aunt Betsey's errant husband was to be buried. At Hornsey Dickens had visited his dying sister Fanny, and at Highgate Cemetery Dickens's parents and his infant daughter Dora are buried. Angela Burdett Coutts had her Holly Lodge estate ten minutes walk from Cromwell House. Cromwell House itself may be considered to have a Dickensian link in its acquisition by Great Ormond Street that is not always recognized.

At the Hospital's anniversary dinner for 1867, one of the speakers was William Gladstone, a cousin of his namesake, the famous Prime Minister. William Gladstone was a Baltic and Russian merchant, a director of the Alliance Insurance Company, and had railway interests, especially in France. At the 1867 Dinner Gladstone strongly urged that Great Ormond Street should be moved or have an establishment 'in the country, somewhere in the neighbourhood of London, where the children would have a better chance of life'. He referred to an institution, a 'moral hospital' which he had been instrumental in moving from the centre of London to the country, and which Prince Albert had thought vastly improved by the change. William Gladstone was an influential resident of Highgate. With Miss Burdett Coutts he was prominent in starting the local church school. The Highgate Literary and Philosophical Society still remember him as one of their early presidents, a friend of the Tsar. The very next year Great Ormond Street acquired Cromwell House and maintained it as a convalescent home for half a century.

The 'moral hospital' William Gladstone referred to in his speech was the Philanthropic Farm School, Red Hill, East Surrey. Gladstone was the honorary treasurer, and was responsible for its establishment at Red Hill, bearing much of the financial burden. The Philanthropic Farm School, which Gladstone modelled upon the French example at Mettray, led to the adoption of the reformatory system throughout England. Sydney Turner, the Inspector of Reformatory and Industrial Schools, said of William Gladstone, 'hundreds of young men both at home and abroad will long and thankfully remember the friend to whom their early rescue from crime and their subsequent progress in honest and independent life have been largely owing.' Sydney Turner was chaplain and master of the Philanthropic Farm School when in 1852 Dickens and Morley visited Red Hill and wrote 'Boys to Mend' for *Household Words*, which appeared six months after 'Drooping Buds'. With the almost inevitable mutual interest in charities for the welfare of the young that we find in Dickens and his circle, it is not surprising that among the vice-presidents of the Philanthropic Farm School are the Earl of Carlisle, the Earl of Shaftesbury, the Bishop of London, the Bishop of Winchester, Samuel Gurney, R. S. Holford, and the great William Ewart Gladstone. All these men were leading supporters of Great Ormond Street.

Richard Rowe, in the third hospital he describes, again is involved in a Dickensian link which can now be claimed by Great Ormond Street – The East London Hospital for Children which Dr and Mrs Heckford started at Ratcliff Cross, Shadwell, after they had worked devotedly and unselfishly among the poor there during the cholera epidemic of 1866. Dickens visited the hospital in November 1868, and wrote an account of that visit in 'A Small Star in the East' which appeared in *All the Year Round* on 19 December. A little later a further description of this 'children's hospital established in an old sail-loft or storehouse, of the roughest nature, and on the simplest means' appeared in 'From an Amateur Beat'. On the very next day after 'A Small Star in the East' was published the first donations began to arrive. Among the first letters one must be quoted here.

> Dear Mr Heckford,
> My mamma has just read to me the story of your hospital. I am only a little girl of six, but I would like to give the contents of my money box for your little children.
> Yours affectionately,
> Little Mary

Nathaniel Heckford died in 1871. In 1875 the East London Hospital for Children was moved to Glamis Road, Shadwell. The name was later changed to The Princess Elizabeth of York Hospital for Children, which in 1942 amalgamated with the Queen's Hospital for Children in Hackney Road, under the new title of the Queen Elizabeth Hospital for Children. The premises at Shadwell were finally closed in 1963. Queen Elizabeth Hospital is now part of The Hospitals for Sick Children Group. And so fittingly Great Ormond Street can consider itself as a sharer in the legacy of Nathaniel Heckford, Charles Dickens and Little Mary. In 1870 Charles West had described the Shadwell Hospital as 'one of our children in whose prosperity we take great interest – that one in the East of London'.

If we are bringing together all the threads that unite Dickens and Great Ormond Street, a commentator* on Sir James Barrie has hinted that the origins of Peter Pan and Captain Hook may be found in Dickens's *Holiday Romance* which belongs to 1868. After all, the poet and novelist Robert Buchanan, reviewing Forster's *Life of Charles Dickens* in 1872, actually claimed that Dickens 'so loaded his soul that he never grew any older. He was a great, grown-up dreamy, impulsive child, just as much a child as little Paul Dombey or little David Copperfield.'

Dickens's last important social engagement was perhaps the final service he rendered to Great Ormond Street, by no means a negligible one. As Lady Houghton told Forster, 'I never saw Mr Dickens more agreeable than at a dinner at our house, about a fortnight before his death, when he met the King of the Belgians and the Prince of Wales at the special desire of the latter.' At the Prince of Wales's special desire! That dinner, as we know from *The Times* Court Circular, took place on the evening of 24 May. On the very next day, to quote the same source again, 'In the evening the Prince of Wales ... presided at a dinner at Willis's Rooms in aid of the funds of The Hospital for Sick Children.' Did that explain why the Prince was so eager to meet Dickens?

The Hospital's dinner of 25 May 1870 was important not only because the Prince presided, although that would normally be a sufficient reason, but because of its being a 'Special Festival'. It was the inauguration of a building fund for the reconstruction of the Hospital. Viscount Gort, chairman of the committee, wrote in the printed appeal for stewards, 'The present occasion is an exceptional one; the Committee can hardly hope ever again to plead for your support under such patronage.' Lord Gort was not to know that every future appeal for the reconstruction of the Hospital would have the patronage of the Prince and Princess of Wales, culminating in the recent Wishing Well Appeal, which owed its unprecedented success to the invaluable support of the present Prince and Princess of Wales.

Dickens's speech and appeal for Great Ormond Street had set an almost unapproachable standard. As Lord Houghton ruefully said, when he presided at a Hospital dinner in 1875, 'It would be dangerous for any man who has any pretension to be a man of letters to compete with the beautiful sketch which many years ago Charles Dickens gave in this chair.' With the knowledge of the task that awaited him the next evening, it would be strange if the Prince did not discuss the hospital with Dickens,

* Roger Lancelyn Green, *Fifty Years of Peter Pan*, London, 1954.

who would have imparted some of his own enthusiasm and knowledge. One sentence in the Prince's speech may have Dickensian undertones:

> I am sure that most of you who know London so well, and pass through so many of those narrow streets and alleys, with which, unfortunately, this great metropolis abounds, and meet at every turn poor, sick and squalid children, must often feel anxious to see some suitable home or hospital provided with a view of ameliorating their condition, and preventing the mortality that prevails among them.

Dr Charles West, speaking later than evening, described the accommodation added to their recently opened convalescent home at Cromwell House, Highgate. This was for a large number of children 'afflicted with chronic diseases, who will be confined for weeks, or months perchance, to their beds, and who, at least, may lie upon their couch there out of town, and see the green leaves dancing in the sunshine, and hear the birds sing'.

Two weeks later his words were echoed when on 8 June Dickens was working on the unfinished *Edwin Drood* at his chalet at Gad's Hill. On the last page he ever wrote, one of the final strokes of Dickens's pen was to amend his description of a sunny morning in Rochester with the phrase, 'Changes of glorious light from moving boughs, songs of birds, scents from gardens, woods and fields'.

That evening during dinner, Dickens had a cerebral haemorrhage, and fell to the carpet. He was placed on a sofa. The local surgeon, Mr Steele was summoned from Rochester. His old friend and doctor, Frank Beard, arrived that evening. The next morning Dickens's eldest son Charley brought a London specialist for consultation, Dr J. Russell Reynolds, who had been one of the first two assistant physicians appointed at Great Ormond Street. It has been surmised that as a boy in Chatham, Dickens watched the younger but sturdier William Jenner at play – Jenner, who was to be physician at Great Ormond Street, and hear Dickens make that most eloquent plea for the children. We *know* that on the very last day of his life Dickens was watched by one of Jenner's old colleagues at the Hospital. But Dickens's last word had been spoken and Russell Reynolds, like the medical advisers in 'Drooping Buds', could only shake his head with vain regret at Charley, Mary and Katey as he came out of the dining-room where Dickens lay on the sofa, and joined them perhaps on the steps where the summer blooms and flowers 'from the one great garden of the whole cultivated island in its yielding time' penetrated with their scents not into Rochester Cathedral, as Dickens had written on that last page, but into his dining-room to 'preach the Resurrection and the Life'.

At ten minutes past six on that evening of 9 June 1870, a tear trickled down his cheek, and Charles Dickens died. For the whole world it was as if one of their own friends had gone. Longfellow wrote, 'I never knew an author's death to cause such general mourning . . . this whole country is stricken with grief.' Once Dr Charles West had described Dickens as 'the master of pathos – he who more than any other living man has brought smiles and tears to every hearth'. Now the tears shed by every fireside were not for Little Nell or Paul Dombey, not even for Our Johnny, nor for the children of Great Ormond Street, but for Charles Dickens himself. During the next few years the Hospital received a subscription of £10 given 'In Memory of Charles Dickens'. The donor is only identified by the initials 'H.F.C.' Was this his lovable if eccentric and sentimental friend Henry Fothergill Chorley, who in a review of *Bleak House* singled out the death of poor Joe as a scene which 'Dickens has nowhere in all his works excelled'?

It is said that it was Lord Houghton who first inspired the article in *The Times* which called for Dickens's burial in Poets' Corner, Westminster Abbey.

> Among those whose sacred dust lies there, or whose names are recorded on the walls, very few are more worthy than Charles Dickens of such a home. Fewer still, we believe, will be regarded with more honour as time passes and his greatness grows upon us.

Although it was kept as a private and unannounced funeral, attended only by six of the family and six close friends on the morning of 14 June, the news quickly spread and thousands came, filing through the Abbey in an endless line to look down on the coffin and heap the open grave with flowers. Among them was Edward Futvoye, who with West, Bence Jones and Bathurst was one of the four originators of The Hospital for Sick Children. No doubt others came from the Hospital, although their names are not recorded as Futvoye's was, by mere chance.

For three days the grave was kept open while the spontaneous procession filed by in an almost unprecedented act of homage paid by the public to a great novelist. After darkness fell on 16 June, and after the last of the public had left the Abbey, Lord Houghton, hearing from Dean Stanley that the grave would not be closed until near midnight, came and looked down at the coffin of his old friend. Only a lantern glimmered on the place which, as Dean Stanley was to say in his memorial sermon, 'would thence forward be a sacred one . . . not of this island only, but of all who speak our English tongue'. And not only these. Forster says that four years after Dickens's death, his grave was still covered with flowers, thrown down by people coming from every place and every land to pay their personal tribute. Today, the Dean of the Abbey still officiates at a short memorial service on every anniversary of Dickens's death, and once again the grave is covered with a wreath. This simple ceremony is often attended by visitors from overseas and of different faiths, who sometimes speak their own tribute, and are obviously deeply moved. In death, Dickens belongs not alone to England but to the world, as the Hospital he so loved and succoured now in a way belongs to all children everywhere and serves and saves them.

Inevitably Lord Houghton, as he stood towards midnight by the open grave, must have thought back three weeks before to the last time he had seen Dickens. Dickens was lame and unable to mount the stairs, but at his most convivial, firing the Prince of Wales with enthusiasm for Great Ormond Street. We have no record of what was said that evening at the Houghton house in Upper Brook Street, but I cannot be far wrong. Five years later, when Lord Houghton was presiding at an anniversary dinner for Great Ormond Street in the very same place where Dickens had once pleaded for the Hospital, besides the praise he gave to Dickens's speech he paid great tribute to the part played by the Prince and Princess of Wales, in words which could be repeated today. Perhaps Lord Houghton, remembering that evening when Dickens and the Prince of Wales met, knew that the handsome new building almost ready in Great Ormond Street really owed its existence to the inspiration of Dickens and the patronage of the Prince.

> The Princess of Wales is eminent for her personal attractions, and still more for the amiability of which her beauty is but the natural expression ... Her Royal Highness has taken a natural interest in this institution. She is a devoted mother herself: she knows what the care of children is ... when in the course of things his Royal Highness ascends to the throne of this country, we shall have a Sovereign who fully understands, and appreciates, and sympathizes with the people whom he is to govern. There is not a small charity which the Prince of Wales now attends, there is not a work of benevolence to which he sacrifices some of his time or attention, there is not a single public object to which he inclines, and in which he interests himself apart from the pleasures natural to his position, but will be remembered in time to come when his mind may be occupied by greater destinies. It is well that he should lay this foundation, and on no occasion has he done so better than when he presided over this institution. For this is an institution of the future; it begins with childhood, it goes on to manhood, and the time will come when children will remember when they are grown up to be men, that the Prince of Wales took share and part in the institution which has relieved and benefited their childhood.

Great changes of glorious light are still cast not only on the walls of Rochester Cathedral, as Dickens described in his last manuscript page, but also on the walls of The Hospital for Sick Children. Walls for whose renewal, as we have seen, children and their elders have collected enthusiastically. Light cast by Charles West, his colleagues and nurses, on the care and treatment of the sick children. Glorious light cast by their innocent patients, good and brave children, sometimes quietly moaning under their afflictions, sometimes chattering like the songs of the birds. Light cast by Charles Dickens with pen and voice, and by his friends upon the deprivation and ignorance of their day. And light cast by modern medicine on some of the hitherto insoluble problems of sickness and disease in infancy and childhood.

Great Ormond Street is not only a place of medical excellence in the forefront of paediatric research and technique, it is also a symbol, a place of hope. It is this symbolic function that has in the end the most significance and the most meaning, the greatest appeal to the public who have given it such unstinting support. It is a place where the spirit and the remarkable patience and bravery of the young still help the doctors and the nurses to perform miracles. Great Ormond Street seems to the anguished mother her last chance to ward off the encroachment of death. Or if it does happen, alas, that the child cannot be saved, she is comforted by the thought that her child was in the right place, was in Great Ormond Street; and the gratitude that such bereaved parents often express has always been among the most tender and moving episodes of its history. This gives it a character of its own, different from other children's hospitals, no matter how wonderful they may be and are.

It is a place for dreams as well as intensive care. As Dickens said in his great speech:

> The dream-children whom I would now raise, if I could, before every one of you, according to your various circumstances, should be the dear child you love, the dearer child you have lost, the child you might have had, the child you certainly have been. Each of these dream-children should hold in its powerful hand one of the little children now lying in the Child's Hospital.

We have seen how powerfully Dickens's dream children aided, and continue to aid, the Hospital. And that other great lover of children and writer of stories for and about them, J. M. Barrie, said in *his* speech, 'At one time Peter Pan was an invalid in The Hospital for Sick Children, and it was he who put me up to the little thing I did for the Hospital.'

If there is an Elysium for all the dream children created by Charles Dickens and James Barrie, it surely must be in Great Ormond Street, where Tiny Tim has thrown away his wooden crutch and been taught to fly by Peter Pan.

INDEX

In this index Hospital = Great Ormond Street Children's Hospital